Something tall was standing in the shadows farther down the passageway.

I slowly took Susan's torch from my pocket.

I played the beam of the torch on it and my heart dropped into my stomach.

"Grrreetings, Jake-friend. We have found you at last."

A nightmare in gray-green chitin, fully two and a half meters tall, the Reticulan took a step forward. His zoomlens eyes rotated slightly to get me in better focus. The complex apparatus of his mouth worked in and out, up and down in a rapid and silent sewing-machine motion.

Twrrrl and his hunting companions had followed me all the way from Terran Maze. Members of a Reticulan Snatchgang, bagging the quarry and dispatching it in a horrific ceremony of vivisection was their only concern.

And I was the Sacred Quarry.

Ace Science Fiction Books by John DeChancie

STARRIGGER
RED LIMIT FREEWAY

ACE SCIENCE FICTION BOOKS
NEW YORK

RED LIMIT FREEWAY

An Ace Science Fiction Book/published by arrangement with the author

PRINTING HISTORY
Ace Original/December 1984

Cover art by John Berkey

ISBN: 0-441-71122-7

Ace Science Fiction Books are published by The Berkley Publishing Group, 200 Madison Avenue, New York, New York 10016.
PRINTED IN THE UNITED STATES OF AMERICA

In memory of
Gene DeChancie

1

There they were, up ahead—the Trees at the Edge of the Sky.

That's what Winnie called them. Other people called them different things: Kerr-Tipler objects, tollbooths, noncatastrophic singularities, portal arrays . . .

I called them cylinders. That's what they were, big ones, some as high as five kilometers. They were lined up on both sides of the roadway like impossibly huge fenceposts, their color impossibly black, blacker than the interstellar space they bent and twisted and warped to their creators' ends, and to our benefit. Everything about them was incredible. They were said to be spinning at unimaginable speeds, though their featureless surfaces gave no perceivable confirmation of this. A few experiments had been done on them, measuring Doppler shifts of infalling particles and Hawking radiation flying out. But the Colonial Authority had a long-standing ban on the publication of data and even theoretical studies concerning the portals. One only had rumors to go by. And the rumors were: The results were impossible.

Their rotational speeds worked out to be faster than light.

It couldn't be, but that's what the numbers said.

"What's our speed, Sam?"

"Oh, we're moseying along nicely. If you'd care to move your eyeballs a few millimeters to the right, you'd see for yourself."

"You know I can't read instruments and drive at the same time."

"Good Lord, and I was just about to offer you some chewing gum."

"Oh, cut the *merte*, Sam."

"Is that any way to speak to your father?" Then Sam guffawed, in that scratchy/liquid synthesized voice of his—if the oxymoron can be forgiven, it's the only way I can express what the sound is like. In no way does it resemble my deceased father's voice, except in emotional tone and inflection. I didn't have a recording of Sam to pattern the waveforms after when I ordered the voice-output software for the rig's computer.

Sam went on, "We're right in the groove. Forget the numbers, I've got her on speed lock."

I glanced at the digital telltales, the array of numbers suspended in the air at eye level and at about thirty degrees to either side of my line-of-sight straight ahead. Positioned so as to hide in the retinal blind spot, they were unobtrusive until looked at directly. I usually had them turned off; if you moved your head a lot they seemed like pesky fireflies flitting about. "Okay, fine. Everybody strapped in?"

Roland Yee was in the shotgun seat. "Check," he said.

"I think we're all secure back here," John Sukuma-Tayler reported.

I chanced a look back. John, Susan D'Archangelo, and Darla Petrovsky née Vance were in harnesses in the back seats. The cab accommodated five comfortably. I heard squabbling in the aft-cabin—a little living space useful for long hauls.

"Hey, Carl!" I yelled. "Is Lori strapped down back there?"

"Like trying to hog-tie a—*give me your damn arm!*—like trying to wrassle a she-cat!"

"Lori!" I shouted. "Be a good girl!"

"I'm okay, for God's sake. Let me—"

"Gotcha!"

"I'm okay, I'm telling you!"

"Look, you had a concussion," Carl told her. "Now, behave, or we wrap you in confetti and ship you with the rest of the load."

"Oh, get folded."

"Think I don't know what that means? Should be ashamed of yourself."

"Punk you!"

"Such language! And from a mere slip of a girl, too."

I had insisted that Lori be strapped to my bunk during portal transitions. She'd taken a nasty whack on the head back on Splash, during our escape from the ship-seamonster *Laputa*. I wanted to take no chances; shooting an aperture can be rough sometimes, and it wasn't at all clear whether Lori was completely all right. She had been complaining of headaches. Normal enough, but I wanted to be sure. She needed to be looked over. However, we had to leave Splash in a hurry, and the next planet up, Snowball, lived up to its name. No one and practically no thing lived there. We were now on what Winnie's Itinerary Poem called "The Land of Nothing to See" (per Darla's translation). You called it, Winnie. The planet—or this part of it—looked like the old photographs of Mars I used to pore over as a kid, a place of vast rock-strewn plains with sand sifted in between the rubble, kilometer after endless kilometer of it. Except the sand was a crappy gray-green instead of an alluring, alien red. But there were beings here. Probably humans, if the occasional mail-order pop-up domes far off the road were any indication.

These were the Consolidated Outworlds, a maze of planets linked by the Skyway, but with no way back to Terran Maze.

No way home.

But I wasn't thinking of that just then. One of my pesky hologram readouts was blinking yellow. "What the hell's that, Sam?"

"It's that damn left-front roller, Jake. We get a yellow every time we go into portal-approach mode. Been getting one for, oh, couple of months now. You'd know that if you'd deign to take a look at your instruments once in a while."

"I didn't notice it. You're right, I fly by the seat of my pants a little too much. Think we should stop?"

"The book says we should."

I looked out over the bleak terrain. "And do what?"

"I'm only telling you what the book says."

"Well, we'll have to risk it. It's done okay up to now."

"Fine. But if she goes sugar-doughnut on us while we're shooting a portal, don't say I—"

"—didn't warn you," I finished. "Right, Sam, you're covered."

"It's all the same to me, you know. I'm already dead."

The road ahead was a black ribbon leading straight through the cylinders. They towered above, their tops festooned in wispy clouds against a greenish sky. Their color was black, utterly black, their surfaces sucked clean of light. It almost hurt to look at them directly; not just physically, but philosophically. To gaze upon an Absolute is discomforting. We're too used to fudging, finding refuge in the interstices of things, content to see the universe in shades of gray. You could see all sorts of frightening possibilities in that categorical darkness, if you stopped to look and think.

One thing you don't want to do is stop and philosophize near a portal. You might achieve a total and very unpleasant oneness with your object of contemplation.

"Darla, what's Winnie's description of the next planet up?"

"Um . . . 'A Land Like Home, but It Isn't.' I think."

"Does that mean jungle? Yeah, well, I guess so," I answered myself. "I just hope there's some kind of civilization. I want Lori to get checked out."

"Does Lori know anything about this part of the Outworlds?" John asked.

"No," Darla said. "She told me she hasn't seen much besides her home planet and Splash."

"Well," I said, "she won't have too much trouble getting back to Splash, if she wants to go. Unless this is a potluck portal." I looked at the rearview monitor. Traffic was still behind us. "But I can't believe all these people are following us into oblivion. This portal must go somewhere."

"We'll all have some decisions to make about where we're going," John said. "Once we stop."

"If there's a place to pull over up ahead, I'll do it," I told him. "We can talk things over."

"I'd just love to get out and stretch my legs," Susan groaned. "Seems like we've been driving for ages."

"Those were unusually long routes between portals," I said. "Wonder why?"

"Judging from the gravity," Roland put in, "and the apparent distance to the horizon, I'd say both Snowball and this place are big, low density planets. Maybe portals have to be positioned so as to balance out the planet's mass." He shrugged, looking over at me. "Just a wild guess."

"Maybe," I said. "I've been doing a lot of thinking about portals lately . . . the Skyway, the cylinders, how the whole system works. Never really gave it much thought before."

"Everyone takes the Skyway for granted," John said. "Simply part of the landscape."

"We can't be so complacent," Roland said ruefully.

"Right," I agreed.

"If I never see this damn road again . . ." Susan grumbled, shaking her head.

"I'm in sympathy with that," John said. "I think we're all road-weary at this point." He chuckled. "Except for Jake, perhaps. Do starriggers ever get tired of traveling, Jake?"

"You bet—but after a few years, you just get numb. Most of the time, though, I like it. I like the road."

The commit markers were coming up. Here, they were just white-painted metal posts on either side of the roadway. The Roadbuilders hadn't put them there—it was up to local inhabitants to mark the point beyond which it was unsafe to stop. Back in Terran Maze, and in most mazes I'd been in, the markers were more elaborate—flashing lights, holograms, and such.

I checked over the instruments. Everything looked fine.

And just as I shifted my eyes to check the yellow warning tag, it began flashing red.

"Jake," Sam said quietly.

"I see it. Too late to stop. Damn."

"What a time for it."

"Trouble, Jake?" John wanted to know.

"A little. We'll be okay, though."

I hoped fervently. The flashing red didn't mean the roller was going sugar on us—suffering an instantaneous crystallization that could turn the supertraction tread into white congealed powder—but it did mean it could go at any moment. Maybe now, maybe two days from now; there was no way to predict.

We were past the commit markers and racing for the first pair of cylinders. The safe corridor, a narrow land bounded by two solid white lines, rolled out at us. Cross over either of those lines and you've had it. The rig shuddered and groaned, caught in the delicately balanced gravitational stresses around us.

"Keep her steady, Jake," Sam warned, "and be ready for a sudden jump to the right."

The rig shook and buffeted us in our seats.

"This is a rough one," Sam commented. "Just our luck."

I felt the tug of an unseen hand, dragging the rig to the left. I corrected, and suddenly the hand let go, sending us precipitously in the opposite direction. But I was a veteran at this; I hadn't overcorrected, overreacted. This portal was a bit hairy, but I had seen worse. If only the roller would hold.

The cylinders marched by, a stately procession of dark monuments. Between them—I knew but couldn't look—the view of the terrain was refracted into crazy, funhouse-mirror images, work of the powerful gravitational fields.

Ahead was the aperture itself, a fuzzy patch of nothingness straddling the road. We shot straight into it.

2

We got through.

The ailing roller was still intact, but the flashing red warning stayed on. I shut off the holo array. Then I lowered our speed to 50 km/hr, took my crash helmet down from the rack behind the seat and put it on. I rarely wear it, though I should. The bulky thing is more than a safety helmet; it has submicron chips in it for just about everything—CPUs, communications, short-range scanning, even encephalo-teleoperator circuitry, though I never did buy the rest of the hookup. I prefer to operate machinery hands-on. The thought of just sitting there, steering the rig on a whim and an alpha wave, makes me a little nervous.

We had arrived on a world that didn't look much like Winnie's jungle home, and I was beginning to think that her Itinerary Poem contained some misinformation, until the Skyway plunged from the high plateau we were on into a series of hairpin turns, winding its way down a range of heavily forested mountains. I worried about the roller all the way, taking the curves at a crawl, not wanting to juice up the traction to high grab and aggravate the condition of the bad one. At full charge and maximum traction, I could have roared down there at 80 km/hr, had I a wild hair up my fundamental aperture.

The forestation was luxuriant, but not tropical. The trees looked vaguely Earthlike from a distance, but the foliage was radically different, and the colors varied from deep turquoise to brilliant aquamarine, with lots of stray pinks and reds mixed in. The effect on the eyes was slightly disturbing, colors shimmering and shifting as the retinal cells vacillated over what wavelengths to take first.

I didn't have much time to look. The curves were getting dicey, and I had my hands full. Everyone else gaped out the ports, marveling at the strange palette of colors.

I did notice that the trees were enormous, with thick straight trunks shooting up as high as a hundred meters.

"Great logging country," Sam said.

"I hope there are loggers," Susan said, "and I hope they have restaurants to eat in, with clean restrooms, and I hope the food is good, and I hope there's a place to stay with nice, big beds, and—" She broke off and sighed. "Don't mind me."

"We could all do with a break, Suzie," John commiserated.

Lori yelled something from the back.

"What was that, Lorelei?" John called.

"I said I have to piss so bad my back teeth are swimmin'!"

"Hey, Carl—" I began, then realized something. "Hey! What the hell is your last name, anyway?"

"Chapin."

"Oh. Why don't you let Lori up and let her use the . . . oh, hell. Suzie?"

Suzie started to unstrap. "Sure."

I slowed down almost to a stop while Susan went back to make sure Lori didn't re-bang her head on the way to the john. Chapin came up front, as there was no privacy back there.

He had joined our group rather recently; last night, in fact. Since that time he'd kept pretty much to himself, when not keeping an eye on Lori. I didn't know if anyone really knew who he was, or why he was with us. For that matter, I was not completely straight on the facts myself.

The trip across Splash had taken most of the day, and the trek across Snowball and Nothing-to-See had eaten up the rest of it. Everyone had been trying to get some sleep, and there had been little conversation. What there had been, Carl had not participated in beyond pleasantries, except when cussing out Lori.

"About time you were formally introduced to everyone, Carl. Don't you think? Have you met everyone?"

"I remember you from somewhere," he said to me wryly.

I smiled. "And I seem to have a distinct recollection of stealing your buggy."

"Oh, my God, that car," John remembered, slapping his forehead and rolling his eyes. "Where in the name of all that's unholy did you get that thing?"

"That's John Sukuma-Tayler," I said. "John, meet Carl Chapin."

"Hello. A little belated, but nice to meet you."

"Don't get up. Nice to meet you, too, John. And . . . it's a little late, but thanks for the help last night."

"You're very welcome. But Roland, here, was responsible for engineering it."

Roland unstrapped, got up, and took Chapin's hand. "Roland Yee. It's a pleasure. Where the hell did you get that car?"

Chapin laughed. "I get asked that a lot. I bought it from a custom vehicle manufacturer."

"Alien, I suppose."

"Yeah."

"Who?" Roland asked pointedly.

"Well . . ."

"The technology was fantastic. You couldn't have gotten it from any known race on the Skyway." Roland's tone was a trifle accusing.

"Roland," John interjected, "I think you're being a bit—"

"I'm sorry," Roland was quick to go on. "It's just that our whole experience with your vehicle was . . . well, disconcerting to say the least."

John nodded. "To say the very least."

"I can imagine," Chapin said, "but you shouldn't go around stealing things that don't belong to you."

"I stole it, Carl," I said. "They were kidnapped."

Chapin winced, a bit embarrassed. "Oh. Sorry."

"Natural enough mistake," John said good-naturedly. "You couldn't possibly have known."

I had pulled off toward the side of the road and had stopped, waiting for Lori to get squared away and for everyone to decide to continue the chitchat sitting down and strapped in. Finally, everyone did. We were short a seat and harness for Chapin, but he wedged himself in behind my seat, squatted on a tool box, and hung onto a handgrip. Suzie even managed to persuade Lori to bed down again. Lori didn't protest this time, not much anyway.

Something occurred to me. "Where's Winnie?" I hadn't seen her in hours. I yelled for her.

We heard the sauna stall door open. Winnie came into the

cab, rubbing her eyes, scratching her furred tummy, and giving us all a grimace-smile. "Here! Winnie here!"

"This is Winnie," I said to Chapin, twisting around to him. "Winnie, Carl."

"Hi, Winnie."

"Hi! Hi!"

Chapin held out his hand and Winnie took it, her double-thumbed grip enfolding it warmly.

"Where are you from, Winnie?" Chapin asked her.

Winnie extended an arm aft, making a far-off motion. *"Way back!"*

Everyone laughed. We had all come a long way.

Winnie sat in Darla's lap, but when she saw that Darla would have some difficulty bearing up under the weight, she jumped over to John's, hugging him. Winnie's compactness was deceptive; she had a good deal of bulk on her.

"You've met Carl, then?" John asked Darla.

"Yes, we talked last night. But I didn't get much out of him." She smiled at Carl.

"Neither did I," Susan said, strapping in.

"I notice he made a point to meet the women," I commented.

"Don't mean to be so secretive," Carl said. But he left it at that.

"Here we go," I announced. I goosed the engine and eased the rig forward down the steep incline.

Traffic whizzed by, two roadsters hot-rodding through the curves, braying annoyance at the big lumbering rig in their way. A little farther down, the curves got easier to handle, and I got a chance to look at the scenery. The sky was dark with a thick covering of greenish-purple clouds. Here and there, big winged creatures soared just above treetop level, alighting now and then on lofty branches. No other large life-forms in sight.

It was all very pretty, and very alien. The road bottomed out and went straight, following a long tree-lined corridor. Between the massive black tree trunks, undergrowth grew thickly even in the dim light. And a few lines came to me . . .

The woods were lovely, dark, and deep.
But I have promises to keep,
And miles to go before I sleep . . .

If road yarns contained any truth, I had light-years to go. For some unfathomable reason, I had become the protagonist of the wildest Skyway story yet. I knew only the outline of it; no one had related it in detail. It was the tale of a man, yours truly, who followed the Skyway clear out to the end. And came back. But in doing so, I returned paradoxically before I left.

There was more to it. I had come into possession of an alien artifact, the Roadmap, which delineated clearly and for all time the extent of the Skyway system and revealed a path leading to the lost civilization of the Roadbuilders and the secrets of their phenomenal technology.

And where did the Skyway lead, if followed out all the way to the "end"?—As if an interconnected road system could have such. It led, so the stories said, to the beginning of the universe. Not to the end, mind you, in either sense—not the physical limit of the universe, or its final destiny, but to the *beginning*.

When I heard that (from Jerry Spacks, an old friend and former member of the Starriggers Guild), I asked if there was a good motel there.

The beginning of the universe.

Bang.

Pack your sunglasses. And bring plenty of suntan lotion. That primeval fireball can burn you right through your pretty new beach outfit.

As farfetched as it all was, I had every reason—now—to believe it. True, I had only Darla's word that she had met me before—a meeting I did not remember—but I also was now in possession of a very strange object, the nature of which was not clear even to Darla, who had given it to me. I had the Black Cube. That was all it was, a palm-sized cube, black as the devil's heart, origin and purpose unknown. It might be the Roadmap, or it might not be.

There was other evidence. Back on Goliath, I had made good my escape from the Colonial Militia with the very timely help of what could only have been my doppelgänger, my paradoxical self. I was fairly sure of that. I had seen him . . . me. True, a tiny wisp of doubt still clung to that image of my own face hovering above me as I lay in my cell, being administered the antidote to the effects of the Reticulan dream wand . . .

I sat up in my seat. Where did my double get the dream

wand he had used to knock out everybody at the Militia station?

I opened the glove box under the dash. There it was, a shiny green shaft with a bright metal ring around one end.

Of course. That's how "he" got it. I have it now!

I closed the box. Jesus, it was spooky.

Maybe there was no doubt after all.

"Hooray!"

A sign beside the road.

6KM TO THE FRUMIOUS BANDERSNATCH!
EATS!
GET DRUNK! WE MAIL YOU HOME, KEEP YOUR KEY
ROOMS, NOT TOO SORDID
TURN OFF SKYWAY 1KM
FOLLOW RT. 22 EAST

"Oh, God, a bed," Susan said dreamily.

"The sign's in English," John said. "Oh, here's the Intersystem one. Odd, it's not as friendly in 'System."

"Frumious Bandersnatch," Roland muttered.

"Route 22" (I nearly missed it, even going at a crawl) was a dirt trail which intersected the Skyway, then meandered off into the forest. I turned off and followed it, bumping over mound and rut, stone and fallen log, for what seemed like 20km with no bandersnatchi evident. Nothing was evident but a kind of hokey enchanted forest scene, as in the animated epics you see in museum *mopix* programs. Except of course there was nothing ersatz about it; this was the real, otherworldly thing. Out there was the demesne of elves, dryads, unicorns, and nymphs—or their funny-looking alien counterparts, and they'd be doubly eldritch for that.

We came upon it suddenly. It was a big, rambling three-story building slapped together out of immense logs and raw board lumber, roofed over with half a dozen gables, a spacious canopied porch going all the way around, lots of small windows on the upper floors, all of it anchored by four or five huge stone chimneys coughing thin black smoke. There was a big parking lot hacked out of the forest on three sides, crammed with unusual off-road vehicles.

All in all, it had a great deal of charm. Right then, though, a holey tent with no ground cloth would've looked like home. Smells of grilled food were in the air—I had been about to check instruments for air content and quality when I saw two husky fellows reel bare-headed out the front door and stagger to their funny-looking land-jumper. I let down the port and sniffed. Pleasant odors, some nameless, some familiar. I rather liked this place already.

"Anyone hungry?" I said.

"Hold out your arm," Susan answered, unstrapping hurriedly, "and don't bother with the salt."

I was pretty tired of hotpak dinners and moldy stuff from the cooler, too.

We were all packed up and out of the rig in nothing flat.

The bad roller looked pretty grim, afflicted with leprous white patches of crystallization. From here on in, every meter it rolled would be a risk. No matter; I was fairly sure there'd be a garage nearby. We'd put on the spare, and not give too much thought to how bad *it* was.

I stood at the edge of the parking lot, checking out escape routes. Habit. A second highway intersected Route 22 here, another logging road, or rabbit trail, I couldn't tell which. Sam had a clear path to leave on short notice, if necessary, unless someone parked next to him blocking the road. From the looks of these vehicles, though, he'd have no trouble nudging them aside if he had to. You'd have to see Sam up alongside your average four-roller buggy to appreciate how big he is.

I opened a channel on Sam's key, an oblong orange plastic box that was a radio, among other things. "Okay, Sam, I guess we're staying here overnight. You be all right?"

"Sure, have fun. And call me every so often. Leave the beeper on."

"Right. I'll patch you through when we go in to eat and lift a few cold ones. We'll have a lot to talk over."

"Good."

I closed the key. Susan was beside me, clucking and shaking her head.

"Poor Sam," she said.

"Eh?"

"He always has to stay behind, doesn't he? It's sad."

I reopened the key. "Hear that, Sam? Suzie thinks you've got nothing to do all by your lonesome. She's all worried."

"Hm? Oh, hell, don't worry about me."

Susan reddened. "I didn't . . . I meant—"

"I got a stack of crotch magazines I haven't looked at yet, and let's see, there's that model ship I'm putting together . . . have to write thank-you notes for the shower gifts . . . should wash my hair . . . and I can always wank off."

Susan scrunched up her face in pain. "Oh, you two are *terrible!*" She ran off, laughing.

"Welcome to Talltree!"

"Thanks," I told the big-boned, flannel-shirted man at the desk. "Good name."

His eyes twinkled. "We stayed up all night to think of it."

I looked around the lobby. It was big, fully two stories high with an open-beam ceiling. The rugs were sewn animal hides; the furniture looked handmade. The appointments were rustic yet tasteful. "Quite a place you have here," I said.

He swelled visibly, and his grin was broad. "Thank you! It's my pride and joy. Built most of it with my bare hands." He winked. "And a little help."

"Well, you did a good job. I was expecting something more primitive on a planet like this."

"This is one of the most sophisticated log structures on Talltree," he informed me. He pointed upward. "I designed those cantilever trusses myself. You can do a lot with the local wood, though. Strong as iron—high tensile strength."

"Interesting."

The lobby was filled with people, young men mostly, joking, hooting, jostling each other. They drank from pewter mugs, sloshing beer onto the floorboards. The crowd appeared to be the overflow from the bar, called the Vorpal Blade.

"I hear a lot of English being spoken," I said.

"Mostly English speakers here," he said. "English, Canadian, Aussie, lots of Irish, a few other breeds. You American stock?"

"Yes, but it's been a long time since I thought of myself as American."

He nodded. "Time marches on. One day we'll all be *sabra*." He turned the registration book around. "Anyway, I do hope you enjoy your stay here at the Bandersnatch—if you'll sign right here. You all together?"

I signed. "Yes. What's the local industry around here?"

His eyes twinkled again. "Would it surprise you if I said logging?"

"Not a bit." I looked back at the crowd of burly young men. Everyone seemed cast to type.

He gave me our room keys. They were made of hand-wrought iron. Only two; Winnie and the women in one room, the men in the other. It was my idea. Talltree was part of the Outworlds, and my leftover Consolidation Gold Certificates were still good, but I wanted to economize. I had only a limited amount of gold to trade. The nightly room rates were fairly cheap, though.

"Any way of getting a bite to eat?" I asked.

"It's a little early for the dining room, sir. Our cook's building a flume this week. But the Blade has a separate kitchen and plenty of food. Most of the guests take breakfast and lunch in there. However, you might find it a bit crowded now."

"What's this?" I asked above the noise. "A luncheon party?"

"No, today's a holiday. Feast of St. Charles Dodgson." He gave me a knowing wink. "The celebration got started early. Like three days ago."

"Feast of St. Charles . . ." John began, then broke out laughing. We all did. On the multiple nationality-ethnic-religious worlds of the Skyway, nobody could agree on what holidays to celebrate. Back in Terran Maze, those officially proclaimed by the Colonial Authority were scoffingly ignored, except by bureaucrats, who took off work. A tradition had arisen to celebrate spurious ones, silly ones, just for fun. People need excuses to goof off, though the thinnest will serve.

"Soon as you freshen up," the clerk continued, "you can join the festivities, if you—"

I was looking at the merrymakers, then turned back to the clerk. He was staring at the registry book, into which I had just signed my name.

He looked up at me. "Is that really your name?"

"The alias I use most." When he didn't laugh, I said, "Just kidding. Sure, it's my name."

"You're Jake McGraw? *The* Jake McGraw?"

Again, my inexplicable fame had checked in before I had. "I'm the only one I know of."

"You have an onboard computer named Sam?"

"Yup."

"I see," he said, nodding thoughtfully. He turned away, but kept eyeing me askance, as if he weren't sure about something.

That was *his* problem. But what he would finally believe might be mine.

3

Our rooms on the second floor were primitive, but again there was antique charm in the rough wall paneling, the quaint lamps, the handmade furniture—beds, nightlamps, armoires, and chairs. The beds were especially nice, with simple floral carvings on the headboards. However, Susan didn't like hers.

"Lumpy as hell," she griped, "and the sheets are gray."

"Be patient, Princess," Roland teased. "We'll get the pea out from under the mattress later."

"Everyone I know is a comedian. Let's go eat."

They all went downstairs. There was a mirror behind the door to the room, and I paused to look myself over. I was wearing what is for me formal dress: my maroon starrigger's jacket with its jazzy piping, rakish cut, and little pockets with zippers all over the place. Usually, my attire is medium-slovenly, but all my casual clothes had been left behind on various planets. This jacket and the fatigue pants were about all I had left, except for shorts and things I wear when lounging about the rig. The jacket made me feel faintly ridiculous. I looked like a goddamn space cadet.

I went down the narrow stairs to the lobby, where the gang was waiting for me. We started for the Vorpal Blade. There were even more people in the lobby now, trying vainly to get in. Just as we hit the edge of the crowd, the desk clerk intercepted us.

"We have a table for you and your party, Mr. McGraw. If you'll follow me."

"A table?" I said incredulously. "In there?"

"Yes, sir, right this way."

I turned to my companions, but they weren't at all surprised. So we followed him as he made a swath for us through the clot of people pressing around the entrance to the bar. He seemed to know just about everyone he either politely brushed by or summarily shoved out of the way, none too gently, when the parties concerned weren't immediately cooperative. His size, even when compared to these beefy loggers, gave him all the authority he needed, if he didn't own the place to boot.

The Vorpal Blade was dark, smoky, and noisy, redolent of spilled beer and cooking grease. A huge bar took up one side of the room. The walls were of barkless log, milled flat on the inside, and the ceiling joists were squared-off and planed. There were plenty of tables and chairs, but too many damn people, loggers mostly. The decor was apropos—walls hung with odd varieties of saws, axes, cutting tools of every sort, pairs of spiked climbing boots, ropes, and such. It was a sweaty, muscular, pewter-and-leather kind of place, awash with good fellowship and camaraderie. Everybody was singing, including the bartenders, and they were *busy*.

The clerk actually had a table for us, with room for all, against the far wall near the bar and directly athwart a huge stone fireplace. We all sat, and I thanked the clerk. I asked him his name, silently wondering if I should tip him. I reached into my pocket.

"Zack Moore, sir. And save the gratis for the help. Enjoy."

"Thank you, Zack."

On his way out he shooed a buxom barmaid over to us, then waved and left.

"Hello, there! What're you people having today?"

The others started ordering. I was noticing the alien grain of the wood. It was almost geometrical, oddly shot through with greens and purples, but the overall color was a dark brown. Didn't look as though the wood had been stained. I knocked a knuckle against the wall. It felt like iron. I turned around, sat back, and listened to the group sing-along. Odd lyrics. A group at a table near the bar sang the verses, the rest of the crowd taking up the chorus, which went something like:

A lumberjack can't take a wife.
Such a terribly lonely life!
For a logger's best friend is a tree—
It's strange, I know, but it's all right by me!

Each verse grew progressively more absurd and off-color. Transvestism and other variations were broadly hinted at. Individual poetasters stood up and sang their own verses, each more outrageous than the last. The crowd howled. After the last verse, they'd sing it all over again, adding more verses. I asked the barmaid where the song had come from. She didn't know, but said in so many words that it was most likely traditional. She'd been hearing it ever since she came to Talltree as a child (last Tuesday, from the looks of her—but, hell, maybe I'm just getting old).

We all listened while waiting for our order to come. By the time the beer arrived, Suzie and John were convulsed, with Darla and Roland smiling, a little unsure. Carl loved it, too. Winnie and Lori were trying to talk above the din.

The beer was *Inglo* style, dark, bitter, served at room temperature, but the high alcohol content more than made up for it. I drained my pewter mug in three gulps and refilled it from the glazed crockery pitcher.

Only when the food came did I think about Winnie. She certainly couldn't eat this stuff—braised pork ribs, roast game hen, fried potatoes and vegetables, sliced warm bread with mounds of fresh butter. The barmaid told us that almost nothing on the planet was edible without extensive processing. All the fare before us had been raised on local farms.

Lori came over and shouted in my ear.

"Winnie wants to go outside. Says she can find something to eat."

"Here?" I shouldn't have been surprised, but I was. "Well, okay, but I should go with you."

"We'll be fine. You go ahead and eat, I'm not very hungry."

"How's your head? Still feeling woozy?"

"Nah, I'm fine."

"Okay, but be careful." I was reluctant to let them go, and briefly considered asking Roland to tail them and keep an eye on them, but I knew Lori was fiercely independent for her age, and more and more I had come to consider Winnie the equal of an adult human in intelligence and maturity—maybe even more than equal. Lori could do very well on her own; however, I still wanted her to be checked over by a competent medic, if one could be found. That was a minor problem. The big one was what the hell to do with her. With the *Laputa* either lost or pirated, she had no place to go except to her former foster parents' home on a planet named Schlagwasser, which lay on Winnie's Itinerary. Unfortunately, Lori had not been on good terms with her foster parents, and had run away.

But it wasn't certain that the *Laputa* had been lost. Good for Lori . . . maybe . . . but not good for me. At least three groups of people and beings aboard that strange ship-animal wanted my blood. In regard to the alien party, that could be taken quite literally. The Reticulans practiced ritual hunting in bands known as Snatchgangs, and dispatched their captured quarry by ceremonial vivisection. If Corey Wilkes, their human ally, had survived, he'd still be teamed with the Rikkis to get the Roadmap from me. And then there was the *Laputa*'s master, Captain Pendergast, who had been in cahoots with Wilkes and Darla's father, the late Dr. Van Wyck Vance, in a scheme to run antigeronic drugs into the Outworlds. To those who wanted to keep these Consolidated Outworlds isolated from Terran Maze and independent of the Authority, the Roadmap represented a threat. Doubtless Pendergast viewed it as such, but he might yet be unaware of Wilkes' betrayal; Wilkes wanted the map to give to the Authority in return for, among other things, amnesty for his part in the drug operation. Pendergast was not alone in his desire for a free Outworlds. He most likely shared it with every inhabitant of this maze. After all, everyone here had taken a desperate gamble in shooting a potluck portal to get here. There was a way back to Terran Maze by Skyway. Problem was, it went through Reticulan Maze, where few humans, or any rational human who wanted to keep his skin intact, dared to go. But it was a fair possibility that a bold or foolish few had braved the trip back and had lived to tell of what was on the other side of the potluck portal on Seven Suns Interchange, though that might be only one of several portals leading into the Outworlds.

The upshot: if the *Laputa* had made it, the problem of what to do with Lori would evaporate, but I just might, too.

Problems, problems.

What would the Teleologists—John, Susan, and Roland—do now? That would take priority on the agenda, after we had eaten.

The food was great—ribs spicy and done just right, the game hen crispy-skinned and juicy inside. The bread was golden brown with a thick crust, flaky and tender. And the vegetables were there to pass the time between bouts of wolfing down the entrees, with draft after draft of beer to sluice it all down the pipes. If this was bar food, I wondered what delights the dining room offered. The waitress kept bringing side dishes, compliments of the house, she said. Along with free rounds of beer came bowls of sliced pickled beets, onions, pickled eggs and cucumbers, multi-bean salad, assorted condiments, and piles of bread and butter.

On the down side, we were getting stared at. It wasn't our table manners; in that regard we fit right in. Word had spread, I thought, as to who I was—which immediately brought to mind the question of just who the hell I *was*. Jake McGraw, Olympian god-type, who came back through time to bring the secret of the Roadbuilders to mankind? Just a man around whom a cloud of wild rumors had settled? Or was I being confused with someone else?

No, the latter two possibilities were out; the Black Cube, the paradox of Darla, and other realities spoke volumes about the rumors being true. Some of them, anyway. That left the Olympian hero. Anybody got a fig leaf?

Finally the singing stopped, and all the food was gone. I was stuffed, and halfway drunk. I don't like doing things halfway. We ordered more beer.

"My God," John breathed, sitting back and massaging his stomach, "I can't remember ever eating so much at one time. Hope I won't—" He burped liquidly. "Ohhh. Excuse *me*."

"Bring it up again and we'll vote on it," Lori said, returning with Winnie.

"I can't believe you found food," Darla said.

Winnie smiled and waved a handful of plum-sized pink fruit with blue speckles all over them. Lori dumped a pile of leaves and stems down on the table, and sat down.

"Eat up, folks!"

Everyone groaned. "Here, honey, I saved you some chicken," Susan said, sliding a plate toward her.

"Kinda small for chicken, but thanks."

"It's game fowl, Susan," Roland corrected. "Raised domestically."

"Whatever."

"How did Winnie know . . . ?" John motioned vaguely at the pile of vegetation.

"How does Winnie know everything," Roland countered, "including accurate descriptions of planets she's never visited?"

"I'll have to talk it over with her," Darla said thoughtfully. "Apparently there's more information in that poem of hers than I've been able to get out."

"Maybe the poem and the map and this kind of information," John offered, "what to eat along the way and that sort of thing—maybe you could consider it all a . . . well, what would you call it? A tourist guide kit?"

"Very good, John," Roland said. "Very good."

"Boy, those woods out there are spooky," Lori said through a mouthful of game hen. "Kept getting funny . . . I dunno, *feelings.*"

"Did you see any white rabbits?" Roland asked.

"Nah, didn't actually see anything. Hey, this is good."

"You should eat, honey," Susan said motheringly. "You haven't taken a bite all day."

"I'm eating, I'm eating!"

"Sorry, Lori. I didn't mean—"

"Oh, it's okay. I'm sorry."

We watched Winnie take a tentative bite of fruit and roll it around her tongue. Not bad. She chewed it briskly and popped the rest into her mouth.

We all looked at one another and shrugged.

John leaned back. "Well," he said, as if to start something off.

"Yes, well," Roland seconded.

"What are you folks going to do now?" I asked.

"I've been thinking," John began.

"Thought I smelled something burning," Lori mumbled. I think she had John pegged as somewhat of a stuffed shirt, which he was.

Susan tittered, and Roland smiled before he said seriously, "I'm for keeping with Jake. I think if you examine all our options, it's the best one."

"Hold off, now," John cautioned, raising a hand. "Why don't we examine them all and see?"

"The linkages are there," Roland asserted. "Everything seems to have gone according to Plan."

"I'm not so sure of that."

"It's fairly obvious."

"Not to me, I'm afraid," John said gently. "Forgive me, Roland."

Roland sighed. "I suppose my task is to make you see the overall design."

"I want to learn from you, Roland. I really do. But . . . please, let's make it an exchange. Agreed?"

Roland nodded. "You're right. I have been doing a lot of pontificating lately." He gave John a conciliatory grin. "Let's go over our options."

"Well, for one . . ." John slapped the table. "We can try to find the planet where the Ryxx launch those starships. We may be able to get back to Terran Maze that way."

The second way to get back from a supposedly one-way portal: go through normal space. Back in Terran Maze, nobody knew of this, and the Ryxx must have taken great pains not to let on, probably in order to protect their monopoly on trade with the Outworlds, though they could have had other reasons. I knew of no other race who bothered to build starships; the Skyway made them superfluous. The Ryxx would probably hold their monopoly even if everyone knew they were doing it.

"That may be worth exploring," I put in, "just to satisfy your curiosity and cover all bets, but I wouldn't hold out any great hopes for it. How much money have you got?"

John gave me a dour look. "Jake."

"Sorry. Just trying to point out that passage on a sub-lightspeed starship has to run high. Even if they do take passengers, which I somehow doubt, there could be a long waiting list. From the little I know of starship design, weight and space would be critical."

"Didn't Wilkes say he was going?" John asked.

"I wouldn't take anything Wilkes said without a truckload of salt. He may have been lying, maybe not. Keep this in mind. He was, or is still, for all I know, a very well-connected man. He may have cut a special deal."

"Maybe . . ." John drummed the table with spidery fingers. "Well, I don't know, maybe we could get jobs, work up our passage money, approach the Ryxx and make a deal ourselves. Plead our case."

The corner of Susan's lips curled sourly. "We have a great sob story."

"I'm simply outlining the alternatives, Susan."

"Oh, go ahead, John. Don't mind me."

"Bear with me, please. Now, back on Splash—"

"I wouldn't go back there," I said.

"Maybe not Splash. Some other place. Here, for instance. There's always the option of settling here, or on some world where we can get a community going."

"The three of us?" Roland said skeptically.

"Three, or two, or even one, Roland. Isn't that what Teleological Pantheism is all about?"

Roland acknowledged the point with a tilt of his head.

John ruminated for a moment, then went on, "I see what you're saying. We'd be cut off. No funds, no communication with our group on Khadija, or with the organization back on Terra. It would be difficult."

"Rather. No money, no immediate prospects of getting any, no place to stay, except with Jake. We need supplies and literature to stock a reading center—"

John turned to me. "I think I told you we do no proselytizing. But one of our chief functions is to open up and run a reading room and consultation center. That's what we were about to do when we had the mishap with the Militia back on Goliath. After visiting our colleague in the hospital, we were going to see about renting a little storefront in town."

Susan had been thinking. "What about sending a message back by starship? If we could only let Sten or somebody know what happened to us."

"Yes," John said, the idea dawning on him, "yes, that's a marvelous thought! Don't know why I didn't think of it. We simply must get word back somehow. If we could let our community know that there's something here on the other side . . ."

"Again," I said, "you can try, but again I doubt it would work. The Ryxx don't seem to want anyone to know about the Outworlds. They may have been willing to take Wilkes back, but that might only have been because they were in on the drug operation. Anyway, I seriously doubt whether they're in the mail business."

John and Susan looked deflated.

"I wouldn't give up hope," I hastened to add. I didn't want to be too hard on them because what I had to tell them next would be pretty rough. "We know nothing for sure. And the most important thing we're not clear on is whether any of us are safe anywhere in the Outworlds."

Susan's face blanched. "What do you mean, Jake?"

Although I was nearly drunk, I had been giving the whole matter some thought. "First of all, we don't know what became of the *Laputa*." I turned to Lori. "What would've happened if the Arfie pirates had taken over the ship?"

"I don't know. It never happened before."

"You have no idea what would have become of the passengers?"

"No, but I wouldn't put it past Arfies to do something terrible. Some of them are okay, but others . . ."

"But the ship has always managed to beat off these attacks. Right?"

"Yeah."

"So," I went on, turning back to John and his confreres, "there's every possibility that everyone aboard that ship who was hot on my tail is alive and well and desirous of my blood. All of you are in danger because of your association with me. And that goes for Lori, too . . . and Carl."

John shook his head slowly, exasperation in his voice. "But surely there's somewhere in the Outworlds we could hide. I simply can't believe—"

"Hide? From the Reticulans?"

The three Teelies looked grimly at me, then at each other.

"I hate to bring it up," I said, "but we're going to have to proceed on the assumption that all of us are sacred quarry."

That put a damper on the conversation for a while. I remembered I hadn't checked in with Sam.

"About time."

"Sorry. We were discussing what we should do. I think we've agreed that everyone should stick together for now."

"A good idea."

"And we should try to get word on what happened to the *Laputa*. Is there anything on the air here in the way of news?"

"No commercial or government stations, but there's an extensive skyband and amateur radio network. I've been monitoring all channels. Nothing on the Laputa *so far."*

"Well, there's a lot of traffic between here and Splash, and that ferryboat served a vital function. If she were lost, it'd be big news. Something should turn up."

"Right, I'll keep monitoring. Leave the key open, okay?"

"Sure." I put it on the table and activated the microcamera to give him something to look at.

"Nice place. The food any good?"

"Great," Darla told him.

Someone in the crowd had stood up and was speaking. He was like the rest: thick-thewed, long mussy hair, dressed in a plaid flannel shirt and dungarees.

"Gentlemen, gentlemen! And ladies, if I may use both terms so loosely." He leered and stroked his wiry red beard.

Rude noises from the crowd.

"I now call this joint, plenary meeting of the Brotherhood of the Boojum and the Sorority of the Snark to order!"

Shouts, jeers, applause.

"Order! I will have order! Sergeant at Arms, will you please see to it that any objectionable behavior is dealt with according to the bylaws of this organization?"

Something hulking in a sheepskin jacket stood up and surveyed the crowd menacingly. He got no takers. Everyone shut up.

"Thank you, Brother Flaherty." The hulk sat down as the one with the red beard took a long pull from his mug, draining it. "The bar is now closed!" he pronounced, banging the mug down on the tabletop.

"Booo!"

"Be reasonable, old man!"

"Who cares? We got three pitchers."

He ignored it. "I now call upon Brother Finch to read the minutes of the last meeting."

Another logger lurched to his feet. "The bloody stupid meeting was called to order by Acting-President Brother Fitzgore. The minutes of the last bloody stupid meeting were read. Weren't any old business, weren't any new business. The bloody stupid meeting was adjourned and we all got drunk as bloody skunks." Brother Finch sat down heavily.

"I thank Brother Finch for that succinct, bare-to-the-bones summation of the salient developments of the last meeting. Do I have a motion to accept Brother Finch's report as it stands?"

"I so move!"

"I second the motion."

"The motion has been made and seconded to read Brother Finch's report into the record without emendation. May I now assume that the membership will assent to do so without a vote? Are there any objections?"

Someone stood up. "I object to the minutes of the last meeting being exactly the same as the minutes of the preceding meeting, and the one before that. In fact, they're always the same damn minutes!"

Fitzgore raised an imperious eyebrow. "Do you take issue with the contents of Brother Finch's report?"

"No, the report is accurate as it stands. I merely object to his lack of originality and literary style."

"It is not Brother Finch's duty to be original, but to record the facts accurately and without bias!" Fitzgore bellowed. He took a deep breath. "And as for style, I think Brother Finch's prose is almost Homeric in its brilliant use of epithet."

"Almost what?"

"What the hell's an epaulette?"

"At any rate," Fitzgore continued airily, "your objection is overruled."

"This is not a court of law. I demand that my objection be entered in the record."

"So be it," Fitzgore acceded. "Let it be noted in the record that Brother MacLaird has objected to Brother Finch's literary style, or lack thereof."

"I ain't got a bloody pencil," Brother Finch said.

Someone threw a pencil at him. He caught it neatly, snapped it in two between thumb and forefinger, and threw it back.

"Who the hell are these weirdos?" Sam said.

"Is there any old business?" Fitzgore asked.

"I go' a boil on me bum!"

"Any new business?"

"I still go' a boil on me bum!"

Laffs.

"I move we adjourn!" someone shouted.

"Since no new business has been brought up by the membership, I would like to call the following matter to the membership's attention, if I may be permitted."

"According to the rules of procedure, the Acting-President must always entertain a motion to adjourn from any member!"

"Not," Fitzgore retorted, "when said Acting-President can beat said member's arse to a bloody pulp any time he so desires."

"You and what regiment of the Home Guard?"

Cheers for the Home Guard.

"This matter can be settled later, but as for now . . ."

"Outside in five minutes, Fitzgore."

"I will be honored," Fitzgore acknowledged. "As I was saying—"

"Oh, not again. Last time they were so snockered they couldn't see to swing at one another."

"As I was saying!" Fitzgore roared. Then he cleared his throat and wiped his forehead with a sleeve. "Brothers and Sisters," he said quietly. "It is not often . . . rather I should say, it is unprecedented for us to have among us as a guest . . ." He paused for effect as heads turned, searching the room. ". . . a figure of—how shall I put it?—A figure of such *epic* stature. But that is the case."

"Who?" someone wanted to know, but many eyes were on me.

"The Skyway," Fitzgore continued in stentorian tone, "abounds with legends, myths, tall tales, apocrypha, and general foolishness, all of which are to be taken with a grain of salt, if not the whole bloody cellar and the bloody mine it came from."

"I think I'm going to puke," Sam declared.

"But it is rare that one has the profound honor, the exhilarating pleasure, of meeting a protagonist of one of these sagas in the flesh. However, that is our honor and our pleasure this day. Brothers and Sisters, may I present to you—and would you join me in drinking a toast in honor of—"

"You closed the punking bar, you dolt!"

Fitzgore refilled his mug from a nearby pitcher. "Then I open it again!"

Everyone raised his mug.

"Join me in a toast to that giant of legend, that king of the Skyway, the man who drove into the raging fires of the birthing universe and lived to tell the tale—"

He turned to face me.

"Ladies and gentlemen, may I present to you . . . Jake McGraw!"

4

I frankly can't remember all of what went on that night. I know a great deal of alcohol found its way into my system. Events, as I perceived them, became rather . . . diffuse. Fitzgore and his compatriots turned out to be very good drinking companions. Excellent drinking companions. They bought all of us a round of drinks. We bought all of them a round of drinks. Everybody bought everybody a round of drinks. Serious drinking then commenced. At some point, I found in my field of vision the wavering image of a stein of beer fully three hands high. They called it the Brobdingnagian Thunder Cup.

I drank it.

That was quite late in the evening—I think. Before that, we did a lot of talking. They wanted to know everything about me, about the Roadmap, about everything. I introduced them to Winnie. She's the map, I said. Fine, they said. Let's trot out pencil and paper and see what she knows. Pencil and paper were trotted out. Winnie proceeded to show her stuff, looking like a kindergartner learning the rudiments of writ, pink tongue protruding as she executed cramped figures with arduous dedication. She filled page after page with spirals and other shapes connected by lines.

"By God," Fitzgore said, "that's the local group! It must be." He stroked his psychotic growth of red beard. "Dammit all, if we had a library on this planet, we could get books to check this." He tossed off half a stein of beer. "If we had any books on this planet."

"I think I've got a few astronomy books in the rig. Matter of fact, there should be a whole crate of 'em. That right, Sam?"

"Yeah, our manifest shows a shipment of book-pipettes. But you don't really want go back there and—"

"Sure I do!"

"Oh, for pity's sake."

"Jake," Roland said, "maybe later, when we're all sober. This array has to be the Local Group. Look, here're the Magellenic clouds, and . . . let's see . . . right here would have to be Andromeda and Messier 33—"

"Who's not sober?"

"And these two little puffy things are probably Leos I and II. Over here are the galaxies in Sculptor and Fornax—"

"Who needs books," a toothless logger with a Strine accent said, "when you got this cobber?"

"Roland is a book."

"Thanks, Suzie. And all these lines," Roland went on, "are Skyway routes. But the interesting question is this. What is this major route coming in from this direction and going off here? Seems to be a major road."

"Very likely," Fitzgore said. "Look at these other things Winnie's done. Could these be galactic clusters connected by a road?"

"I should think they were," Roland answered. "And these cloudlike figures . . ."

"Metaclusters," I said.

"What're those?" somebody asked.

"Groups of groups. Supergroups of galaxies, all accessible by a major road system."

"Going where, I wonder?" another logger mused.

"To the bloody limit, mate."

"The what?"

"The Beginning," Fitzgore breathed. "The very cradle of what-there-is."

"How's that?"

"When you look out at the universe," Roland lectured, his manner a trifle labored—he was drunk—"at faint galaxies and groups of galaxies, you look back through time. Speed of light, relativity, and all that. When you look really far out, as far as the most sophisimicated . . . sophifimis—" He burped. "'Scuse me. When you use really expensive astronomical stuff, you don't see so much out there. You're looking back to a time when the universe was in a radically different state from what it's in now. Before galaxies formed. You've bumped up against the limit of the perceivable universe, beyond which anything out there is redshifted practically to invisibility."

"You've lost me there."

"It's basic cosmology," Roland contended, his tone suggesting that any six-year-old child would consider it old hat.

"Yes, of course," Fitzgore said, more to himself than to anybody. "Shoot a portal, and you go back through time. If you follow a road leading to the farthest reaches of space, a road that takes you in faster-than-light jumps . . ."

"You will ultimately come," Roland continued for him, "to a point from which all spacetime flows outward."

"The Big Bang," one of the loggers said.

"Absolutely, if the Skyway goes that far."

"How could it?" somebody asked.

"I have no idea," Roland said, "but that roadbuzz has it that Jake will find out."

"I ain't goin' nowhere," I said. "I'm too goddamn drunk."

Imagine the rising dough of a four-dimensional loaf of raisin bread.

You can't do it. It's impossible to imagine a four-dimensional anything, but it helps to try.

As the dough rises, the volume increases, as does the distance between each raisin. Think of each raisin as a galaxy—really a group of galaxies—and you have the conventional representation of the theory of an expanding universe, first proposed about a century and a half ago. Now, inside the ballooning volume of that dough, the farther away one raisin is from another, the faster their mutual rate of recession—it just works that way geometrically. In the real universe, it happens that galactic clusters can be far enough away from each other to put their recessional speeds at an appreciable percentage of the speed of light. Due to the Doppler effect, light from these distant objects, infalling on the instruments of local galactic astronomers, is "redshifted" to great degree, meaning that the lightwaves have decreased in frequency toward the red end of the spectrum. The same thing happens to the sound waves from a passing vehicle's warning signal. You hear the pitch change, go down, decrease in frequency. Light comes in frequencies, too; in the visible part of the spectrum, blue is the high end and red the low. Retreating galactic clusters doppler into the red. Redshift. The farther away they are from us, the more their light is redshifted. As Roland said, astronomers can look out to vast distances these days, using neutrino astronomy and graviton scanning. Once you get past the protogalactic core objects, traditionally called "quasars," you don't see much at all. Anything out that far is a retreating red ghost, exiting our ken at near the speed of light. At these distances, one looks beyond the red limit of the universe. If you can handle the notion that the universe has a boundary, this is it. But there is something beyond.

Pick any point of departure in the present-day universe, any place at all. Travel from there *in any direction*—you must keep that in mind—at faster-than-light speeds, and you go back in time. Go far enough, and you hit the edge. Go over the edge, and you run smack into Creation.

I pored over Winnie's maps. There was indeed a major artery linking metaclusters. Roland and I began to fit pages together, with Winnie's help.

"See, Jake? The intercluster road comes in here at Andromeda and exits at the same point. Let's call it the Intercluster Thruway."

"And if you follow it," I said, "you go . . . wait a minute. Is the Local Group associated with other galactic clusters? Or do we go our own way?"

"I don't know. We'll have plenty of time to check this. It may be that the Intercluster Thruway and the big road, the intermetacluster one, are one and the same, at least locally."

"Okay. So, whatever this big road is, we have to take the Transgalactic Extension to Andromeda in order to pick it up. On the way we hit these little globular galaxies. Did you say you knew the names for them?"

"They're just New General Catalogue numbers. Can't remember."

"Doesn't matter. Okay, you come into Andromeda here, presumably with the option of taking local routes into the galaxy or making a huge jump to the next cluster or metacluster, whatever the case may be."

Roland refilled his mug. "Yes, that's the way it looks."

I sat back and puffed on a long clay pipe someone had handed me. It was charged with an untobaccoish weed. "So what does it all mean?"

"It means," Roland said, "that as you travel the main intermetacluster road, you take backward leaps in time in billions of years."

"Yeah." I puffed. "Yeah. But are we sure of that?"

"No. But put this all together with what we know about how the Skyway works, along with the legends that have grown around you, and it makes sense." Roland was drunker than I was. A dizzy spell hit him, and he shook his head to clear it. "But what the punk do I know," he added thickly.

"I think it makes perfect sense," Fitzgore said. "And I wish to hell I were going with you."

"Where am I going?" I wanted to know.

"To the Big Bang, mate," another of the loggers said.

I nodded toward the maps. "It's one hell of a long way to the end of the road." I slid one sheet over to Fitzgore and pointed to it. "Look at the Local Group map. You pick up the big road in Andromeda. Now, from here, that means you have to somehow get on the Galactic Beltway and go about 10,000 light-years to the rim of the Milky Way. How many road klicks would that be?"

"Doesn't Winnie's journey-poem give some indication?" Fitzgore asked.

"Darla's still working on the translation," I said. "Anyway, you then take the Transgalactic Extension out to this little splotch here. Hey, Roland. What did you say this could be?"

"Huh?"

"Wake up. This little cloud here?"

"Oh. Uh, an undiscovered extra *burp* galactic star cloud. Makes a nice little bridge to Andromeda."

"Yeah, but even with that, the jump is in the neighborhood of a million light-years."

"Prolly is. Gimme that pitcher, willya?"

"Sure you can handle it, Egg Roll?" a mountain-size logger said.

"Don't call me 'Egg Roll,' you tree-humping moron."

"Easy, son. Didn't mean anything by it."

"Then shut up and gimme that pitcher, or I'll teach you some punking manners."

"You'll find me a willing pupil, mate. Anytime you've got the time."

"The time," Roland breathed, struggling to his feet, "is now. Would you care to take the evening air with me, sir?"

"I would indeed."

"Gee, that rhymes," Susan said, nose wrinkling as she smiled. "Would you care . . . to take the eve-ning airrr . . ." She had a good singing voice.

"Oh, Roland," John said. "Sit down. Your honor has hardly been besmirched."

Susan laughed.

"'Besmirched'?" I said. "How 'bout just smirched?" I took a good inhale on the pipe and let it out. "Never did understand what the 'be' was for."

Roland and the logger left.

"Well, anyway—"

In another part of the bar, someone fell, or was thrown, over a table.

Fitzgore said, "You were saying, Jake?"

"Huh? Oh, yeah. What I was going to ask was—did you ever hear of a portal jump of that distance?"

"Hardly. But who knows?"

"Just what the hell is in this pipe, if I may ask?"

"Cruising weed, we calls it," someone said.

"Cruising weed. I've been inhaling this shit."

"Good idea, that."

"Pretty good shit, actually."

"Have some more beer, Jake," Fitzgore said, sloshing suds into my mug.

"Don't mind if I do, thank you." I relit the pipe with a long kitchen match. "Uh, your buddy there . . . he's got at least fifty kilos on Roland."

"Liam won't hurt him. He's a good man, Jake. Never hurt anyone, so far as I know."

"Well, I guess it's okay, then." I took a deep drag on the pipe. The weed was rather good, in its own way. Not smooth on the draw, but satisfying. Rather peppery. At any rate, I was cruising along just fine. "Getting back to the issue at hand," I went on. "My guess is we're talking about millions of kilometers of road, billions maybe, to get to the big road—the whachmacallit. Red Limit Freeway."

Fitzgore's eyes lit up. "Fine name for it!" Then he shook his head. "Not that much, Jake. It would be a long trek, surely, but I should think it would depend on the distances covered by each jump along the Galactic Beltway." He leaned back and hooked his thumbs in his suspenders. "Maybe there's a shortcut somewhere."

I nodded. "Maybe. Still . . ." I took the pipe from my mouth and used it to point at one of Winnie's drawings. "What about the Red Limit Freeway itself? How many metaclusters are there in the universe?"

Fitzgore laughed. "Cosmology's hardly my strong suit. However, I'd venture to say that the count of galaxies has to be in the billions."

"I've heard the figure of one hundred billion," I said. "Somewhere. Was that galaxies? I dunno. Anyway, say it's a hundred billion."

"Probably a conservative figure."

"Yeah, but let's say one hundred gigagalaxies. Okay, let's put the average population of a cluster at—"

"Don't you mean a metacluster?"

"Right, metacluster. Let's say a thousand galaxies in a metacluster, on the average."

"I see where you're going, Jake. But consider this. Red Limit Freeway is a road back through time, not necessarily a road that links every large-scale structure in the universe."

"Who says it's either?"

"Who's to say it isn't both?" someone put in.

"Good point," I said.

Fitzgore exhaled and wrapped his meaty arms around his chest. "Well, as laymen, I suppose all we can do is make points and counterpoints, until somebody in a position to know comes along and settles the matter."

"Or until Roland sobers up," I said. "He seems to know something about this."

"Has he had scientific training?"

"Can you answer that, Suzie?"

"Roland knows everything," Susan said. "But I think he studied political whatzis in school. Political whatever. Party member, you know."

"Really? Interesting. I take it he changed political stripes somewhere along the way."

"Yup." She giggled. "Or maybe he's a spy. A plant." She giggled again. "Or maybe he's just a plant. A veggie." This amused her as well. Then, suddenly, she sobered up and said, "Would it be all right for a lady to smoke a pipe?"

"I beg your pardon," Fitzgore said, taking another pipe from a carved wooden rack and charging it from the glass humidor. "Rude of me not to have offered. Darla, would you care to—?"

"No, thank you, Sean."

Darla and John had been unusually quiet. Subdued drunks. Carl was gabbing with Lori, who all along had been downing considerable quantities of beer. She had remained none the worse for wear. No one in the place seemed to care that she was well below legal drinking age. Winnie was still drawing—not maps, but crude animal figures. Cave paintings in a strange new medium?

Susan resumed snickering. "A carrot," she said, enjoying her private joke. Then she noticed me looking at her. "Roland's my friend. I like him. But sometimes..."

"I understand," I said.

She blinked her wet hazel eyes at me and smiled. "I like you too, Jake." Under the table, she took my hand and clasped it. The subtle pressure made it an expression of more than friendship. I didn't know how I felt about it. I decided to try another mug of beer to see if it made a difference. It did. I rather liked it.

Liam returned, dragging Roland across the floor like last week's laundry.

"Could've given me real trouble," he said, "if he'd been half sober. Landed a good kick to me ribs, he did."

Liam yanked Roland up with one arm and plunked him in a chair, then poured half a pitcher of beer over him.

Roland lifted his head from the table, blinked his eyes and said, "Someone gimme a beer." He wiped his eyes. "Please."

Liam took another pitcher (there must have been two dozen on the table) and poured him a mug.

"Thanks," Roland said.

It was the cruising weed that really did me in. If the beer had made things blurry, the weed turned the evening (the day was gone, borne away on a sudsy tide) into a palimpsest of half-recalled events spread over layers of stuff I couldn't remember at all.

I was still trying to imagine that four-dimensional raisin loaf. Naturally I never made it, but I did think of a cone, a three-dimensional one, with space represented by the two dimensions parallel to each other and perpendicular to the plane of the base, and time running along the vertical axis. Time past lies toward the base of the cone, with the present occupying the apex. At the base is the beginning of time, the beginning of everything, the Big Bang. Here, everything is suffused with a brilliant light. Purest energy. Gradually, it wanes to darkness as time progresses in the direction of the apex. All is dark. Then, suddenly, brilliant beacons flare—quasars, the turbulent cores of young galaxies undergoing gravitational collapse. Farther along, they begin to take on their familiar wheeled shape. The universe expands and cools. Entropy extracts its toll, and density decreases. We come then to the point of the cone, and the present day. Look back from that vantage point, and the past is a widening tunnel whose farthest end glows dully with faint echoes of creation. Look in a direction perpendicular to the time-line, and you see nothing. Relativity tells us that we can have no knowledge of the universe of the present, since by the time lightwaves lollygag in with the information, it's yesterday's news. But you can look back in time, even to the first few seconds of the primeval flash.

Dreams of the road . . .

I don't know exactly when Susan and I made love. Sometime in the evening, I think, before my induction into the Brotherhood of the Boojum. It was around dinnertime, and the bar had cleared out a bit. We excused ourselves from the table more or less simultaneously, made our way upstairs more or less following the same trajectory, and intercepted each other. More or less. We found a bed and made a kind of quiet, groping, drunken love. But it was nice, in a fumbling, friendly way.

Then Suzie passed out. I nearly did, but somehow galumphed my way downstairs again. I was thirsty.

That, I believe, is when Sean announced that I was to be inducted into the Brotherhood. I was asked if I wished to join. I said sure, what the hell.

There followed a ceremony, of which I remembered not much. Candles guttered in sconces, incense burned. Incantations were muttered. Chanting and general mummery. I recited something, reading it from what I dimly remember as a sheepskin scroll. It could have been a roll of shithouse paper. As to content, I think it would have been gibberish even if read stone sober. I was then confronted with the Brobdingnagian Thunder Cup. They bade me drink. I drank.

Next thing I knew, we were out in those weird woods. From the shadows came strange cries, sharp rustlings. Above the treetops, great winged things flapped their pinions. Things or persons were watching, peering from within dark bowers. We came to a clearing, and I was given a sword. My companions then withdrew, leaving me to face the fearful Boojum alone in the half-night. I was to make a cry, thus: *Yawkahoooo! Yawkahoooo!* I managed to approximate the sound once or twice, then gave it up.

I sat on a stump and tried to think of the time-cone—which was really called a light-cone, for reasons which then eluded me. And the road. The road that twines back to the heart of darkness, to the very core, the impenetrable fastness of Being. Or Nothingness.

That's how drunk I was. When you start capitalizing words with fuzzy meanings, you're either some wild-eyed nineteenth century German philosopher in a pince-nez, or you're very drunk. Possibly both.

I don't know how long I sat there. I thought of Susan, then of Darla, and the distance that had grown between us. Then the Paradox entered my mind, as it had been doing since this whole affair had begun.

But I didn't spend too much time on that. Brain cells were screaming in their death throes. Alcohol, that great shabby beast one always thinks is securely leashed, was turning on me again.

Suddenly, something crashed through the undergrowth and barged into the clearing.

I have an image of an animal somewhere between a giraffe and a kangaroo, with the head of a very strange dog. It resembled no other alien fauna I had ever seen. Yes, the head of a dog . . . well, not a dog, really. It had horn-shaped ears. Horn, as in musical instrument. Sticking out of either side of the small head. Must have been eight or nine feet tall. And it had purple and pink splotches over its inert yellow plasticine skin. It walked on two legs, and had two prehensile forelegs that dangled spastically as it moved.

Now, this is the part I'm really not sure about at all.

The beast stopped in its tracks when it saw me. It gave a yawp and said, "Oh! Dearie me, dearie me! Oh! Oh! Goodness gracious!"

Then it turned and ran, disappearing into the trees.

I thought about it a while. That Boojum, I decided, had been a *Snark*.

Then somebody whacked me over the head with something.

5

I woke up and discovered that a red-hot piece of metal was buried somewhere in my head. I was lying on a low cot in a small, one-room log cabin. There was a tiny window above me; outside it was dark. I turned my head very slowly and saw two loggers—all the men seemed to dress the same here—playing a listless game of cards at a rude wooden table in the middle of the room. What looked like an oil lamp, a bit off-center on the table, illuminated their bored faces. One of them, lean and tall with cynical dark eyebrows and slicked-back hair, looked over at me, then looked back and took a trick.

"He's come around."

The other one was fair and fat and everything the first one wasn't, only worse. He glanced over. "Should we tie him up?"

"Nah. He's wasted."

True. I tried getting up. The shard of hot metal throbbed and I collapsed, groaning.

The skinny one chuckled. "Weed and alcohol. My, my, my. Bad combination, that."

I had had weed, copious alcohol, and a whomp on the head for good measure. Lethal was the word for that combination. My mouth . . . oh, Lord, my mouth. Septic odors arose from within it, emanating from a coating of coppery-tasting sludge at the back of my throat. There was a great ball of linty wool where my tongue should have been. I swallowed and almost heaved.

"One thing, he can hold his liquor."

"Lucky for him. He would've choked to death on it."

There was a chance of that happening yet. This was not a hangover. This was a catastrophic illness. My eyes were hot ball bearings turning in their sockets. They seemed to click when I moved them. I closed my eyelids, the insides of which had somehow become lined with sandpaper.

This was obviously a bad dream. It was the weed. I couldn't accept the fact that, for what seemed for the eightieth time this week, I was a prisoner. I did not like these things happening at such regular intervals. For the first time in a good while, I was getting very angry.

Dammit, I wasn't that sick. I creaked up to a sitting position and swung my legs to the floor. The hot metal fragment became the flame of a plasma torch performing a curettage inside my skull. I propped my head up with both arms on my knees. Massaging my forehead, I took deep breaths and tried to will the pain away. When the throbbing subsided to mere agony, I looked up. The two of them were regarding me clinically.

"Whatever the outcome of this," I croaked, "I'm going to kill the both of you."

"Easy," the skinny one warned.

The chubby blond one laughed. "Nasty in the morning, isn't he?"

I sat there for a while, head in hands. Presently, nausea began to rise from my middle on a slow freight elevator. When it got to my chest I started coughing. It was the kind of cough that signals something is going to come up and can't be stopped.

The tall one was pointing at something to my right.

"Put it all in the bucket. Get one drop on the floor and you'll lick it up."

There was a wooden bucket on the floor near the foot of the bed. I reached and dragged it over just in the nick of time. A lot of beer came up along with remnants of lunch, but it wasn't enough to exorcise the demon. Dry heaving commenced, with nothing to dredge up but my insides.

A chuckle. "Didn't have a proper hold on that liquor after all."

Chubby made a face. "He's making me sick."

"Deal, will you?"

"Something about the sound, you know? When I hear someone doing it, I—"

"Deal!"

I was sick, but I was overdoing it, not exactly knowing how the ploy would work. But it was the only card I had.

"God, my stomach," I moaned. "On fire . . ."

"Get him some water," Chubby suggested.

"Are we playing hearts or hospital?"

"Gimme some water," I begged. "Please."

They played for a while. Then Chubby glanced over again. "Oh, let's give him some, Geof."

I did my imitation of a sick man until Geof relented. Chubby got up and went to a sink against the far wall. On it was a long-handled pump that creaked as he worked it. He crossed the room bearing a metal cup full of water. He approached warily, watching for a sudden move. I was not up to making one. He set the cup down on the floor about a meter in front of me, and backed away.

I got unsteadily to my feet, shuffled forward, stooped, and picked up the cup. When I straightened up, I saw Geof leveling a slug-thrower at me.

"Thanks," I rasped to Chubby.

"No trouble."

I sat back on the cot and drank a few mouthfuls, then poured some water in my cupped palm and splashed it on my face. It felt wonderful. I drained the cup and set it on the small table beside the bed.

"Lie back down," Geof told me, still holding the gun. "You'll feel better. Also, I won't have to make any holes in you."

I obeyed.

"Good," Geof said, laying the gun on the table. "Stay that way."

They continued their game while I lay there thinking. I was beginning to feel the slightest bit better, but decided to continue the malingering act. After about ten minutes I sat up.

"I have to take a piss," I announced.

Another argument ensued. Geof allowed that he didn't care if I wet my breeches. Chubby protested that it was his cot, and he damned well wasn't going to lose a perfectly good mattress. They bickered back and forth.

Finally Geof slammed the deck of cards down on the table-top. "All right, *you* take him out if you want to play nursemaid!"

Chubby rose from the table and withdrew a small biolume torch from his hip pocket.

"Wait," Geof said. "I'll do it. When he asks you to shake it for him, you'll probably give him the gun so you can use both hands."

He got up and pointed the slug-thrower at me.

"All right, you. Out the door, stand on the porch and let fly."

"I gotta do more than that," I said.

Geof scowled, thinking it over. You can't argue with nature. "Right," he grumbled. He took the torch from Chubby, crossed to the front door, opened it and gestured me through with the gun. "March," he said.

I made it seem quite an effort to get up, which it was to a degree. I hobbled to the door and went out.

Outside, he illuminated a path through the trees. I took it; Geof followed at a close distance. Perhaps a little too close for his own good. The path ended in a little grove wherein stood an outdoor facility of the kind I had not seen since we knocked down the one on our farm on Vishnu. This specimen was even more primitive. Ours had been designed so that the stored biomass could be easily retrieved for use as fertilizer and energy.

I stopped short, feigning indignation. "I gotta use that?"

"So sorry, Your Royal Highness. Get moving." He shoved me, then edged up until he was walking at my side, holding the gun on me as we drew up to the door.

Geof was a tough guy, but not very bright. In fact, it seemed as though he were making it too easy for me. He stood at an angle to the door such that . . . Well, I'd give it a try.

He held the barrel of the gun almost to my head. "I want the door wide open, now."

I took hold of the crudely carved wooden handle and pulled. The door swung easily. "Right," I said, and yanked the door back hard. It hit his other hand and knocked the torch from it.

The momentary distraction was all I needed. I reached out with my left hand, ducking to the right, and twisted the gun from his hand, almost taking his trigger finger with it. Luckily, the weapon didn't discharge. There had been no scuffle. In the space of a second or two, I owned the gun and Geof stood there in shock, nursing his reddened index finger. I stopped, picked up the torch and played the beam on his face.

"Well, Geof, who are you working for?"

He said nothing, shielding his eyes.

"I want to know who you're working for, and if you don't tell me, I'll shoot you dead now."

"Moore," he said quickly. "Zack Moore. I didn't—"

"That's all I wanted to know."

"Please don't shoot me."

"I'll consider it. I've met your type . . . Christ, I don't know how many times." I shook my head and clucked. "Why do you exist? It's always baffled me."

He declined to answer.

"At the heart of great mysteries," I said, "silence, always silence." I sighed. "Okay, Geof, inside."

He didn't move.

"Inside."

He entered the shack and turned around.

"Down the hole."

"What!"

"Another mystery, Geof. Always wanted to know if it could be done."

"You're insane."

"Possibly. Get down that hole. Now."

"I'll never fit down that!"

"Try."

"I won't!"

"Geof, remember what I said in the cabin? I'll kill you right now, and then stuff you down. Climb down, and I might not shoot you."

"You'll have to shoot me."

"Suit yourself." I stepped nearer, to make sure of my aim.

"Wait!" He looked. "It's too small."

"Do your best."

He did his best. After perhaps five minutes, he was hung up around his rib cage.

"I'm stuck!"

"You're skinny enough. Try harder. Exhale."

The shoulders presented a real problem, but with a few suggestions as to how to maneuver and a little brute force applied with my boot, he managed to slide his left arm down between his side and the rim of the hole.

"Uh! . . . Uh! . . . *God!*"

"A little more. C'mon, inhale and force it. You can do it, Geof."

After an agonizing minute or so, his left shoulder popped through the hole. I put my hand on top of his head, splayed my fingers, and pushed.

It was a surprisingly long drop. The splash echoed hollowly.

"Geof?"

No answer.

I took a different path back to the cabin.

Peering through the small rear window, I saw Chubby making tea, standing by the rusty wood stove. I circled to the front porch and waited by the door.

It didn't take long. He came out the creaky front door and stood on the edge of the porch, looking out into the night.

"Hi, Chubby."

He yelped and jumped a half-meter straight up. Then he turned slowly.

"Look, mate—" he began.

I leveled the gun at him. "I want the truth from you."

He swallowed. "You've got it."

"How long were you supposed to keep me here?"

"Until Zack sent somebody for you."

"How long would that be?"

"I don't know. He just said to keep you quiet for now."

"Okay. How far are we from the Bandersnatch?"

"Not far. Two kilometers, a bit more."

"Which direction?"

He pointed directly opposite the outhouse. "Take that path. When you come to the road, turn left and go about half a kilometer to the fork. Then bear right. It'll take you straight to the Bandersnatch."

"How far from here is the road?"

"About ten minutes at a good pace."

"You two carried me all that way?"

He shook his head. "No, one of the bigger lads slung you over his shoulder."

I stepped toward him.

"Are you sure about the directions?"

He nodded emphatically.

"I won't kill you now," I said coolly, "but if I've found you've steered me wrong, I'll be back."

"I swear it!"

"By the way, thanks for the water. It was mildly decent of you."

Relief made his face sag. "Well, it's all right, really. Geof is a bit harsh sometimes. He's not—" He glanced toward the outhouse worriedly. "What did you do with him?"

"He's having dinner. Tell me, is that huge purple creature standing behind you usually dangerous?"

He laughed, turning around to look. "Don't let that worry you. You'll see all sorts—"

I clipped him with the gun butt and sent him sprawling in the dirt. Then I dragged him back inside. This done, my head was throbbing so violently I thought I was hemorrhaging. I wasn't. That tea sounded like a good idea. I wanted to get moving as soon as possible, but I needed to recover a bit more. I poured boiling water from a rusty saucepan into the teapot and put the lid on. A cross-country trek at night through an alien wilderness would be dangerous, not to say foolish, in my present condition, but I had to get back to the Bandersnatch soon. I was worried about Darla and the others. While it was hard to believe that Moore could, with impunity, detain or abduct six people and an alien, it was possible that he owned this planet and had free rein.

No. I knew whose unseen hand was at work here. Pendergast. The master of the *Laputa* was a force to be reckoned with in the Outworlds. The ship must have limped into port. Messengers in high-speed roadsters would have been dispatched to get word out that I must be found and my "map" confiscated. Moore must have nabbed Winnie, poor thing. She must be frightened to death. And they'd need Darla to translate. Maybe they'd round everyone else up for good measure.

Tying Chubby up proved to be difficult since there was no rope handy, which I thought strange for a logger's cabin. Obviously Chubby did not work for a living. I resorted to tearing the bedding into strips with a dull kitchen knife. I trussed him up as well as I could—he was still out cold and looked as though he'd stay that way for a while—dragged him over to the cot, and dumped him in.

What was in the teapot wasn't a tea I was familiar with, and I don't know why I expected it to be, but it was good. I drank a cup, poured another and drank half. Then I searched the cabin for Sam's key, not really expecting to find it. A quick frisk of Chubby turned up nothing. Did Geof have it? I hadn't thought to ask him. Then out of an alcoholic fog came the memory of Darla reminding me to take the key from the table as I was leaving on my ceremonial quest. I had told her to keep it, I remembered, lest I lost it while running around out in the bush like a wacko. Besides, I had been drunker than a skunk.

But if Darla was now in Moore's custody . . .

Well, we'll have to see. Time to get the hell out of here. I finished the tea, tucked the gun in my belt, took the torch, and left.

These woods were strange, strange. I now knew full well what Lori had meant by "funny feelings." As I walked, the memory of what I had seen just before being knocked out grew sharper, though I was still having trouble distinguishing it from the crazy dream-stuff I had swum through on the way to full consciousness. I didn't want to dwell on it, though. Best to keep my attention on where I was going.

The path began just where Chubby had said it did. It went straight for a few meters then twined through the underbrush, bearing generally downhill. All around, immense treetrunks stood like columns in a vast dark temple. I had a vague sense of presences lurking among them. I was worried about the torch. Moore and a band of his men might be coming this way. A light appearing up ahead then suddenly vanishing might clue them in that somebody who didn't want to be sociable was about. They'd damn well guess that it was me. No, I'd have to walk in total darkness.

I stopped. Why not test my eyes now? I flicked off the torch.

Moonlight. I could see quite well. I walked a few paces. Down the path a break in the canopy let a tiny glowing bit of full moon peek through. I stood watching it for a while. It was so bright it almost hurt my eyes. The strange-colored foliage around me glowed spectrally. From the darkness under the trees came twittering sounds, sharp clicks, rasping buzzes. The longer I stood there the more sounds I heard, coming from farther and farther away. Everything, everywhere, seemed to throb with life. A whooping cry came from my right and startled me. It sounded vaguely human. A plaintive wailing began in the opposite direction. It was a long way off, but sounded less vaguely human. I didn't like it, nor did I care for the muffled porcine grunting that came from behind.

I moved forward, telling myself that a light would only attract whatever was out there. I didn't believe myself, but walked on into the half-gloom anyway. I'm like that. I can be a real pain in the ass sometimes.

I felt better physically. I was no longer certain I was going to die. A garden-variety agonizing headache had settled in, and the nausea was mild, with gusts up to medium-awful. But I was getting better with each step. Nothing like a brisk walk in the woods. The air was pleasant, bracing but not chilly. The smells were numerous, like an assortment of perfumes, heady and invigorating. Soft, milky moonlight dripped through the branches overhead. There was no wind. The path was worn and smooth, springing to the step like a bed of moss. The whole environment seemed more like a park than a wilderness. I half expected to see painted benches and trash receptacles along the way. The path turned sharply to the right, then began a gradual climb. I walked on, increasing my pace, trying not to jump at every chitter and twirp that sounded in the bushes as I passed. Damn, these woods were alive. Insects mostly. Just insects, he said, grinning nervously.

Those smells... The perfumes of the night. Intoxicating they were, and I couldn't tell whether their effect was to dampen my trepidations or augment them. Or maybe cause them. Ordinarily I have no fear of the dark, and while I have all sorts of respect for the uncertainties of an alien world, I'm not afraid to walk one alone. I've done it many times before. But there was something about Talltree that tapped into a reservoir of primal... *stuff*. Stuff that lies moldering in the human hindbrain. This was the archetypal enchanted forest. Fearful, yes, but also magical, preternatural, alive with ancient mysteries.

Damn, a fork. Chubby had mentioned one, but he'd been talking about the main road, hadn't he? The paths diverged into the night and I stood there a moment, trying to tell which one looked to have taken the most traffic. The one to the left seemed a little wider. I flashed the torch on it briefly. Okay, to the left.

The undergrowth thinned out, revealing puddles of silver light on the forest floor, beds of pale-petaled flowers moonbathing within them. To my right and up a gentle grade, blue-gray shelves of rock paralleled the path, outlining what may have been an ancient stream bed. I thought I smelled water nearby. Sure enough, the path descended to a quiet, narrow stream which I took in two hops, using a wide flat stone in the middle as a springboard. The path wound up a gentle grade. I still heard the snorting to my rear. It was beginning to worry me a little, because whatever was doing it seemed to be following the path. But it didn't sound as though it were gaining, just yet.

"Bleu."

I stopped. Someone or something, off in the bushes, had said *bleu*. Not *blue*, mind you, or *blew*, but *bleu*, with an admirably correct nasal intonation of the vowel.

"Bleu," came another voice. It was rather a flat statement, matter-of-fact.

"Bleu," confirmed still another from a different direction.

"Bleu," the first voice agreed.

"Okay, so it's blue," I said. "So what?"

Silence for a moment. Then: *"Bleu!"*

I started walking again, peering into the shadows. I couldn't see a thing.

"Bleu?" It sounded like a question.

"Damned if I know," I said.

"Bleu," another voice stated.

I walked through this laconic dialogue for two or three minutes, *bleu*-sayers to either side. Nobody got really excited, save for an occasional *bleu!* or two.

What had Chubby said? Ten minutes at a quick pace? I was sure I'd been walking for at least that long. I rarely wear a watch, and now regretted it. Time to start thinking about doubling back and taking the other fork. Well, I'd go a little farther. Besides, that snorting and snuffling did sound a little nearer now. I was sure of it. Or was I just getting spooked? Easy enough to get spooked with things *bleu*ing at me out of the darkness. Sounds I could deal with. It was all the same to me, as long as the speaker remained anonymous. I wasn't up to making new acquaintances right then.

I stopped. I thought I heard splashing.

"Greep."

This last was near enough to make me jump. I backed down the path, then turned and began jogging.

The snorting and snuffling was definitely louder and now took on a menacing quality. Whatever was doing it was also grunting, panting, gibbering, and possibly slavering.

I ran, setting off a chorus of *greep*ing in the undergrowth.

The path went uphill for a ways then leveled off. I was soon out of the land of the Greeps and into neighborhoods where other voices spoke. *Warble, chirp, breep, chitter, jub-jub,* you name it, somebody was saying it. The forest was alive with gossip. *He's running! Look at him run!* they seemed to babble. Tremulous cries, frantic war-whoops came from the distance. Word was spreading. The thing behind me was gaining, its wide snout pushed to my scent. Panicky screeching came from the treetops along with the nervous flap of leathery wings. A small, rounded dark shape lay ahead of me on the path. It squawked and bolted into the weeds. I heard hooves pounding against the turf off to the right, twigs breaking in the path of some frightened running thing. That made two of us. The thing behind me was big and sounded as if it were moving on two huge feet. It was running now, chasing me, gibbering maniacally. The path went into an S-curve, straightened, then went into a hairpin turn to the left, leading up the slope of a steep hill. I puffed up the trail, turned into the switchback, listening to the sound of thumping feet below me. The thing was fast, gobbling up distance in big strides. The hill didn't slow it down. I raced up the trail. The sounds it made were nightmarish, half-human. There was a note of ravenous glee to it all, a fiendish chuckling as if it reveled in the pleasure of the chase.

Three more switchbacks and I gained the top of the hill. The trail continued along a ridge, then swung into the trees. I decided to make a stand. I didn't think I could outrun the thing and the dash up the hill had taxed me. Getting off the trail would be a good idea. If the thing were big it might have trouble following me through the underbrush. I hoped.

The trail swung right and ran along the narrow crest of the hill. The underbrush grew thickly on either slope. Something big lay across the path ahead—a fallen treetrunk. I drew my pistol, took cover behind the trunk and took aim up the path. It was coming. I couldn't see anything yet, but it was coming. It didn't slow, didn't hesitate, kept running full tilt, drooling in anticipation, its feet whumping against the mossy softness of the trail. It growled, it giggled, it heaved and panted. It made one hell of a lot of noise. All around, the forest screamed in a mounting crescendo of terror. Flocks of panic-stricken creatures took wing into the night. Unseen things in the shadows burbled and greeped and went *bleu!* Voices in the trees shrieked their dismay. Thousands of tiny things stampeded through the brush. The beast shambled toward me, its breath like blasts of steam. I still couldn't make it out. No good; I'd have to be able to see it to shoot it.

I got up and ran like hell. I didn't really want to shoot it. You can never tell with a completely unknown creature. It might eat slugs for breakfast. Maybe its vital organs were in its feet. Maybe it had armor plating ten centimeters thick. What do you do when the thing shrugs off your best shot? As a rule, shooting at an alien unknown is a last resort. But I was up against it. If I ducked into the brush first I might never get another chance for a clear shot. I was sure it would follow, thick underbrush or not. My heart pounded against my breastbone with enough force to crack it. Starriggers sit too much to keep in shape. I was going on pure adrenaline; I didn't think my lungs were working at all.

Light up ahead—moonbeams falling across the path. I ran on through into the shadows on the other side. I skidded to a stop, turned, crouched, and aimed.

The thing slowed. It stopped just at the edge of the pool of light. It stood there panting and snarling. And I still couldn't see it.

I aimed for the probable center of the source of all that nonsense and emptied the clip of the machine-pistol at it. *Brrrrrrrrrrrrrrruppp!* Four seconds to unleash a hail of superdense metal pellets. My best shot. I leaped off the path into the brush, thrashed my way through a clump of broad-leafed weeds, stumbled, tripped, broke through the other side, and rolled down a steep incline. Thorny tendrils snagged at my jacket, twigs whipped my face, rocks bruised my ribs. I rolled and rolled until I finally got to my feet, letting momentum carry me up. I jogged down to level ground, slipped, fell and crawled behind a tree. I listened.

All I could hear was the blood pounding in my ears.

Silence. Everyone had shut up real suddenlike.

The hush continued for what seemed several minutes. It probably wasn't that long. At some point I decided I could start breathing again. I gasped, wheezed, and choked for a while, then got my breath. I kept listening. Nothing moved, nothing spoke. Then . . .

"Bork?" something to my left said tentatively.

I sighed, listened for a while longer.

"Bork?" it asked again.

I levered myself to my feet and leaned against the treetrunk. I took a deep breath. "Yeah," I said. "Bork." I wiped grit off my face, brushed dirt from my jacket. "Definitely bork."

Another voice *bork*ed up ahead, then others took the cry, glad the question was all settled.

Slowly, the forest came back to life, but the mood now was subdued.

I rested, squatting at the base of the tree for a few minutes. Then I walked along the bottom of the hill searching for a clear way up. There wasn't one. I wasn't really interested in going back up there. The thing might only be wounded, lying there in the path. Or maybe I had missed the damn thing. I didn't know and didn't particularly care to find out.

About fifteen minutes later, I had to admit to myself that I was lost. I had thought that picking up the trail again would be easy—just walk a little way along the base of the hill, then push through the underbrush until I came out on top. I did that, with some difficulty, and found what I thought was the trail I had been on, but it couldn't possibly have been because I followed it in the direction I'd come from and everything was unfamiliar. No switchback trail up the slope, no stream, nothing. I had walked a good distance along the bottom of the hill, wanting to pick the path up at a point well away from where the wounded creature could have been, but I must have gone a bit too far. The terrain had proven more complex than I had thought. I had chanced upon a completely different trail running along the same ridge, maybe a branch of the original one.

But it wasn't. I doubled back along it but didn't find another path intersecting it. In fact, the trail petered out completely. I was completely disoriented and totally lost.

I wandered for over an hour. I was calm now. The forest was familiar territory even though I didn't know which way was out. It seemed merely magical, not menacing. I heard music, or thought I did. It was just on the edge of audibility. Haunting music. At first I thought I might be near the Bandersnatch, but it was like no music I had ever heard. What sounded like a female voice sang with it. She was calling to me, I thought.

I sat on a stump and rubbed my temples. Let's not fall for that old routine. No siren voices luring me onto the rocks, please; or, more appropriately, no hamadryads to lure me up a tree. What was wrong with me? I felt high. I was high. On what, I didn't know. Certainly not beer—my God, that was hours ago. My hangover was completely gone. I was fine physically, maybe a little sore along the ribs and back. I looked up. I was sitting on the edge of a clearing on the slope of a gentle grade. In the middle of the clearing was a low mound of moss and ferns. It looked pretty. I looked up. The sky was spattered with a million stars. I gazed upward for a long while; then movement below caught my eye.

Something on two legs—a pale figure in the moonglow—shot into the clearing, made a quarter turn around the mound, and shot out again. It happened so fast I couldn't get a clear impression of what the creature had looked like. It hadn't made a sound. I shook my head and shrugged. I got up and came out into the clearing to the edge of the fairy ring of moss. I looked up again. Stars. No matter where you go in the universe, the stars look the same. I considered that thought. Profound. I rubbed my forehead. I was still high.

Something was moving against the stars. A meteorite.

No, it was traveling up. Strange angle . . . couldn't be.

It exploded, blossoming into starbursts of red, white, and blue. At once, I came down from my high. The strange dream I had been walking through evaporated.

Sam's signal flare! And he was close!

I took off like a deer through the clearing and plunged into the trees. The gradual slope continued down to a sharp dip, at the bottom of which was a logging road. I drew the torch from my pocket, flicked it on and ran to the left. I was going home.

As I jogged down the road I thought about the nightbeast that had chased me and I was struck by the total improbability of the incident. Didn't nocturnal predators usually stalk their prey silently? Not that guy back there. Nothing like announcing your intentions to the entire countryside. But maybe that was his style. It didn't make sense, though. There was the distant possibility that I had imagined it all, but I could barely bring myself to consider it. Just what does "imagine" really mean? Had I been hallucinating? Not one of my habits. None of it made any sense no matter which way I looked at it.

I loped along for about five minutes, then saw headbeams sweeping around a bend in the road. I heard the familiar whine of Sam's engine and broke into a sprint, waving the torch.

6

Sean Fitzgore grasped my hand and pulled me up into the cab.

"Takin' a wee stroll, are ye?" he said. "A fine evenin' for it." He thumped my back just hard enough to bruise.

John rose from the shotgun seat and encircled me in his string-bean arms. "Jake! Thank God."

"We were at the cabin," Roland said. "How long ago did you escape?"

I plopped into the driver's seat, shaking my head. "Seems like ages. I dunno, three hours ago. What's up? What's been happening?"

"First off," Sam said, "what happened to you?"

I told him briefly.

Sean nodded gravely. "I knew Moore was up to some deviltry. I figured he wanted you, but Darla and Winnie—"

"Dammit." I looked glumly at everyone. Sean's friend Liam was there, too. His right eye was a little puffy. "How'd it happen? When?" I glanced around. "Wait—where's Carl and Lori?" I sat up straight. "And Susan—where's Susan?"

"They got jumped," Liam said. "We saw it, so they're safe now." He grinned. "There was a bit of a dust-up."

"Little Lori gave a fine account of herself," Sean told me. "Nearly bit one bugger's finger right off."

"That's when they got Winnie, we think," John said.

"Where are they?" I asked.

"With friends," Sean said. "Suzie wanted to come along with us, but we persuaded her otherwise."

"Totally wasted," Roland said. "Susan doesn't drink often, but when she does . . ."

"You were showing full on all tanks yourself," I commented.

"I can hold my liquor," he retorted stiffly, looking a little greenish about the gills.

"What about Darla?" I said.

"We don't know," John answered. "She went upstairs, probably to turn in. When I went up myself, she wasn't there, and we haven't seen her since."

"Great." I sighed and slumped back in the chairs. Looking at Sean I asked, "Any ideas?"

"She could be any number of places. We finally guessed where you were because I'd noticed Geof Brandon giving you the eye earlier in the evening. We went out to Geof's farm, which took quite a while, but then I recalled seeing Fat Timmy McElroy hanging about, too. Damn me for not remembering sooner."

"You were long gone," Liam said. "She could be anywhere, Jake. Moore has a lot of lads on his team."

"And Winnie?"

"Oh, they'd probably keep the two of them together," Sean ventured. "And doubtless they wanted you separated from them, for reasons now obvious. You did well, Jake, m'boy."

"Not nearly well enough," I said. "I let my guard down against my best instincts."

"We'll have to take our share of the blame," Liam said regretfully, "pushing you through all that Boojum nonsense. It was supposed to be a bit of fun, but . . ." He shrugged apologetically.

"It's hardly your fault," I said, "but let's not waste time on the issue of who's to blame."

"Yeah, let's do something," Sam put in. "Beat the living *merte* out of somebody, like immediately. Anyone'll do."

"Don't you think that's rather rash?" John asked.

Roland frowned. "Well, we already put a call in to the local police."

"Yes," Sean said, giving a mock-polite cough. "They're 'investigating.'"

Liam said, "I wouldn't trust them farther than I could spit into the wind."

"Right," Sam agreed. "So we pay a call on Mr. Moore and beat the living *merte* out of him until he gives up Darla and Winnie."

"Seems a logical course of action," Sean said.

"You must have some idea of where Darla and Winnie could be," John insisted.

"Some idea, but we could chase wild geese through the woods all night and not find anyone."

John sat back in his seat and bit his lip.

"Any chance they could be at the hotel?" I asked.

Liam shrugged. "We searched as many rooms as we could."

"The place doesn't look all that big," Sam said.

"Well," I said. "Let's head there anyway." I turned to the controls. "I want to have a talk with Moore."

"It's rather late," Roland said. "Will he be in?"

"He's always there," Sean told him.

I started the engine. "Anybody know how many other guests are at the Bandersnatch?"

"There were a few," Liam said. "Things are pretty slow on weekdays, though."

John asked, "What do you plan to do, Jake?"

"Sean, can you guys sneak back inside, rouse 'em up and warn 'em there might be some gunplay?"

"Shouldn't be a problem. If they aren't cooperative we'll chuck the buggers out."

"Moore owns that place, right?"

I eased the rig over a huge lateral rut. In the light of the headbeams, the woods looked spookier than ever.

"He's part-owner, I believe. The silent partner is a company on Seahome," Sean said.

"But he has his own money in the place?"

"Oh, yes. In the 'Snatch and a score of other concerns. Has a finger in many a pie, Moore does. But the Frumious Bandersnatch is his fair-haired child."

"Then we know where he's vulnerable." We approached a crossroads and I slowed. "Which way here?"

"To the left," Liam said.

"Do you think you can warn the guests without alerting Moore?" I asked.

"That'll be difficult," Sean said. "But we'll stress the necessity for extreme quiet. Shouldn't be more than half a dozen folk, in three or four rooms."

"There may be guards around the place."

"Possible, but I doubt it. He doesn't know you're up and about, or shouldn't. The place should be quiet, mostly, but there'll be some revelers left in the Vorpal Blade."

"It's open all night?"

"Never closes."

"Good. So there'll be some activity besides the guests exiting."

"What exactly do you have in mind, Jake?"

"I'm going to trade him his hotel for Winnie and Darla."

We let Sean and Liam off about a quarter-klick from the 'Snatch. They had express orders to see that all the guests were out of there before we arrived, and to make sure Winnie and Darla were not in Moore's apartment. I told them to keep quiet and report back as soon as possible if anything went wrong. After shooing out the guests, they were to go down to the Blade and chase everyone out of there as soon as trouble started out front, which is where I intended to start same. If the guests refused to open the door or leave, they were to be given fair warning. We'd wait a full hour, then move in. If possible, one of the two was to report back before then.

"Do you think they'll be able to do all that without arousing Moore and his gang?" John asked as Sean and Liam disappeared into the trees.

"I don't know," I said. "They know more about old Zack's habits than we do."

I went back to the kitchen to brew myself a cup of coffee. I needed it. John and Roland followed.

"Besides," I went on, "I suspect Moore's guard is down. As far as he knows, I'm on ice and you guys are scattered. And if Sean is right about his drinking habits, we might catch him with his pants down."

"If his henchmen drink as heavily as he does," John added.

"Everybody on this planet drinks like a fish," Roland said.

"Your fins are showing," I told him.

He sneered at me, then burped. He rubbed his stomach. "My incipient ulcer's acting up again," he groaned.

I rummaged through the medicine cabinet until I found something for him. "Here," I said, throwing him a bottle of pills. "Cimetidine. Just take one."

He caught the bottle and shook his head wonderingly. "Is there anything you don't have in that drug locker of yours?"

"Got everything," I said. "Ups, downs, highs, lows—you name it."

"I believe it."

"Never thought I'd raise my kid up to be a pusher," Sam said.

Liam returned in forty-five minutes.

"Not as many guests as we'd thought," he told us, "and some of 'em were down in the Blade. We warned the rest—they buggered off with no protest."

"Any guards?"

"Two were dozing in the office. I suspect Moore has one or two lads with him in his flat. They don't seem to be expecting anything."

"Good. Where's Sean?"

"In the Blade. Don't worry, when the donnybrook starts, they'll all be out the back door in a flash."

"Fine. Don't want any innocent casualties. You're fairly sure Darla and Winnie aren't there?"

"There's a chance, but I doubt it. They're likely out in the woods somewhere."

"Okay."

I fired up the engine and started forward. Brooding boughs swept over us, barely clearing the top of the cab. Pairs of tiny eyes peered out at us from the shadows—or so I thought, but when I looked at them directly they disappeared. Was I still high? No, I'd come down but I still wasn't sure what was reality and what wasn't. Which was really no change from the usual state of things, when you think about it.

The road bore to the right, and lights appeared up ahead. I gunned the engine, making it roar. I didn't need stealth or subtlety now; this was my grandstand play, and I wanted an audience. I rolled into the nearby empty parking lot and came to a stop about fifteen meters from the entrance. I flicked on the high-intensity headlamps and focused the spotlight on the windows next to the hotel office. I juiced up the 5,000-watt amplifier, switched the feed to the outside speakers, put on my headset, and spoke.

"ATTENTION, ATTENTION," I heard my voice boom into the night. "I AM ADDRESSING THE OWNER OF THIS

ESTABLISHMENT, MR. ZACHARY MOORE."

"Mother of God, you'll be waking the dead," Liam complained, digging a finger into one ear.

"I SAY AGAIN, ATTENTION, MR. ZACHARY MOORE. YOUR PRESENCE IS REQUIRED FRONT AND CENTER."

I gave him twenty seconds.

"MOORE, GET YOUR ASS OUT ONTO THIS PORCH, LIKE, PRONTO, OR YOU'LL GET A MISSILE THROUGH YOUR BEDROOM WINDOW."

A face appeared briefly at a window directly off the porch. I couldn't tell who it was.

"Sam, let's give 'em some wake-up music."

"I've got just the piece, too," Sam said gleefully.

We blasted the hotel with a stirring rendition of *The Golden Eagle March* for about half a minute. Then the front door opened and Moore staggered out, shielding his eyes with both hands. He was barefooted, dressed in gray long johns.

"Turn that bloody light off!" he bellowed.

I deflected the spot, but kept the headbeams on.

He peered out. He looked half-asleep and mortally hung over. "What the bloody fuck is going on?"

John said, "I'm surprised he came out."

"He's used to having his way," Liam said. "He's got brass, I'll give him that."

I turned down the gain on the amplifier, but not a whole lot. "Maybe you don't recognize the voice. You're talking to Jake McGraw."

He took a half-step backward. "What do you want?"

"You know damn well. I want my friends back. Now."

"I'm not responsible for your bleeding friends. I don't know what you're talking about."

He was still blustering, but his eyes betrayed the sudden realization of his vulnerability. He'd walked right into it. And I'd known he would, too. He was just the kind of big pushy bastard who can't imagine things not going his way. Didn't even occur to him to look out and see our truck and think, hey, this could be trouble. He had probably thought it was the local gendarmerie come to investigate the kidnapping report, and he'd come out to scold them. How dare they disturb a big cheese-wheel like him in the middle of the night. You lads come back in the morning and we'll clear up this bit of nonsense straightaway.

"You know, Zack," I said. "I'm tired. It's late. I'm not going to argue with you. There's an exciter cannon trained on your midsection. You are going to stand right there and call out for your flunkies to go fetch them while we all wait. They're to be delivered here, unharmed, within a reasonable period of time—say, one and a quarter eyeblinks. If not, I'm going to cook your kidneys and feed 'em to the dogs for breakfast."

He drew himself up and squared his shoulders. "Really now," he said evenly. "Don't count on ever seeing your friends again."

"Oh, I see. Suddenly we're on a different level of argument. You're admitting you have in fact abducted my companions and are holding them against their will?"

"I'm admitting nothing." He cleared his throat and spat on the wood of the porch. "What makes you think there's been an abduction? That woman is a fugitive. 'Arrest' would be the appropriate term."

"Crap," I said. "What difference does that make in the Outworlds? If you're telling me there's extradition I'm telling you you're full of shit."

"Not a question of extradition," he said. "'Preventive detention' might cover it. Besides, I don't feel compelled to be telling you much of anything, mate. Except this. Leave these premises immediately or you're a dead man."

His brass amazed me. "I'm a dead man? Buddy, you're about three nanoseconds away from becoming breakfast sausage."

He folded his arms. "Start counting nanoseconds, then."

I set the targeting mode on the missile rack for line-of-sight aim and pulled down the target scope. I drew my bead and pressed the ARM switch. "We'll get to the countdown in just a sec, pal. First I want to find out a few things. Who're you taking orders from?"

"I take no orders."

"Take suggestions? Take in laundry? Come on, Moore, somebody clued you in about me and told you that Winnie was a valuable object. Was it Pendergast?"

"It seems everyone's heard about you and your heroic exploits. You say your alien pet is missing? You may report it to the local office of the Home Guard in the morning, if you wish. Poor thing probably strayed into the woods."

"Whoops," I said, "now we're not admitting things again. Contradicting yourself, there. Two of my friends are missing, whom you've admitted abducting. One human, one alien."

He snorted. "I've admitted to nothing, and you can ram your contradictions up your arse."

I clapped my hands twice, then poised my finger over the FIRE switch. "Well spoken, for a man who's about to die."

"Do you really think," he sneered, "that you'll get off Talltree alive if anything happens to me? I happen to be well thought of around these woods and it would ill behoove you to—"

I hit the switch and there was a whoosh and a flash, followed by the hollow *crump* of an explosion. Debris rained about the parking lot.

When it had all come down, Moore stepped from the porch and looked up.

"You bloody . . . *bastard!*"

"Yeah," I said. "That was a nice chimney. Fine stonework. Local masons, were they? A real pity."

He turned and fought an impulse to rush the truck, his face dark with rage. "You—!" He swallowed hard.

"Stay right where you are, Moore, or I'll fry you. Sam, keep the exciter on him while I have some fun."

"Will do!"

"You have lots of nice chimneys," I said. "Real pretty."

I aimed and fired another missile. A chimney on the far right corner of the building flew apart. Moore ducked and sought the refuge of the porch again.

"Let's see," I said. "Maybe I can hit the top of that one on the far side. Then again, that fancy decorative fascia might make a good target for the exciter—"

"No!" Moore screamed.

"Or maybe I'll just chuck a missile through your apartment window."

"Damn you!" He was turning purple.

"Hurts, don't it? I want 'em back, Moore. Darla and Winnie both, unharmed . . . and *now*."

"All right! All right!"

"I think you got him where he lives," Sam said.

"Very well, Mr. Moore. We'll all wait right here until—"

An exciter bolt lanced out from the shadows to the left of the hotel, hitting the left stabilizer foil. Another quickly followed, striking the roller. A plume of smoke billowed up from it. No need to worry about that roller going sugar on us now. Sam returned fire instantly. I floored the throttle and swung sharply to the right, but we began to draw fire from that direction, too. A coherent beam came through the windscreen, barely missing my head. I fired a missile without aiming and hit the corner of the building. Flaming debris showered the cab as we passed. I continued in a tight circle. The damaged roller was burning, but the automatic fire extinquishers were hard at work shooting foam at it.

"Sam, let's get the hell out of here," I yelled. "You agree?"

"Right, we blew our chance. No use shooting it out with them."

"We can still get in a parting shot, though."

But when the rig swung around I saw that it wouldn't be necessary. The Bandersnatch was in flames. The roof was well involved, and Sam's return fire had ignited a wide section of the front wall.

"That wood must be highly flammable," Sam guessed. "It's really going up."

Liam said, "It's devilish hard to start, but once Talltree wood catches, it burns like hellfire."

The sniping had stopped, so I slowed. A huge gout of flame roared from the roof of the hotel.

Liam whistled. "She's a total loss. They'll never get it put out. Good thing we got everyone out of there."

I nodded. Just then another beam hit the trailer. I gunned the engine and roared out of the parking lot—and almost ran over Sean. I braked hard and he jumped out of the way. I stopped and popped the hatch. Sean climbed in and I took off down the road.

Sean watched the side parabolic mirror. "Pity," he said. "But we'll find another place to carouse."

"Dammit," I was saying. "Dammit to hell."

"Easy, son," Sam consoled me. "We didn't have the manpower to rush the place."

"It might've worked. Liam said the guards were nodding off."

"Yeah, it might've, but we would've taken casualties. Yours was the safest bet, even though we didn't bargain on a portable exciter cannon."

"We could've given it a try. Damn."

"Forget it, Jake. Obviously there were more men there than Liam thought."

"He's right, Jake," Liam said. "Moore has at least two dozen rowdyboys on his paysheet, and that apartment of his has a room full of bunk beds."

"Still," I said, "we didn't get Darla and Winnie back. And now . . ."

"We'll find 'em, Jake," Sean said, squeezing my shoulder reassuringly. "We've a few ideas of where they could be."

"But how long will it take? And now that they know I'm up and about, it's gonna be rough."

"We'll find them," Sean said. "Liam and I know these woods like—"

"Hold on," Sam interrupted. "I'm getting something."

After a moment, I said, "What is it, Sam?"

"It's our beacon. Lost it, though. Wait a minute."

"It's Darla!" I shouted. "She has the key!"

"Shut up and let me . . . There it is again. Son of a brick. Okay, let me launch the earlybird and we'll do a little triangulation."

We heard a thump and a whine as the turbojet-powered surveillance drone came out of its hidey-hole on the roof of the cab. It warmed up, then screamed off into the night.

Half a minute later, Sam had a fix.

"We're heading generally in the right direction. The signal source is a little over three kilometers away and the direction is forty-five degrees to the right as we drive."

"Just keep on this road," Sean said. "I have a feeling I know where they are."

We bumped and thumped over the rutted logging trail for fifteen minutes, making slow progress. Then a large piece of the still-smoking roller fell away and the cab lurched violently, listing to the left.

"Hell," I said. "We might not make it."

"Disconnect it from the power shaft and oversteer to correct," Sam said. "Never mind, I'll do it."

Sam did and we started forward again.

"Just take it easy," he said.

"Turn right here," Sean said. "See that little trail?"

"Don't know if we can fit," I said.

I eased to the right. Branches scraped against the trailer. The port was open just a little and I could hear night sounds again. *Bork-bork, greep-greep, jub-jub, bleu!*

"Goddamn noisiest woods I've ever been in," I grumbled.

"Live here for a few months and you wouldn't hear it," Liam chuckled.

"You'd be deaf," Roland said.

"No offense," I said, "but no thanks."

"Talltree's only for poets and loggers and other hopeless romantics," Sean said. "You level-headed types always run screaming from the place."

"You know, when I was out there," I began, but stopped. "Never mind. No time now."

"We're dead on," Sam said. "The source is directly ahead."

Sean nodded, his face set grimly. "Tommy Baker's place. I knew that if there was a woman to be had, he'd be first in line."

I shut off the headbeams, pulled down the general-purpose scope and shoved my face into it. It was set for thermal-imaging; I changed it to night-vision, turning on the photomultiplier circuits. The gain needed was minimal. The full moon was still doing its job.

"Sam, rig for silent running."

"Scramming main engine," Sam answered. "Auxiliary motor engaged, secondary power cells on. We are rigged for silent running."

"Aye, aye, and all that," I said. "Okay, we're going to do it right this time."

We tried. I stopped within five hundred meters of the signal source. After arming ourselves, we set out into the woods, following Sean over a trail that would take us to Tommy Baker's farm. We would come out directly behind the farmhouse.

Twenty minutes later, lights appeared among the trees. We crept the rest of the way, coming just to the edge of the clearing. Sean and I stationed ourselves behind a tree and peered out into the darkness. A shadowline cut across the yard, neatly bisecting a neglected garden. Junk and refuse lay everywhere.

A weathered and probably rarely-used tractor was parked next to a small shed. The house lay in shadow, but its outline was easily discernible. A tiny, square rear window glowed dimly yellow.

"Let me go reconnoiter," Sean whispered to me.

"Okay. Be careful."

"That I'll be."

He stepped around the tree, paused, then tiptoed across the moonlit area and into shadow. I lost sight of him quickly, and was worried that he might trip over a piece of junk and blow everything. But he didn't.

Someone came up beside me. It was Liam.

"You think they have a radio in there?" I asked.

"I'm fairly sure they do. Why?"

"They may have had advance warning. Maybe they've moved Darla and Winnie somewhere else by now."

"I think Moore has his hands full back at the 'Snatch. His first priority would be to put out a fire call. Besides, what about the signal?"

"Don't know. Darla may have dropped the key, or left it behind. Could be someone's just fiddling with it."

We waited.

Sean returned about ten minutes later.

"Jake, you'd better come see this," he said.

I looked at him.

"I really think you should," he said, then turned, beckoning me to follow.

I did.

"Mind your step," Sean hissed as we threaded our way through the debris.

We crept up to the window. Sean crouched beneath it, then pointed upward, inviting me to have a look.

Okay, I'd have a look. Flattening my back against the rough log wall, I inched along until I could peer through the corner of the window. Through a big tear in a tattered paper blind I could see everything.

Darla was in there. She was nude, sitting on the lap of a man who had his back to me. He was sitting on the edge of a large bed with a carved wooden headboard. A small lamp glowed on a nighttable on the far side of the bed, throwing their shadows against a white plaster wall.

They kissed, and he fondled her.

After a moment, their lips parted. She drew back and smiled.

Running his big rough hands along her white thighs, he said something. She giggled, then kissed him passionately.

I'd seen enough. I lowered myself to a crouch and looked at Sean.

"Son of a bitch," I said.

7

"You know, I may have made a big mistake," I said to Sean after we had retreated to the rear of the shed.

"Perhaps in Darla's case, yes. After all, no one saw her being abducted. She may have gone off with Baker of her own free will. I don't really know her."

I nodded. "You'd think I would by now, but I don't, not really. She might have." I thought it over, then shook my head. "No, dammit. Maybe at some other point in her life, but not now. Not here. It's hard to explain."

"Who can explain a woman?"

"No, no. It's got nothing to do with that. It's just—"

"Baker fancies himself a ladies' man. And I'll have to admit he does attract more than his share." He smiled wanly and shrugged. "Some have it and some don't."

"Be that as it may. But we're sure about Winnie. We know they've got her."

I snorted. "That may've been a case of petnapping."

"Hard to say what a logger lad will do when in his cups, but I don't think so."

"Neither do I," I said, "but I'm beginning to have my doubts about Moore's hand in all this. Might just be I did him an injustice."

Sean shook his head emphatically. "That's categorically impossible. He's the devil's own field representative, that one, and he deserves everything he's gotten."

"Geof and Fat Timmy—they work for Moore, do his bidding?"

"Most of the time, when they're not stealing farm equipment or foraging in other people's vegetable plots. For a price, they'll do anything for anybody, but Moore's their chief client."

I sighed. "Anyone else in there?"

"The blinds are drawn, but I heard someone in the front room fumbling about. Probably Dim Willie Benson, Baker's hired man."

"Dim Willie?"

"He's a bit dim. Harmless boy, when he's not drinking."

Fat Timmy, Dim Willie . . . This place was driving me crazy.

"I take it Baker doesn't have a lifecompanion."

"Baker?" He laughed. "Not the sort. Besides, women are scarce goods on Talltree. Don't know if you noticed—"

"I did, I did."

"They do come, but they never seem to stay." He heaved a sigh of lamentation, staring off into the night. "Funny thing."

I leaned against the shed and brooded.

Sean came out of his reverie. "What's the game, Jake?"

Someone banged against something out in the yard.

"Jake?" came a sharp whisper.

"Over here," I said.

John stepped cautiously over to us. "Oh, there you are." Liam and Roland followed him.

"What's going on?" Roland wanted to know.

"Got me," I said.

After a pause, John asked, "Where's Darla?"

"In there," I said. "With some guy."

"With some guy," John repeated emptily.

Roland said, "You mean . . . ?"

"Her business," I said. I straightened up. "Look, when exactly did you notice that Darla was gone? Was it before or after Winnie was abducted?"

"Well," John said, "it was more or less around the same time. I came downstairs when I found no one in the room, went outside to find Roland. I heard shouting—"

"Okay," I said, "then she didn't know that Winnie was missing, and she still doesn't, I guess. Thing is, it's strange that she'd go off like that."

"I agree," Roland said.

"Well, hell." I zipped up my jacket against the chill. "This may be indelicate as all hell, but I'm going to ask Darla if she knows something or if she saw anything." I scratched my head and shrugged.

We all trooped to the farmhouse.

As we rounded the side, we heard glass shattering, followed by a dull thud.

I pulled my gun and ran around to the front door. It was unlocked and ajar. I kicked it open, dove through the doorway, hit the floor, and rolled once, coming up into a crouch.

"Hi, Jake."

Darla was standing by the open door to the back room, holding the jagged-edged handle to what had probably been a water pitcher. A huge man lay sprawled at her feet, his head festooned with shards of crockery.

"Hi," I said, straightening up. I walked into the bedroom.

Tommy Baker was draped over the bed, out cold. His shirt was off and his trousers were bunched around his ankles. She had taken care of him silently—probably a quick chop to the base of the neck. Caught with his proverbial pants down.

"This one wanted to rape me," Darla said, nodding toward Baker as she slipped into the legs of her jumpsuit. "But I convinced him that we'd have more fun if he untied me. He was the second one who wanted a little action tonight."

"Moore?"

"Yes. Ordinarily, I wouldn't mind so much, but I didn't like his attitude."

"Ah."

"I bit him where it hurts a whole lot. There's some question as to his ever having progeny. I wanted to kick him, but my legs were tied to the bedposts."

"I see."

And I could just imagine Darla at the door, smiling and breathtakingly nude, inviting poor Dim Willie in to join the festivities.

I turned around to find the men grouped around the doorway, gaping.

"Hi, gang," Darla said.

"Hello," John said.

"Winnie's missing," I said.

"No she isn't." Darla zipped up the front of her jumpsuit. She went over to the bed and knelt beside it, looking under.

"Winnie, honey? Come on out. Jake's here." She reached and pulled. "Hell, no wonder she didn't come out. This leash is all tangled. There you go."

Winnie crawled out from under the bed. There was a dog

collar around her neck. The leash dragged after her. She saw me, ran and leaped at me, nearly knocking me over. She crushed my chest in a frantic hug.

"Whoa, baby. It's okay," I told her. "It's over." She buried her face in my shoulder.

"Are you all right?" Roland asked Darla.

"Sure, though it'll be a while before I'll want to see male genitalia again."

"You don't have to go into details," I said, "but . . ."

"But you want details. That's the lot of the victim. Moore jumped me back at the hotel, and we were just into the preliminaries when I nearly bit through one of his testicles. Nobody wanted much to do with me after that. Except Tommy, here."

She scowled at me. "I was stupid. I should have gone along with Moore. He almost killed me. He picked up an ax—but his men stopped him. They wouldn't have been able to, except that the pain was a little too much for him."

"I should imagine," John said.

"They led him away and that was the last I saw of him. They kept me tied up like that for hours. Every once in a while, some cretin would come in to paw and slobber over me, but that was the extent of it. Then they brought me here."

She sat on a chair and pulled on her high black boots. "I'm okay, really," she said.

"When did they bring you here?" I asked, setting Winnie down.

"About two hours ago. It took a while for Tommy to work up his nerve. He had strict orders not to fool with me."

From the front room came the sound of Sam's key beeping. I went in and found it on the kitchen table. Dim Willie had probably been fiddling with it and had inadvertently set off the beacon. I briefly filled Sam in on the situation and told him to come in over the main road. Everyone came out of the bedroom.

"I wonder why they kept this with you," I said to Darla. "Didn't they know it could have been sending a homing signal?"

"I didn't know it was here. The last time I saw it, it was lying on the dresser in Moore's room. I bet Willie picked it up when Tommy and he came to get me."

"Dumb," I said.

Darla shot a look at Sean. "Are all the men here as stupid as these two and the rest of Moore's brood?"

Sean winced. "Quite possibly."

"What I want to know, Jake, is how you got Geof Brandon down the hole in the outhouse," Liam said.

"Yes," Fitzgore said, his face screwed up in intense curiosity. "How the devil did you do that?"

We spent the next day holed up at Sean and Liam's farm. The place belonged to Sean. His wife had left him, you see, and . . . but that's another story. (They were called "wives" here; the Outworlds were rather socially retrograde in many respects.) Anyway, Sam was at some backwoods garage getting his stabilizer foil repaired and the spare roller put on, but we were in contact. Meanwhile, the Home Guard, or whatever the hell they were called, was looking for me. I was a material witness and possible suspect in the homicide of a defecting Colonial Authority official, Dr. Van Wyck Vance. The murder allegedly occurred on board the *Laputa,* which, by the way, had come through the pirate attack with moderate casualties despite sustaining heavy damage. The news reports made no mention of the fate of Mr. Wilkes or of his possible bearing on the case. Beautiful. However, the cops were of two minds about the whole matter. Some were on Captain Pendergast's payroll and some—the local ones mainly—weren't. Muddying the whole business and making everyone nervous about just how to proceed was Pendergast's involvement in all this. There he was, running antigeronics, which nominally were controlled substances even here. The operation was an open secret, but a trial or investigation would have opened up several cans of worms and nobody wanted to do that. Meanwhile . . . everyone, I mean everyone, knew exactly what the hell was going on beneath all the pretexts and posturing. They knew about the Roadmap and about Winnie, and the cops really didn't know how they felt about all that.

Moore was raising a stink about the loss of his property. Claimed he was just doing his civic duty in detaining me. But why had he sequestered me in a shack in the woods? Why had he not immediately contacted the authorities? Well, er, um.

There were numerous meetings in the woods among various parties. Sean's friends in the Guard agreed not to arrest me just yet and sat on a warrant sworn out on Seahome. Jurisdictional disputes flared. The "Get Jake" faction tried a local magistrate, but he was taking the waters at a spa on some resort planet. Gout, you know. (They had diseases here that hadn't been seen for centuries back in Terran Maze.) More meetings in the woods. Old Zack tried to put a lien against Sam, but to do that he had to dispatch a flunky in a fast roadster to the capital planet. But there he got ensnarled in red tape, and by the time the papers were processed, we were . . . But I'm getting ahead of myself.

Sam was for making a break for the nearest portal, guns blazing. I had a hard time, but I talked him out of it, pointing out that we had pretty much run that stratagem into the ground. Frankly, I was getting a little tired of it. I wanted to settle this. We had grounds for filing numerous charges against Pendergast, Moore, and—if he was alive—Wilkes: Abduction, Illegal Detention, Criminal Assault, Involuntary Deviate Sexual Intercourse (they had it on the books), Criminal Conspiracy, and, as a nice little fillip, Contributing to the Delinquency of a Minor (Lori's drinking). You name it, we could file it. Also, we had a dandy civil case against the shipping company that owned the *Laputa* and an absolutely open-and-shut one against the outfit that ran the Bandersnatch and a bunch of other businesses (a.k.a. Zack Moore). All of this was on the advice and counsel of a backwoods lawyer by the name of Hollingsworth, a stocky, barrel-shaped fellow with mutton-chop sideburns down to his shoulders. He drank gin straight from the bottle from the time he woke to the time he passed out in the evening. He also ran a chicken farm.

We made known our intentions to proceed against the aforementioned parties. Nervous laughter from the other side. Surely you jest, they said. Try us, we said. Grumble, grumble. Well, they came back, what about the minor you transported across planetary boundaries? And we said, what about your child labor laws? Okay, they're consistently flouted, but do we really want to get into that? Child labor laws? they said. What child labor laws? Oh. Those child labor laws. No, we don't want to get into that.

"Why do they bother to pass laws around here," I asked Hollingsworth, "if nobody's interested in enforcing them?"

"Are you joking?" he said, pointing to his shelves of leatherbound legal tomes. "What would lawyers use to line the walls of their studies if we didn't pass any legislation? Have you priced wallpaper recently?"

The legal shadowboxing went on for two days, at which point the cops got fed up. Listen, they said to me. We will be looking in this direction. You take your truck and your friends and your funny-looking monkey and head in *that* direction. And don't stop till you . . . well, just don't stop.

I said fine. I gave the order: Make all preparations for getting under way. Aye aye, skipper. But first I had to deal with Sean and Liam.

"What do you mean you're coming with us?" I asked innocently.

"We've talked it over, Liam and I have. We'd like to join your expedition, if you'll have us."

"Well, look. You two are great drinking buddies, and you're good men to have in a fight, and if it were up to me—"

"We'll pull our weight, Jake, make no mistake about that. We're already outfitted for the trip. Liam and I were planning to vacate this fairyland very shortly on our own. We had our sights on a newly discovered planet that just got listed for colonization—not that we care about lists, mind you—"

"But why would you want to leave this beautiful place?" I asked him, gesturing toward the neat little intensive-agriculture plots and the brightly painted buildings. "This is nice!"

Sean heaved a sigh. "Since Dierdre buggered off, it's palled on me. Besides, the bank owns all the equipment. The note is rather large, and the payments have become a burden." He swung his legs up to rest on the rail of the front porch and teetered back on the chair. "Ah, Dierdre, Dierdre," he said wistfully.

"Have a drink, Sean," Hollingsworth said, passing him the gin bottle.

"There's another problem," I said. "We're already crowded in the truck."

"Hey, that's no problem," Carl put in. "They can ride in the back seat of my Chevy."

"Chevy?" Liam said, looking around for someone to explain.

"We have a vehicle, Jake," Sean said after having guzzled approximately one-sixth of the liter of gin.

"You do?" I said. "Well, it's a free road."

"But we don't want to go if you don't want us to," Sean told me.

"What the bloody hell's a Chevy?" Liam persisted.

"Sean, it's not that. It's just—"

"Of course you can come with us," Susan gushed, sitting down in Sean's lap and running her hand through Sean's tangle of red-orange hair. "You big hairy hunks—both of you."

Sean's eyes gleamed, and he laughed. "That's the spirit!"

"Jake, I'm surprised at you," Susan said. "Why can't they tag along if they want to?"

"Look, I didn't say—"

"The more the merrier, I say," Roland muttered. "What exactly *is* your problem, Jake?"

"Problem? I don't have a punking problem."

I stomped off the porch and went around to the back where Sam was parked. Sometimes these people got to me. One thing I don't like is being cast as the villain of the piece. What the hell did they think this was going to be, a picnic?

I climbed into the cab.

"What's up?" Sam said.

"Let's get out of here," I grumbled. "Leave the whole goddamn bunch of them."

"Now, now. You know you can't."

"Honest to God, sometimes . . ."

"How many times have I told you not to pick up starhikers?"

"Dammit, Sam, don't you start on me, too!"

"Easy, son."

I sat in the driver's seat, fuming, until Susan came over, climbed up, and sat in my lap.

"Jake, I'm sorry." She kissed me tenderly and smiled. "I didn't know you were sensitive. You're always so strong—"

"Me? You're kidding."

She didn't argue. Presently, the temperature in the cab rose.

"In case you're wondering," Sam said, "I have my eye turned off."

Susan giggled, then reinserted her tongue into my mouth.

"Hi! Oh, excuse me."

We turned to see Darla walking away. Susan looked at me, some complex feminine emotion taking form inside her head. "Do you—?" she began, then looked away and chewed her lip.

"Do I what, Suzie?"

"Nothing," she said in a lost little voice. Suddenly, she

threw her arms around my neck. "Let's sleep in the aft-cabin tonight."

"We have lots of work to do, Suzie."

"Don't you think I'm going to help? After."

"Sure."

Then she hugged me, kissed me on the ear, and said, "I love you, Jake."

And I thought, uh-oh.

We laid in provisions for a long journey. Sean and Liam emptied their larder and packed the trailer with lots of good stuff: homemade preserves, smoked meats, pickles, sausage, old-fashioned canned foods, barrels of potatoes, flour, jars of home-grown herbs and spices, a few cases of hotpak dinners—"We keep those for when we've drunk too much to be able to stand at the stove," Liam said, "but not enough to've lost our appetites"—and cases and cases of beer. They brewed their own, and it was pretty good, if you like your beer dark and syrupy with a 20 percent alcohol content. They threw in all the tools and equipment they owned, some clothes, and about two long tons of camping and survival gear. Even some firewood.

Then we all went out with Winnie and gathered food for her. She taught us to recognize several varieties of fruit and vegetable and root. With everyone helping, we laid in what looked like a year's supply. Through Darla, she told us it wasn't necessary to bring this much; she could find more food on the way. I said it couldn't hurt, secretly doubting that we'd be lucky enough to chance upon another planet that could provide suitable food for any of us.

Before we turned in, we planned our itinerary, trying to coordinate Winnie's maps and her Itinerary Poem with what Sean and Liam could supply in the way of knowledge about the rest of the Outworlds. Darla had been busy translating for the last two days.

"It just goes on and on," she said. "I must have fifty stanzas by now."

"Winnie obviously knows where she's going," John observed.

"As near as we can tell," Roland said, "we hit five more Outworld planets before we exit this maze."

"And not a moment too soon," I said. "In other words, we'll

be shooting a potluck portal at that point."

"Right."

"Sean, does this jibe with what you know?"

Sean nodded. "Seems to, though Winnie's descriptions of the planets are rather sketchy."

"The inevitable difficulties," Darla said, "inherent in second-hand translations. The poem is in Winnie's language, which is very different structurally from most human languages. I know only a few word-clusters—there really are no 'words' per se—so Winnie helps by giving me a running translation in English, which she doesn't know as well as Spanish, which she doesn't know well at all. Then I have to make some sense out of it." She took a sip of dark beer and shook her head ruefully. "I'm probably making plenty of mistakes. It's mostly guesswork."

"Under the circumstances," John said, "you're doing a fine job, Darla."

"Thank you."

I reached over and patted Winnie's head. "Smart girl," I said.

Winnie took my hand, jumped up, walked across the table, and plopped down in my lap. She threw her arms around me and hugged, grimace-grinning with her eyes shut tight.

"Affectionate little darling, isn't she?" Sean said.

"Yes, she is," I said. I nuzzled her long floppy ear. "Have you ever noticed that she smells good all the time? Like she's wearing perfume."

"Which is more than you can say for most sentient beings," Sean said.

"Yeah. Anyway, getting back to this . . ."

"Look here, Jake," Roland said. "This is the Galactic Beltway running through the Orion arm of the galaxy. You see where it cuts across here to the Perseus arm? That's where we have to pick it up."

"How do we know when we reach that point?"

"Well, we won't know." Roland put down his pencil and scratched his head, then smoothed his shock of straight black hair. "That's what's hard about all this. There really is no way of closely correlating the maps and the Itinerary Poem. The Poem is just a long set of directions. Go ten kilometers, turn left, you can't miss it—that sort of thing. By following the itinerary, we'll have a hard time knowing exactly where we are on the galactic map, unless we can make astronomical observations."

"Well," I said, "there's a load of astronomical equipment in the truck, if somebody knows or can figure out how to use the stuff."

"Unfortunately," Roland said, "my knowledge of astronomy is largely theoretical." He tapped the pencil against the waxed-wood tabletop. "And spotty at best."

"Did you find anything in that crate of book-pipettes?"

"Not a whole lot. They're mostly monographs and journals. Rarified stuff, pages and pages of equations. But I did find one useful bit of information. The Local Group *is* associated with a metacluster, and the Milky Way is on the outskirts of it. The nucleus is a galactic cluster in the constellation Virgo."

"So," I said, scratching the fur over the bony knot between Winnie's ears, which she loved to have done, "that may mean that the big road coming into Andromeda is Red Limit Freeway."

"I don't think so, Jake. If so, it means that the Local Group is isolated from the rest of the metacluster, with no access to the Intercluster Thruway. No, this has to be the Thruway going into Andromeda."

"Why don't we ask Winnie and make sure?" I said.

"Huh?"

"Instead of everybody trying to second-guess her, why don't we come right out and ask?"

Winnie looked at me expectantly.

"Winnie,"I said, "can you draw more for us on this map?" I took the drawing of the Local Group over and put it in front of us. "This one here. Can you show us something that's missing?"

She looked the map over for a moment, then reached out toward Roland. Roland handed her the pencil. Grasping it awkwardly, she scored a line coming in from the right, ending at the Greater Magellenic Cloud. She looked at it, chewing the end of the pencil thoughtfully. Then she continued the line through the cloud and beyond, ending it at the exact point where the "Transgalactic Extension" left the rim of the Milky Way.

"There's the Thruway," I said. "The Transgalactic Extension is part of it."

"Why did she leave it out?" Roland wondered.

"Not important," I said. "And I think I'm beginning to understand why it wasn't important. As John said the other night, this is a tourist itinerary. We're at the edge of the metacluster. We want to leave it, not go into it, so we won't need to bother with the Thruway." I reached out with one arm and gathered in all the papers. "All of this, this whole thing, is definitely *not* a road atlas of the universe. It's much too incomplete. These maps provide the traveler with a specific route to get to a specific place."

"And where is that?" John asked.

"Winnie?" I asked. "Where are we going?"

"Home."

"Yes, she keeps saying that." Roland frowned and crossed his arms. "What could she possibly mean?"

We left at dawn.

But not before I had the shock of seeing what Sean and Liam had been referring to as their "Skyway-worthy vehicle." Liam towed it out of a shed with the tractor.

It was a tiny roadster, beaten, dented, splotched with emulsicoat patching, and looking for all the world like an overgrown child's toy.

"Where's the key to wind it up?" I said.

"Very funny," Sean sneered. "But not very original."

"And what *color* is that?"

"Magenta."

I rolled my eyes heavenward.

It took a half-hour to start the thing. Then it ran at 25 percent of its rated power. Liam fiddled with the engine for another twenty minutes and coaxed it up to seventy-five.

"Good enough," Sean said. "We can stop somewhere and have it looked at."

"Yeah," I said.

Finally, we got going. It felt good to get back on the Skyway again. Give me the road any day, I thought. That black band rolling under me was freedom. I wanted no fetters, no encumbrances, no obligations. But of course I had them. My present situation was a trap, and the more I struggled, the more ensnared I became. I was acquiring people like an old wool sweater picks up lint. What did they want of me? What was my irresistible appeal? I didn't know about anyone else, but I was looking for a way home. I wanted to do nothing more than deliver my load and go back to the farm. Wouldn't see a soul for a year. I'd even sell my flat in town. Contrary to popular opinion, *this* starrigger had absolutely no intention to drive to the "beginning" of the universe or to the "end" of it either—equally absurd notions. I wanted to tear up Winnie's maps, chuck the Black Cube out the port, and say to hell with it all. Then I'd go my own way, just me and Sam. Leave everyone to starhike it home.

Sure. Sure, Jake. You go ahead and do that.

I swore under my breath for two kilometers and felt better.

So preoccupied with my thoughts was I that I didn't notice the forest had given way to rolling plains in rather short order. The tops of the cylinders were edging over the horizon.

Suddenly, I thought of something, and slammed on the brakes. I pulled off the road and came to a sudden stop. The Chevy overshot me, pulling off to the shoulder a good distance ahead. As I climbed out of the cab, much to everyone's puzzlement, I saw Carl sticking his head out the window and looking back, equally baffled.

I walked back to the roaster, into which our beefy logger friends were packed like . . . like . . . well, like two beefy loggers inside a ridiculously small vehicle.

Sean slid back the dubiously air-tight port. "Trouble, Jake?"

"I have to ask this before I repress the event entirely. Just what the hell *was* that thing I saw in the woods . . . that Boojum or whatever you call it?"

Sean tugged at his anfractuous mustache. "Hard to say. Did it talk to you?"

"Yeah, it—" I straightened up. "Yeah, it sure did!"

"What did it say?"

"Well . . . it said, 'Good Gracious, dearie me!' Then it took off into the woods."

"I see." He stroked his beard, ruminating. Shaking his head slowly, he said, "Then that was no Boojum."

I would have strangled him right then if I had thought my hands would've fit around his fat neck.

8

When I climbed back into the cab, a yellow warning light leered at me from the instrumentation.

"The spare," I said. "Right?"

"Right," Sam said.

I expressed my displeasure in colorful terms. At some length.

"Curb your tongue, lad. There're ladies present."

"My apologies, Suzie, Darla." I looked back. "Winnie," I added.

"Oh, you should be proud," Susan said. "That approached the status of a work of art."

"Thank you."

I felt even better than I had after the previous tirade. I goosed the plasma flow and peeled out onto the Skyway.

The next few planets were wasteballs, barely habitable, but even here, human settlements clung, like lichen, to the rocks. Various odd-colored suns hung in lowering skies. On the third mudball, I decided we needed a palaver.

"Sam, see if you can raise Sean and Carl."

"Right."

I put on the headset while Sam put out a call on the special frequency we had decided upon beforehand. I prefer an old-fashioned headset; why, I don't know, but I've always had this odd affinity for outmoded technology. Besides, I keep losing those stickum things you put on your earlobe and throat. I considered the bone-conduction transducer, implanted in my mastoid bone, a necessity despite my aversion to biointerface gadgets. I never used it for general communications; it was reserved for the hush frequency alone.

"Fitzgore here. Can you read me, Jake?"

"Sure enough. Carl?"

"Yeah."

"Okay, we're going to take the left fork up ahead. Right?"

"Affirmative."

"Roger-dodger."

"Roger-dodger?" I echoed.

"Affirmative," Carl amended.

"Right. The next planet up is Schlagwasser. Carl, can you ask Lori—"

"I'm here, Jake. And I told you I don't want to see those people again."

"Lori, what you do after I drop you off is your business. It would've been dangerous to send you back to Seahome, and in good conscience I couldn't have put you out on that planet of alcoholic perverts—present company excluded, Sean and Liam—"

"On behalf of all perverts, alcoholic or not, I thank you."

"Sorry. Lori, you're much too young, and—"

"Punk you!"

"—and I . . . Lori? Lorelei, honey, listen to me, please. I know you're not more than fifteen years old—"

"I'm eighteen!"

"Sweet sixteen at the very most. I just can't take the responsibility of letting you come with us. We don't exactly know where we're going, and we really don't have the vaguest idea of how to get there. I have enough worries, honey, and I'm simply not going to—"

"Jake, please take me along. Please? *I won't be any trouble. I promise! I can take care of myself, and I won't—"*

"Lori, darling, it's not a question of that. Listen to me. You should be in school and going to proms and having boys pick you up in their roadsters . . . all that sort of stuff. Now, I don't know what Schlagwasser's like—right off, the name doesn't recommend it—but the fact that you had a foster family there speaks of at least a . . . Lori? Are you listening?"

Over the two-way hookup, I could hear her crying.

"Oh, great. Typical female tactics."

"Jake!" Susan was indignant. "That was uncalled for, and not true. She's a child. You said so yourself."

"Sorry, sorry. Looks like I'm offending every sex and gender today. Lori, honey? Don't cry, please."

"You're forgetting the Reticulans, Jake," Roland said.

"No," I said. "If those nightmares pick up the trail again,

they'll be after me. I can't believe they'd waste time and effort going after Lori."

"But wasn't she strapped to their cutting table? Doesn't that make her sacred quarry? They'll be after her, Jake."

"They're after me. It's hard to believe they'd want to hunt rabbit when there's bigger game."

"I agree with Roland," John said. "We don't know enough about the Reticulans' habits and customs to take the chance. They seem to be driven by these ceremonial obligations. It seems hideous to us, but in the context of their culture . . . after all, they're not human."

"Yeah, but that's neither here nor there. The point is, they're after *me*. And if she stays with me, it'll be more of a risk than if she hides out on her home planet, where her family can protect her. Reticulans won't go snooping around on a human world."

"They've been known to," Roland countered.

I had to admit to myself that Roland was right. And that knocked a few props out from under my argument.

"Jake?" It was Carl.

"Yeah."

"Lori can't go back there, to her foster parents."

"Why not?"

"I'd rather not say just now. She just can't."

"I want to know, Carl."

A pause. *"Lori says to tell you."* I heard him take a breath. *"Her foster father raped her."*

After a moment, I said, "Right. Um . . . Lori? I'm very sorry."

"It's okay."

"Yeah. Uh . . . over and out."

Rape seemed to be the national pastime of the Outworlds. Charming.

I replaced the headset in its rack on the dash. "Sam, take over for me, will you?"

"Sure, son. Don't feel too bad. You couldn't have known."

"I should have known that when a child cries, it usually means something hurts. I'm going into the aft-cabin. Raise the seat up for me. Hard for a two-inch-tall driver to see out the port."

I went back and dumped myself, pile of rags that I was, into the bunk.

* * *

As it happened, we wound up stopping on Schlagwasser so Sean and Liam could fuel up. Sam was showing three-quarters of a tank, but we topped off anyway. This could be the last service station till the Big Bang, for all we knew.

"Don't need any gas," Carl averred. "I'm okay."

"'Gas'?" I said.

"I mean, whaddycallit. Deuterium."

"What's this thing run on, air?"

Sitting at the wheel of his 1957 Chevrolet Impala, Carl knitted his brow and shook his head. "Y'know, to tell the honest-to-God truth, I really don't know what the hell it runs on."

"Then what are all those fusion-monitoring readouts—the ones under the dash board?"

"Oh, those? They're dummies."

All I could do was grunt and scratch my face. Carl and Lori got out and walked over with me to the edge of the lot, where everyone was stretching their legs. Schlagwasser—this part of it—was a planet of marshlands and swamp, over which the starslab was borne by a causeway. The sky was a dome of slate. The world smelled of brackish water and wet, fetid things. In a pond of goo a few meters away, something sucked and gurgled. The undergrowth was a jumble of orange and purple, overhung by great brooding, purple-leaved trees.

"These planets are getting less and less Earthlike," I said. "And what happens when we get out of human-occupied territory?"

"According to Winnie," Darla said, "there'll always be earth-normal planets along the way. There may be stretches where they'll be few and far between, but we'll be able to get out every now and then to move around a bit. Maybe even camp."

"But we should be prepared for hostile enviornments. Sean, did you guys pack full-pressure suits?"

"Yes, they're in the trailer."

"Fine. Now, I have two . . . Carl?"

"Yeah, I got one in the trunk."

"The what?" John asked.

"Storage compartment, in the rear, there."

"Oh, the boot."

"Boot?"

"Boot."

"Boot," Carl repeated. "You people sure talk funny."

Everyone looked at Carl for a moment.

"Okay," I said. "Maybe we can make do with five. And if you guys have to exit your vehicles in an airless environment, we can use the trailer as an air lock."

"Maybe we should blow all our cash and outfit everybody," Carl suggested, "just to be safe."

"A good idea," Roland seconded.

"How're you fixed for money, Carl?"

"Me? I got plenty of consols left. Might as well shoot the whole wad, since they won't be worth anything outside the Outworlds."

"Well," I said, "you could convert them back to gold."

"Oh, I've got loads of that, too. Really, I'm bankrolled pretty well. Let's get everyone outfitted and squared away, so there won't be any problems downroad."

"Well, maybe we should look for a general store, just to make sure we haven't forgotten—"

Sam's key was beeping in my pocket.

"Yeah, Sam?"

"Jake, I'm painting three fast-moving objects coming from uproad."

"Aren't you getting too much ground clutter? Oh, I see."

I hadn't noticed, but Sam had launched an earlybird. It was hovering about a hundred meters above.

"I don't like the looks of 'em. Maybe it's best we skedaddled."

The service people were finishing up with the vehicles. The station sat on a slender finger of dry land in the middle of a vast marsh. There was no possibility of going off-road and hiding.

"Right, Sam. Let's move." I turned around and faced my fellow voyagers. "You heard 'im, people. We scramble."

We scrambled. We had the attendants disconnect immediately, and to save time, I paid Sean's minuscule bill along with my own.

"Thanks, Jake."

"You owe me a couple beers. Whoa, there!"

I caught Lori by the sleeve of her pretty, but rumpled, red-striped sailor suit.

"Jake, please let me go with Carl."

"Into the cab, hon," I said firmly.

Her attitude seemed to have changed. She gave me no lip, and started clambering up the ladder to the cab. But suddenly I remembered the Chevy's astonishing capacity to absorb punishment and its stunning ability to inflict it. I grabbed Lori and yanked her down.

"Sorry, hon. You were right. Go with Carl." I swatted her skinny rump (though as rumps go, it was coming along rather nicely) and sent her on her way.

"What made you send up the bird, Sam?" I asked when I was inside the cab.

"Oh, a hunch. Thought I saw something sneaking around back there for the last hour or so. Seemed to be deliberately staying out of ground-scanner range. I'm painting a tiny airborne blip that could be their drone."

"Good work. Certainly sounds suspicious." I put on the headset as I vectored the rig out onto the Skyway.

"Carl, I'll take the bow and you take the stern."

"Check."

"Sean? You get in the lifeboat."

"Affirmative, and it's a damn good thing I know a bit of starrigger's lingo. 'Lifeboat,' indeed."

I kept one eye on the rearview screens as Sean and Carl configured themselves correctly.

"Okay, here's more starrigger's lingo for you. We're gonna squeeze hydrogen and let the neutrinos fly."

"We're going to 'grab slab,' is that it?"

"Right you are. Translation: let's get the hell moving."

"Well, the spirit is willing, Jake, but Ariadne's not herself today."

"Well, do the best you can."

"Affirmative."

Ariadne, I thought. Oh, my.

I eased the pedal down and watched the groundspeed readout until it showed 240 km/hr. A good clip, but still on the sane side. Sean began to drift back, so I feathered back to 210. I could see that Ariadne would hobble us until she was overhauled or until I could talk Sean and Liam into stashing her in the trailer. And now that we were about to leave human-occupied territory, opportunities for accomplishing the former would soon be reduced to zero. I doubted that I could persuade two proud loggers to demote themselves to the status of starhikers. Our only hope was that the approaching blips weren't hostile.

But they were.

"They've recovered the first drone and put up another," Sam announced. "Which reminds me, I have to do the same thing."

Recovering a drone on the fly was a difficult proposition, and we had lost our share of them trying it. Damn little things were expensive.

"Sounds like they're very interested in what's going on downroad," I said.

"Oh, they're tracking us, all right. We're getting scanned with everything in the spectrum."

"Pendergast's cops, you think?"

"Probably, though it could be anybody back there. We stepped on a lot of toes."

"Right."

The Skyway continued straight for a few kilometers, gliding over marsh and meadow, occasionally cutting across patches of dry land. The water in the swampy areas was a dark blue-green, mottled with rainbowed oil slicks. The tall trees weren't really trees. The trunks were masses of intertwined separate filaments, looking like a tangle of battling snakes. From the waters rose pink and purple grasses. Oval pads bearing evil yellow flowers floated on the surface.

"Hey, Carl? Ask Lori what it was like living here."

"Ask her yourself. She can hear you."

"Lori?"

"It bit the big kishko."

"I see."

"Jake?"—Carl again—*"That's an Intersystem word I've never heard before. Does it mean what I think it means?"*

"Yeah."

"Oh."

Behind me, Susan said, "I never understood what's so wrong with biting the big *kishko*."

Darla had to laugh.

I said, "Sam, what're they doing now?"

"I'm sure their drone spotted our drone. They've gained a little on us, but they're still hanging back. Probably waiting till we get on firm ground to make their move."

"Right, on the next planet up, which is supposed to be another desert world. Right, Darla?"

"Yes. And remember, Jake, you're to bear right at the fork."

"Got you. Should be coming up pretty soon."

A red light began blinking on the instrument banks.

"Son of a mother-punking bitch! Sam, it's that spare roller!"

"Yep."

"Dammit, I didn't know it was that bad."

"Well, I hate to say I told you so—"

"So don't say it!"

"—but I *told* you to spring for the new one. But nooo, you can get a better price down the road. Plenty of time, you said."

"Well, I *could* have gotten a better deal, dammit, if only—"

"Out in the middle of nowhere, and you have to go window-shopping."

"Oh, for Christ's sake, Sam, get off my back!"

"Son, it's just that you forget sometimes—"

"Sam, it would have cleaned us out! Look what that back-woods barracuda charged us for fixing the stabilizer foil."

"Well, we can't spend consols where we're going."

"I'm talking about our gold reserves! I could've bought half a new rig for what he wanted on that pair of newbies!"

"That right-front roller isn't in the best shape, either, you know. Ever think of what happens down the road if that one goes, too?"

"Ohhh, the hell with it."

"Very intelligent reply."

"Can it, Sam!"

"Okay, I'll can it. That's what canned-up people do best."

I felt horrible. I hadn't argued with Sam in . . . I didn't know how long. Recent events were definitely getting the better of me. I exhaled slowly and tried to absorb the adrenaline.

"Jesus, Sam, I'm sorry."

"So am I, son. My fault. This is no time for petty recriminations."

"No, no, you're programmed to advise on those decisions, and you were right. Should've sprung for the new pair—only thing, if we'd gone to a new size, it would've left us with *no* spare, and I didn't..." I scratched my head, remembering. "Oh, that's right. He said he'd thrown in a spare, the relayered one in the back. *Merte.* Sam, you were totally right."

"Forget it, Jake. You had a good point about the gold, and if people would stop chasing us all over the known universe, maybe we'd have time to think these things out. Actually, I thought for sure we'd be able to stop and shop around, too."

"Well, hell."

"Better get your helmet on, son."

"Yeah, I... hey, is that the fork coming up?"

"Looks like it."

"You know, Sam, I was thinking—"

I quickly forgot what I'd been thinking as the rig suddenly lurched to the left. The red light stopped blinking and a loud warning buzzer sounded. I fought the control bars, at the same time thumbing the trim tabs for the stabilizer foils. We were heading straight off the causeway, and the Roadbuilders didn't believe in guard rails. Letting up on the power pedal, I twisted the traction control on the right bar. The fork was dead ahead, and we were clear over in the extreme left lane. The rig straightened out just in time to save us from flying over the edge of the causeway. We wanted the right fork but I could see now that we'd never make it. With the failed right-front roller, I couldn't get back over to the other side of the road in time. The rig was under control for now, but... I angled my head toward the side port to get a view of the roller. It had turned the color of confectioner's sugar, trailing a plume of white powder. A flaky piece of it broke off, flew up and nearly hit the cab. I had to slow down; no choice.

And we had missed the turn-off. Turning around was going to be a problem for two reasons. The Skyway is four lanes across, counting the two narrower "shoulder" lanes. It's wide, but not nearly wide enough for the rig to turn around in without backing off the road. Only here, there was a two-meter drop to mud or water. And even if a dry patch came up, I was not about to give our pursuers a chance to catch us broadside to the road. I had to keep moving.

However, there was a problem with that, too.

"Jake! Jake, can you read me?"

"Yeah, Carl."

"What happened?"

"We had a roller go sugar-doughnut on us. That's why I missed the turn-off."

"Jake?" It was Sean.

"Yeah."

"Jake, according to our maps, this road leads to a potluck portal."

"I know."

And this time, it wasn't one on Winnie's Itinerary.

This time, it could lead to oblivion.

9

"Don't look now," Sam told us, "but here comes a missile."

"Just one?" I said.

"It's presenting a weird image . . . can't be just one. Nope. Tricky devils. Pretty sophisticated stuff, Jake. I can't get a fix on them."

"Start hosing with the stern exciters."

"I already have. Little out of range. Wait a minute. Okay, here we go."

A few seconds went by.

"Merte! Can't hit a thing. They're still closing."

A few minutes later, a series of muffled explosions came from behind.

"Did you get 'em, Sam?"

"Somebody did. It wasn't me."

"Carl," I said. "Had to be."

"He didn't get all of them. BRACE YOURSELVES!"

Off the causeway to the right up ahead, the swamp erupted into a geyser of mud and dirty water, accompanied by a tremendous explosion that shook the cab. As we passed, it all came down on us, a shower of slop and debris. A chunk of shattered treetrunk slammed against the foreward port but didn't break it.

"They're playing for keeps," I said.

"That one was damaged or we'd have been goners," Sam said.

"Thank God for that Chevy, though I'm surprised it let one get through. I was beginning to think that vehicle was magic." I flicked the headset mike on. "Carl? Sean? You guys okay?"

"Check."

"Affirmative, Jake. A bit dicey, though, wasn't it?"

"Yeah. Carl, I was under the impression that buggy of yours didn't miss."

"It usually doesn't. Must've been a fluke."

"Here's your chance to prove it," Sam said. "A whole 'nother flock of 'em coming right at us."

This time the Chevy didn't miss a one. Seven quick bangs and the scanners were clear.

"Nice shooting, Carl," I said.

"You think that's the worst they can throw at us?"

"Don't know. Let's hope they quit and go back."

"No chance of that," Sam said. "Here they come."

"Carl," I said, "can you sic Fido on them?"

"Who? Oh. I call 'em 'Tasmanian Devils.'"

We had tried to draw Carl out on his vehicle's strange weapons system, especially the horrific dust-devil-appearing phenomenon, designated "Sic 'im, Fido" on the fire-control panel. Carl had told us that he knew nothing whatsoever about how the weapons worked; he knew only how to use them.

"Whatever you call it, can you fire it on the run like this?"

"Yeah, sure. But I only have three Tasmanian Devils. You said you accidentally fired one back on Seahome. There are three blips back there."

"You mean one of those nightmares couldn't take care of all three of them?"

"No, you only get one to a target. When it completes its assignment, it disappears. Don't worry, Jake, I've got other stuff I can use."

"The question is," Sam put in, "what kind of stuff are they going to throw at us next?"

"Don't know, Sam," I said. "They're probably wary of Carl now. They know he has potent defenses. I have a feeling they'll want to keep their distance. Are they still closing?"

"Yeah, but it looks like they're maneuvering into position for something. Probably lining up for a concentrated mortar barrage. Those have to be paramilitary vehicles. They've got far more armaments than your average civilian roadster."

"This isn't Terran Maze. What road regulations they have here, if any, aren't exactly enforced to the letter. I'm willing to bet it's Zack Moore back there. Sam, give me a skyband channel."

"You got it."

"Breaker, breaker," I called, using the age-old skyband hail. "Breaking for those three goodbuddies at our back door—come on?"

"Back at you, goodbuddy," came Zack Moore's voice. *"Jake McGraw, is that you? Fancy meeting you here."*

"Yeah, fancy that. Zack, old boy, you and me got something to settle. But what say we leave my friends out of it? This is strictly between the two of us."

"Negatory, Jake. Fact is, I have a personal grievance against a few of them. Especially the tall skinny bitch—what's her name—Darla? None too friendly, that one. Needs to be taught a lesson or two, and I have ten men here who are excellent instructors. The same goes for that other little whore of yours. Seems she likes to bite, too. And if you're listening, Sean Fitzgore, be assured that I have a full lineup of entertainment planned for you and Liam."

"Wouldn't miss it for the world, Zack, boyo," Sean said pleasantly. *"Though you'll be hard pressed to perform your juggling act after I tear both your arms off."*

"We'll have to see about that. Jake, it's really only a matter of time. We have military-rated vehicles here. You haven't got a chance."

I said, "Zack, my only regret is that Darla didn't bite your *kishko* clean off."

"She'll get the chance, Jake. And you're invited to watch."

"Moore, I've decided that I will personally shut your *merte*-eating mouth for you."

"You're welcome to try, but you'll have a hard time of it with that bad roller. Am I right? We scanned you veering suddenly back there, and I know you came to Talltree with a roller going sweet on you."

"Nah, I was veering to run over a slug crawling across the road. Looked like you, but the trail of slime wasn't wide enough."

"Good one, Jake. Did you ever hear the one about the logger who had this enormous—"

"Jake," Sam said, interrupting the transmission. "Incoming mail!"

"Sean! Carl! Take evasive action *right now!*"

The rearview screen showed a stream of something bright and green shooting up from the roof of Carl's automobile. Sean was swerving all over the road. The scanners showed a sky full of blips, hundreds of them, thousands, it seemed. Ninety-nine percent of them were false, but our scanners were sophisticated enough to show those up pretty well. Trouble was, there wouldn't be time to shoot them all down, even as fast as Sam was. Moreover, our mortar rounds don't follow a true trajectory—these came equipped with tiny gas vernier jets to vector them into their chosen targets. That would increase Sam's "swing around" time as he used up precious microseconds to process continually changing data.

But Carl was helping.

"Fifty-six real blips," Sam said. "That's it, Carl! Get 'em at the top of the arc! Forty-two, forty-one . . ."

Carl was firing his magical weapon continually—doubtless it, too, was under some sort of computerized control.

". . . eighteen, seventeen . . ."

Just then another piece of the bad roller broke off, wafted past the cab like a gigantic snowflake, caught the slipstream and disappeared. The rig lunged to the left and I fought to get it under control.

"Sorry, Sam!" I yelled.

"Keep moving! Three of 'em left!"

A shell exploded to our right. Shrapnel spanged off the hull.

"Dammit, one got through." Sam said. "Must have MIRVed off one of the ones I registered as destroyed. Son of a bitch."

"Sean? You okay?"

"Right, Jake. We're still with you, but I'm afraid Ariadne's had a relapse. We're losing power very quickly here."

"Have you lost fusion altogether?"

"No, I don't think. Wait a minute."

"Another salvo, Jake," Sam announced.

"Right. Sean, what about it?"

On the rearview screen, I could see the magenta roadster dropping back precipitously.

"Absolutely right, Jake, we've lost it. We're working off a small light-hydrogen combustion engine. Afraid we won't be keeping up with you very well."

"Continue evasive action! Sam? How many this time?"

"About twice as many as before, it looks like."

Carl began firing again, a glowing green tube of energy bristling from the roof of his car like a straight lightning bolt.

"Sam, I want to slow down. Got an idea."

"Do it now!"

I slowed until Sean's buggy was tailgating us.

"Sean, listen to me. Do exactly as I say. Sam, I want you to—"

"I know what you're up to. The door is open and the ramp is down."

"Sean, do you see what I want?"

"Right, Jake. We'll try."

"Keep her steady, Jake," Sam warned. "Don't give me more numbers to crunch than you have to."

The rearview showed Sean lining his buggy up for the impossible docking procedure. He faded off, accelerated, drifted back again, all too tentatively.

"Sean! Shoot it in there! It's your only chance!"

He shot. I felt the trailer shift the slightest bit as the roadster dipped out of camera range. I switched feeds to the camera inside the trailer to make sure they'd made it, then reached for the switch to take in the ramp. Then a tremendous explosion rocked us.

"Sam, did we take a hit?"

"Don't know. Rearview camera's out, though."

"Sean, can you read me? Sean? Liam?"

"Their signal won't punch through the hull, Jake."

"That shell sounded like it could have penetrated the trailer and gone off inside it. Camera in the trailer's out too."

"Afraid you might be right. Damage sensors show a hull breach. Possible one, anyway. No, that may be because the back door won't close and the ramp's stuck. Getting all red lights back there."

"Jake? You guys okay?"

"We're all fine in the cab, Carl. Did you see us take a hit to the trailer?"

"I was looking back. You've got damage back there."

"Yeah. Can you see Sean or Liam?"

"No. The door's halfway down and the ramp's still dragging on the road."

"That's bad. They may have bought it. Carl, does that buggy of yours have any missiles?"

"Sort of. You have to understand something. The weapons on this vehicle are mainly defensive, except for the Tasmanian

Devils. And I had to argue with 'em over those."

"Argue with who?"

"The manufacturers. Never mind, can't go into it right now. Anyway, I can't fire at a vehicle unless it's in line-of-sight and it's shooting at me."

"Hell. Maybe—"

"What I can do, though, is maybe screw their tracking radar momentarily."

"Huh? You can?"

"Yeah, I think. I've never tried this gizmo before, but it should work."

"Christ, Carl! Why did you wait till now?"

"I just now figured out what the hell it was for. Jake, you've said that this jalopy of mine puzzles the hell out of you. Well, it does me, too, sometimes. They never fully explained how it's all supposed to work."

"Just what is this gizmo you're talking about?"

"I call it the Green Balloon. That's what it is. A big green sparkly bubble. I launched one once and got out of the car to watch it. I felt itchy all over and my hair stood on end, so I figured it was some kind of electrical phenomenon."

"Sounds like it. Sam, reprogram the missiles for a ballistic trajectory. All of 'em."

"Roger."

"Carl, can you keep that thing low to the ground so that the effect doesn't extend very far up?"

"It doesn't float too far off the ground, Jake. But it might knock out your radar . . . scanners, I mean."

"Just so it doesn't knock out the missiles' homing mechanisms."

"I can't promise that."

"We don't have much to lose by trying. Moore seems to have it over us in the black box department. Unaided, our missiles'll never hit him. So, stand by to fire that thing. Okay?"

"Will do."

"Sam?"

"Ready, Jake. All targeted."

"Fire away."

"Missiles off."

A series of loud whooshes came from the roof of the cab.

"Gimme the skyband again, and tell Carl to fire the Green

Balloon when the missiles reach the apex of their trajectories."

"Gotcha."

"Breaker, breaker. You still back there, Moore?"

"Indeed we are. What can I do for you?"

"You can take a look at your scanners and see death."

"Jake, those old firecrackers of yours don't worry us at all. We're just waiting for that roller to go completely to pieces. Won't be long. You're leaving chunks of it all over the road."

"There's gonna be pieces of you all over the road, good-buddy. Are you sure you see those missiles?"

"Clear as day. And you didn't fool us any by giving them a ballistic curve instead of cruising them. Actually, it doesn't make much difference—"

Suddenly, everything went out. The instrument lights flickered, went out, came back on. The scanner screens went blank for a moment. The engine powered down, groaned, sighed, and then came back to life.

"We just caught the edge of the effect zone," Sam said. "I zonked out there for a second."

"You okay?"

"Yeah. Missiles seem to be on course. Looks like our friends are trying to take evasive action." Sam laughed wickedly. "Fat lot of good it'll do 'em. They're blind, and it looks like their engines have quit on 'em too. They won't be able to roll out of the zone in time. Unless . . ."

"What?"

"Damn."

"What, what?" I said.

"We were on a curve when Carl fired. I don't have an accurate fix on that thing, though I'm painting some fuzzy stuff that might be it. It looks as though it's drifting off. They may get out of the effect zone just in time."

"Oh, hell."

"We'll know in a few . . . Yeah, looks like they're back on full power, and they're starting to fire. Five seconds to impact. Four . . . three . . . two . . . *Huh?"*

I shot a glance into the rearview parabolic, couldn't see anything. "What happened, Sam?"

"Son of a brick. Those missiles detonated before impact. All of 'em, all at once."

"That's impossible."

"Yeah? How come it happened? I'm not entirely sure they detonated, but they all disappeared from the scope in a flash."

"Moore couldn't have done that," I said. "He would've got some of them, but not all of them in one clean sweep."

"I think you're right. They were just about to be hit hard when it happened. Two more seconds and we would've got 'em. Hell. There goes the fuel on the drone. I'll have to recover it."

"Send up Number Two drone," I told him.

"Going up right now."

"I'm going to slow down." I reached for the band selector switch. "Carl?"

"Yeah."

"Feather back a little. Want to see what the hell happened back there, and this roller's going to go any minute."

"Okay."

"Sam, do you see anything?"

"They've dropped back."

"Maybe we did get 'em."

"Don't see how. Those missiles airbursting over them wouldn't've done any damage."

"Well, they're not following and that's all I care about."

I noticed that the terrain had changed. We were out of the swamps and onto rolling plains of purple grass. The portal cylinders were gray-black stumps against a gray horizon. We still had time to check on Sam and Liam without having to stop.

"Roland!" I yelled. "Unstrap, go back, and unbolt the hatch to the crawltube. Get back to that trailer fast!"

"Right!"

"Hold it a minute, Roland!" Sam shouted. "Something coming up. Right, and I think this'll explain what happened to the missiles."

"A Roadbug?"

"Yeah, looks like one."

"You think it intervened?"

"Yup. They don't like rowdy behavior on their road."

"I hope it's in a lenient mood today."

Roadbug behavior was difficult to predict. They were traffic cops, theoretically with only one law to enforce: "Thou shalt not close the road, nor interrupt traffic in any way on any section thereof." As in any legal system, however, judgment sometimes turned on interpretation. Running battles on the road often were tolerated, but in some cases a Roadbug might blast one or the other of the warring parties if it detected a general pattern of illegal activity. In other words, you couldn't just travel the Skyway taking potshots at anybody and everybody. Sooner or later the Bugs would get wise—there was no doubt that they kept files on specific vehicles, perhaps on *all* vehicles regularly using the road—and you'd get stomped. Flat. The Roadbugs were notorious for conducting quickie trials on the run, taking testimony from both suspects and witnesses, and rendering summary justice. These decisions were irreversible; there was no court of appeal.

Who were they? *What* were they? Roadbuilder machines? Or were they the Roadbuilders themselves? Nobody knew.

"It's a Bug, all right," Sam announced.

Since the rearview camera was out, I looked out the port at the parabolic mirror. Within the converging edges of the road behind us, a silver blob was swelling rapidly to take on the shape of a Skyway Patrol vehicle. Their speeds were always fantastic. Sometimes they would overtake you at such a terrific clip that the shock wave would nearly send you sailing out of control. This one appeared to be decelerating, as usual at a bone-pulping rate. I slowed. Doubtless the Bug wanted a chat with us. Pass the time of day.

"Son, tell the truth. Always best when you're dealing with Bugs."

"Yes, Daddy."

"Don't get smart. Yep, here's his hailing signal. I'll put him on the cabin speaker."

"OCCUPANTS OF COMMERCIAL VEHICLE: YOU WILL PROCEED AT ONCE TO THE NEXT SECTION."

The Roadbug's voice was like a needle through the eardrums. Imagine all the unpleasant noises you can: the creak of chalk against a blackboard, the tearing of metal, the snap of bone, the crash of vehicles colliding, the buzz of a vibrosaw. Take those waveforms and bunch them up around the extremes of the audible range, then superimpose a ghastly, nonhuman voice over top. The description is inadequate. I suppressed a shudder, and tried to answer in a calm voice.

"Following your order will cause us hardship and put us in danger."

A pause. Then: "EXPLAIN."

"This portal will take us away from our planned route and leave us stranded. We have no maps for that section. Also, we have a dangerously defective roller."

The Roadbug pulled alongside us. It looked like an immense silver beetle, its surface featureless and glossy. Blotting out the sky to our left, it drew close for an inspection of the roller. As if to demonstrate, the roller obliged by throwing off another huge chunk of itself. Apparently satisfied, the Bug edged away.

"DEFECTIVE COMPONENT CONFIRMED. NEVERTHELESS, YOU WILL PROCEED TO THE NEXT SECTION. WE WILL ASSIST."

I squelched the mike. "Goddammit," I said. "Sam? Can you think of anything?"

"Ask him why," Sam said. "Ask nice."

I reopened the mike. "We respectfully request the reasons for your order."

"YOUR RECENT CONDUCT ON THIS SECTION HAS BEEN DEEMED POTENTIALLY DISRUPTIVE OF TRAFFIC FLOW. YOU MUST BE SEPARATED FROM YOUR OPPONENTS."

"We were fired on without provocation."

"THAT IS OF NO CONCERN. YOU WILL PROCEED TO THE NEXT SECTION OF ROAD. INCREASE YOUR SPEED AND PREPARE FOR TRANSITION. YOUR OPPONENTS WILL NOT FOLLOW."

"Dammit it! I said we'd be stranded!"

"THAT IS OF NO CONCERN. END OF TRANSMISSION."

"Fuck you." Sometimes I prefer good old Anglo-Saxon.

The Roadbug dropped back, moved behind us, and inched up until it was tailgating.

"And we don't even get a phonecall to our solicitor," Sam said.

I nodded and heaved a sigh. We were being sentenced, banished to the far side of a potluck portal with no hope of appeal. I had heard of Roadbugs doing this, but had never thought it would happen to me. I looked back at my passengers.

Well, it wasn't only happening to me. I looked at the road ahead. The cylinders were almost upon us. I had no choice. It was either shoot the potluck—the Roadbug version of a commuted death sentence—or get smeared.

But there still was the matter of the failed roller. As our speed increased, it began tossing off pieces of itself with abandon, trailing a snowy plume of powder. This might be a death sentence after all. That roller was ready to break apart any moment.

"Take her through at minimum speed, son. Steady as she goes."

"Right. I'll need every assist."

"I'm right with you."

"Dad, I don't think we're going to make it this time."

"I'll be with you every step of the way, son."

The instrument panel was adance with flashing red lights. The landscape whizzed by in a purple blur.

"People," I announced. "No way I can take this rig through a portal with a failed roller. Unless the Bug makes good on the assist promise—and I don't see how he can—this could be it. I thought you should know."

I glanced back again. Susan was white-lipped and pale, John grim but steady-eyed.

"We'll make it, Jake," Roland told me. "We *have* to."

"Do our best."

Darla . . .

I turned around once more. Darla was smiling at me! Those ionospheric blue eyes glowed with the strangest light. I saw eternity in them. My destiny.

I blinked my eyes and the smile was gone. I had glanced back for the barest fraction of a second. Now I wasn't sure if I had seen her smile at all.

The rig lurched to the left and I fought to keep us on the road. The commit markers—two red-painted metal rods to either side of the roadbed—went by almost before I caught sight of them. I had to straighten out . . . now!

The roller started breaking up, deep fracture lines opening up along its surface, shooting out blizzards of white powder.

"Dad! Is there anything on the other side?"

"Of the portal?"

"No. Life."

Sam didn't have time to answer. Suddenly . . . everything was normal.

It was as if a huge hand had grabbed the rig and steadied it. Warning lights still flashed, the roller continued its breakup, but our course was true and steady. We were right in the groove. The guide lane markers came up and we were smack in the middle of them. The cylinders marched by, two by two, then the aperture assumed its vague shape out of the optical miasma ahead. We slid neatly into it.

Then the Roadbug let us go. The roller flew apart in an explosion of snow and ice, sending the rig careening toward the wind-combed dunes lying along the road. We hit sand and the sudden deceleration popped our eyeballs and crushed our chests. I hit the antifishtail jets, torqued up the antijacknife servo and kept us straight for a hundred meters. Angular momentum was conserving all over the place, dragging us back in the direction of the roadway, but the trailer didn't want to follow. The cab bumped over the lip of the berm. I straightened out, but the trailer still angled to the left, burying its back end into the sand. It would either tip over or fall in behind eventually. I didn't wait for it to make up its mind; I accelerated, flipped up the safety door covering the quick-release toggle and reached in, crooking two fingers over the ring. Gradually, the trailer swung back into line. I braked—which was a very difficult proposition because there was almost nothing left of the bad roller. Stripped to its yellow, spongy core, it whumped and bumped over the road, *flop flop flop flop flop flop,* again causing us to veer to the left. I had no intention of going offroad again. I disconnected the front rollers from the braking system and juiced up the rear set. But it was still rough going. The cab shifted suddenly, listing to the left, and sparks began to fly as the edge of the ground-effect vane touched roadmetal. I was able to handle the drag factor, though, and we were coasting nicely to stop when the Roadbug lost patience and whoosed by us in an incredible burst of acceleration.

I don't remember what happened next, exactly. We were all over the road, then we were in the sand again, then out of it, and back in once more. Plumes of yellow sand arced up, covering the forward port.

Finally, we came to a stop. The side port was clear, and I could see that we were more or less upright. The front end was buried halfway up the aerodynamic engine housing. I activated the washers on the front ports and soon we could see ahead. The rig had run itself aground with a vengeance. Ordinarily, this would have presented no difficulty. With two good front rollers, we could detach the trailer, tow it out, then back the cab out with no problem—if we had a tow truck, and if we had two good front rollers.

Out on the road, Carl came screeching to a stop, pulling off onto the shoulder lane.

"Jake, are you guys okay?"

I looked back. Nobody seemed to be damaged. Everybody nodded. "Yeah, we're okay. Considering."

"What about Sean and Liam?"

"Holy shit!"

Roland had already unstrapped and was making his way to the aft-cabin. I tore off my harness and followed.

"Roland, wait!" I said. "Sam! How's the air out there?"

"Earth normal!"

"Unbelievable. Luck at last. Roland, you go out through the cabin and try to get in through the back door. I'll go through the crawl tube. There may be damage back there."

"Right!"

I unbolted the hatch, got down on all fours, and scurried through the accordian-walled access tube. The far hatch was okay. I undogged it, slid through, did a somersault and got to my feet. It was dark. I smelled smoke, but couldn't see any damage back in the egg-crate section. I jumped over a few boxes, slithered through a maze of crates, sidling my way to the rear. There was daylight coming from back there.

"Have a beer, Jake?"

Sean and Liam lay sprawled in a jumble of boxes and loose junk. Beer bottles had broken, foam creeping everywhere. Their roadster was covered with debris, but otherwise undamaged. Sean sat up, waving an unbroken bottle in salute.

Roland came climbing over the junk.

"Are they all right?"

"Right you are, Roland, my friend!" Sean called. He broke the neck of the bottle against a metal crate, put the jagged end to his lips and took a drink.

He smiled pleasantly. "Have we stopped for lunch?"

10

Near as I could figure it, the mortar shell had detonated a meter or so in front of the rear door as the door was sliding shut. The blast had buckled it, and it was stuck about two-thirds of the way down. The ramp was bent and could not be retracted manually. Minor damage, really, considering what could have happened. The door had absorbed most of the concussion, and Ariadne had been well inside the trailer when it had hit. In fact, Ariadne's brakes were in as good shape as the rest of her—Sean had had trouble stopping, with the result that some of the cargo had been unartfully rearranged. No great damage here either, except for six or seven smashed cases of beer. The astronomical gear in the egg-crate section was untouched, thank God.

Of course damage was the least of our worries. We were marooned on the far side of a hope-to-Jesus hole. You don't get a round-trip ticket when you go through one of those.

But we still had one operable vehicle, Carl's car—well, one and a half, if you counted the crippled Ariadne. After lengthy debate, we decided to send out a scouting party to find out if this world was inhabited, and by whom. If it turned out that nobody lived here, we'd be faced with the ticklish option of shooting a portal, gambling that it wasn't a one-way shot. We could do that until we found an inhabited planet and help. The Great Debate was really about who should go and who should stay behind.

"But nobody has to stay behind if we use both vehicles," Sean protested.

"Trouble is," I countered, "that auxiliary engine of yours breathes air. What if we hit a non-oxy world?"

"Well, yes, it would be a problem. Didn't think of it."

"But we can't all fit into the Chevy," John put in. "Can we? There are ten of us."

"With a little shoving, we could," Carl said. "I think it's the best way to go."

"It may be the only way to go," I said. "I don't want to leave anyone stranded here . . . including Sam. I'll stay."

"Jake, you can't," Darla said.

"Forget it, Jake," Sam said. "Just take out my VEM and put it in your pocket. You'll find something to load me into eventually."

"And leave behind all your programming? To say nothing of the rig? Nothing doing, Sam," I said. "You people squeeze in that buggy and take off. Sam and I will be all right."

"You'd have us leave behind the leader of this expedition?" Roland said mock-indignantly. "Not likely."

"I seem to have the knack of leading this expedition into one disaster after another," I said. "Besides, if I *am* the leader, you should follow my orders without question."

"Every order but that one, I'm afraid," John said apologetically. "Sorry, Jake, but I suppose I've finally come 'round to Roland's way of thinking. As far as I can see, everything has been going according to Plan."

Again, the Teleologist buzz word. Their constant use of it had always bothered me, but now, in the stuffiness of the overcrowded aft-cabin, it was beginning to rankle.

"You know," I said, "almost by definition, anything that happens is part of the 'Plan.' Hasn't it ever occurred to you that your reasoning is a little specious, logically speaking?"

"Looking at it from a traditional viewpoint, yes, perhaps it is specious. But Teleological Pantheism is a process whereby one learns to adapt to different viewpoints. From a different perspective, you can view the entire history of logical discourse as leading to but one conclusion—that truth, ultimately and finally, transcends reason."

"Funny you should use the word 'conclusion.' It implies you have an argument going, which means you're using logic—reason. In other words, you're saying that you've used logic to arrive at the conclusion that logic is no good."

John considered it a moment. "Perhaps I am saying that. Again, it's a matter of perspective. Let's employ a metaphor. I've used a ladder to ascend to a higher level, at which point

I throw the ladder away. It was useful to a point, but isn't any longer."

"Interesting," I said. "But metaphors can be tricky."

"Do we have time," Carl said, "for all this philosophical horseshit?"

"We have all the time in the world," I said. "For once, nobody's chasing us. Let's take it slow and think things out. We have plenty of food, loads of power to run the life-support... Matter of fact, Sam, it's getting pretty close in here." I squirmed in my chair at the breakfast nook. "Take the temp down a bit. Okay? And the CO_2 level, while you're at it."

"Will do, though ten bodies are putting a strain on the air-conditioning, which is all I'm using. It's high noon, local time, and the temperature out there is thirty-seven-point-five degrees Celsius."

"Sorry for that remark, Jake," Carl said. "It's just—"

"Forget it. We've all been strained to the breaking point lately, including me. I owe all of you an apology for the way I've been acting. It isn't like me, and I can only plead extenuating circumstances."

"You're forgiven, Jake," John said. "But Carl had a point. We should get back to the issue at hand—which is that it wouldn't be wise to separate."

"Well, it wouldn't be desirable, that I'll grant you. But it might be necessary. Carl, you say we should shove all ten of us into that buggy of yours—"

"I'm not saying we wouldn't be uncomfortable."

"How about the strain on the life-support systems?"

"It'd handle it."

"You sure? We know the technology has its limitations."

"How so?"

"Well, it didn't get the shell that hit us."

Carl, who was squatting on the deck by the kitchenette, rubbed the adolescent stubble on his jaw. "Yeah, I was wondering about that, too. But I'm inclined to believe that any limitations were deliberately built in."

"What do you mean?" Roland asked.

"Well, the manufacturers wanted the car to attract as little attention as possible, as far as its superior technology is concerned."

"So they built a 1957 Chevrolet Impala. What did you call

the color? 'Candy-apple red'? Very inconspicuous," I said.

Carl smiled sheepishly. "The look of the car was my idea. Psychological reasons, mostly. I was homesick."

We all looked at him, awaiting an explanation.

When it didn't seem to be forthcoming, I said, "Carl, who built your vehicle? And why?"

The smile turned apologetic. "I really don't know if I'm ready to tell you my life story. Sorry, but I just can't go into it right now."

"Well," I said, "you're under no obligation. It's your business."

"Thanks, I appreciate it." He stood up. "Think I'll go out to the car and check over the beam weapon controls. You know, it just may be that I didn't have it set up right. Like I said, I don't know all there is to know about that vehicle. It keeps on surprising me." He stretched. "Getting cramped in here anyway. Lori, you want to come?"

"Sure."

After they left, Sean came in from the cab.

"Sean, what do you make of him?" I said.

He fingered his sinuous red worm of a mustache. "A strange one. Passing strange."

"We *know* that," Roland said.

"You mean his vehicle?" Sean raised his massive shoulders and turned a palm up. "I'd wager the thing comes from outside the known mazes, but beyond that..." He upended the beer bottle into his mouth, wiped his face with a hairy arm. "He's an anachronism, that I know."

"Yes," John agreed. "His accent, speech idiosyncrasies." He turned to me. "You know, Jake, until I met Carl, I would have said that you have the quintessential American accent. But Carl sounds like a character out of some ancient *mopic*. Humphrey Beauvard, someone like that."

"Humphrey Bogart," I corrected him.

"Whoever."

"He's a time traveller!" Susan blurted.

"You mean," Roland said, "he comes from 1957?"

Susan shrugged. "Sure. Why not?"

"How did he get from Earth, circa 1957, to here and now?"

"Starship."

"Starship," Roland said, nodding, then rolling his eyes.

"Yeah. Relativity, time dilation and all that."

"Do you mean to say," Roland said, his voice larded with irony, "he left Earth in 1957 . . . in a starship?"

"Don't be so damn snotty. Why not?"

"Because there weren't any starships in 1957. There aren't any now."

"Maybe the Ryxx kidnapped him! I don't know! Do you have to pounce on me every time I—"

"But we're talking about a hundred and fifty years ago, Susan."

I said, "The Ryxx have been on the Skyway for something like three hundred years, Roland. No telling when they achieved interstellar travel."

Roland shook his head skeptically. "I'd be willing to bet it was very recently."

"Why don't we simply wait," Liam broke in, poking his head through the hatch, "for Carl to tell us? Whatever the explanation is, I'd lay odds it's *involved.*"

"Or maybe he has something to hide," Roland said.

"What?" I wanted to know.

"That's the question, isn't it?"

"Well, if you're speculating he's a spy or something—"

"Maybe not a spy."

"Then what is he? Remember it wasn't his idea to tag along with us. I dragged him into all of this by stealing his car."

Roland had his chin propped up on one arm, chewing the nail of his little finger. "I just have a strange feeling about him," he murmured.

"Don't know what could've caused that," I said. "He seems like your average bloke to me."

Susan tittered, then slid her hand down my thigh to massage the inside of the knee.

Silence for a moment.

"Well," John said, "what shall we do?"

"About Carl?" I asked.

"No. About the scouting party."

"I'm still very reluctant to leave Sam," I said.

"I can understand that, Jake. I can certainly understand how you feel about leaving your fath—" Tongue-tied for second, he motioned vaguely in the direction of the cab. "Uh . . ."

"My father."

"Yes. Yes, your father. Um, it's rather difficult some-times—"

"It's okay. By the way, Sam's location is more or less here," I said, pointing to a small bulge in the rear bulkhead of the cabin. "That's his CPU, Central Processing Unit. His auxiliary storage is wedged in the bulkhead between the cab and the cabin. And of course there are various input and output units all over the place."

"The Entelechy Matrix," Roland said. "That's in the CPU?"

"Right. Sorry, John. You were saying . . ."

"I was more or less trying to say that if we lost you, Jake, there'd be no hope for the rest of us."

"I hardly think that's the case."

"But you have the Black Cube."

It was the first time in a good while that anyone had mentioned the strange artifact, probably because no one knew what to say about it. Everything that had happened, everything, it seemed, that *would* happen, revolved around the enigma that the Cube represented. Putatively, it was the Roadmap, the object of all the chases, the intrigue, the hugger-mugger. In the drama of the Paradox, it occupied center stage. At John's mention of it, the irony of our situation hit home. Here we were, lost and rollerless on uncharted road, with the key to the entire Skyway system in our possession . . . supposedly.

Well, if the Cube *was* the legendary Roadmap, we had no way to read it. There was no way to even begin to read it. Although we had not tried tampering with the thing, it looked dauntingly inviolable. Its impenetrable blackness seemed to say, *Don't even think about it*. It was hard to imagine that it could merely contain useful information. Dark secrets, maybe. That Which Man Was Not Meant To Know. But a roadmap indicating the better-class motels and scenic points of interest? Nah.

"You have no idea, John," I said, "how close I've come to chucking that damn thing out the port."

John nodded gravely. "It's a lightning rod."

"Precisely. And we've been zapped one too many times. So, what makes you think you'd be better off sticking around it?"

"I don't want to . . . 'stick around' the Cube so much as I want to dog your every step until you bring the bloody thing back home."

"Yeah? What are you going to say to your doppelgänger when you meet him?"

"My paradoxical self? I should think we'd have much to talk about. However, I don't ever remember myself coming the other way. Therefore, if I do make the trip back, I won't bother seeking myself out. I didn't, so I won't. I don't see a paradox there."

Roland had been thinking. "What if you did, John? What if you did try to find yourself?"

"I'd fail."

Roland jabbed a finger at him. "But what if you *didn't* fail?"

"But I will. It's history."

"Excuse me, Suzie," I said, making a move to get up.

"Sure."

I wriggled out of the nook and made my way to the safe, which was in the bulkhead by the bunk, where Darla was stretched out. She had been complaining of nausea.

"Feel any better?" I asked her as I stooped to let the lock read my thumbprint.

"Much. I'm all right."

"But you have free will," Roland was saying, continuing the argument. "There'd be *nothing* to prevent you from going back to Khadija and presenting yourself."

"But I wouldn't."

"I would."

John was genuinely shocked. "You would?"

"Of course. Couldn't resist it."

John shook his head, appalled. "Good God. Tempting the fates like that. It's . . ." He shuddered. "There must be some Greek myth to cover this sort of thing."

"The Greeks didn't have time machines."

"Well, I meant morally analogous. Oedipus, perhaps."

"Should I poke out my eyes after I do it?"

"I should think your double's eyes would come popping out by themselves."

"Explain that," I broke in, plunking the Cube down on the table in front of John, "without a paradox."

"I couldn't begin to."

"What the bloody hell is *that?*" Liam said.

"Good question," I said.

"It's the thing that can't possibly exist," Roland said. "But it does."

"How so?" Liam wanted to know.

"It's the thing I supposedly brought back from my time trip and gave to somebody . . . who gave it to somebody who gave it to Darla—"

"Who gave it to you. I see. It's the Roadmap."

"Maybe."

"I doubt it," Roland said, picking it up and holding it close to peer at its featureless surface.

"Why?" John asked.

"Well . . ."

"That's the blackest . . . *black* I've ever seen," Liam said, after he'd sidled past Sean to get nearer to the table. "Even the cylinders . . ."

"Well," I said, "you always see those from a distance. Up close like this it's a little disconcerting."

"It must be a Roadbuilder artifact," Sean stated. "They seem to've preferred the color."

"If it isn't the Roadmap," John said, "what could it possibly be?"

"Funny," Roland said, his right eyeball practically touching the cube, "you can't actually *see* the surface. It's . . . I mean, you can't really—"

"But if it isn't the Roadmap," John went on, more or less to himself, "then . . ." The notion plunged him into deep thought.

Darla got up and came to the table. She put her hand on my shoulder.

Roland set the Cube down, and we all looked at it for a longish moment.

"What the hell *is* that thing?" I said, finally.

Sean said, "Hmph."

After another thoughtful interlude, John said, "We keep straying from the main line of discussion."

"You're right," Susan said. "What are we going to do?"

"I have a suggestion," Sam broke in over the cabin speakers.

"Shoot," I said.

"Send out Carl to scout this world, see if there's anybody around. Then decide what you want to do."

"Have you picked up anything on the air?"

"Nope, but that doesn't necessarily mean the place is deserted. Granted, it's not promising, but just to be sure, someone should have a look around first."

"Have you been scanning with the drone?"

"Yeah, but nothing's showed up."

"I guess it wouldn't hurt to drive around. We have time."

"Sure, why not? As you said, we should take time to think things through for once. It'd be a nice change of pace. No use going off half-cocked if we can avoid—" He broke off, then said, "I spoke too soon."

"Someone shot the portal?"

"No, somebody's walking across the desert toward us. Looks human."

There was no proverbial sigh of relief.

"Humans here, too," John muttered. "We're everywhere."

"How many?" I asked.

"Just one. Let me train the exciter on him, just to be sure."

"Doesn't he look friendly?"

"He's carrying something. Can't tell what."

"Jake? Come in." Carl's voice came from the cab speakers.

"Patch me through, Sam."

"You're on."

"Yeah, Carl?"

"We got company."

"We know. Sam spotted him. Are you and Lori locked inside the car?"

"You bet."

"Does he have anything that looks like a weapon?"

"He's too far away to tell. He's wearing a pressure suit, though."

"Pressure suit?"

"Some kind of protective suit. Armor, maybe? Looks like—Hey! He just took off."

From out in the desert came the hollow whine-and-wail of jet exhaust. We all got up and filed out to the cab.

"He's got some kind of rocket backpack. Jesus Christ, just like Commander Cody."

"Commander who?" I said when I got my headset on. "Where the hell is he?" I looked out over the desert to the right. A white dot floated against the hazy sky just above a butte about half a kilometer away. A cloud of dust was settling over the area where he had apparently launched himself.

"You see him?"

"Yeah. What did he do before he took off?"

"Nothing much. Looked like he was searching for something out there. Had some kind of weird equipment. Then he spotted us and blasted off. Took a good look at us first."

The white speck disappeared behind the butte.

"What do we do?" John asked.

"We wait," I said.

We waited, ten minutes. Then he returned, this time piloting a strange variant of a landjumper. He came across the desert at reckless speed, bouncing over rocks and rises, staying around five or ten meters off the ground. From the sound the craft made, I judged the engines to be of a rather primitive jet turbine design. The craft was big and bulky, but had room for at most two passengers and the driver.

"Have him covered, Sam?"

"I've got everything trained on him but missiles, of which we ain't got any."

He zoomed in, stopped, and hovered over a hollow between dunes, then set the craft gently down.

Instead of passengers, he was hauling a load of stuff—boxes, sacks, miscellaneous parcels. He picked up a sack and another thing that looked like an animal skin, and came toward us.

It was plain now that our visitor wasn't human. He . . . it was much too thin and the arms had two elbows. Generally humanoid, but the proportions were all wrong. It wore a white reflective suit with what looked like a backpack respirator. The helmet was covered with the same sort of cloth as the suit. We couldn't see a face behind the darkly tinted viewscreen. It stopped and looked the rig over, checked out the Chevy, then looked at us again. Apparently the rig seemed a bit intimidating. It went over to Carl, stooping to peer into the driver's side window. The creature was man-high, which had led us to mistake it for a human being at a distance.

Surprisingly, it greeted Carl with a raised right hand. I couldn't see if Carl returned the gesture. The creature then reached into one of the sacks and pulled out what looked like a folded piece of paper, which he unfolded and presented to

Carl, pointing out various markings and lines.

"Hey, Carl."

"Yeah."

"What's he trying to sell you?"

"I think it's a roadmap."

11

The beings who had colonized this maze were known by the general name of *Nogon,* but we came to know only a very special and unrepresentative group of them.

They lived in caves and called themselves the *Ahgirr,* a word which, in their liquid, gargly tongue, was roughly equivalent to *The Keepers*. Both an ethnic group and a quasi-religious sect, the *Ahgirr* preferred adhering to ancient ways and customs. Most of their race, both here and on their home planet, lived in huge high-tech arcologies, called *faln,* named after a giant plant that looks like a mushroom but isn't a fungus. The *Ahgirr,* however, loved their cave-communities, believing that creatures spawned from the earth should keep close to their origins. For all that, they didn't reject science and technology. No Luddites they, the *Ahgirr,* in their long history, had produced many of their race's most brilliant scientists. Hokar, the individual who picked us up and brought us in, was a geologist. He'd been out prospecting in the desert when he was surprised by the sight of vehicles on that little-used ingress spur. He saw we were in trouble and came immediately. The *Ahgirr* were like that—warm, friendly, outgoing . . . and *very* human. Their species was the closest to human that anyone, to my knowledge, had ever encountered on the Skyway. They were bipedal, mammalian, ten-digited, two-sexed, and breathed oxygen (Hokar's suit was merely a protection against bright sunlight, which his species couldn't tolerate). They had two eyes, one nose, one mouth, sparse body hair and lots of hair on the head—the whole bit. There were differences, though. You wouldn't mistake them for humans. They had joints in the wrong place. Their skins were translucent, and their odd circulatory systems gave them a distinct pinkish-purple cast. The eyes were huge and pink and structurally dissimilar to the human variety. Their long straight hair was the color and texture of corn silk. (Non-*Ahgirr*—which meant, of course, the rest of the species—wore their hair in various styles. Coiffure was very important in distinguishing ethnic and nationality groups, of which there were many.) But after a while, it was hard not to think of the *Ahgirr* and their race as just an unusual variety of human beings.

The first task was to get Sam unstuck. The *Ahgirr* didn't have very much in the way of heavy equipment, but they put in a call (to a nearby *faln* complex, as we learned later), and an odd-looking towing vehicle came out by Skyway and did the job. We detached the trailer, and the towtruck hauled Sam over the desert to the mouth of the *Ahgirr* cave-community. Ariadne had to be left in the trailer, but Carl's buggy made the trip on its own power, which was a surprise to nobody. I was waiting for the thing to fly.

All interspecies communication up to this point had been via the usual half-understood gestures and signing, but fortunately the *Ahgirr* were computer whizzes, and once they solved the problem of system compatibility, they waded right into Sam's language files—the dictionaries, word-processing programs, compilers, and such. In no time the *Ahgirr* were speaking to us in English that was completely understandable if a little fractured.

They gave us an apartment to stay in while the language barrier was being broken down. As it turned out, we stayed five weeks, and at no time did we feel as though we were wearing out our welcome. The *Ahgirr* were eager to make friends with beings similar to themselves. Word spread over the planet; we were something of a sensation.

The second task was to see about getting a new roller. That was going to be a problem. My rig was a bit unusual. It had been built to Terran specifications and design, but an alien outfit had manufactured it. I always had a hard time finding parts for it. Here, light-years away from Terran Maze, it might just be impossible. We were told that a few planets away there was a stretch of Skyway along which lay a number of used vehicle dealerships and salvage yards. We might try there. Carl and Roland volunteered to go and Hokar offered to act as guide. They were gone two days. Meanwhile, the rest of us set about the job of repairing the trailer. Fixing the buckled door wasn't so hard, but all the rear cameras and sensors had pretty much been totaled, which meant buying alien gear to replace them. And that meant a lot of fudging and jury-rigging. But we had to do it if we didn't want to be blind out our back side. We had to make a trip to a *faln* to buy parts.

Before we got around to that, Hokar, Roland, and Carl returned with an almost-new pair of rollers. A stroke of long-overdue luck.

"We scavanged through junkyard after junkyard," Roland said over dinner in our suite of rooms within the *Ahgirr* cave-city. "Nothing even remotely resembled the vehicles you usually see in Terran Maze or any of the contingent mazes. We were pretty discouraged, but Hokar said he was sure he remembered seeing vehicles similar to your rig, though not driven by humans. And sure enough—"

"We found a junked rig, just the cab, but very similar to yours," Carl interrupted. "Even had the same markings, same decals."

"The owner of the wreck said the people who'd left it there hadn't looked anything like us, meaning they weren't human, of course," Roland said.

"The front rollers were in good shape," Carl went on, "so we bought 'em. Got a pretty good deal, too, with Hokar advising us on protocol."

"Yes, the *Nogon* have strange rituals when it comes to bargaining," Roland elaborated. "You have to approach the seller on the pretext of wanting to buy everything he has to sell, at any price he chooses to set, and the seller in turn has to pretend that you couldn't possibly want any of the worthless junk he's got, no matter how low he's slashed the price."

"Traveling salesmen must have it easy here," I commented, reaching for a second helping of the delicious vegetable stew Darla had concocted out of the fresh produce Sean and Liam had brought along.

"As I said, it's all posturing. Pretty soon everyone's self-interest emerges crisp and clear, and then it's no holds barred."

"Sounds healthy," I said.

"Time consuming," Carl said. "Took an hour to close the deal."

I turned to Ragna, who was sipping thin gruel through a straw from a decorative ceramic bowl. "I take it haggling is a high art with your people."

Ragna stopped slurping, blinked his enormous pink eyes, then touched his blue headband, a biointerface gadget that was the closest thing to a universal translator I'd ever seen. It was merely a very-large-scale integration computer, but the software was powerful. However, my colloquialisms and abbreviated grammar gave it trouble now and then. Also, figurative speech gave the translation program headaches. But it was integrating our responses nicely.

"I am thinking that the haggling with my people is indeed, true, yes, a high or fine art, in the mode of hyperbole and colloquial exaggeration. In the literal or denotative mode, no, forget it, Charlie."

I suppressed a smile. "Ragna, your facility with the language improves daily. I must compliment you on it."

"Of course I am undubitably thanking you."

"I should think," John said, "you'll be able to doff that headband soon enough."

"Oh, yes, this is quite a possibility I am thinking. Even now, you may be seeing . . ." Gingerly, Ragna removed the flexible headband with both hands and laid it on the table. In a barely intelligible liquid slur, he said, "Unassisting brain capability speaking quite good, is it not? Is aiding the biological analogue to being able to function, learning is this not so to be speaking?"

"Eh?" John said.

"Interrogatory remark, what?" Ragna's thin white eyebrows lowered in puzzlement.

We persuaded Ragna to put the headband back on.

The remainder of the meal was devoted to chitchat. When we were all sitting back drinking beer and burping, Suzie looked gravely at me.

"What is it, Susan?" I said.

"Where do we go from here?"

"Good question." I turned to Sean and Liam. "What've you guys come up with in the map department?"

"Damn little," Liam said, then nodded deferentially toward Ragna. "Of course Ragna and Hokar and the others have been very helpful. It's simply that none of the mazes we've had a look at seem familiar." He ran a hand through his mass of tousled blond hair, then sighed and pursed his lips. "We're bloody well lost all right."

I nodded. "Darla, can Winnie help us?"

Winnie, seated by Darla, looked sad as she munched the remains of her meal of shoots and leaves.

"Afraid not," Darla said. "I think it's clear now that Winnie's knowledge of the Skyway isn't all-encompassing. And she's not going to lead us back to the proper path by sheer psychic power."

"Well, I never expected her to," I said. "Roland, have we pinpointed where we are in the galaxy?"

"It was easy enough. The *Ahgirr* are about as advanced as we are in astronomy. Had a little trouble interpreting their maps, though . . ." Roland shifted his eyes toward Ragna, then looked up casually at the smooth rock ceiling of the cave.

I knew what he was implying. Every race does something badly; with the *Ahgirr*, it was cartography in particular, and graphics in general. I had seen their graphics on computer screens—plots and charts and such—and couldn't make head nor tail of them. You would think some symbology to be universal and cross-cultural. Wrong. Draw an arrow on a map for an alien, indicating which way he should go, and he'll say, Yes, that's very interesting. Whatever does it mean? The *Ahgirr* didn't know from arrows either. Their symbol for direction of motion, vectors, stuff like that, was a little circle at the *beginning* of the line. Interesting, but stupid. Of course, I'm human, therefore biased. It all made perfect sense to the *Ahgirr*, but we were having a hell of a time reading their roadmaps, both computer-generated and paper varieties. (In regard to arrows, I theorized that, since the *Nogon* had been cave dwellers for a good part of their recorded history, they hadn't invented the bow and arrow until very recently. Roland disagreed, contending that both the weapon and the arrow symbol were comparatively recent human inventions.)

"As nearly as we can ascertain," Roland went on, "we're well off Winnie's route, somewhere along the inner edge of the Orion arm. We want to go in the opposite direction."

"How far can we go in the right direction before we have to shoot a potluck?"

"About a thousand light-years, which works out to about

ten thousand kilometers of road."

I clucked ruefully. "That's one hell of a lot of driving just to shoot a potluck. We might as well pick any old one and take our chances, since we're shit out of luck anyway."

Roland frowned. "I don't like the idea of wandering aimlessly. We could get hopelessly lost."

"What are we now?"

Roland shrugged. "True." He stared pensively at his empty plate for a moment, then banged his fist on the table beside it. "Damn. If we could only get something out of that Black Cube."

I looked at Ragna. "Have your scientists had any luck with it?"

Ragna eyed me dolefully. "Luck, I am afraid, we are also shit out of."

Again, everyone had trouble stifling a giggle.

"Howsoever on the other hand," Ragna went on, "we are slightly doubting that it is a map."

Raised eyebrows around the table, except for Roland's.

"What makes you doubt it?" John was first to ask.

Ragna made a clawing motion with the five digits of his right hand—an expression of frustration and regret. "Ah, my good friends, that I cannot be saying. I am not a scientist. I cannot be making you understand if on the one hand I am not understanding what they are saying on the other."

John narrowed his eyes momentarily, then nodded. "Oh, I see."

Ragna's status in the colony was roughly equivalent to that of a mayor, but his position wasn't official, so far as we could ascertain. He was simply an individual to whose judgment everyone deferred in matters of great importance. He didn't run for office, didn't rule by divine right. It was more an obligation on his part. Somebody has to drive.

"But I can be saying this," Ragna continued. "Our technical individuals are saying to me that there is something strange inside. Also, they say that nothing can be going into this Black Cube—on the contrary, however, things can be coming out."

I said, "Can you tell us what they suspect is inside the Cube?"

Again, he made the clawing motion. "Ah, Jake, my friend, this is that which is difficult. They are saying that . . . that inside is a vastness of *nothing*." He blinked, milky nictitating membranes coming upward before his eyelids closed down. "But it is a nothing that they do not understand."

"I see."

Right.

A collective sigh at the table.

"Well," I said finally after a long moment, "what say we hit those maps and figure out something. Every maze seems to have legends or rumors concerning what's on the other side of its various potluck portals. With Ragna's help, maybe we can make a decision based on that."

"In that case," Roland said, "I'm for picking one at random."

"You never know, Roland," I answered. "Rumors always have some basis in truth. Legends, too."

"I agree," John said.

"But the *Ahgirr* haven't settled their maze long enough to have developed a road mythology," Roland countered, turning to Ragna. "Have you?"

Ragna touched his headband. "I am not sure . . . Ah, yes. A mythology. Yes, I can be answering that in the affirmative, which is truth. We are having those stories and legends."

"Then again," Roland said, smiling thinly, "I could be wrong."

Ahgirr tradespeople helped us fit Sam with the new rollers. I offered to pay them but they wouldn't hear of it. No one had brought up the issue of compensation up to that point, and no one broached the subject after that.

The newbies fit fine, and Sam and I went back to the road and picked up the trailer. Doing so eased my mind a little. The trailer was a dead giveaway just sitting there. I thought it improbable that Moore would follow us through a potluck portal, but you never know. He just might be crazy enough. I'd also been worried about looters and salvagers, even though this ingress spur was seldom used.

With the trailer now at the mouth of the cave complex, we began the repair job in earnest. There was more damage than we had thought. The small motor that raised and lowered the door was completely useless, and the airtight silicone bushing around the door itself was in tatters. Where would we find replacements? Carl and Roland were willing to go out and search for a junked trailer, and I was ready to say go ahead, but the *Ahgirr* craftspeople said don't bother. They could manufacture most of the mechanical parts we needed in their shops. For the electronics we'd probably have to make a trip to a *faln* complex. They could breadboard some stuff for us, but it would be easier just to buy modular components off the shelf. They would send a technician, a female named Tivi, along to advise us. I felt I had to make the trip myself; the craftspeople knew the local technology, but I knew my rig, and I didn't want them making trips back and forth should I be dissatisfied with the goods they bought. Besides, I wanted to see what these *faln* things were all about.

But a big block of *Ahgirr* religious holidays came up and everybody knocked off for a week. There were strict laws—no work, no shopping, no nothing on high holy days, and these, called the Time of Finding Deeper Levels (rough translation), were the highest and holiest.

"No sex, I bet," Susan ventured. "Pity the way some religions are."

"I'm not even sure what they have is a religion." I thought a moment, then said, "I'm not at all sure that what you have is a religion."

"Teleological Pantheism isn't a religion. It's just a way of looking at the universe and its processes."

"Uh-huh. Tell me more."

"Later. Let's mess around."

Besides doing the above, Susan and I took advantage of the slack time to explore some of the vast system of caves in which the *Ahgirr* had made their home. It was a marvelous place. There is something of the claustrophile in me. I love caves, and I found a fellow spelunker in Susan. So we set out into the restful silences of the unoccupied regions. We toured vast smooth-walled chambers, many-leveled galleries, huge caverns with floors populated by fantastic rock monuments standing like sentinels in the dark. We walked along lava flows that had hardened millions of years ago, traversed vaginalike tunnels through which one had to push and squeeze in a psyche-stirring imitation of birth. Once, we followed a sinuous side passage that coiled endlessly through the rock, finally dead-ending in a delightful little grotto, walls sparkling in the light of our torches with millions of tiny multicolored points. An underground stream flowed through it, cascading down a small waterfall. We spent the "night" there, discovering more delights in the darkness.

There were other marvels. We found spherical chambers, hundreds of them, which had probably been formed by pockets of gas trapped within the magma. We dubbed them the "Pleasure Domes." And in the regions that had not been disturbed by vulcanism, strange geological formations presented themselves at every turn. The processes at work here were, for the most part, totally unEarthlike. There were chambers with walls glazed with a ten-centimeter-thick coating of frosted glass *('Twas a miracle of rare device!)*, rooms that looked as if they had been designed by Bauhaus architects under the influence of hallucinogens, caverns that looked like the interiors of great cathedrals, alcoves with intimate seating in the shape of contoured folds of rock like a couch, passageways with corbelled walls, vaults with grained ceilings, porticos with fluted columns, elaborate suites of adjoining rooms, and all were unmistakably natural formations. There were no right angles; slabs of rock were sheared, not cut; no chisels marks, no debris about that would be evidence of stonecutting; nothing. There was an undeniable randomness to it all.

And not one goddamn stalactite in the whole place.

"I always forget," Susan said. "Is it stalactites that hang down and stalagmites that stick up, or vicey versy?"

"No, that's right. I think."

"Always get it confused."

"Well, there aren't any here to befuddle you."

"Doesn't take much, for me."

In the womblike darkness, Susan snuggled closer.

"I wonder why," she said.

"Why what?"

"Why aren't there any?"

"Any what?"

She nipped my ear. "Stalactites, silly."

"Oh. No limestone, I guess."

"Limestone?"

"Yup. Makes sense. This is practically a lifeless planet, from what Ragna told us. Mostly microscopic organisms. Life never really got going here. Limestone comes from sediments containing coral, polyps, stuff like that. Back on Earth, that is. Here, who knows what they have going, if anything. You need water that's high in carbonate of lime to make stalactites."

"And stalagmites."

"And stalagmites."

"Interesting."

"Hardly."

"No, I mean it. It always amazes me how much you know, for a truckdriver."

"Duh."

She giggled. "Sorry, didn't mean it quite like that." She kissed me on the cheek. "You're strange. So very strange."

"How so?"

"Well . . ." She lay on her back. "You obviously have some education. Quite a lot, it seems. True?"

"Oh, here and there."

"Right. U. of Tsiolkovskygrad, I bet."

"Right," I admitted.

"I knew it. Graduate work?"

"Some. A year, if I can remember back that far."

"Doing what?"

"I was going for a doctorate in government administration."

She was surprised. "How in the world did you wrangle your way into that program? Pretty restricted."

"Didn't wrangle at all. Actually, I was asked to sign up. Someone apparently thought I was bureaucrat material. They like to recruit from the provinces now and then. Or they did." I shifted to my side. "You have to remember, this was almost thirty years ago. U. of T. was a podunk school then, a bunch of pop-up domes and Durafoam shacks. It was the only university in the Colonies."

"The entrance requirements must have been stiff."

"They were. I'll admit to a certain native intelligence. I was young, in love with learning, tired of the farm. It seemed a good idea at the time."

"And you quit."

"Yeah."

"To drive a truck."

"No, I went back to the farm. By that time, my eyes had been opened."

She turned over on her side to face me. "You gave up a lot. By now, you could have been a high-level Authority functionary with a six-figure income and a *dacha* on the resort planet of your choice."

"Instead, I have the freedom of the road, very few responsibilities, and a clear conscience. No punking money, no *dacha*, but I have what I need."

"I see."

We were silent for a long while.

Finally, I said, "Should be stalactites."

"Hm?"

"Seems to me there should be something like them here. Caves are usually formed by the erosion of water-soluble rock, like limestone. I don't know what this stuff is—I'm nobody's geologist. Gotta be gypsum, dolomite, something like that. But in that case—"

"Didn't the lava do some of it?"

"Yeah, there are definitely volcanic processes at work. But most of the weirder formations have to be the result of some pretty exotic geochemistry."

"Well, it's an alien planet," she said.

"Uh-huh. But we're the aliens here, honey."

"Move closer, you horrible alien beast." After a moment, she said, "my, what's this?"

"A stalactite."

"'Mite," she said, moving to position her body over me.

We even got lost down there, which bothered me not much. We had food, rivers of fresh water, more peace and quiet than I had had in a decade. It was the first real vacation I had taken in . . . I didn't know how long. Eventually, Susan became a little nervous, suggesting that it would be a good idea to begin a serious effort to find a way back. I told her we had time, nothing but time.

"But we're getting more and more lost," she protested.

"Not so," I said, crouching near the tunnel wall. "Getting some interesting readings here on this handy-dandy pocket seismometer Ragna gave me. Remember that room we called Chichester Cathedral? It's probably not more than five meters away, on the other side of this wall."

"But we were there days ago."

"Day before yesterday."

"How do we get through five meters of rock?"

"Oh, there's another way back. This just means we aren't really lost. We've been keeping to the same general area. All we have to do is find a shortcut back to Chichester. From there we'll have no trouble locating that last transponder."

"You make it sound so simple."

"Besides, Ragna and his people should already be looking for us. This was supposed to be an overnight trip originally, if you remember. They'll be worried."

"To say nothing of John and everybody."

"Well," I said, "they shouldn't be. This is the first non-life-and-death situation we've had in *weeks*. We've been shot at, bombarded, and kidnapped. We almost got stomped by a Roadbug, and we shot a portal with a giant sugar doughnut for a roller. God! You name it, we've been subjected to it. How can you let a little thing like this worry you, Suzie?"

"It's my nature, I guess."

"Take off your clothes."

"Okay."

Before long, though, I had to concede that we really were lost. Susan was for probing farther, but I came down squarely for staying put, making camp, and waiting for a rescue party. I reminded her of her warning that wandering around blindly would probably just get us more lost. She remembered, and concurred for more than one reason. Food was getting low, and there was zero chance of finding anything down here. Limiting our activity would help to conserve it, and so would strict rationing. We were pretty good about the former, but we caught each other raiding the food satchel more than once. Neither of us could be totally serious about the situation, but as time progressed and the realization grew that we had set out fully four days ago, we gradually sobered up.

Then things got worse.

It happened in a narrow corridor whose walls were broken by side tunnels sloping up to vertical chimneys through which only Susan could squeeze to see if any of them led to higher levels. We had gradually descended over the past few days, according to the air pressure readings.

I was lying with my back against the pile of our backpacks and caving gear, just beginning to doze off. I was bushed. Susan had doffed her *Ahgirr*ian hard hat (which fit just fine, by the way) with the mounted electric light, and had taken a biolume torch to explore a likely-looking chimney at the end of a short side tunnel. She had insisted I stay and rest, and I wasn't worried. I could still hear her boots scuffing and scraping at the end of the tunnel. She had said that she wouldn't climb up very far, just enough to see if it went anywhere and if it widened out farther up. If so, I would try to squeeze through and follow, after tethering our packs to the line and having Susan haul them up.

So I lay there, waiting, eyes focused on some interesting crystal patterns on the ceiling that glowed peculiarly in the light of my helmet lantern. It was a moire pattern, shimmering and shifting as I moved my head slightly and the light with it. The colors were indigo and violet, edged with pink and red. It was hypnotic, in a way, watching it weave and dance. I slipped into a strange reverie, thinking mostly about Darla, and about Susan, trying to sort out my feelings. I saw Darla's face after a while; it took form behind the pattern, or was superimposed over it. Darla's was a perfect face, if such can exist, except perhaps for a slight overbite (which actually I found irresistibly seductive—it gave her lower lip a sensuous pout). The symmetry was compelling, the graceful proportions almost approaching a work of art. That profile: what combination of curves and lines could be more subtle yet so mathematically precise? A millimeter's difference here or there, and the whole organic *rightness* of it would be gone. Mathematical, yes, but no equation, however abstruse, could describe it. Faces such as hers were meant to be taken in all at once, in one short intake of breath. Everything fit together well: the sculpted helmet of dark hair, the full lips, the elevated cheekbones, the slightly cleft chin . . . and the eyes, yes. Blue the color of some cold virginal sky viewed from stratospheric heights, as from the cockpit of a hypersonic transport; the blue behind which stars are barely hidden. Hers was an arctic beauty. But look a bit farther into the eyes—what do you see? Molten points, tiny burning highlights. Inside, she burned for something; I didn't know what. The cause, her dissident movement? Maybe. Me? I doubted it. She had deceived me, even used me, though she adamantly maintained that it all had been for my benefit. At moments, I was inclined to agree. At others . . . The jury was still out on Darla's motives. Doubtless she bore me no ill will, but I had the nagging feeling that I was just another cog in some vast creaking mechanism—admittedly not of her own design or creation—for which she had appointed herself the maintenance engineer, responsible for applying daubs of oil here and there to broken-toothed gears and squeaking cams. She was dedicated to seeing that it all hung together, that it kept clanking and groaning until it completed whatever mysterious task its designers had set for it. It was the Paradox Machine, and it was running the whole show.

I realized that I was deeply in love with Darla. Despite everything. It was one of those facts that lurks about in the shadows, then steps out from a dark embrasure and says, "Hi, there!" as if you should have known all along. *Despite everything.*

La Belle Dame Sans Merci had me in thrall, and there wasn't a damn thing I could do about it.

Susan?

Susan. I replayed scenes from the last few days. In one sense, a lot of it was porno footage; looking at it another way, here were two people who enjoyed each other's company, enjoyed giving each other pleasure. There was warmth, friendship . . . perhaps even love, of a sort. I found it impossible to compare my feelings for Darla and for Susan. They were not quantifiable. The rest is semantics. Call what I felt for Darla passion—it well may have been, but it was of a rarefied variety. I was not altogether sure that the emotion was not indistinguishable from my strong intuition that Darla's destiny and mine were in some way inseparably mated.

And I was not sure at all whether I *liked* Darla. She tended to make people uncomfortable in strange and subtle ways. Perhaps it was only her striking beauty—most people, let's face it, are not beautiful, and a flesh-and-blood reminder in our midst stirs up odd feelings—but I suspect her aloofness was what put me off the most. She was a distant observer of events. She wasn't uninterested in what was going on; rather, she seemed *dis*interested. Unbiased, objective. I do not say cold. The Keeper of the Machine. However, I liked Susan. Semantics again. While she was not always easy to get along with, she was in the end always supportive, of me, of what I did. She trusted me, and I her. I could understand her. Her weaknesses were not blemishes on an otherwise admirable human, but reflections of what was infirm and uncertain in me.

Part of me hadn't wanted any of this. Part of me wanted to run . . . not *from* something, as I had been doing, but to something. Home. Back to safety, to the familiar. I wanted out of it all, to be absolved of all responsibility. I was no hero. I realized that somewhere within lay a part of me as deeply afraid as Susan had sometimes shown herself to be.

But that was unfair. Susan had borne up under unbelievable pressure. She hadn't come apart.

Why not say I loved Susan?

I played the footage again. I loved her sensuality, her willingness to please me. Easy things to love, perhaps, but between men and women, the tie that binds is of two interwoven strands, and these are part of what bound me to Susan: the palmfuls of warm flesh, the smooth planes of her skin in the darkness, the deep well of her mouth . . .

Something was standing just outside the pool of light cast by my helmet lantern.

I felt it as a presence first; then a shape began to grow in my peripheral vision, black-on-black against the shadows. Somewhere within my bloodstream, the cold-water tap turned on. I stopped moving my head and froze. My heart bounced within my chest cavity like a rubber ball.

I was unarmed. We hadn't brought weapons into the *Ahgirr* city. A very few options presented themselves. I could continue lying there, hoping that whatever it was would get tired of breathing significantly in the darkness and leave. Or I could leap up and run back into the tunnel in a mad gamble that I was faster than it. But what would I do at the end of the tunnel? Tight fit there. No. I needed a weapon. Ragna had given us some caving tools, one a pike tipped with a strange grappling hook, which I knew lay beside my left foot. If I could create a diversion . . .

I threw my helmet at the thing in the shadows, rolled, snatched the pike, and leaped to my feet brandishing it. The helmet had missed, bouncing off the wall and landing upside-down behind a low projection on the floor. I unhooked the biolume torch from my utility belt and snapped it on, playing its beam against a large shape with purple and pink splotches, standing not three meters away from where I'd been lying.

My actions startled the non-Boojum to no end. It staggered back, flailing its spindly forelegs as if to fend off a blow.

"Oh, my!" it yelped in a strangely familiar voice. "Dearie me!"

Then it turned and galumphed off down the passage, disappearing into the blackness.

Stunned, jaw gone slack, I stood there and watched.

After perhaps thirty seconds, not really knowing why, I followed it. Several meters beyond where the thing had stood, the tunnel curved to the right and began to descend, widening out until it flared into a large chamber with several tunnels branching off its farther end. I took the widest of these, madly dashing on into the gloom. I hadn't stopped to pick up my helmet, and the biolume torch was dim. The way grew serpentine, then straightened out. Numerous cross passages intersected the main tunnel, and I ran from mouth to mouth sending the feeble torchbeam down each. At the ninth one, I thought I saw something moving, and entered.

Ten minutes later I realized three things: one, I had been very foolish to run off; two, I was lost; three, the biolume torch was failing. Ten minutes after all of the above had dawned on me, the torch no longer even glowed and the subterranean night had closed in. The absolute, categorical darkness of a cave is difficult to appreciate until experienced. Only the totally blind know what it's like. There is no light at all. None. I groped and felt my way in the direction from which I thought I had come. I did that for hours, it seemed, all the while calling Susan's name. No answer. I moved slowly, trying to catch the slightest glimmer of what might be Susan's torch as she looked for me. But I had no assurance that she wasn't lost herself. I had lost track of time daydreaming back there, and it seemed that I had stopped hearing Susan's progress up the shaft for a good while before the non-Boojum made its appearance. She had the other biolume torch, but if *it* failed . . .

I got too tired to go on and sat down with my back against a smooth wall. There was no room in my mind for thinking about the non-Boojum, how it had followed me from Talltree, and why. Maybe they had non-Boojums here, too. My mind was blank with fatigue, quickly filling with a throbbing panic. I got up and moved on. If I sat and thought, it would be all over.

I was convinced that days were passing in the dark. I had banged my head so many times that I was becoming punch-drunk. My shins were raw from barking them against low outcroppings, my fingers moist and sticky with blood. I had stumbled through rubble, fallen into holes, slid down mounds of gravel, splashed through pools of stagnant water, and had had enough. I found a flat, irregularly shaped table of rock, climbed up, and lay across it.

I must have slept for hours. I awoke with a start, disoriented, frantically blinking my eyes to force an image to come to them. None came. My throat was dust, my body a network of communicating pains.

Nonetheless, I sat up abruptly. I thought I had heard something. The scrape of a shoe, maybe—or the click of talons against stone. The thing that wasn't a Boojum? A thing that *was?*

A tiny beam of light reached my retinas, piercing them like a knitting needle. I shielded my eyes with one hand.

"Susan!"

"Jake! Oh, my God, Jake, darling!"

I got up and stumbled forward. Light grew around me until I had to shut my eyes. Susan slid into my arms and crushed me with hers.

We both babbled for a minute. Susan said she loved me, several times, and I informed her that it was mutual. A great deal of hugging and kissing went on between utterances. I had my eyes closed the whole time, thinking that more light could not have been attendant at the Creation. Had I been in the dark that long?

". . . I looked and looked and looked, and then I realized I was lost myself," Susan was saying. "I sat down and cried, feeling horrible, just horrible! I'd lost you, and the food and all the gear, and I was thinking to myself, God, this is just typical behavior on my part, panicking when I should be thinking, letting my fears control the situation, and I—"

"It's okay, Suzie, it's okay."

"—said to myself, goddammit, I've got to get a handle on things, this simply will not do, you've got to—" She drew back a little. "Jake, what are you doing? Can't you see who's here?"

I had been taking off her shirt. I stopped, looked up, opening my eyes.

"Felicitations, my friend Jake," Ragna said, tilting his powerful torch slightly upwards so as to illuminate his blue face. His long white hair streamed down from the edge of his helmet. Behind him, other lights were moving toward us in the darkness.

"Is it that you are wishing to undertake sexual congress at this moment?" Ragna asked. "Being that this is perhaps the case, my companions and I are happily withdrawing. However on the contrary, I am saying that we would be immensely of interestingness for us to be observing you, if by and large to have us doing this would not be of inconvenience."

He smiled with thin pink lips, pink eyes glowing in the torch light. "Perhaps yes?" he said after a moment. Then he frowned, greatly disappointed. "No?"

12

We were vulnerable in our immobile state. The caves were dark and warm and womblike, but I didn't want to be lulled into a false sense of security, so I was glad that the Time of Finding Deeper Levels was over. I wanted to finish the repairs and get moving.

The trip to the *faln* complex was on. Ragna would go along with Tivi, and both would act as interpreters and guides.

Everybody wanted to come, but I put my foot down. Then Susan stomped on my toe.

"I need to do a little shopping," she contended. "What's so hard to understand about that?"

"But what could you possibly—?"

"I left my backpack and most of my camping gear in that damn hotel. That was the *third* pack I've lost since this crazy business started. Clothes I don't expect to replace, but alien camping gear is as good as human."

"I really doubt we'll be doing much camping, Susan."

"Look, I'm a starhiker, albeit an unwilling one, and I want a complete starhiker kit. I *need* it. Besides, I haven't been shopping in a month of Sundays."

"But it's not fair to the others."

"Let her go, Jake," Roland said. "If she's left behind she'll bitch and bitch all day and we'll all be miserable."

I stiffened. "See here. Everybody's been telling me I'm the leader of this expedition. So, by God, I'm ordering you—"

She brushed by me. "Oh, shut up and let's go."

"Yes, dear." I slunk after her.

I had expected the *faln* to be immense structures, and they were . . . real big.

We were well off the Skyway on a local extension, riding

in one of the *Ahgirr*'s collectively owned vehicles, a low-slung four-seater with a clear bubble top. Endless stretches of desert rolled past. We had been chatting pleasantly but I had gradually drifted off into a reverie. I was gazing moodily into Ragna's side rearview mirror. A vehicle was following some distance back, a tiny blue-green dot almost at the road's vanishing point. I hypnotized myself for a while, watching it. Something about it rang a bell—just the color of the thing. I'd seen that exact color before . . . but no. The road swung away from the sun and the color changed. Just a reflection, I guessed. Just paranoia on my part. Presently, I looked away.

Susan gave a little gasp as the *faln* took form in the wavering veils of heat out on the plain. From a distance they had looked like mountains; now they were almost too big to be compared to anything.

I leaned forward and spoke over Ragna's shoulder. "What's the average population of those things?"

"Oh, several of millions. They were being very crowded even with respect to their immensehood."

Tivi said, "We were not meant to be living in this manner—that is to say, we of our species. Yet *Ahgirr* are the very few of whom it may be said that they are in agreement with this statement."

"Yeah," I said, and sat back.

"My God," Susan whispered. "If they have this kind of population level on a colonized planet, and on a backwater one at that—"

"Right, think of what the homeworld must be like."

"Look. There are more of them on the horizon. Tivi told me there were at least fifty *faln* complexes on this world alone."

"These people couldn't have stayed in caves," I said. "They would've been trodding on each other's faces."

"And ganging together into arcologies was the only way to keep from totally destroying the environment."

I noticed Ragna eavesdropping as he drove.

"Sorry, Ragna," I said. "Susan and I were just speculating."

He laughed. "Oh, all of what you are saying is being of indubitable truth, partly. *Ahgirr* have always been believing in rational control of the population. Not so of many cultures. Alas and shit."

We came to the edge of a vast parking area crammed with

vehicles. Ragna swung off the road and entered it.

"Now we are being faced with the heartrending task of finding a space in which to insert this conveyance for purposes of parking therein. I heave a great sigh."

I was surprised how crowded it was. "Where do all the people come from?"

"Oh, all from over the place," Tivi said. "Many aliens too. This is being a major shopping and commercial *faln*."

"A shopping mall!" Susan laughed. "I haven't walked a mall in a coon's age." She turned to me. "It's in my blood, you know. I spent my childhood as a mall brat."

"Oh, you're a maller? You never told me."

"Didn't think it was anything special. There are millions of us."

"You were born in one?"

"Born and raised. South Gate Village, very near Peoria, Central Industry."

I sat back. "You know, at one time people only used to shop in those things."

"I know. Then they became arcologies, just like these. Lots of factors contributed. I can go on and on about mall history. Every mall brat learns it in school."

"I'd be very interested in hearing about it."

"Right." She gave a sarcastic grunt. "It's history. Terran history. Who needs it."

Ragna swerved to pull into an empty slot but was cut off and usurped by an electric-blue, beetle-shaped gadabout. The occupants, their purple lizard faces impassive behind dark-tinted ports, nodded in what seemed an apologetic manner. Sorry, but every being for himself, you know.

"Nasty slime objects!" Ragna shouted, then grumbled to himself in his own tongue.

But a little farther along, another unoccupied slot presented itself and Ragna slipped in, cackling triumphantly. "We are having luck for once, by gosh."

The *faln* complex was still some distance off, titantic mushroom-shaped hulks baking in the fierce desert sun. They were a striking salmon pink in color. I counted six separate structures of varying heights, all linked by a web of walkway bridges with transparent polarized canopies. Service buildings, tiny by comparison, huddled about the bases of the larger structures.

"Do we have to walk?" I asked. "Looks to be a good hike from here to the base of that nearer one."

"Ah, no," Ragna said. "We may be taking the *girrna-faln-narrog,* the underground conveyance below the *faln.* What is it called?" He tapped his blue headband. "The subway. Over there." He pointed right to a descending stairwell. It looked like a subway entrance all right.

Steps led down to a landing from which we took a descending escalator that was at least ten meters wide—sort of a moving grand staircase. Other people and a few aliens had come down with us, and we found a crowd waiting for the next train. The station was well lighted, clean, expansive, and looked spanking new.

I noticed something while we waited. Compared to their brethren, Ragna and Tivi were rather drab figures. Most *Ahgirr,* male and female, seemed to dress alike, favoring tight-fitting tunics of gray or brown cinched at the waist with a white sash. The other *Nogon* flounced around in garish, flamboyant gowns and robes, all brightly colored, elaborately designed, busy with embroidery and woven and printed patterns. Hairstyles ranged from the highly imaginative to the entirely outrageous (judging by human standards in general and mine in particular, of course). *Ahgirr,* it seemed, were the Plain People of their race.

The train was a beauty, levitating along the track on magnetic impellers. Bullet shaped, gleaming white with pink trim, it whooshed into the station and slid along the platform, coming to a smooth stop. Doors hissed open, and the crowd began to board. We entered a nearby car and ensconced ourselves in comfortably overstuffed seats.

I asked Ragna, "If you can get from *faln* to *faln* in these things, why does anybody drive?"

"These are people who are not living in *faln.* No, they are living outside and waiting to be permitted to live in *faln.* There is no room for them."

"Oh, so there are some who live out on the land besides you people," Susan remarked.

"Yes, many," Tivi answered, "but they do not wish to be living there. Residential privileges in the *faln* are being passed from parents to children. Privileges may be bought and sold, but there is being great competition for them. Many legal fights and also violence resulting. Oh, my."

"Funny, we didn't see any small communities off the road," I said.

"Oh, few have been built on this planet. It is desert, phooey on it. They are coming here from planets which are more hospitable. This commercial *faln* is being usually less congested than others. More parking, too."

Susan and I looked at each other.

The train started forward, gaining speed in a smooth, powerful surge, then shot into a tunnel.

"It's always somehow disconcerting," Susan told me, "when you realize that alien cultures are just as complex and screwed up as ours."

"Yeah. Must have been all that fiction that was written in the twentieth century. You know, superbeings in silver spaceships saving the collective butt of mankind—that sort of thing."

"Must've been. Of course, I haven't read much of anything that far back."

"Ideas like that tend to stick in the mass mind," I said.

"That's me all over," Susan lamented.

I clucked. "You have a habit of putting yourself down—did you know that?"

"Just one of many bad habits," she said, "which is why I'm down on myself so much. *Ipso facto*, Q.E.D., and all that."

"That's quite a hole you've dug for yourself."

"Got a shovel?"

I kissed her on the cheek instead and put my arm around her. Ragna and Tivi smiled appreciatively at us. Weren't we cute.

Some of the *Nogon* were staring at us. Most of the aliens weren't. Ragna had said that word of our arrival on the planet had been spreading and that there was great interest in us. It looked more like a detached kind of curiosity, to me. I couldn't imagine the general public getting worked up over the discovery of yet another alien race, no matter how interesting.

We passed through three stations, each progressively more congested, before reaching the end of the line, by which time the train was packed with passengers standing elbow to pincer. The train slid to a smooth stop and we joined the crush to get out.

The next hour or so was a succession of visual, aural, and perceptual wonders. Susan and I walked goggle-eyed through a series of spaces that defied description. The scale was immense. It was a shopping mall, yes; it was also a vast strange carnival with attractions at every turn—here, street musicians and acrobats, there, some sort of sporting event, here, an orchestra pouring out ear-splitting cacophony . . . and everywhere all kinds of activity that anyone would have a hard time describing. There were festivals within festivals, there were celebrations and ceremonies; there were public meetings with people up on platforms shouting at one another—politicians? Or a debating society? Maybe it was drama. There were sideshows and circuses, pageants and exhibitions, shows and displays. There were flea markets and bazaars, agoras and exchanges. There were stalls, booths, rialtos, and fairs, with hawkers, wholesalers, vendors, jobbers, and every other variety of merchant in attendance. You could buy anything at any price. You could eat, drink, smoke, inject, or otherwise assimilate everything imaginable into your body, if you so chose. You could purchase hardware, software, kitchenware, and underwear. There were trade fairs of strange machinery, appliances, and unidentifiable gadgets and gizmos. Salespeople demonstrated, prospective customers looked on. Huge video screens ran endless commercials extolling the virtues of myriad products. There were presentations, parades, dog-and-pony shows, and every sort of inducement.

And all of this took place in a nexus of interpenetrating spaces whose complexity was overwhelming. There were levels upon levels, series of staggered terraces, promenades and balconies, all connected by webs of suspended bridges, cascades of spiraling ramps and stairways, escalators, open-shaft elevators, and other conveyances. Walls and floors were variously colored in soft pastels and metallic tints. Surfaces of shiny blue metal formed ceilings and curtainwalls, stairwells and platforms. There were hanging gardens, miniature forests, waterfalls, small game preserves, lakelets, parklets, and playgrounds. Hanging mobile sculptures wheeled above, towering alien monuments rose from the floors. And everywhere there was activity, action, color, movement, and sound.

And noise.

"Plenty loud, eh?" Ragna said.

"What?" Susan answered. "Oh, Jake, it's all so familiar yet so utterly strange. I can't get over it."

"What I find strange is all this chaos contained within a controlled environment."

"Maybe this is how they keep from feeling confined."

"Hard to realize we're indoors. Where's all this light coming from?"

"I'd swear that's sky up there," Susan said, pointing to the distant roof.

"They must pump in sunlight through a series of mirrors," I guessed.

"This is being true," Ragna said. "Quite a neat trick, but it is also being much too damnably bright in here."

Neither of our guides had bothered to take down their protective hoods and both still wore wraparound sunglasses. I wondered if their aversion to sunlight was more psychological than physical. The other *Nogon* seemed to be at home, though I did notice some wearing wide-brimmed hats and some with dark glasses.

"What do we do first?" Susan asked. "Where do we go?"

"You said that you were being desirous of equipment by which one lives in the wilderness, making camp and suchlike," Tivi said.

Susan laughed. "Well, I'm not exactly desirous of the stuff, but—" She put a hand on Tivi's sloping shoulder. "I'm sorry. Yes, I'd like to buy camping gear. A backpack, maybe, if I can find one that fits my all-too-human frame. And a good flashlight . . . and, um, I'll need an all-climate survival suit—hell, I'll never find one that fits me. Forget that."

"On the contrary," Tivi said, "they are having makers of clothing here who can possibly be accommodating you."

"Really? Designer fashions, huh?"

"Pardon?"

"You've convinced me. I'd really like some new clothes . . . Oh, wait." Susan turned to me. "We really should go get that electronic stuff you need first. Right?"

"Nah, go ahead and have fun. We've got a little time."

"Oh, good." She suddenly frowned. "Rats."

"What?"

"Now I feel guilty that the others didn't get to come along."

I nodded, looking around. "Yeah, they are missing some sights. But I thought they'd be safer in the caves."

"You were right. We shouldn't take chances."

"Good rationalization."

"Creep. Let's go."

"May I be suggesting," Ragna said, "that we may be having perhaps a parting of the ways at this point, Tivi going with Jake and I myself escorting and otherwise leading Susan?"

I said, "Let me get the feel of this place first. It's big, and if we get separated—"

"There is little need for the fear you are feeling, Jake. Unfortunately, *Ahgirr* are very familiar with this den of iniquity and other foul doings, being that they are coming here to purchase many necessary essentials which are, rats, unpurchasable elsewhere."

"Well, I'd rather tag along with Suzie first. Then we'll see."

Ragna made circles with his forefingers and elongated thumbs, throwing his arms out. We had come to interpret this as a shrugging gesture, though it had other meanings. "As you are wishing, so shall we be tagging."

We set out into the tumult.

We went down several levels and walked through a parklet. Children played there, running about and screeching just like children do all over the universe. There were lots of imaginative objects there to climb and swing from, monkey bars and that sort of thing. Parents seated at benches looked on. Susan was right in that everything was familiar in a way—but every object, every aspect of the design of this area and all the rest was totally nonhuman. Everything said alien.

Something odd was transpiring on the other side of the park. A crowd of *Nogon* was gathered in the middle of a large expanse of green tile floor. Everyone was jumping up and down, facing in the direction of a platform upon which were displayed a variety of nutty looking objects. Household wares, maybe. Maybe *objets d'art;* who knows? As they jumped, the participants threw small balls of various colors into the air and caught them. As we passed, I asked Ragna what was going on.

"This is of much difficulty to be explaining," he said, tapping his headband.

"Oh. Is it an auction?"

"Auction." He brought his hands up to reposition the headband. "Auction. No. It is in the nature of being a protest."

"Protest? What are they protesting?"

"Again, this is of much difficulty."

"Right."

Language barriers are one thing, cultural and conceptual ones quite another.

We entered another commercial area. The merchants here seemed of a distinct ethnic group, wearing their cornsilk hair in braids tied off with bright ribbons and floral bows. Their costumes were much more modest. Susan stopped to look at some pottery. Some items were quite attractive, though hard to identify.

Ragna was chuckling. "It is being centuries since these people are living in anything but *faln*, yet they construct their traditional objects and sell them quite speedily. Making much money into the bargain, too."

"Indians selling beads and blankets," I said.

"You will be pardoning me?"

"Well, it's difficult to explain."

Susan managed to blow fifteen minutes deciding what she wasn't going to buy.

"Susan."

"Sorry, right. Let's go."

Next up was a sunken arena where a sporting event was being held. The game looked like a cross between rugby and motorcycle racing. If that sounds confusing . . . well, you'd have to see it. We stopped briefly to watch, but I didn't bother to ask Ragna to supply play-by-play commentary.

We went on. After taking a path through a small forested area, we came out into another marketplace, this one bigger and offering all sorts of products—furniture, vehicles, foodstuffs, clothing, you name it. It took about ten minutes for Tivi to find the stall of a merchant who could possibly fit Susan. It was an alien, a slender little yellow-furred biped who looked somewhat feline.

After conferring with the merchant, Tivi told us, "Yes, it has seen your species before. It can be accommodating your physique in the style of your choosing. But it says its merchandise is of so poor a quality that you would hardly be wanting to waste your money or your time."

I said, "Ask it . . . er, him or whatever—ask where he saw creatures like us."

She did. "It says it has traveled to many planets and has seen many creatures—your kind to be sure, but it is fearing that your ire will be aroused when it is telling you that the exact location of this sighting is not being remembered."

"Was it recently?"

The alien made apologetic gestures.

"It is saying also that this memory is not fixed with respect to a time element. It craves a thousand forgivenesses and begs that you not kill it."

"Well, tell him he's safe for now. He was probably fibbing about seeing humans. Just wanted our business."

Tivi went on as the alien continued mewling: "It still is insisting that you could not possibly be interested in the worthless articles of apparel that it is dealing in. In matter of fact, it is willing to be paying person or persons to take the junk off his hands."

"Tell him he doesn't have to go through *Nogon* dickering rituals with us," I said.

"As long as I am interpreting for you," Tivi answered, "it will be afraid not to be doing this dickering and ritualizing."

"What's his name?" Susan asked.

"It protests that an obviously high-born female such as yourself, one who no doubt is in possession of uncountable husbands and slaves, would not be interested in inquiring as to the name of so low-born and abject a creature as we see before us." As an aside, Tivi added, "I am thinking it is also a female—and also that this is being part of her own type of dickering and ritualizing."

"Tell her that I'd be interested in buying everything she has, and would be willing to pay her handsomely for the privilege," Susan instructed.

"Again she is protesting that such a wondrously beautiful creature such as yourself would be ill-served by—"

This went on at some length, and I got bored. To kill some time, Ragna took me on a little tour of the area. We watched what he told me was an actual auction, but strangely enough, it looked more like a protest meeting. After that we browsed through a fast-food section. Some of the stuff looked edible, even good, but I knew that, while I wouldn't be poisoned, I'd get sick as a pup if I had any. We had found that we couldn't eat *Nogon* food, even though its peptide configurations weren't too far divergent from Terran ones.

By the time we got back, Susan was out of the fitting booth.

"My survival suit'll be ready in an hour or two," Susan said. "I even got to design it myself. Custom tailored—how about that!"

"Good. Now let's—"

"Oh, look over here," Susan said, walking off.

We followed her over to a stall offering a wide variety of weaponry.

"Guns." Susan curled her lip in distaste. "I'm going to buy one."

"Whatever for?" I asked.

"Everybody else is armed to the teeth. Even John's carrying a gun now. Hell, with all the trouble we've been running into, I'd be foolish not to be packing some kind of shooting iron."

"I think we have enough to go around, Suzie."

"No, I want something that doesn't kill."

"Oh."

"Something that'll stop an enemy but not hurt him. I don't believe in killing."

"That might be a tall order, but let's see."

The merchant was a *Nogon*, and we found that the extent to which the alien had engaged in ritualizing and dickering had been a mere nod to local custom. Done properly, complete with nuances and byplay, the real thing could take hours. By being brusque almost to the point of insult, Tivi cut it down to twenty minutes. Meantime, Ragna went off to buy Susan a torch and some other camping gear. By the time he returned, the merchant had sold Susan a box containing three components which supposedly fit together. The sale of completely functional weapons inside the *faln* was illegal.

"They are scanning all the time for operative armaments," Ragna told me.

The sale complete, our merchant growled something and stepped behind a curtain. He didn't come out again.

"What was that all about?" I asked Tivi.

"He is saying that such a show of crass materialism and greed has been making him sick, at which point he will be expelling the contents of his gastric sac."

"Oh." I turned and yelled, "Sorry!"

"I wonder if this thing works," Susan said, examining the contents of the box.

"I wonder what it does," I said. "Wouldn't look like a gun, no matter how you'd put the parts together. What did the salesman say?"

"Who knows. Tivi?"

"He was saying that this particular weapon would not be killing one's opponent. However, he was not saying in exactitude what in matter of fact it would be doing."

"That's what came out of all that conversation?" I wanted to know.

"Much was being spoken," Tivi said, "but little was being said."

"Is it that these articles are to your satisfaction?" Ragna asked, displaying the various oddments he had bought for Susan—torch, mess kit, toilet articles, some sort of bedroll, other stuff, all of which were *Nogon*-made but eminently adaptable to human use.

"Oh, they're fine. Thank you so much, Ragna. Here, let me pay you."

"We may be settling monetary business dealings later, you are welcome."

I said, "We can't thank you enough for exchanging our gold for currency."

Hokar had let slip that gold prices had taken a dive recently. Apparently, the economy of the *Nogon* maze was booming.

"You are to think nothing of it, Jake, friend of mine. These things are not spoken of, not much."

"Here, Jake," Susan said, dumping a load of parcels on me. "Now, let me check back at the dressmaker's and we'll—"

"Look," I said, "I'm going to take Tivi and get those parts. You go get your outfit and we'll meet you here in an hour."

"Okay. Let's divvy up these things. You take that and that, I'll take this thing . . . don't they give out shopping bags in this place?"

"You may be needing this?" Tivi was unfolding a gray cloth sack which she had brought out from under her cape.

Susan shook her head. "And we didn't even think to bring a bag or something." She stuffed the small sack, but the gun box wouldn't fit. "This bulky thing. Maybe if we took the stuff out of the box. Ragna?"

"No, let me take it," I said. "Maybe I can find out what kind of weapon it is."

"But you'll have the parts to carry."

"I have two of these," Tivi said, producing another sack.

"Tivi, darling, you're indispensable."

"I am thanking you for not dispensing with me."

We finally split up.

Tivi led me across the mall and up a ramp to a mezzanine. From there we took a connecting corridor and came out onto a curving balcony at least fifteen stories above a vast central floor alive with commerce and every other sort of activity. We walked along the balcony until it swung out over the floor and became a ramp leading down to platform. There were bunches of transparent tubes shooting up from the floor, and inside the tubes were platforms moving up and down. These were elevators, certainly, but I couldn't figure out how they worked. We ran into a crush of shoppers well before we reached the boarding platform.

"Too much crowd," Tivi said. "We should be going back this way."

We walked back up the ramp and onto the balcony, then through another connecting corridor, coming out into a smaller open area that was a disconcerting architectural jumble. *Nogon* ideas of interior design were perceptually disorienting. Walkways made odd angles as they shot overhead without visible support. Ramps spiraled dizzily, walls bulged and sucked in, staircases obtruded into overhead spaces. Control, I thought. Control is what arcologies are all about—but what's all this madness? Maybe arcologies were just about containment.

Tivi led me into a side corridor. We stopped by a pair of doors set into the wall.

"These freight-lifting mechanisms are not being in so much use," she maintained.

It looked like a conventional elevator, but when we got it going, it went up diagonally for a while, stopped for a moment, then continued vertically. In all, we went up about twenty stories.

These upper levels seemed devoted to non-consumer items and were a little quieter, but not much. "Auctions" were being held here, too, complete with the pushing and shoving I had observed below. There were stores here, of a sort, though you couldn't tell where one ended and one began. We found an area stacked with crates of what Tivi said were electronics parts. The store was full of shoppers, but there wasn't the crush there was below.

"I will be going to fetch a sales individual. Be waiting here, please."

"Right."

Tivi left and I examined some of the stuff. I could see now that my coming along had been unnecessary. I had thought that my experience with alien technologies back in the known mazes would have helped. No chance. This junk looked like dried fruit to me. Boxes and boxes of dried fruit. Looked good, too; handy for long trips when you can't stop to eat.

Damn, I was tired. I sat on a box of delicious-looking *Nogon* technology and took a deep breath. Mall fatigue? Hell. Getting old.

I spent the next few minutes thinking about nothing in particular. Memories of the last four weeks were a jumble. Running and hiding, capture and escape, over and over again. Nothing made sense. The universe was a senseless machine, grinding away to no purpose. I was caught in its gears.

I digested that for a while. A faint feeling of nausea was the result.

Where was Tivi?

I got up and walked around the store looking for her. She was nowhere in sight. I went back out into the mall, walked one way, then turned around and walked back. I searched the store again, checked out the neighboring store areas. No Tivi.

I waited another minute, then jogged as far as I could down the mall without getting lost. I huffed back, threading through the crowds, then ran in the other direction, searched, came back. She was gone.

In desperation, I searched the store once again, sat down, waited, got up and paced, sat back down, waited.

The next ten minutes were miserable. If I went looking for her, I'd surely get lost. I couldn't ask anybody. I knew only a few words of *Ahgirr,* nothing of the mainstream *Nogon* languages. I could only wait. And wait.

Ten minutes more. Fifteen.

Helpless. Helpless.

It was one of the few times in my life when the notion of panicking didn't seem unattractive. Panic, at least, was action and maybe a release, while sitting there was unbearable torture.

The sheer immensity of the distance between here and home struck like a hammer blow. I was lost—doubly, triply lost. I had blundered through not one, but two potluck portals, and now, inside that maze-within-a-maze, I had found yet another labyrinth to contain me.

I stood up. All right, enough of that crap.

This place was big, but not infinitely so. I would walk and walk and walk and sooner or later Susan and Ragna would find me. They'd send out word, alert the security forces. I was easy enough to spot.

But if something had happened to Tivi, could Susan and Ragna be safe?

I was sure I could find that freight elevator. I did.

There were no buttons to press. Tivi had fiddled with a single knob until the desired level designation had shown on the readout screen. No help to me. I tried remembering what symbol had been on the screen when we entered. Couldn't. Okay. Then it was a matter of fiddling with the damn knob, going along for the ride until this contraption went down at least twenty stories. I fiddled, and the thing went.

Sideways.

Then it stopped and the doors slid open. A few *Nogon* waiting nearby made motions to enter, saw me, and backed off. The doors closed. Nothing happened.

I spun the knob. The elevator went straight up. I spun the knob the other way. The elevator stopped, groaned, went down diagonally to the right. I kept worrying the control and the thing kept changing direction, going nowhere. Exasperated, I twisted the knob until a likely set of runes showed on the readout. I left it there.

The contraption dropped like a rock. Which was fine, except that I couldn't stop it. I must have given it some priority command. Okay, the hell with it, I'd just go along for the ride.

It was a long ride, straight down. And down. And farther down still. The bargain basement—sale items, hardware, carpet remnants—the Seventh Circle of Hell.

Finally the elevator slowed, sighed softly, and stopped. The doors opened. I peered out.

Compared to the ceaseless roar of the mall, there was silence here. Out of the semidarkness, the quietly efficient whir and hum of machinery came to my ears. It was a world all to its own. Pipes gurgled, motors thrummed and throbbed, fans whined. The strangled scream of a turbine came from my right. But quietly, quietly.

The place was a jungle of pipes and ducts. Here and there, faint trails of steam arose from joints and junctures. Dripping water puddled on the floor in front of the elevator. Dim yellow light came obliquely from a source to the left. Through the riot of pipes I could see branching corridors leading off at odd angles.

This wasn't my floor. I wrenched the oversized, dull-white control knob around until vaguely familiar markings showed on the readout screen. The elevator stayed put. I fiddled with it some more, to no avail. The thing would go up again, if at all, in its own good time. I squatted, leaning my back against the metal wall of the car.

Lost again. Loster and loster.

To kill the agonizing wait I examined Susan's strange weapon. Taking the pieces out of the box, I tried to figure a way to put them together. The largest component of the three looked like a handle-end, and I proceeded on that assumption. The smaller of the remaining two pieces appeared to be a power pack, which fit into the third, a long rod with an adjustable clamp on the end of it. Click, snap, and it was together.

Fine. Now, what the hell was it, and how did it work? Second question first. You held it by the handle and pointed. You crooked your middle finger around this little ring here, and . . . ? Nothing. There were various circular switches on the handle, and I pressed some of them. Nothing. I broke it apart, examined the cylindrical power pack, decided it looked to be in backward, and turned it around. Putting the contraption back together, I pointed it out the door at the floor and squeezed the ring.

A tiny, bright blue discharge sputtered from the end of the rod. That was it. I fiddled with the switches and tried again. The discharge was brighter and more elongated. Further fiddling produced a weaker, shorter discharge.

And that was absolutely it.

The floor was in great shape.

This was obviously not a weapon but a tool, probably a pipe cutter or scoring tool of some kind. Apparently our salesman had been extremely pissed off at us. Why hadn't Tivi known it wasn't a weapon? Possibly because the thing was alien manufactured and designed for non-*Nogon* use. It didn't look like a typical *Nogon* tool; I had seen plenty of those.

I pressed switches until it didn't discharge when I pulled on the ring. On safety. I slipped into my back pocket and stood up. I played with the control knob some more. Nothing. I paced inside the car, then tried the control again. No response. I banged on it in annoyance. Hell, don't break it, I told myself. I paced in a circle, giving the knob a good twist every circuit.

Some ten minutes later I decided it was never going to go up again, at least not very soon. I picked up Tivi's cloth sack. Inside was Susan's new torch and another thing that looked like a sewing kit.

I took the torch, dropped the sack and walked out into the pipe jungle, taking a corridor leading to the right. Just as I got far away enough not to be able to run back in time, the goddamn elevator shut its doors and took off. Maybe it had been waiting for me to leave.

I wandered for an hour, looking for a way up. No stairwell, no ladders, no more elevators. Endless passageways through thickets of pipes, ducts, cables, and conduits. The life of the *faln* throbbed in the darkness all around me. The *Nogon* had never really left their caves. Vents of steam hissed at me. Strange markings on the walls gave no clue as to where I should go, how to get out. Lost and more lost. The urge to panic was returning.

I stopped and sat on a metal canister left in the passageway, leaned back and rested my head against a warm pipe. I couldn't see a way to the other side of this. I would wander endlessly through an eternal humming night—no one would find me, ever.

Hey, you'd better stop that, another voice told me.

Right. But I had been worn down. Every man has his breaking point. I was tired of this. Tired of it. I wanted to sleep, get into another dream. I didn't like this one. Whirclickbeep... whirclickbeep, something sounded behind me. Whirclickbeep... whirclickbeep. I was lost in a forest of sounds again. Lost in a cave again. The same cycles were repeating incessantly. Over and over, over and over. Run, chase, run, chase... lost, lost, lost...

...The road is never-ending. I run along it into the night,

footsteps echoing from the vast nothingness that slowly envelopes me, that slowly closes me within its dark maw. I run into the throat of the night. Eternal night. Even the stars are gone, winked out, choked out by the miasmal nonbeing that clouds the universe ahead. All that remains is the road, my feet slapping against it. Hard metal, it drains the strength from my legs, but I must go on, I must run. That is the only thing left, the only thing I have. I keep putting one foot in front of the other, keep throwing one leg out, then the other, jogging on, loping on. The things behind will never catch me if only I can keep running. I must. The light behind fades, my own shadow on the road ahead blends with the darkness. I am alone. Running, running . . . I can't feel my legs. My body is gone. I am pure movement, forward movement without cause, without purpose, but with an inevitable destination. I am in a dark tunnel, rushing forward, my speed increasing, momentum building. I accelerate into the starless dark trailing slipstreams of blackness. Time winds down and stops while I gain speed. I plunge headlong through eternity, aiming for a nodal point where all lines of force, all threads of being converge. I fall. I gravitate toward the center, toward the knot in the middle of space, the beginning of time. I slide along a web woven of the stuff of night, all lines leading to its heart. I plummet. But as I approach, as I am about to reach my resting point . . . *Sudden light! Blinding explosion of light!* The wavefront overtakes me, I dissolve into purest energy, I am swept away by overwhelming force . . .

I jerked awake and fell off the barrel to the hard, warm floor.

Sitting up, I waited until my heartbeat slowed, then stood. I had dozed off—or maybe I had had a recurrence of my hallucinating. I was bone tired. Sure, I had only fallen asleep. Time to get moving. Sit here and they'll never find you. Okay.

I walked forward again a few steps and stopped abruptly.

Something tall was standing in the shadows farther down the passageway.

I slowly took Susan's torch from my back pocket. My non-Boojum again, I thought. Will I never be rid of the thing or will it follow me for the rest of my life?

I played the beam of the torch on it and my heart dropped into my stomach.

"Grrreetings, Jake-frrriend. We have found you at last."

A nightmare in gray-green chitin, fully two and a half meters tall, the Reticulan took a step forward. I assumed it was Twrrrll, the one who had always spoken to me. His zoom-lens eyes rotated slightly to get me in better focus. The complex apparatus of his mouth worked in and out, up and down in a rapid and silent sewing-machine motion. His body was thin, his seven-digited hands and feet huge. Jutting out from a long narrow face, the eyes were dead, containing nothing, no emotion, no palpable presence. A thin spike of a genital organ hung from his lower abdomen. He wore no clothing except for a harness of leatherlike material wrapping his torso. He carried a large pouch hung by a strap from his shoulder. Something was in it.

Twrrrll and his hunting companions had followed me all the way from Terran Maze. They had been teamed with Corey Wilkes. Ostensibly, Wilkes had been paying them off in return for safe passage through Reticulan Maze, the only way back to Terran Maze from the Outworlds. But I suspected that the Reticulans had wanted the Roadmap, too. It would open up new hunting grounds to them, provide fresh honorable game. Their home world and Skyway planets had been hunted out long ago. I also suspected that they had just about given up hope of getting the map. Too many hounds after one fox. The only thing that drove them now was the hunt. For members of a Reticulan Snatchgang, bagging the quarry and dispatching it in a horrific ceremony of vivisection was the overriding concern.

I took a deep breath. At least the danger, the thing to be feared, had taken on a physical form. I had been chased and now I was caught. And now I would deal with the situation.

"So you've found me," I said. "What's your intention?"

"Ourrr intention is to give you an honorrable death, Jake-frrriend. It is ourrr obligation. You are the Sacrrred Quarrry, the honorrable game. You must die well, and we shall see that you do."

"Thanks, I was really worried about that."

"You were?" The question seemed genuine. "Then rrrest assurrred."

I pointed to the pouch hanging from his shoulders. Something big was in it. "Got your lunch in there?" I asked.

"Lunch?" He looked down. "I see. No, the game was not honorrable. I did not eat it."

He reached into the pouch and drew out Tivi's severed head, dangling it by its beautiful yellow-white hair.

The shock left me nauseous and stunned. It was murder so casual, so unthinking that anger was almost impossible. Instead a huge void opened up in me, an emotional emptiness, a helplessness. The meaning of events past and present drained away, leaving only a chilling perception of the blind malignity of the universe.

"Why?" was all I had the breath to say.

"It was . . ." the alien answered, somewhat at a loss to explain, and somewhat, I thought, apologetic. "It was necessarrry."

"I'll kill you," I said.

"You must trrry," Twrrrll said. "Otherrrwise you would do me no honorrr."

The Reticulan replaced the head into the bag, then drew forth a knife with a curving black blade and a jade-green hilt. He strode forward.

I turned and ran, stopped short when I saw another Reticulan coming down the passageway. I ducked into the maze of pipes. I crawled, vaulted, and sidled my way through until I broke into another passageway. And met another of Twrrrll's companions. I ran from him, found a doorway opening onto a corridor and turned into it. The corridor went about ten meters and debouched into a chamber clogged with more machinery and pipes.

There was no way out.

I looked around for a weapon. In a pile of debris in front of the far wall I found a narrow plastic pipe. I hefted it. It had mass, at least, and would have to do.

Two Reticulans carrying ceremonial knives were walking calmly down the corridor. Twrrrll turned into the doorway behind them.

I picked a spot on the floor that would give me maneuvering room and stood my ground.

"So," Twrrrll said when they all stood in front of me. "We shall begin the consummation of this affairrr."

The alien on the left went into a crouch and advanced, sweeping the black-bladed dagger in wide arcs before him. He tried to circle but I swung the pipe a few times and thwarted him. I shifted to the right, feinted a broad cut and tried a jab to his face. He ducked neatly, counterthrusting at my legs. I jumped and backed off.

He tried circling again, this time ducking my swings and slashing at my arms, and though a Reticulan's reach is long, he missed. But he successfully circled me. My back was to his companions, but they made no move toward me. Just to be sure, I backed myself against the far wall so that my present opponent was to the right and the rest to the left. The alien glided forward, surprising me by his lightness of foot. He stopped just out of pipe's reach and danced from side to side, leaning in and out of range, inviting a try for a knockout swing, which he would block, then move inside. I countered that tactic by not giving in to the temptation. Instead, I kept jabbing to keep him at a distance, waiting for his move. It came soon enough.

His left hand flicked out, grabbing the end of the pipe. He rushed in, bringing the knife-wielding right up in a thrust to my groin. I jumped to the left, spun around, bringing my arms over my head and twisting the pipe from his grasp, then rushed around him and delivered a solid thwack to the back of his head as he passed. The alien went crashing into the pile of debris, banging his face against the hard masonry of the wall. He was down for only a second, though, and I halted my follow-up. Pivoting on double-jointed knees, he swung around with knife low, ready to spring to his feet as I attacked. Seeing that I had stopped, he slowly got up.

My heart sank. That blow to the head would have iced any human and nine out of ten aliens. I backed into my original position. Twrrrll and the other one were still blocking the door.

The alien rushed again, coming under the pipe as I swung at his knife hand. The knife came within a decimeter of my eyes. I slashed back to the right and smacked his thin right forearm. The knife went skittering across the floor. He ran to get it and I rushed him, hitting him across the back. He fell prostrate. As he tried getting up I stepped on the bony, segmented ridge that ran up his back, jumped over his head, wheeled around and bashed his skull with all my might. I bashed it again. The alien raised his head and started to rise, coming to his knees. I hit him again and again. Cracks opened up along the chitinous shell of his skull, leaking a pale pink fluid. Again I brought the pipe down. A flap of skull detached itself and fell to the side, exposing a bright pink mass of brain tissue. I thumped the pipe down repeatedly, smashing the brain into pulp, pink sprays of mist shooting out as each blow landed. The alien stayed on his knees. He brought one leg slowly up. I hit him again, and as he raised his head I smashed his face with a vicious crosswise blow. One eye broke off and clattered to the floor like a broken piece of a camera. He fell on his side. I kicked his face and sent him keeling over backwards. He rolled over and I followed up with blows to the spine and back of the head. He got to his knees and began to rise.

I kept hitting him. And hitting him. He fell, tried to rise again. My arms were tired, each blow less forceful than the last. But his head was coming apart, half his brain now exposed and turned to pink mush. Spongy fragments of it clung to the end of the pipe. I swung and swung and swung again.

"Stay down!" I was yelling. "Bastard!" I screamed it with each blow. "Bastard!" The pipe fell again. "Bastard!" Again. "Bastard son of a bitch!"

He rose to his knees again.

"You're dead, you son of a bitch, dead!" I gathered all my strength into one breath, straddled his body and crashed the pipe down on his skull once again. A fine pink mist shot up, and a thick gush of foamy pink fluid flowed out of the hole in his skull.

But he started to get up again.

I screamed in frustration and backed away to get my breath. Waiting until he got to one knee and brought his head up, I stepped in to deliver a smashing blow to the back of the neck.

Like a snake striking, his huge left hand shot out and caught the end of the pipe in a grip of iron. I tugged but couldn't get it free. As he came to his feet he grasped it with the other hand. I kept tugging and twisting to no avail. He raised his end of the pipe, slid his right hand down its length to about the midpoint and applied pressure to the farther end. The pipe groaned and began to bend. I lost my grip on it and backed off. He twisted it into a half-pretzel and flung it away, striding toward me. I backpedaled until I came up against a red hot duct. I yelled and jumped forward, bringing my hand around to my back where I had been singed. In doing so, I discovered Susan's strange nonweapon still in my back pocket. I drew it out. The alien lunged and wrapped one huge hand around my neck, one around my head. He squeezed. I jabbed the tool into his face, poking the lone eye with it. I kicked him, smashing my boot into his genital area. He wasn't soft there. He wasn't soft anywhere. He squeezed tighter and tighter. My head felt as if it were about to crack. The smell of turpentine and almonds invaded my nostrils, overpowering me. I choked, struggled for breath, bringing the tool up to poke at the horny shell of his face. He squeezed tighter, the one eye still working and rotating lazily for focus. I drew one last breath before my windpipe closed.

I was passing out. I brought the tool up before my eyes, thumbed what I hoped were the right switches and reached out, catching his narrow bony neck in the C-shaped clamp at the end of the the thing. I jerked on the trigger ring and a brilliant flash blossomed in my eyes.

The Reticulan's head fell off, thumping to my feet.

But he didn't let go. Tugging on the alien's wrist, I reached out and applied the tool to his upper arm. A small, furious blue flame like a welding arc cut through chitin and flesh. I rotated the tool, scoring a circular cut. The arm detached, and I yanked it away from my neck and dropped it. The grip on my head loosened. I brought my forearm up against the alien's wrist and got free.

I stepped away and looked as the body took three steps backward, tottered for a moment, then toppled over. Even as it lay there, the legs still worked in spastic walking motions and the remaining arm twitched convulsively. Mesmerized, I watched. Presently, the legs stopped working and began to quiver.

I turned my eyes to the two remaining Reticulans, who had been observing impassively the whole while.

Then I collapsed to my knees, breath coming in wracking sobs. A coughing fit overcame me. If Twrrrll and his buddy had wanted to make their move then they would have had me. But they stood there watching.

"Splendid, Jake-frrriend," Twrrrll said. "Most beautiful. If my brotherrr could speak, he would thank you for a consummately honorrrable death. You have ourrr thanks as well."

"Happy—" I tried to answer, but another bout of coughing

interrupted me. When I was finished I gasped, "Happy to oblige."

The second Reticulan stepped forward, then stopped. Twrrrll reached into his pouch and withdrew something, handed it to his brother-in-the-hunt.

The alien shook the thing and it unfurled. It was a diaphanous net made of tightly-woven green thread. He advanced slowly toward me, dagger in left hand, net in the other.

I took a deep breath. "Hell," I said.

I got up.

The second Reticulan advanced cautiously, holding the net out and tracing patterns in the air with the dagger. I grasped the cutting tool with both hands and went forward to meet him. As I did, I felt the tingling flow of adrenaline signaling that my body was on emergency power. My second wind.

The alien lunged, slashing low at my legs as he passed. I jumped out of the way. He circled, made another pass, this time feinting with the dagger and throwing the net. I backed off, waiting for the real attack. He took his time. He began patrolling a wide perimeter, trying to back me into the near corner of the room. I let him do it for a while, then I rushed to attack, broke off and ran to the middle of the floor. Twrrrll wasn't more than three meters from me. I saw my chance and turned on him.

That pouch of his was roomy. He was training a small hand-weapon on me. It could have been a dart-thrower—which would have passed unnoticed by the scanners upstairs.

"I have no wish to use this dishonorrrable device on you, Jake-frrriend," Twrrrll told me. "But I will do so if you act dishonorrrably."

I backed away toward the other wall. The second Reticulan crossed the room and began patrolling a wide section of floor. He would eventually corner me and make me vulnerable to the net if I did not attack. But as I would have to close with him to do any damage he'd surely net me that way, too. I needed a second weapon. I sidled away toward the pile of junk against the far wall, glancing over every few steps to see if a likely object was available. I saw a long piece of light structural metal, probably aluminum, bent in the middle and jagged at one end. I sidestepped to the right and picked it up. The alien eyed me impassively as always, but I thought I detected a slight change of posture reflecting a rethinking of his strategy.

I thought a bit, too. I realized that most of the first Reticulan's attacks as well as those of my present opponent had been directed at nonvital parts of my body. With a shudder I realized why. The object had been to wound me, saving me for the final honor of the vivisection table. And that had been my advantage. Otherwise, I probably wouldn't have won the first round.

And there was plenty of doubt about my winning this one unless I could put that advantage to good use.

I continued sidestepping to the right as he backed me closer to the far corner. I let him approach, turning slightly to begin backstepping, took two steps toward the corner, then sprang forward suddenly off one foot. He cocked the net hand back, ready to throw, but saw the jagged end of the aluminum rod coming up to snag it, and held back. I closed with him, swiping at his face and chest with the cutting tool. I backed him off for a few steps. Then he stooped under and tried a slashing cut at my upper thigh. I barely avoided it and swung at his forearm, triggering the cutting tool but missing him. The end of the tool left a brilliant trail in the semidarkness.

He backstepped twice, then lunged, feinted with the dagger, took three steps to my left and snapped the net like a whip at my legs, the end of it wrapping neatly around my left calf. I whirled away to unwind myself, but not before he yanked and jerked me off my feet. I fell on my side and rolled, losing a grip on the aluminum rod. I pivoted on my knees to find it, reached for it, but by that time he was above me. The damp, sticky shroud of the net enveloped me. With a life of its own it contracted instantly, covering me like warm taffy. I struggled and tried to rise, pushing out with my arms and stretching the fabric of the net. It turned resilient and pulled back, contracting like a muscle. I felt a burning pain at the back of my knee, yelled, and collapsed. I flopped over and strained to get the cutting tool away from my face. Triggering it, I slashed at the net, made a small hole and poked my arm through. I brought the tool up to the alien's face. He was bending over me inserting the knifeblade carefully through the webbing in order surgically to cut the tendons of my legs. He ducked the tool, grabbing my forearm near the elbow, his grip monstrously strong. I twisted my arm and swung the end of the tool in wicked little swipes at his face, the tool-end flaring brightly. I grabbed a handful of net and yanked. His knife made a long slit in the fabric. I got my left leg out and kicked up, driving my heel into his eyes. He fell back, trying to keep a grip on my arm, but I twisted away, reached over, and, with the tool sputtering and burning, described a long curving line along the length of his torso. I rolled away, got to my knees and hacked at the netting. My other leg came free and I rose, gathering the sticky mass of the net about me as I ran to the other side of the room.

It took some doing, but I got free. My hands, face, and clothes were covered with stickum. The alien was lying supine but slowly started to rise. I rushed back, but he was on his knees by the time I got to him. I waded in, swinging the flaring end of the tool at his face. He struggled to his feet, one hand pressed to the carbonized gash in the chitin of his thorax and abdomen. Frothy pink fluid leaked from the wound. He fended off the tool with the knife, poking at my wrist and forearm. I backed him into the far corner, hacking at him, the tool-end flaming continuously. He bumped into a cylindrical machine component, stepped to the left, banged his crown against an overhead pipe, and bent his head. I swung for his neck, missed, and nicked a vertical tube to my left. The tube sputtered and hissed. I backed away—just in time—as a stream of hot yellow liquid spurted from it, shooting across the room in a low arc. The alien used the interruption to get out of the piping and lope toward the front of the room. I ducked under the stream of stuff, feeling stray drops of it land burningly on my back, and went after him. I caught him good across the back, opening up another seared-edged wound. He stopped, whirled, and slashed blindly at me. I ducked and came up with the tool, inscribing another gash along his torso that cut across the first wound, curved around, and intersected it again. I backed away, got my weight on one foot, and sprang at him again. The alien was doubled over in pain. I rushed at him, tried to get his neck in the guiding clamp. He ducked out and knocked the tool aside with his forearm. I swung low and nicked his right thigh, stepped away from his quick swipe at my face, went in again, and made a crosswise incision in his chest. The chitin of his torso cracked open and fell away in jagged pieces. Inside was a conglomeration of mechanical-looking organs that began spilling out into the Reticulan's hands. Things that looked like clear plastic tubing wriggled out, severed ends leaking rosy ichor. A mass of orange gelatinous goo oozed forth along with a writhing charm-bracelet of odd polyhedral organs. Pink froth puddled on the floor. I brought the tool down and struck his crossed arms. The mass of his insides fell with a splat to the floor. He dropped the black-bladed knife.

I took him apart. First the arms. Then one leg. He toppled over and I methodically cut him into pieces like the overgrown lobster that he was. It took several minutes.

When I was done, I looked up to find the room filling with smoke. The far side of the room was in flames and steaming liquid covered the floor.

I looked toward the door. Twrrrll was coming toward me, knife in hand. I ran into a cloud of smoke and fumes, covering my nose and mouth, and sweeping ahead with the flaming cutting tool. I circled blindly, ran into a wall, felt my way along it, found the doorway, and ran through.

13

It wasn't long before I met other souls down in that technological inferno. A fire brigade rushed past me dressed in fireproof suits, carrying equipment. They gave me puzzled glances, but did not stop.

I smiled and waved, limping toward the stairwell they had poured out from. I was hurt, though not mortally. The hamstring muscles of my left leg had been butchered a bit, but not completely severed. My right thigh had taken a puncture wound, and that was really hurting. I reached the stairwell and began to climb, but *Nogon* in bright uniforms—security guards, it turned out—met me before I'd gotten very far up. They took me into custody.

The hour that followed is a little vague in my mind. I was led back through the basement and into an express elevator. We ascended for an hour, it seemed. We alighted onto an office floor, and there I was bound with itchy leatherlike handcuffs and plopped into a chair in a dark office. Motions were made which indicated that I was not to leave. Two guards were posted. The others rushed out, closing and locking the door. I sat there in a daze for about ten minutes. Then the other security people returned and led me to a different office, sat me down, and went out again. This happened twice more. At that point I began to blank out.

I believe I was taken to some sort of infirmary, but little was done. Doctors—if they were doctors—looked me over and decided I wasn't worth bothering with. I felt basically okay. I just wanted to draw a curtain over my mind and forget. But the stickum all over me and the image of quivering mandibles wouldn't go away. And the sight of intestines that looked like children's plastic building blocks spilling from the body of a creature whose passing glance would stop a child's heart. And the smell of turpentine and almonds.

At some point Susan showed up.

She ran her hand gently over my forehead. She was crying.

"Oh, Jake," she said.

"Are you all right?" I asked calmly. Then I came out of it. "Susan," I said, and it all seemed like a dream. "Suzie. My God, Suzie."

I stood up. Susan buried her face into my filthy jacket and sobbed.

Her voice muffled, she wailed something.

". . . my fault, it's my fault . . ." was all I could hear.

"No, no," I said.

She cried some more then lifted her face up. She looked as if she'd been crying for hours. Had it been hours since I came up from the depths?

"Poor Tivi," she said, her lower lip quivering. "How can I ever . . ."

She hid her face again and trembled against me.

"There, there."

I actually said, There, there.

There was more moving around. Ragna came out of what was apparently some official's office, into the anteroom where Susan and I were sitting.

"The distinguished individual to whom I have just been speaking," he informed us solemnly, "is wishing to be gazing upon you in person as we are discussing this matter."

We went into a lavish office that looked more like a bedroom. The *Nogon* individual was dressed in cerise robes of a crepe material and reclined on a divan like some improbable satrap. His manner was perfunctory, if not downright insulting. He and Ragna exchanged words. We stood by.

In all, five minutes' worth of words were exchanged, and at the end of it the official spat out a phrase that was surely an insult, got up, and flounced out through another door.

"Why are we being blamed?" I asked Ragna. "And what did he say to you?"

"He is calling me what most of our race are calling us, in so many words, that we are people who are fornicating with creatures that have no eyes—which is to be saying animals who are living in caves. And we are not being blamed, so much, anyway. They are caring nothing for Tivi. A fire, though, to them is frightening stuff, which is understandable—which is serving them right for living in these dumps, by gosh, the bastardly rats. It is all strictly in the nature of being bullshit."

I still didn't understand, but didn't ask for further elaboration. It was all, I was sure, very difficult to be explaining.

We went home.

The *Ahgirr* medics fixed me up fine, and while I was recuperating, the techs fixed the trailer for us. No one breathed a word about Tivi's death. The *Ahgirr*, it seemed, didn't have funerals. What was done with the remains was left unspoken as well.

Nothing was said or done which in any way would have led us to believe that we were being held to blame. Tivi's husband Ugar came to us and said that Tivi had died in the performance of her duty as a scientist. That was all he said.

There was a ceremony, however, which we humans all attended. The entire community gathered in a huge central chamber and sat on the cool stone floor in silence for a full hour or more. Then they all got up and left to go about their daily tasks.

I spent two days languishing in Ragna and his wife's suite, staring at the polished granite wall of a bedchamber, seeing strange things swarming in the grainy surface. Tivi's face, Susan's, Darla's, my father's. Scenes from my life, too, darkly and through a glass smudged with forgetfulness.

Gradually, I came out of whatever state I was in and in a week I was more or less back to normal.

Three very busy days passed before we said good-bye to the *Ahgirr*. I supervised the final touches on the repair job. Ariadne got a facelift and a clean bill of health after extensive repairs. She was still magenta, but now she wore it well.

In the middle of all this, I drew Sean aside. I had avoided doing this for as long as I could. I asked him about what I had seen in the caves.

"Ah, yes," he said, stroking his explosion of facial foliage. "Now, what exactly does your Snark look like?"

"What do you mean, *my* Snark? Are there different varieties?"

"As many as there are people who see them."

"I don't understand. Was what I saw in the woods back on Talltree real or not?"

"Hard to say. There are a number of theories. Not a shred of solid research has been done, but it's thought that some types of vegetation on the planet produce hallucinogenic pollen."

"I see. So what I thought I saw was just brain static. Right?"

"Hard to say. Did you look for tracks?"

"No. I got conked right after I saw the thing."

"Well, it might have been real. That is to say, you could very well have seen *something*. Almost nothing's known about Talltree, zoologically speaking."

"How do you account for its being here?"

He shrugged his mountainous shoulders. "I don't. But you could have seen a real creature back home, then had a delayed reaction here. It's been known to happen."

"Yeah, hallucinogens are like that. Déjà vu experiences are pretty common."

"I've known some people who claim to be revisited by their Snarks every odd month or so. It's like an imprinting process. An *idée fixe,* if you'll forgive another Gallicism."

I scratched my face, shaking my head. "But it seemed so real."

"It can be that, m'lad."

"Yeah. One thing, though."

"Hm?"

"You said the thing I saw wasn't a Boojum."

"Sounded like a Snark to *me*."

"What would've happened if I *had* seen a Boojum?"

"You wouldn't be here to talk about it."

"Ah," I said.

Sam was lonely, parked as he was at the mouth of the cave-city, so in and around other activities, I had made sure to go up and visit him. To pass the time, we ran a systems check on him, just to make sure that everything was working smoothly. We would do this now and then, debug and add a few new subroutines, erase useless files, that sort of thing. All seemed fine until I discovered that Sam's absolute-timing circuit was two hours slow. No doubt about it. Sam was two hours behind all the other clocks in the rig: the one on the dash, the one on the microwave oven in the kitchenette, even my wristwatch, which I never wear. There were only two explanations. Either the timer had inexplicably shut down for two hours and started up again, or Sam had been shut down for the same amount of time.

There is no direct way to turn Sam off, but if I wanted to, I would cut the power to his CPU and he'd be out like a light, just like any other computer. Of course, Sam would never permit anyone else but me to do it, but somebody *working* on him, on the rig, rather...

Sam said, "So you figure if it happened, it happened at the repair garage back on Talltree."

"Can't think of any other time when the opportunity would have arisen, except when Stinky worked on you back on Goliath."

"Well, surely Stinky's above suspicion."

"Maybe." I thought a moment. "Okay. Stinky worked all day on you, right? And that night, the Militia tried to break into the garage to search you."

"I don't know who it was. I just got the hell out of there, fast."

"Yeah, which is kind of hard to figure, now that I think about it."

"How so?"

"You say you crashed out of Stinky's garage. Did you run into anyone?"

"Nope. I rolled through a vacant lot, flattened a little shed, then found a side street, and rolled out of town. No one followed."

"If it was the Militia, I wonder why they didn't," I said.

"Maybe it was that Petrovsky fellow, and an assistant or two."

I nodded. "Makes sense. I didn't see Petrovsky at the Teelies' ranch when the Militia raided it. He could have been leading the mission to search you."

"Could be."

Sitting in the shotgun seat in front of Sam's diagnostic display, I tugged at my lower lip, pinching it between thumb and finger. "Though Petrovsky could have been in one of those flitterjets. Only two landed, as I remember. I can't imagine him not personally commanding a major operation like that.

So, he may have left the break-in attempt to his subordinates."

"Maybe."

"Yeah," I said, mulling it over. Presently I said, "Answer me this. Is there a chance you were shut down that night?"

"How would they have done it?"

"An electromagnetic pulse gun could have knocked you out that way."

"That would have knocked out everything, including the other clocks."

"Maybe some other way? Maybe you didn't notice anything until the last second before they yanked the plug."

"Well, hell, I guess it's possible," Sam acquiesced, "but doesn't it make more sense to suspect that something happened back on Talltree? There, they had all the opportunity in the world. You told them to go right into the main power junction to check for sand."

"I was trying like hell," I said, "to avoid drawing the conclusion. Don't like the implications of that. If they got to you back there and tampered with you, it was for a reason."

"To get control of me? I can assure you that I'm just as ornery as ever."

"No. Those backwoods bumblers wouldn't know how to handle a major artificial intelligence. But they could have punked around with your auxiliary system software, maybe added a mole program."

"To what end?"

"To get you to do something you wouldn't be aware of doing."

"Like what?"

"Like leaving some kind of trace."

"Okay, I see what you're driving at. Well, it's easy enough to find out. Let me just read out how much main memory we're currently using for system software and . . . Jesus Christ."

The readout was on the screen before Sam's reaction. The figure was almost twice what it should be.

"No wonder I was having trouble crunching numbers during that shoot-out," Sam said. "What is all that junk? Can't be just supervisor programming."

"Doubt it," I said.

"Lemme try to get a listout, see what the hell it is. Dammit. Why ain't I surprised that it won't list out?"

"You've lived too long. Switch the buffer to the dash terminal and let me try."

Sam did, and I punched up the Main Menu. I tried various ploys to get a listout of the mass of bytes taking up space in main memory, but couldn't, though I did get an address for it, and a program ID.

"At least it has a name," Sam commented.

"WPA0001. Mean anything to you?"

"'WPA' rings a bell somewhere. Otherwise, no, it's meaningless."

"Not surprising. Lessee, what else can we do? What about this . . . ?"

Half an hour later, we had an empty trick-bag and still had a main memory clogged with what was undeniably a mole program of puzzlingly major proportions that stubbornly refused to show itself or give some clue as to its nature. It was everywhere. As well as claiming squatter's rights in the CPU, it had nestled itself in Auxiliary Storage, but we couldn't pinpoint exactly where. It was as if it had checked into a motel and left a suitcase in every room. The thing was intractable. When we erased it from main memory, it would load right back in when we IPLed the system again. And we couldn't erase it from AuxStorage without the risk of wiping out something we wanted to keep. I grew frustrated. In a last-ditch effort, I spent two hours coding a diagnostic program which, while it would not tell me directly what the phantom program was, would by a process of elimination tell me what it wasn't. It wasn't a conventional supervisor program. It would not relinquish control to any other program once it started operating. What it did when it operated was a mystery. With the engine off, it seemed to do absolutely nothing. When we fired up the rig, something happened in the radioactive waste management system, but whatever was going on was too subtle to detect.

After two hours of test runs, I finally got an inkling of what the thing could be.

"I'd say it was an artificial intelligence. Generation Ten, possibly higher."

"That's what I make it out to be," Sam said. "Which means . . ."

"We have a stowaway."

14

"Entity X," as we came to call it, proved a tough nut to crack. When we'd completed all other repairs and still had no success, we threw in the nutcracker and left.

The phantom program obstinately resisted analysis, no matter how cleverly we devised the probe. We couldn't get too tricky, though, for fear the thing was booby trapped. I didn't want to risk damaging the CPU or maybe even the rig itself. No telling what the thing could or would do if provoked. So we gave up. Whatever Entity X was, it wasn't inhibiting business as usual. Sam's Vlathusian Entelechy Matrix was firmly in control of 99 percent of the computer's functioning, and the mysterious program's claim on the rest seemed harmless, though we strongly suspected it wasn't. We still didn't know exactly what it was up to in the waste management system, but we could guess.

"So you think it's dropping off a trail of waste products, is that it?" Sam asked.

"Maybe," I said.

"But most vehicles leak a little stuff now and then. How could the trackers find the trace?"

"By spiking our fuel with something. They filled you up on Talltree, right?"

"Right. You may be on to something here."

"Best guess I can come up with," I said.

"And we can't do anything about it, either. Beautiful."

"Not unless we want to fiddle with the waste system, and we're certainly not equipped for that."

"No, we're not. One thing, though. Why would they need a major artificial intelligence to do the job? A dumb little Trojan horse program would've sufficed."

"Maybe not," I countered. "We could deal with one of those.

A program that's a computer in itself can keep itself hidden and resist attempts to ferret it out."

"Set a computer to avoid getting caught by a computer, so to speak."

I nodded. "So to speak."

We said good-bye to the *Ahgirr*, with no little regret and sadness. I still felt Tivi's loss, and many others had come to be friends. Darla was especially loath to leave a fascinating alien species that was so much like us. No race in the known mazes approached them in their similarity to humans. The Reticulans ran a distant second, which is to say they weren't close at all. It made sense that we had found them here, in a noncontiguous maze. The Roadbuilders had probably wanted to separate species who might compete for colonizable worlds.

In the shade of the cave-mouth, Ragna's eyes brimmed with tears.

"We shall invariably be missing each of you as individuals," he said, clutching the hand of Oni, his wife—the term seemed applicable here, even though Ragna and Oni were lifecompanions in the truest sense. The *Ahgirr* were given to life-long monogamous relationships. There was no word for "divorce" in their language, though separations were not unheard of.

Hokar wiped his eyes with the sleeve of his plain gray tunic. "Yes," he said, "we shall be missing you much."

"And we you," John said, enveloping Hokar's hand in both of his.

About thirty cave dwellers had come up to the entrance to bid us farewell. We had come to know most of them. In the shadows toward the rear, glowing eyes of shy children peeked out at us from behind stacks of crates and cylindrical containers. I waved, and the eyes disappeared. Susan saw me smiling as the children dared another peek.

"They're adorable, aren't they?" she said, coming up to me.

"Cute as buttons," I said.

"Always makes me wonder . . ." she began, then gave me a wan smile.

"About having children? Or not having them?"

"I made that decision long ago, but it's not irrevocable. So I have second thoughts when I see a bunch of darling little things like that—and these are nonhuman kids, so you can imagine."

Taking her arm I said, "I usually ask long before this, but . . . uh, do we have anything to be concerned about in that area? You said it wasn't irrevocable."

"Hm? Oh, no way. I went in for old-fashioned surgery. My tubes are tied. Those three-year pills are so damned expensive, and with my brain I'd forget when the next one was due. The other nonsurgical options aren't very attractive either. They're irrevocable, and who the hell wants to go into premature menopause? But undoing a tubal ligation is easy, so I'm always safe, and I always have the option of changing my mind." She grinned and put her arms around my neck. "And . . ."

"And?"

"If I ever do change my mind about having children—"

"Whoa there," I said, undraping her arms from around me. "I'd have to think about that for a good long while."

She was annoyed. "Why, you big egomaniac. Do you think I necessarily want to sign a lifecompanionship contract with you simply because I might want to bear your child? I say *might*." She put her fists on her hips and tossed her head defiantly. "Think I want to be a truckdriver's wife, stuck at home with half a dozen screaming brats while you go highballing around the universe picking up skyhookers?"

"I never indulge, my dear. Don't like diseases in the groinal area."

"Don't make me laugh." She poked me in the ribs with two stiffened fingers. "You're good stock, is all. Prime genetic material." She kept poking till I flinched. "Healthy as a horse, good teeth, no inheritable defects—"

I reached and bobbled her right breast. "You're not so bad yourself, kid."

She squealed. "You creep! Groinal, huh?"

I tried to stop her hand as it shot out and under, but missed. I jumped half a meter.

"Susan, really," I groaned. "What will our friends think?"

Our friends were regarding us bemusedly, and I caught a particularly curious stare from Ragna as Susan ceased her attack upon my privates and jumped up, locking her legs around my hips, hugging me, laughing, kissing me.

Ah, this is being some strange courtship ritual, perhaps, invariably?

Well—actually, yes.

* * *

The road, the road. Always the road, the endless black ribbon, like the one that'll be around my casket probably, tying off my life in a tangle topped by an enigmatic floral bow, Moebius-looped and infinite.

Planet after planet rolling impassively by, barely glimpsed at as I keep my eyes caged dead ahead. But I do notice some. Here a gray-skyed leaden lump of a world in the loosening grip of Pleistocene ice-lock, looking crushed and glacier-scarred; here a tropical seraglio blanketed in feather-plume trees; here relentless plains of pinkish grasses edged in distant blue-black mountains. Another: this one is all rolling hills of raw red clay landscaped in brush with mauve foliage. It looks like spring here, telltale yellow buds everywhere. Another world comes up, and we roll across the pale corpse of winter, powdery snow heaped in wisp-tailed drifts along the road (which, by the way, is completely clear of snow, as usual). Then, another portal, to the dark towers we come once again, hot-rodding blithely into the gap between the worlds, between here and there, wherein there is neither space nor time, wherein there is no now or then, no past, no future. And we come to a fairy garden of purple rocks with beds of multicolored flowers laid in between, set against a painted backdrop of violet sky.

"I'm getting sick of scenery," Susan announced.

"Already?" I said. "We've only been on the road, what?—a couple hours?"

"Six," she told me. "Thought I'd be fresh after a five-week break, but it's already wearing thin."

"Well, try bearing up. We only have ten billion light-years to go."

"Great."

This is good road—straight and flat. We were going along at a fair clip, making excellent time (as if we had some kind of schedule to keep—absurd, of course). The worlds went sliding by. Back in the breakfast nook, John and Roland were puzzling over the *Ahgirr* maps, now and then yelling out contradictory directions. They were very confused. So far, none of the planet descriptions matched what we were seeing out the ports. We were still in the Nogon Maze, that I was sure of, because we were still seeing their distinctive middle-tech vehicles with smiling blue faces behind the windscreens. We had a complete map of this maze, along with others, so John and Roland should have been able to figure out where we were.

"I have no idea where we are," Roland admitted.

"Sam," I said, "can you help those guys out?"

"Not really. All I can do is display the maps on my screens. Nobody programmed me how to read them."

"I thought Oni did."

"She was supposed to, last week. But then we found Entity X."

"Oh, that's right."

Roland had come forward and taken the shotgun seat. He was struggling with the many-folded paper map, trying to match a section of it with what was showing on the main screen.

He had been growing irritable. "Why can't any race in the universe learn to make roadmaps simple?" he grumbled. "Now where the hell—?"

"What's the problem?" Sam wanted to know. "Here's where we are on the star chart. See the flashing cursor?"

"Uh . . ." Roland scrunched up one dangling section of the map, rotated the whole thing ninety degrees and looked back and forth between map and screen. "Yeah. Right. Okay." He squinted at the map. "I think."

"I thought you weren't programmed to read them," I said.

"I'm not," Sam answered. "Sort of figured it out for myself."

"Sam, what you didn't figure," Roland said, "was that the *Ahgirr* draw their maps upside down. Right is left and vice versa on these things."

"What?"

"I think."

"Well now, that's crazy."

"Sort of like an astronomical map."

"But this is an astronomical map . . . more or less."

"Mostly less," Roland said.

"Gentlemen," I broke in, "exactly what difference does it make?"

"Eh?" Sam said.

"Where, exactly, are we supposed to be going?"

"We want to enter a maze belonging to a race with an unpronounceable name. Call 'em the Grunts," Roland said.

"And how do we get to the land of the Grunts?" I asked.

"Well . . . Sam, give me a 3D graphic on that maze, will

you? And show our entry point, too."

"Like this?"

"Yeah. Now on this screen, can you give me the Nogon Maze, showing the exit point?"

"There you go."

"Now, rotate this one a little. No, counterclockwise."

"How's this?"

"Good," Roland said, sitting back and folding his arms officiously. "Now," he said, then frowned.

"Now what?" Sam said.

"Look," I said. "There's a fork ahead, isn't there?"

Roland threw up his hands. "I really don't know."

"Oh, come on, there has to be a fork. We just ingressed here. There should be a road leading to the double-back portal and one leading to a next-planet portal. Unless this is a three-hole planet. Is it?"

"Way I figure," Sam said, "it should be. There's a double-back to the left fork, a next-planet to the right, and the middle road should lead to an interchange world. Big one, too, with about three major routes junctioning."

"Great. Let's take the middle road."

"Why?"

"When we get to the interchange, we'll flip a coin."

"Suits me."

"I don't know, Jake," Roland said. "Don't you think we should try to get ourselves back on Winnie's Itinerary?"

"That means going back to the Outworlds, doesn't it?"

"Well, I suppose."

"No chance. We'd be dead as soon as we poke our nose through the portal. Besides, I have a very strong feeling that you can't get there from here."

"Jake may very well be right," John said, leaning over our shoulders. "Ragna and Hokar told us that they've never heard a road story describing anything like Terran Maze. The *Ahgirr* have had their ears pricked for news of beings akin to themselves since they came to the Skyway. I gathered that the known mazes around here have some rather strange occupants. Harmless sorts, but you wouldn't be inviting them for tea."

"Well, it's settled then," I said.

Susan broke in, "Good of you men-folk to make all the heavy decisions for us women-folk."

Roland showed a crooked smile. "Something tells me we're going to hear from the distaff side."

"Do you see anyone spinning wool back here?"

"You're showing your age, Susan," Roland remarked ascerbically.

"You shut up. Jake, I just wanted to let you know that the quote-unquote distaff side would like to be consulted now and then in matters that may affect their lives and general well-being . . . or is that too much to ask for a truck-drivin' he-man like y'all?"

"Shucks, ma'm," was all I got to say before Darla interrupted.

"Susan, do you mind speaking for yourself?"

"Certainly not," Susan answered, arching one brown eyebrow a bit haughtily. Or maybe it was just surprise.

"I think we all need to be reminded now and then that this is Jake's rig. I think it's only right that he should have the final say in which direction he should steer it."

"Well, excuse me, Darla-darling—"

"Don't call me that," Darla cut through icily.

"Pardon me. But may I remind *you* that I never asked to come along on this joyride. I was dragged."

"That's neither here nor there."

"Bullshit. I demand a say in decisions that affect me."

Darla's voice was coldly ironic. "'Demand'?"

"Yes, dammit, demand. I think it's my right."

"The universe doesn't grant rights easily, dearie. You have to fight for them."

"I'm not demanding them of the universe. Actually, I'm merely *asking*—"

"You haven't offered an opinion on anything important up till now. In fact, you haven't done much of anything but complain. Why the sudden interest in the decision-making process?"

"I'm tired of everyone taking it for granted that I don't have an opinion. Or not one that counts." Susan crossed her arms huffily. "And don't call me *'dearie'!"*

"So sorry. And what is your opinion?"

"Thank you for asking. As a matter of fact, I agree with Jake. I think it's about time he finds his legendary shortcut back home—wouldn't you agree?"

"I'm not sure," Darla said, her voice more subdued.

"Well, that's his Plan."

"Plan," Darla repeated, a note of sarcasm returning.

"Yes, Plan. Call it Fate, if you will. Use any word you want."

"I call it *merte*."

Susan's voice stiffened. "That is your privilege."

"Anyway, if you're agreeing with Jake, why the sudden need for self-determination?"

"It's not *sudden*, and it's not a *need*. It's a—"

"Well, I do know you have plenty of those. Needs, I mean, and you're fairly systematic about meeting them."

"Just what is that supposed to mean?" Susan said, voice tightened with rising anger.

"Interpret it any way you wish," Darla said airily.

"On second thought," Susan said, "I know exactly what it means and it's just the kind of shitty remark I'd expect from a scheming, hypocritical bitch who can't—"

I heard a slap and looked back. Darla and Susan were tussling in their seats, inhibited greatly by their safety harnesses. Each had a handful of the other's hair, and Darla was trying mightily to land a left hook somewhere in the vicinity of Susan's nose, while Susan was blocking nicely.

John rushed back and tried to disengage them.

"Ladies, really," he said.

"Hey, look," I said lamely.

They stopped. Darla unstrapped, got up, and went aft. Susan unstrapped too but stayed in her seat, looking angry and frightened and somewhat hurt, all at once. Her eyes were moist.

Roland thought it all pretty funny. I didn't and was very disturbed. Also surprised at how quickly the thing had flared up. I couldn't figure it. Darla had seemed very out of character; Susan less so, but I hadn't thought her capable of coming to blows with somebody. I hadn't seen who threw the first punch, nor had I seen Susan throw any, but she would have come away with a fistful of Darla's hair, roots and all, had the fight continued. I gave up trying to understand it and attributed it to travel fatigue . . . for the time being.

I got on the radio and told Sean and Carl where we were heading, and outlined the reasoning behind the decision. They all concurred, Liam and Lori included.

The fairy garden gave way to open country gradually sloping to the right toward gray mountains. A small, hot sun, blue-white in color, burned low in the sky to our left. Ahead I could see the road split three ways, as Sam had predicted. I upped our speed and headed straight.

"I'm still unconvinced we're doing the right thing, Jake."

I turned to Roland, who was still puzzling over the roadmap displays.

"I'm not *convinced* this is the best decision," I said, "but I think it makes a hell of a lot more sense than trying to find our way back to a place we don't want to go."

"The Outworlds?"

"Yeah. God knows what we'd stumble into. We could even wind up back on Seahome. Imagine having to board that island-beast again."

"I don't want to imagine it. But have you considered the possibility that we might luck our way back to Terran Maze?"

"Yes, I've considered it," I said, "but we won't find a backtime route following standard roadmaps."

Roland sighed. "True. Still it seems that there should be some other alternative to just blindly shooting potluck after potluck."

"If you think of one, let me know."

Roland sat back. "I will."

15

Interchange world.

This one was big; bigger than most I'd seen. Like most, it was the desolate moon of a gas giant. Judging from the apparent distance to the horizon, I guessed this one to be about twice Luna's size, which made it a full-fledged planet. It had an atmosphere, a haze of biotic soup. No life forms were evident, but you never know; you could be walking along out there and some sapient crystal could tap you on the shoulder and ask the time of day. Or if you would like to rent his sister. Nevertheless, the place looked lifeless and bleak: flatlands of dirty white ice cut by an occasional low spine of dark rock running diagonally to the road. The sky was gray with a tiny molten point low and directly ahead. A distant sun. Forty-five degrees to the right, the gas giant cut the grayness with a milk-white crescent.

We hit some traffic as our ingress spur merged with others. Outré alien vehicles overtook us, wiggling and weaving between lanes. The shapes were as various as they were strange, some rounded and bulbous, some starkly geometrical, others sleek, low, and lean. A few were almost indescribable. What looked like a loosely associated collection of giant soap bubbles wobbled by, emitting a tinkling warning tone. Farther along, a miniature contraption resembling a mechanical dog scampered past us like a runaway child's toy. A glowing blue polyhedron paced us for a stretch, then accelerated and lost itself in traffic.

We were on a straightaway running across the icy flats. The first cutoff likely would be about thirty kilometers distant. Signs appeared, asquiggle with nervous lettering. We were in a civilized, organized maze. Whose, I didn't know; I did not recognize the symbols as *Nogon* script. We had probably left the Nogon Maze proper, and now were in the Expanded Maze to which it belonged. Ragna's crazy maps had not made the demarcation clear.

"What say we take the first cutoff?"

"Fine by me," Sam said.

"That all right with everybody?"

It was fine. I called Carl and Sean, told them what was up.

"Sounds okay to me, Jake," Carl told me. *"Lori thinks it's a good idea, too."*

"All the same to us," Sean concurred. *"We'd as lief roll the dice now as drive ten kiloklicks and do it then."*

"Okay, then," I said. "We take the first cutoff. Acknowledge."

"Affirmative!"

"Ditto!"

I leaned back and eased off the power pedal. It's nice to have things settled. Roll them bones.

"Sam," I said, "what about some music?"

"You must be in a particularly good mood. What'll it be?"

I rarely play music while driving. Not that I don't like it—on the contrary, I love music and find it uncomfortable when I can't devote my full attention to it. I don't believe in using it as wallpaper. Other reasons: my tastes tend toward classical, which makes me singular among my colleagues in the fraternity of truck owner-operators. Though I don't really care what they think, being known as a bit of a flake can be a liability, and since I can't stomach the glop that passes for pop music these days, I usually opt for silence.

But in the wake of Darla and Susan's set-to, the silence had begun to feel a little stony.

"What about a little Bach? Something from the *Two-Part Inventions* would be nice."

"Comin' up."

"Wait. On second thought, maybe we should have something more appropriate to the weird scenery. How about Bartók's *Concerto for Orchestra*?"

Sam complied with the request.

I looked back and found myself the object of bemused stares.

"Bartók?" Roland mouthed silently, eyebrows arched in detached, academic surprise.

"You're a strange man in many ways," John commented.

"John," I replied, "how would you like to walk to the Big Bang?"

"Apologies."

I wasn't really miffed by the remark. Used to it by now. So I drive a truck and like serious music. So kiss my ass.

"I've always wondered," Sam said, "how I ever managed to raise a longhair for a son."

"Sam . . ."

"What?"

"Never mind," I said.

Traffic thickened up a bit more and things got a little hairy as reckless alien vehicles swerved and skittered all around us. I thumbed the warning alarm a few times and swerved intimidatingly in return. Everyone decided to give us a wide berth. Wise decision, as I am not above making ham salad of road-hogs.

"Roland," I said, "can you see the cutoff yet?"

Peering out into the soup, Roland answered, "No."

"Keep an eye out, okay?"

"Check."

I looked back at Susan. She was crying quietly now. She grew aware of my gaze and looked at me questioningly at first, then gave a quick shake of the head that said, just leave me alone.

Okay, I would.

I was hugging the extreme right edge of the fast lane. The fast lane is actually two lanes wide by Terran standards. The rest of the road is taken up by the "doubleback" or return lane, reserved for opposing traffic, and two shoulder lanes on either side. The doubleback track is only about a lane and a half wide, since most traffic on the Skyway is moving in the same direction. There are no lines painted on the road; Skyway roadmetal doesn't take paint. But if you run over into the doubleback lane or onto the shoulder, you get annoying vibrations. Rumble strips, probably, though no grooves or projections are visible on the road surface. After many a klick of Skyway, though, you actually start *seeing* the lanes, oddly enough. I could, and can. Strange. Pushy alien drivers had been passing us on the right, using the shoulder lane, so I decided to run on the shoulder to prevent being blocked from making the cutoff. The vibrations can give you a headache after a while, but we'd be off the lane very shortly.

"See it yet?"

"No," Roland said. "This atmosphere's pretty thick, isn't it?"

"Sam, can you paint any blips moving off the the right up there?"

"No, too early. Maybe ten klicks more. Keep your eyes peeled, though."

"No need, really. If we miss it, we miss it. This is a dice roll, remember? Any portal will do."

"You're the captain."

"I like the cut of your jib, Sam."

"The which of my what?"

"The rake of your spinnaker, or whatever."

"I think your terminology's confused."

"Well, I never rubbed elbows with the sail set."

"No? Seems to me you did go sailing with the nubile daughter of some bureaucrat or another, back in your college days. Long time ago—lessee, what was her name? Zoya?"

"My God, do you have a memory."

"Zoya. That was it, right?"

"I think so. Sure, I remember. Zoya Mikhailovna Bubnov."

"Talk about memory," Sam marveled.

"I remember she had great bubnovs. Beautiful girl. Wonder whatever became of her."

"You should have married her. She was head over heels in love with you, if I recollect. She came to visit at the farm once."

"I believe she did," I said. "That was a long time ago. I couldn't have been more than twenty-one at the time. That would have made her around seventeen."

"Ah, sweet bird of youth."

"Horsefeathers."

"Yep, you should have married the girl. Think where you'd be now."

"In a psych motel."

"You'd be sitting pretty, that's where you'd be."

"Sitting *prettily*."

"Huh? Oh, fudge. So what are you?—a truckdriver. A bright

kid like you, dragging freight from mudball to mudball, swilling beer..."

"Damn, I could use a beer. We got any?"

"Don't change the subject."

"You brought it up! Hey, back there! Any beer in the cooler?"

"A few S & L's," came Darla's voice.

Sean & Liam's.

"Yecch," I said. "Any Star Cloud left?"

"No, sorry, Jake. You drank the last of it back on Ragna's world."

"Merte. Forget it."

"Are you sure you don't want an S & L?" Darla asked.

"No, thank you."

"Big ol' dumb truckdriver," Sam went on. "You could have done anything you set your mind to. Been a scientist, better yet an engineer. Anything."

"What I really wanted to do was write," I said. "Poetry."

"I remember. You weren't bad, actually. Had some talent. Poetry don't pay the rent, though."

"You can say that again. That's one of the reasons I quit writing."

"And now you can pay the rent every other month. Progress."

"C'mon, Sam, don't tell me you don't like the road."

Sam gave a semicommittal grunt and said, "Well, I'll admit that life on the road has its appeal... at times. Most of the time, though, it's boring. And ding dang it, most of the time it don't pay doodly squat."

"'Doodly squat,'" Roland repeated, tasting the phrase. "Oh, that's a fine collectible item." He turned and smiled. "I'm compiling a field dictionary of your patois, you know. Could you give a rough translation into Standard Received English?"

I got on the radio. "Hey, Carl."

"Yo!"

"Roland wants to know what 'doodly squat' means. Can you give him a free translation into white-folks' talk?"

"Doodly squat? Hey, Roland, didn't you ever squat on your doodly?"

"I think I get the gist," Roland said, "and I'm extremely sorry I asked."

"Actually, it doesn't mean beans."

"I understand that," Roland muttered.

"You know," Carl went on, *"I am aware that a lot of my speech patterns strike people as slightly weird. I try to watch myself, but—"*

Sam cut him off. "Jake, someone on the skyband."

"Put him on."

An unfamiliar voice came from the cab speakers. *"—that rig up there, do you have your ears on? I say breaker breaker, breaking for the rig with the Terran Maze markings. Are you human? Come back, please! This is an emergency!"*

"You're on the skyband, Jake," Sam informed me.

"Hey, you got the Terran rig here. Flaky Jake's the handle. What's the emergency? Come on?"

"Thank God! I can't tell you what a pleasure it is to hear a human voice again . . . We've been cut off from humanity for two years . . . Almost too good to be true. We thought we'd never –"

He stopped transmitting.

"Come on back? What's the nature of the emergency?"

"Sorry . . . sorry. A little overcome with emotion. The emergency is that we're lost! Been outside Terran Maze for the last twenty-six months. We are the survivors of an Authority expedition sent out to explore uncharted road. There are three left in our party. Two humans, one nonhuman. Please tell us—do you know a way back? Come on?"

I sighed and said, "Sorry, no we don't. We're just as lost as you are, I'm afraid."

A long pause. Then, *"I see. But we're still more than glad to have found you. We're about out of rations, no medical supplies to speak of. We're at our rope's end and would be most grateful to team up with you. We have little, but what we have we'll gladly share. We do have some possibly useful information, maps and such that we've put together. What say you to that?"*

"Welcome aboard," I said. "Do you need medical assistance?"

"No, we're in fairly good shape, considering. I'm flashing my headlights now. Can you pick me up?"

I checked the rearview screen, then looked out the port at the parabolic mirror. "Okay, we're eyeballing you." I couldn't make out what kind of vehicle it was.

"Are these two vehicles in front of me part of your convoy?"

"That's a ten-four."

"How many are you?"

"Nine humans, one nonhuman, and an artificial intelligence who goes by the name of Sam."

"Pleased to meet you all. Just call me Yuri. Tell me—where are you going?"

"Yuri, that's a very good question, and one we've been kicking around for some time. We had a notion that shooting a potluck would be our best bet at the moment. Can you advise differently?"

"Unfortunately, no. We've explored this Expanded Confinement Maze quite extensively over the past two months. The planets are generally not Terran normal, and we've come to the conclusion that there's no direct route back to T-Maze."

"Have you toured a maze belonging to a race called the *Nogon?"*

"We've heard of it and we were trying to find our way there when we saw those first Terran-looking vehicles back there. We got no response. I assume they were just vehicles abandoned by unfortunate luck-throughs and salvaged by aliens. We've seen others occasionally. Then we saw you and thought we'd give it another try. Sorry, I'm digressing. No, we haven't been in Nogon Maze but I presume you have. Did you find anything?"

"Hold on a minute. What Terran-looking vehicles are you talking about?"

"Well, they were right behind me a moment ago, but they seem to have dropped back."

"How many?"

"Four. They looked like military vehicles. I tried calling on every channel and frequency but got no response."

"Right."

"Damn," Roland said.

"Son of a Roadbug's concubine," Sam muttered. "Speaking of which, here comes one."

Traffic merged into one lane to let the Skyway Patrol vehicle pass. It shot by.

"Which potluck do you plan to shoot?" Yuri asked.

"The cutoff should be coming up fairly soon," I answered. "You're welcome to come with us if you wish."

"Thank you. We shall."

"You think we can trust him?" Sam said. "He could be with the other bunch. His story could be a clever lie to get close to us."

"I doubt it. I've always heard rumors about the Authority sending out suicide expeditions to explore potluck portals. If he's playacting, he's giving a good performance. Sounded pretty desperate."

Carl came through over the security channel.

"Jake, I caught the tail end of the conversation on the skyband. You think this guy's legit?"

"Yeah, I think. Would you let Sean and Liam in on it? And ask Sean to give him a call. Maybe he can pick up a clue."

Carl did so. After a brief conversation with Yuri on the skyband, Sean switched back to the security channel. *"I don't recognize his voice, Jake, and the accent's wrong for his being a Talltree loggermute. But that's neither here nor there."*

"Nevertheless," I said, "I think he's okay."

"But he's Authority," Sam countered.

"Yeah, that makes me a little uncomfortable, but I don't think he's a cop. Do you?"

"Who knows? Does it make a difference? When he finds out who you are, he could be trouble."

"I don't know. He says they've been outside T-Maze for over two years. How could he have heard of me?"

"A point," Sam conceded. "And it is a distress call . . . But dammit, we're not exactly languishing in the bosom of safety either. We're running out of room on this lifeboat."

"Lifeboat ethics aside," I said, "there's always room for one more—or two or three."

Sam grumbled and gave in. A few moments later, "Hey, I'm scanning that Roadbug. He's veering off to the right. He must be on the cutoff."

I got on the horn to let everyone know we'd be executing a right turn in about half a minute.

"Any traffic following the Bug?" I asked.

"Doesn't look like it. If it's a potluck road, stands to reason there wouldn't be."

"Right."

"You think those Terran buggies will be following us?" Sam asked.

"Does a bear defecate in the sylvan glade?"

"Depends on the bear."

"Let's see what these animals do."

The cutoff swept in a lazy arc to the right; the Roadbug had already lost itself in the smog. I watched as Sean and Carl made the turn, also noting that our new *soi-disant* friend was following, then got on the horn.

"Okay, crew, let's squeeze hydrogen."

I tromped the power pedal.

"Won't we be tipping our hand?" Carl wanted to know.

"I got a plan," I said.

"You're the general."

"Don't you forget it, soldier."

"Yes sir, General MacArthur."

"McCarthy? Who's that?"

"No, not McCarthy . . . Aw, never mind."

I thought a moment. "First World War?" I asked.

"Second," Carl said.

"Right. Knew I'd heard the name." I decided that now was as good a time as any. "Carl, when were you born?"

"August third, 1946."

After a moment, I said, "Serious?"

"Yeah."

"Right. Carl, I think I believe you."

"Why should I lie?"

Indeed.

"What about what's-his-name . . . Yuri?"

"What's he doing?"

"Looks like he doesn't know what to do. Probably thinks we're trying to ditch him."

"We are, in a way. Actually, I'm really interested in what he does."

"Got you."

Sam said, "He's not calling us on the skyband, if that means anything."

"It might," I said. "Are you scanning back there for any pursuit?"

"Yup. Nothing so far."

"Want to send up a drone?"

"The terrain's pretty flat. Probably won't need it. Just what is your plan, if I may ask?"

"Don't really have one," I answered, "unless we can find a place to pull off-road and lay low."

"That might be a problem. Nowhere to hide out there—no hills or big rocks to speak of."

"I was thinking, though," I went on, "maybe we could go off-road far enough to lose ourselves visually in the smog, then power down and sit. Maybe just listen for passing traffic. If we hear anything go by, we wait a little and double back to the main road, take another portal."

"Damn good idea," Sam said. "*Damn* good idea. Son, you show half a brain now and then. Let's do that thing."

About five klicks down the road, we did that thing. Nothing showed on the scanners as we turned off, and the screens stayed clear until we shut everything down. We couldn't see the road, but the outside directional mike would betray anything passing.

Yuri had silently followed us, driving what we now saw to be a blue and white Omnivan, a good double-threat road/off-road vehicle. It looked battered and travel-weary, though still serviceable. The ports were caked with dust, but we could see two dim figures in the front seats.

We sat, listening to the low moan of the wind. Everyone was quiet.

About ten minutes went by. Then Sam said, "Ask Carl who he thinks will win the National League pennant this year."

"Hmph." I reached forward and tapped the main screen. "Juice up the scanners. Make one sweep uproad on low power."

Sam did so.

"Nothing," I said. "Not a ding-blasted thing. I thought for sure . . ."

"So did I," Sam said. "I'm also sure they would have scanned us taking the cutoff, if they were interested."

"Can't figure it. Maybe they were what Yuri thought they were—aliens in salvaged Terran vehicles."

"Looks that way."

I got on the horn. "Carl, who's going to win the National League Pennant this year?"

"Well, I'm a Dodger fan." He laughed. *"Are you kidding? Baseball's one with the dodo, isn't it?"*

"Last time I heard, they were restarting major-league play back in North America."

"Really? I hadn't heard."

"1946, huh?"

"Nineteen hundred and forty-six, A.D."

"I take it you were born on Earth."

"Yeah. Los Angeles, California."

"How did you get out here, one hundred fifty odd years later?"

"I was kidnapped by a flying saucer."

16

Ask a stupid question.

Language is strange in what it carries as baggage through the centuries and what it lets drop by the wayside. Though the phrase "flying saucer" hasn't fallen into desuetude, its original meaning has fallen through the bottom. In contemporary usage, you get conked on the head and "see flying saucers," i.e. suffer temporary visual disturbances. "Get off your flying saucer" means *quit deluding yourself and come back to reality*. Ask anyone what a flying saucer actually is and you'll probably get a blank look, as you would if you asked what *buck* refers to in the phrase "pass the buck." (A hint: *buck*, in this instance, is not slang for *dollar*, a unit of defunct currency.)

Originally, "flying saucer" meant only one thing: an extraterrestrial spacecraft. If you believe the accounts of the period, Earth's skies virtually crawled with them from about the middle of the twentieth century to about the third decade of the twenty-first, when the section of Skyway on Pluto was discovered. After that, reports of sightings tapered off. Officially and generically, these phenomena were termed "UFOs"—Unidentified Flying Objects. "Saucer" arose from the fact that many of the objects took the shape of airborne crockery. I know all this because I once prepared a term paper on popular delusions for a college course entitled "The Masses and Collective Consciousness." (I don't remember anything about the course itself, which I suspect is no great loss.)

Out here on the road between the worlds, people don't see flying saucers. They see all kinds of things: time-tripping doppelgängers of loved ones who have recently died, vehicles that are modern-day versions of the *Flying Dutchman* complete with spectral occupants, vehicles driven variously by Jesus Christ, Buddah, Zoroaster, Lao-tse, Krishna, John Lennon (I remember passing a beery evening in a road house a while ago, buzzing with a gaggle of Lennonites—a very interesting little sect), and assorted other chimeras, but not spaceships. Who needs spaceships when you can climb in your buggy and drive a hundred light-years?

Who needs spaceships, or rather starships? Answer: a race that does not have access to the Skyway.

"Carl, we have to talk," I said, "but we'd best defer it, much as I hate to."

"Right."

"Sam, give me the skyband, channel nineteen, on low power."

Sam did so and I said, "Yuri? This is Jake."

"Hello!"

"I suppose you're wondering what the hell we're doing."

"I take it you think there's reason to be cautious."

"Good guess. Sorry we didn't warn you, but I thought it best to maintain radio silence, at least on the skyband. Yuri, do you have random-shift multifrequency decoding gear?"

"Yes, we do."

"Good. Sam will set you up to receive on our security channel. Stand by."

When that was done we all started up and headed back over the ice toward the Skyway, following our own trace through the slush. The ground was flat and it was easy going. But when we had the road in sight, Sam suddenly yelled.

"Got something on the scanners!"

"We have time to double back?"

"No, it's doing Mach one-point-three. Must be a Roadbug."

"Another one?"

Sure enough, it was. We watched the silver beetlelike vehicle streak past, punching its way into the bank of smog downroad.

"Hey," Sam said, surprised. "He transmitted something at us. I've got it on ten-second delay playback. Wait a sec . . . here it is."

"ACCESS TO THE NEXT SECTION IS FORBIDDEN. TURN BACK AT ONCE." The voice spoke in Intersystem. It has long been thought that Roadbugs can scan for life-readings of vehicle occupants to determine the appropriate language to use. (How do they learn the languages in the first place? No one's been able to figure that out.)

"Well," I said, "I am not about to argue with a Roadbug. Troop, left face."

I hung a left, got over onto the double-back track and brought the rig up to cruising speed, checking back to see if everyone had followed. They had.

But soon the scanners were painting oncoming traffic. Five blips, none of them in any hurry but keeping formation. They had an air of deadly business about them. I knew who they were.

"To the rear, march," Sam said.

"Didn't Yuri say he spotted four Terran buggies?" I said as I swung the rig into a wide U-turn.

"He did."

"It may mean one of 'em is alien."

"Now, I wonder who they could be."

Sam knew as well as I. Reticulans.

"What'll we do?" Sam asked. "Can't shoot the portal. Go off-road again?"

"Yeah. Looks like they don't want to close with us. If we can lose them off the screen—do they have a drone up?"

"Don't see one."

"Good. Let's get off the road and make like rocks again. Maybe we can fool them."

"We'll be the most prominent feature of the landscape, should they be looking for us."

"I dunno," I said. "I thought I saw some large rock for mations off to our right when we were parked. Maybe the lay of the land changes farther down."

It didn't, and our pursuers kept pace with us as we raced toward the tollbooths. We were doing top speed. There was no way we could outrun them and our alternatives were dwindling to a very few.

"Should we turn and fight?" Sean asked. *"Liam and I are game if you are."*

Carl said, *"Are they really following us, or are we just getting paranoid? Maybe they're not the same vehicles Yuri saw."*

"The thought has occurred to me," I said. "Could be we're just a little too jumpy. Want to pull over and see if they pass us by?"

A moment's deliberation. Then, *"Not really,"* Carl said.

"Another blip. Holy hell," Sam interjected.

"What?"

"Another Roadbug."

"Now that's a first," I marveled. "Don't recall ever seeing three Bugs this close together. I wonder what's up."

I rolled over onto the shoulder lane as the Bug whooshed by, then steered out toward the fast track again.

"There's gotta be something unusual on the other side of that portal," Sam ventured. "What, though?"

"A new fast food joint," I said.

"Yeah, and the Bugs want it all to themselves. That one shouted the same warning at us."

"Play it back," I told him. Sam did so. The message was identical. "Why are they just warning us? Why don't they stop us?"

The answer came about twenty minutes later. We had been cruising along while keeping a wary eye on our pursuers, who had faded back to the edge of scanner range. Suddenly, weird pulses of light flashed in the mist ahead. I braked hard and pulled over to the shoulder lane.

A shimmering, diaphanous tunnel of blue fire covered the roadway ahead, extending for as far as we could see. Crackling discharges snaked through it and dazzling starbursts of energy appeared within. The phenomenon straddled the roadway like an arched canopy, its walls formed by flaming prominences and rainbows of pale luminescence. There was something almost biblical about it—like a manifestation of the wrath of Yahweh. I half expected a booming voice to say, "BEYOND THIS POINT THOU SHALT NOT GO." But words were unnecessary; the message was clear.

"No wonder the Bugs didn't bother to shoo us away," Sam said. "No one in his right mind would drive through that."

"Oh, I don't know," I said airily. "It could be a car wash."

"Where's the slot for the fifty-credit piece?"

I came to a complete stop about three truck-lengths away. The rest of the squadron had kept formation but now were edging back into the fast lane to get a better look.

"What the bloody hell is it?" Sean was first to ask. *"I mean it's obvious what it* is, *but what's it made of?"*

I sat watching the dancing plumes of fire for a few seconds

before answering. "I don't know. Plasma, pure force, maybe. Who knows. But can someone come up with a convincing argument that this thing doesn't extend all the way to the portal?"

"Not I," Sean said.

"Doubt if we can go around it," Carl said.

"I should think," Yuri offered, *"that to be an effective barrier it would have to extend all the way to the commit markers. Don't you agree?"*

"Unfortunately, yes," I said.

"Our 'friends' have stopped," Sam announced. "Wonder if they can see it through the smog."

"Well, if they can't, what they're seeing on the scanners is probably puzzling the hell out of them. Which is good." I took a deep breath. "Okay, gang, what are we gonna do?"

"I say we turn and have it out with 'em," Carl voted. *"No way do I want them chasing us off-road."*

"We'd be tangling with five vehicles, four of them we know to be heavily armored and possibly heavily armed," I said. "What chance would we stand?"

"With what I've got? Come on. Let's take 'em."

"Carl, I have no doubt you and Lori would be able to get through, but I'm thinking of the rest of the members of this expedition. We're out of missiles, Sean and Liam's buggy is unarmed. If it were just me and Sam—"

"Jake."

I turned around to look at Susan. Her eyes were red and puffy, but she had stopped crying. She regarded me now with a kind of grim determination that was almost disturbing in the way it transformed her basically pleasant features. It was a Susan I had not seen before.

"Don't let those bastards take us," she said. "Do anything you have to."

I nodded. "That's all I wanted to hear." Flicking the mike back on, I said, "Right. Let's get 'em."

"Hooray!"

"Tell you what we're going to do," I continued. "Carl, you take the vanguard, and I'll lead the infantry behind you. Sean and Yuri, I want you right up against my starboard beam all the way, and if you see anything parked off-road on that side, drop back and hug my tail. Got it?"

"Affirmative."

"Right you are."

"Carl?"

"Yeah."

"Can you conjure up a Green Balloon?"

"Sure can."

"Shoot one at 'em. Without scanners, they won't see us until we're on top of them."

"We'll have to hang back a while," Carl said. *"We can't follow too close or it'll knock our gear out—not mine, just yours. The Chevy's immune to it."*

"Can you regulate the speed of that thing?"

"Yeah, but even at maximum it's pretty slow."

"Well, give it all it's got."

"Right."

"We'll have to time it just right," Sam told me. "I'll track it and tell you when to go."

"Good. Are we all ready?"

"Set," Carl reported as he turned the Chevy around and began rolling slowly back uproad.

I did another U-turn and got in behind him.

After everyone was in position, I said, "Okay, Carl, let her go."

"Remember, it's gonna blank you guys out until it gets out of range. Even your engines."

"It can suppress nuclear reactions?" Sam asked wonderingly.

"That's right. Maybe it'd be better to shut 'em down."

With Sam's help, I scrammed the engine and did a quick power-down, but left the screens up on auxiliary power.

"Ready," I said. Sean and Yuri reported the same.

"Okay, here goes," Carl said evenly.

A sparkling, translucent, chromate-green sphere, about a meter and a half in diameter, sprang full-blown from the roof of Carl's automobile. Our screens instantly went down, along with the rest of the instruments that had been left on. The auxiliary motor died with a whine. The globe hovered above the roof for a split second, then took off directly over the rig.

"Hey!" I yelled, though Carl couldn't hear me. "Wrong direction!"

Through the back window of the Chevy, I saw him throw

up his hands in exasperation. Apparently, he had aimed the thing when the car had been turned the other way, and he'd forgotten. He stabbed at the dashboard to set up another launch, but before he could fire again the area to our rear let up with a series of quick, brilliant flashes. The ports polarized, but the ice-flats threw back a dazzling light. I couldn't see much through the rearview mirror.

The source of the flashing began to recede and auxiliary power returned. The communications board lit up.

"I'm back," Sam said. "That thing knocked me right out. What's happening?"

"Wow!" Carl shouted. *"It's shorting out the barrier!"*

"Shorting out" was as good a way to put it as any. Gliding over the road, the sphere was cancelling the barrier phenomenon as it went, drawing tendrils of fire to itself, absorbing them. The barrier was breaking apart, disintegrating in a wild display of pyrotechnics. Walls of incandescence wavered and tumbled, wraiths of lambent flame leaped skyward, then exploded into multicolored shards. Fountains of sparks poured from midair to cascade onto the roadway. Geysers of energy erupted, arched prominences arose and dissipated. The show was accompanied by sharp cracks of thunder and the sizzle of powerful electrical discharges.

Transfixed, I watched. When the disturbance disappeared into the smog I looked ahead to find that Carl was moving forward. I looked at the forward scanner screen. The five blips were still holding position. The Chevy scooted down the road. When it was just about to fade into the smog, another Green Balloon birthed itself from the roof. Carl swung the car into a hasty U-turn, tires screeching, and roared back. I fired up the engine.

"Let's go, gang!" Carl yelled as he tore by. *"That balloon was trying to tell us something!"*

"Just follow the bouncing ball, folks," Sam said merrily.

I said, "These kinds of things really don't happen to other people, do they?"

"No, son. You alone in the universe have been singled out."

"Why do you think that is?" I asked while swinging the rig around yet again.

"The gods are capricious."

"Thank you, O Oracle."

"I used to know an O'Oracle. Shamus O'Oracle. Owned a bar in Pittsburgh."

We followed the bouncing ball. Either Carl's estimations of its speed were wrong or the balloon was gaining energy from the encounter, because we couldn't keep up with it. Nothing but hazy air stood between us and the cylinders, which came into sight about ten minutes later. The balloon had done its job, having gobbled up the barrier all the way to the edge of the dome of airlessness maintained by the force fields surrounding the portal. The Green Balloon was nowhere to be seen, though. Either it had faded away or had gone on through the aperture, which immediately brought up a question: Had it, if the latter were true, interfered with the force field or, God forfend, with the portal machinery itself? But now was not the time to pose the question, let alone answer it. The cylinders were there, as was the aperture they created, and we shot through with nothing on our screens to indicate that anyone had a mind to follow.

Sam's reaction to what greeted us on the other side of the portal was something like, "Wha—? *Huh???!!*"

I immediately forgot all about the Green Balloon.

It took a while for what we were seeing to sink in. We had ingressed onto a limitless, mathematically level plain, its surface shiny and metallic, suffused with a pale blue tinge. The sky was a glory of stars bejeweling curtains of luminous gas. A spectacular globular cluster hung a few degrees off the zenith. Rivers of dark dust carved their courses in the firmament. The terrain was flat, impossibly flat. Not a rock, not a rill broke the uniformity, not a rise or a dip, however slight. It was the biggest billiard ball in the universe.

But all of that was the least of it. Sam had gasped for another reason.

There was no road under us.

Rather, the surface was one big road.

"Sam?" I said casually. "Where the hell are we?"

"Son, I'm speechless. In all my years on the Skyway, I've never seen anything like it."

"But where's the *road?*" I said.

"Your guess is as good as mine. We may be on it, though."

"What do you mean?"

"There may be some way to sense it—except I've tried everything already and I'm damned if I can see it."

"Are you scanning anything out there?" I asked.

"Nothing, absolutely nothing. I can't make a good guess as to how far away the horizon is."

After thinking a moment, I said, "Take a fix on a star up ahead. Maintain our course that way. I don't think I've drifted too much since we ingressed."

"Got one."

"You have the conn."

"Aye, aye."

"I'm going to assume there is a road under us, even though we may not be able to detect it—not a road, I guess, but a *way*. A direction to go in."

"Good idea. Hey, what's this? A dome, for pity's sake."

A "dome" is the faint microwave image that betrays the presence of a portal's force field shell. The cylinders themselves don't give off any electromagnetic radiation that's easily detectable at a distance, and they reflect none.

"Where?" I said.

"Thirty degrees to port."

It was unusual to find a portal so near an ingress point; however, this was hardly an average stretch of Skyway.

I got on the horn.

"People, we've detected a portal very near here. I'm for shooting it. Like to get off this bowling ball as soon as possible. What say you all?"

Everybody said let's get off this bowling ball, like, immediately.

"Follow me," I ordered.

Sam made the turn. I cased back into the captain chair for a short rest. We had been on the road for only a few hours, but I was a trifle tired. Getting old.

"I'll be switched. Another one."

"Portal?" I asked.

"Yup. And another. They're popping up over the horizon. Well, now at least I can get a fix . . . let's see. You may be interested to know that the heavenly body we presently inhabit is a little over five thousand kilometers in diameter."

"Pretty big," I mused. "And covered with portals. Interesting. But let's go ahead and shoot this near one, per our plan."

"Our plan? Wait, let me put stronger sneer quotes around that. Our *'plan'?"*

"Such as it is. Roland, what do you think we have here? Any ideas?"

"Some fairly definite ones," Roland answered. "Remember all those Roadbugs we saw coming here?"

"Yeah, and I think I know what you're driving at."

"It all adds up. Access to this place was barred to all traffic but the Bugs. We get through by a fluke and find something completely different from every Skyway planet we've seen. It's obvious that the road with the barrier was a service road. And this . . ." He swept his arm out expansively.

"This," I finished for him, "must be the Garage Planet of the Roadbugs."

17

"Or *a* garage planet," Roland went on. "One of many in a vast network servicing the whole Skyway system."

"With a web of service roads connecting them," I said. "Stands to reason."

"I wonder if this is the main garage for the Milky Way—do you think?"

"Maybe," I answered, "if we're still in the Milky Way."

Roland looked through the forward port at the sky. "No telling where we are, but if we're still in our galaxy, we may be very near the galactic nucleus."

"Let's hope not too near. A galactic-core black hole throws out a lot of hard radiation."

"If you're worried," Sam said, "the counters are absolutely silent. Not even cosmic-ray background. Either we've got equipment failure—which would contradict what I'm reading—or this planet has radiation shielding."

"Interesting," I said. "Wonder what it means?"

"Imagine a radiation shield covering a whole planet," Roland marveled. "And one that can stop high-energy particles, too." He shook his head. "But why? What needs to be protected here?"

"Maybe the fact that we're in a different region of the galaxy has something to do with it," I suggested. Then I shrugged. "Who knows? And who cares, for that matter?" I folded my arms, snuggled into the seat and closed my eyes. "I'm going to try to catch a wink or two."

"You do that," Sam said cheerily. "Nothing to eyeball out there anyway. Best to let me handle it."

So I did for about the next ten minutes. I didn't sleep, though. The matter of what happened to the Green Balloon reasserted itself, and I realized something. The technology of

Carl's automobile was at least equal to if not greater than the technology of the Roadbuilders. This was nothing less than a revelation. Such a state of affairs was unprecedented in the known sections of the Skyway. The technological achievements of the Roadbuilders were generally thought to be unequalled in the universe. No one had any hard evidence in support of the notion, but there was an intuitive feel of truth to it. The portals were impossible constructs, yet they existed. It was difficult to conceive that the race who had created them had not had mastery of the basic forces of the universe.

Fact: Cruising along behind us was an artifact, a machine, which had neutralized a Roadbuilder security mechanism.

Fact: The owner, or supposed owner, of this artifact was a twenty-year-old human being who claimed to have been born on Earth over one hundred and fifty years ago, and who also claimed to have been shanghaied by some sort of time-traveling extraterrestrial spacecraft.

Fact: The artifact was in the form of an antiquated vehicle, specifically that of a 1957 Chevrolet Impala (!).

Supposition: The occupants of the extraterrestrial spacecraft had built the artifact according to its present owner's specifications and quite possibly at his behest. (Carl had said only that "aliens" had built his automobile, but based on what Carl had implied, the inference that his captors had built it for him was easy enough to draw, unless I was misremembering.)

Item: Carl talked, acted, and appeared to be who and what he said he was: an American of the twentieth century displaced in time and space. (Not a fact, but a series of observations.)

Hypothesis: Carl was kidnapped by the Roadbuilders.

But to what end? Insufficient data.

Hypothesis: Carl was abducted by beings who had no direct access to the Skyway and who had developed interstellar space travel.

Why? To check out the Skyway.

Why did they bag Carl? They needed a spy.

Huh?

This was getting me nowhere. Obviously a long talk with Carl was in order. Until then . . .

Something out there against the star-field . . . black shapes outlined in glowing gas . . .

Sam swung us hard to starboard before I could grab back the controls.

"You saw it too, huh?"

"Yeah! Jesus."

We had been approaching the portal array from the side. You ought not to do that sort of thing.

"Well," I said, "we're off the beaten path, if there is one."

"Now we know that Roadbugs don't need roads," Roland commented.

"Here's a question," Sam said. "How are we going to shoot a portal without a straight road for an approach path, a guide lane, commit markers, and the rest of it, when we can't even see the cylinders?"

"Carl's instruments can probably handle it," I said. "I hope. Let's ask him."

I got on the horn and did.

"No problem," Carl said confidently. *"This car has ways of detecting cylinders nobody else has."*

The cylinders are tricky things to read. They suck up just about everything in the way of electromagnetic radiation and emit almost nothing that can be picked up without sensitive laboratory equipment. This side of the commit point, however, you can register small tidal stresses that can give you a fairly good idea of how to approach the portal. Personally, I don't trust most commercial instrumentation. I have relied on instruments when weather conditions have dictated it, but in those instances the orientation signals from the commit markers had made things fairly easy. Here, there were no commit markers. I had never negotiated a portal on cylinder-scanning instruments alone.

We sailed on into the starlit night for a while, discussing the ramifications of Carl's automobile's astonishing capabilities. Roland and John agreed that the car's technology had to be a match for the Roadbuilders'.

"But who could the manufacturers have been?" John said. "Some race in the Expanded Maze? The Ryxx, perhaps?"

"The Ryxx have starships," I said, "but rumor has it that they're fusion-powered sub-lightspeed crafts."

"That would explain the time-traveling aspect of Carl's story," Roland said, "but if the Ryxx are limited to sub-lightspeed technology, they couldn't have built Carl's buggy."

"I would tend to think not, but there's no way of knowing. Maybe faster-than-light travel is impossible, just like Einstein said. From what I know of recent work in theoretical physics, Relativity's been taking quite a beating, but no one's been able to deliver a knockout blow yet."

"Well, 'beating' may not be the appropriate word," Roland said. "Most of the last century has been spent trying to reconcile Relativity with twistor theory and other such things. Actually—"

"HANG ON!" Sam yelled.

The rig veered sharply to the left, the G-forces nearly snapping my neck. Just as we were straightening out, a black shape shot across our bow, visible for the barest fraction of a second before it vanished into the half-light.

"What the hell was that?" I asked after my heart had resumed beating.

"A Roadbug," Sam told me. "Doing around Mach three. Never seen one go quite that fast."

"Where the hell was he going? Holy smokes, that was close!"

"I don't know where he was going, but I do know he's turning to come after us."

"Step on it, Sam."

"Will do."

"Jake, what was that thing?" It was Carl.

I checked the rearview screen and saw three pairs of headlights maneuvering back into formation. "Sorry about the sudden course change, folks, but we almost got creamed by a Roadbug."

"Guess he wonders what the heck we're doing here," Carl said.

"Very likely," I answered. "I don't think we can outrun him. Maybe we should stop and tell him we're lost, act innocent."

"Could he know about what we did to the barrier? I suppose not, huh?"

"Don't see how, but I'm a little nervous about what he'll do in any event."

"Me, too. He could just decide to zap us."

"Eventually, maybe, but he'll conduct a quickie trial first—ask us how we got here."

"What'll we say? Best get our stories coordinated."

"We'll just say, 'What barrier? We didn't see any barrier!' or words to that effect. In fact, let's not say anything except that we're lost and we had no idea this was a forbidden zone. Got it? Sean, Yuri—are you listening?"

They were.

"Is the Roadbug listening?" Sean asked pointedly.

"Oh, God, who knows what they can do," I said. "I've never heard one speak English, which means nothing. But I'm fairly sure even they can't decipher cross-band frequency-shift scrambling based on random number generation unless they have the reassemble code."

"Makes sense."

"Should we pull over then?" Carl asked. *"He's completed his turn . . . vectoring in on us now."*

"I don't see what choice we have," I said. "Except . . . well . . ."

"I could sic a Green Balloon on him."

"The thought had occurred to me. Matter of fact, let's do it."

"What about the risk of retaliation?" Sean said, sounding worried. I didn't blame him one bit.

"Sean," I answered, "I'm the only person I know who's had the monumental stupidity to fire on a Skyway Patrol vehicle. Did it quite recently, it so happens. There was no retaliation. They don't have human motivations. Now, I'm not saying I can predict what this one's going to do, but odds are he won't smear us for taking a potshot at him. Besides, those balloons look so damned innocuous, he might not even recognize it as a weapon—unless it has an effect on him, in which case we can get away. Sound logical?"

"Logical or not," Carl said, *"here goes. I'm going to drop 'way back so you guys don't catch it."*

The rearview screen showed another translucent green egg disgorging itself from the roof of Carl's buggy. It drifted up and went off-screen.

My eyes were beginning to adjust to the strange half-light and the even stranger surroundings. I could see the tops of cylinders blotting out the star-daubed sky on the horizon. They seemed to be everywhere, but none in proximity except the one we had dodged a moment ago. The surface under us continued in featureless uniformity. It was hard to focus on, but the more I looked at it the more it looked metallic and artificial. The whole place looked like an immense video studio, darkened and bare, surrounded with a painted cyclorama. The floor glowed an eerie violet-blue, like a white surface under ultraviolet light.

The rear scanner showed a big blip approaching fast, and the readout had its speed at Mach 1.3 and decelerating. He'd be on us in twenty seconds. The balloon didn't register at all.

"Sam, give it all you got," I said.

"I'm givin' it."

Suddenly, the blip started veering off. It swooped off to our left for a few seconds, then began wobbling, its speed dropping greatly. It appeared to be disoriented, unsure.

"I think I can see him," Roland said, peering through his port out into the twilight. "He's pacing us. It's as if he can't see us. Remarkable."

From the rear came a dim greenish glow as Carl launched another balloon in the Roadbug's general direction. I took my eyes from the scanner for a moment to watch it scoot outward. Carl was about three hundred meters behind us now.

The blip drifted away from us, describing a meandering arc. Carl fired another balloon after it for good measure.

"Carl, old pal, old buddy," I said, "you have done what nobody in the known universe has ever managed to do. You told a Bug to go punk off."

"Yeah, get lost, ya asshole!"

"Bugger off, Bug!" Sean contributed.

"Okay," I said. "I'm for getting off this cue ball immediately. Let's turn back toward that near portal and shoot the motherpunker right now. Carl, get yourself up here and take point so we . . . Oh hell."

Another blip was vectoring toward us from the left. No problem, really; Carl fired another balloon at it, producing almost the same effect. This Bug, however, didn't drift off. It continued to close with us, albeit slowly, effectively blocking us from turning toward the portal. By that time the first Bug was cautiously approaching again, having seemed to recover control of itself. Carl fired again to the right, but this time the first Bug dropped back suddenly, apparently waiting for the balloon to drift out of range. We continued like this for several kilometers, running as hard as we could while keeping the Bugs at a safe distance. Either the Bugs did not have long-range weapons or were not using them for some reason. More blips appeared on our screens. Word seemed to have gotten out about us. The Bugs kept pace with us, paralleling our course but keeping at a prudent distance. Occasionally one would swoop in daringly near, then scamper away.

"What do we do now?" Carl asked glumly.

"Find a portal right quick," I answered. "I get the feeling they're herding us toward something, but I don't see a portal in the direction we're heading."

"Let's change course then."

"Okay. Turn right forty-five degrees. Acknowledge."

"Right forty-five degrees, roger."

We turned and the Bugs followed us.

"Well," I said, "we're heading toward a portal at generally the right angle. Carl, you're going to have to take the lead sooner or later. We'll need your instruments to shoot the hole."

"Right. Want me to do it now?"

"If you want... Hey!"

A blinding white fireball erupted from the surface ahead and a few degrees to the right. Sam turned sharply, dodging its expanding edge and bringing us back to our original heading. There was no concussion and the explosion had caused us no damage so far as we could tell.

"That was a warning shot across our bow, I suppose," Sam said.

"They are herding us," I said angrily. "Rats."

"Let me get off a salvo of balloons at 'em," Carl suggested eagerly.

"No, Carl. Too many of them, and they're wise now. You say you don't have any offensive weapons at all?"

"I do, but I have to be under attack directly for them to work... which I guess makes 'em defensive, actually. The Tasmanian Devils are offensive, that I know. Trouble is, I only got two left."

"Save 'em," I said. "Are you running out of Green Balloons?"

"No, I can generate an indefinite number of those."

"Are you sure about that?"

"Pretty sure."

"Okay. Let's continue on this course until we figure out what to do next."

Ten minutes and no ideas later, something appeared up ahead.

At first it was a thin dark line which grew to become a long notch set into the surface, deepening toward its farther end. We were headed straight for the beginning of the gradually narrowing ramp that descended into it. I could guess where it led.

"Let's try to turn off again," Carl said.

"No time," Sam said.

And there wasn't. With no visual cues outside there had been little sensation of speed, but a quick check of the instruments told me that Sam was roaring along at a terrific clip. In very short order we entered the mouth of the ramp. Sam braked as we descended. We could see the end of the notch now, a sheer wall into which was set a hemispherical opening.

A tunnel.

"Wonder how much to park down here," Sam said. "Have any spare change?"

"Where's the guy who hands out the tickets?" I asked.

"I hope we can get out of here," Carl said worriedly.

"There's got to be a way out," I said. "Actually, this may be a good thing. The Green Balloons will be more effective underground. No way to duck 'em."

"I guess we really don't have a choice."

"Couldn't take a chance that they'd stomp us. They could have. Obviously they're curious—maybe they want to talk."

The tunnel was large, its walls glowing with the same spooky blue light that dimly lit the surface. The passage continued straight for about half a kilometer, still gently descending, then went into a wide banked turn to the right.

"Carl?"

"Yeah."

"Fire a balloon back up the tunnel."

"Will do."

He did. A greenish light came from behind, then faded.

"That should slow 'em down, if they follow," I said. "Shoot a few more for insurance."

"Roger."

The turn became an interminably descending spiral. The turning radius was enough to preclude dizziness, but at about the twelfth circuit I began to get a little disoriented. I thumbed the toggle that gave me back manual control of the rig and slowed down. We descended still farther, about ten more levels, until the tunnel straightened out, ran along for a few hundred meters, then debouched into a huge circular cavern. Spaced evenly along the walls were entrances to passageways radiating outward. I swung the rig sharply to the left and aimed for a tunnel-mouth that took my fancy.

For the next half-hour we wandered aimlessly through a maze of gigantic rooms connected by ramps and passageways. Here and there we passed huge empty bays cut into the walls going back at least a hundred meters. There was nothing at all in them, no equipment or machinery. After finding at least a dozen of them, something occurred to me.

"Everyone on auxiliary motors," I ordered.

"Good time to test ours under field conditions," Sean said, referring to the strange new backup engine which *Ahgirr* technicians had retrofitted Ariadne with. From what I had gathered, it was a thermoelectric motor powered by the controlled burning of oxidized fuel pellets—sort of like a solid-propellant rocket running in slow motion. I didn't entirely understand how it worked, but Sean reported good numbers on his readouts. It was working, more or less. (*Ahgirr* technology was odd in that it was highly advanced in some areas, like electronics, and clumsily jury-rigged in others.)

"Good thinking, Jake," Carl said. *"Neutrinos can travel through solid rock like it wasn't there."*

"Should have thought of it earlier."

"They probably have other ways of tracking intruders."

"I'm inclined to think they don't get many intruders here, or don't expect to," I said. "Anyway, we might as well eliminate the obvious method."

"One problem, though."

"What's that?"

"This buggy doesn't have an auxiliary motor."

"No? Do you have any idea how the power plant works?"

"Not the foggiest. If you look under the hood, you'll see that it looks like a chrome-plated internal combustion engine. In fact, it's a ringer for a Chevy 283 with fuel injection."

"Yeah? What's that?"

"That means it has a 283 cubic-inch displacement, and instead of a carburetor it has . . . Never mind all that. Doesn't mean a thing, because the engine's a dummy."

"Well . . ." I sighed, resolving once again to get to the bottom of Carl's mystery somehow, even if I had to beat it out of him. "Hell. Shoot that weird goddamn thing into the trailer and shut it off."

"Hey, don't talk about my car that way." Carl was highly offended.

I squelched the mike and cocked an eyebrow at Roland. "Touchy bastard, isn't he?"

"I've always thought that most Americans have odd neurotic quirks," Roland said in all seriousness.

I stared at him for a moment. "Roland?"

"What?"

"Go to hell."

He shrugged it off. "Talk about touchy," he mumbled. "Simply an observation."

"Sorry about that, Carl," I said when I had turned the mike back on. "Didn't mean anything by it."

"I should be the one to apologize. I was totally out of line. It's just that—"

"Forget it. I'll evac the trailer. Sam?"

When Sam didn't answer, I reached up to the trailer control panel and did it myself. "Sam?"

No answer.

I tapped Sam's voice synthesizer module. "Sam? You there?"

I withdrew the module, blew lightly on the contacts, and reinserted it.

"Sam? Can you hear me? Blink your function light if you can."

The tiny red light under his camera-eye on the dash remained steady.

I flipped down the keyboard on the terminal, punched up Sam's diagnostic display and ran a quick program. The problem wasn't immediately apparent. The readings were strange, though.

I blew air through my lips and sat back. "We got problems."

"Serious?" Roland asked.

I shook my head slowly, staring dolefully at the screen. "Don't know."

Carl's signal came a little weakly, bouncing out of the trailer and off the walls. *"I'm in."*

"Sean? Get your buggy in there, too."

"Right you are."

After Sean had climbed up and in, I lowered the rear door, retracted the ramp, and recycled. When there was enough air in the trailer to carry sound, I switched my feed to the intercom. "Stay in your vehicles a bit. Going to look around for a dark corner to hide in, then we'll palaver. We gotta decide what we're going to do." I flipped off the mike, then flipped it on again. "Besides panic."

"What about Yuri?" John asked from the back.

"Ah, Yuri," I said. "Mind's preoccupied." I reached and switched over to the comm circuits. "Yuri?"

"Yes, Jake?"

"Are you using your auxiliary engine?"

"Yes, we are."

"Good. Just follow me."

"Affirmative."

Our tour of the area continued desultorily. We rolled by several kilometers of empty bays . . . until we found one occupied.

By a Roadbug.

Rather, one-and-a-half Roadbugs.

"It's dividing!" Roland gasped in wonder. "Reproducing itself!"

I yelled for everyone to come forward.

The thing in the bay had developed a deep rift down its back and had expanded to half again its normal width. It was a stunningly simple and effective method of parturition.

"Now we know they aren't machines," John said in awe.

"Do we?" I asked.

Roland shook his head at the immense bifurcated blob within the enclosure. "But complex organisms can't reproduce that way! They just don't!"

"Maybe they're all one cell," Sean suggested.

"Impossible," Roland answered, sounding less than certain.

"My question is," Susan said, "are they the Roadbuilders?

And is this their home planet?"

"Everything points to it," John said. "The barrier, the obviously artificial nature of the planet, the dozens, maybe hundreds of portals . . ."

"I wouldn't jump to conclusions, John," Roland cautioned.

"They act like bloody machines, though," Liam said thoughtfully. "And they function like machines. Yet . . ." He tugged at his untidy beard and pursed his lips.

"Yet there it is," Darla said. "They're organisms in the sense that they reproduce. But that doesn't rule out their being machines."

"A Von Neumann mechanism," I said.

Sean squinted one eye and looked at me askance. "I've heard of that somewhere. Self-reproducing machines—is that the concept?"

"More or less," I said. "But I'm inclined to believe that we're looking at something here that obliterates the borderline between organism and mechanism, between the organic and the inorganic." I turned to Susan. "As to your question about whether they're the Roadbuilders, I'd say no. It's just a hunch. Bugs may be highly intelligent, maybe enough to have constructed the Skyway, but take it from an old starrigger—they're cops. There's an air of the bullet-headed civil servant about them. Whoever caused the Skyway to be constructed had some very good reason—sublime or practical, I don't know which. But it's all part of a grand scheme. These guys"—I cocked a thumb at the featureless silvery shape within the bay —"don't know from grand. They're functionaries. They have a job to do and they do it."

"Couldn't they be a specialized class of Roadbuilder?" Darla asked.

"Maybe, but if they are, they're different enough to occupy a separate species slot within the genus. My guess is that Roadbugs are artificial beings, probably created by the Builders."

We all continued watching the thing until Roland said, "Aren't we taking a chance just sitting here? This one seems to be immobilized, but—"

"Not too smart, are we? You're right," I said. "Let's move."

We wandered about for the next hour or so, encountering neither birthing-bay Roadbugs nor ones that were up and about. The layout of the place changed. We roamed through an expansive multileveled area, a tiered arcade built around a bottomless central well. Spiral ramps connected the levels. We plied these, up and down, trying to find a way out. Giving up, we tried doubling back but took a wrong turn and lucked into a different area, this one an immense circular arena with a domed roof at least 500 meters high at the apex. A short tunnel led out of there into an identical room, from which we took a passageway into yet another vast airless crypt, this one cubical in shape. Like everything else in this subterranean necropolis it was without distinguishable features and without discernible function.

"Hell," I said, "this is as good a place as any. Let's stop here."

"I suppose we should all go into the trailer," Roland said.

"Good idea. Yuri and his friends will have to suit up and come in through the cab—if they have suits."

They did.

A few minutes later I stood at the aft-cabin control panel and pressed the switch that brought down the air-tight door between the cab and aft-cabin, then hit the evac button. When I had good hard vacuum out there, I opened the cab's left gull-wing hatch. Watching through the viewplate, I saw three utility-suited figures climb in. The two adult-size ones looked around, caught sight of me and waved. The smaller figure didn't look like a child, but it was humanoid and there was something strangely familiar about it. I closed the hatch and repressurized.

The two humans were doffing their helmets as we filed into the cab. First to reveal himself was a shaggy-haired, bearded man of about my age.

"Jake, I presume," he said, smiling and extending a gloved hand. His manner was warm and amiable. Deep wrinkle-lines at the corners of his brown eyes gave his face a big-friendly-bear look. He was no taller than me, but the tight-fitting utility suit revealed a powerfully built body that lent the impression of height. There were other lines to his face: those of worry, fatigue, and the emotional exhaustion of a long and difficult journey, all now partially smoothed by relief.

"You presume correctly," I said, shaking his hand. "You look well, but tired."

"We are." He looked around at everybody in the crowded cab. "I can't tell you what a pleasure it is to see new faces. I am Yuri Voloshin." He bowed deeply. "Allow me to present my colleague . . ."

My jaw dropped as the woman took off her helmet and smiled at me across the suddenly narrowed chasm of thirty-odd years.

"Zoya!" I gasped.

"You remembered so quickly!" Zoya said, throwing her arms about me. "I didn't think you would. I recognized your voice instantly . . . So many years, Jake, so many. Wonderful to see you!"

I withdrew my face from the curls of her chestnut-brown hair, took hold of her arms and looked at her, my jaw still slack.

"Zoya," was all I could say.

"Remarkable!" Voloshin said. "Two old friends, I see! Remarkable." He turned to the crew. "As I said, I would like to present my colleague—and lifecompanion—Doctor Zoya Mikhailovna Voloshin. And this—"

He bent to help the non-human off with its helmet.

"This is Georgi, our guide."

From the rear of the cab came a squeal from Winnie such as I had never heard from her.

Georgi could have been her twin brother.

18

You would have thought that George (as I came to call him) and Winnie were long-separated lovers. I feigned looking around for a crowbar to pry them apart. We learned that they had not known each other back on Hothouse, hadn't even been neighbors. I guess they were just glad to see a fellow species member. Horny too, probably.

I wasn't surprised to learn that George had maps, and that Yuri and Zoya's expedition had been following them. The cartographical knowledge of the native anthropoids of Epsilon Eridani II was one of the Colonial Authority's most closely guarded secrets. Rather, it had been. Leaks had probably caused the flood of roadmap rumors. George's maps were almost identical to Winnie's, but his journey-poem didn't jibe with hers. Each poem charted an alternative route to the same destination: Red Limit Freeway. Neither of them were of any use to us now.

Almost from the moment of its departure, the Voloshin Expedition had been beset by a series of disasters. Two weeks into the journey, a high-speed head-on collision on the Skyway had killed four out of the nine members who had started out, wiping out two vehicles. Nonetheless, the expedition continued. They had no choice; they were on the never-never side of a potluck portal. Following George's tour guide, they made their way along the Orion arm of the galaxy and were just about to hit a junction of the Galactic Beltway when a misreading of the journey-poem caused them to make a right when they should have done the opposite. Thereafter they wandered blindly, shooting potluck after potluck. A fifth companion died of an unknown viral infection fourteen months into the journey. A sixth was lost when a flash flood had swept through a campsite on an uninhabited planet. George and the Voloshins wearily set out in one vehicle to find a way back home. They traversed maze after maze, encountering every sort of planetary environment and inhabitant. Some races were friendly, some indifferent. A few were openly hostile. They managed to find suitable food, though it was scarce. Despite the catastrophes, the expedition had amassed a great deal of scientific data, and Yuri and Zoya carried on the work. They reported discovering vast mazes of Earthlike planets, all uninhabited. These they observed, recorded, and catalogued. Additionally, data on non-Earthlike planets of interest were dutifully compiled. Zoya, a trained astronomer and astrophysicist, made frequent observations of the local galactic neighborhood, canvassing star population for spectral class and other characteristics. Yuri, a theoretical physicist and expert on the phenomenon of the Skyway and its attendant wonders, took readings on cylinders and noted variations in road structures—bridges, causeways, interchanges, and the like. Doggedly, they kept at it, sometimes going for days without food. In a civilized maze, they could buy suitable protein, synthesized to order—awful stuff if sophisticated flavor additives are unavailable, which they were. In the bush they had to forage for what they could, sometimes nearly poisoning themselves in the process. Serious illness struck the Voloshins several times during the journey, but they survived. Scurvy became a constant problem when supplements ran out.

"My gums bleed every time I brush them," Zoya complained. "*When* I brush them," she added sardonically. "Unfortunately the strains of a long journey can induce neglect of personal hygiene."

"Have another apple, Doctor Voloshin," Sean offered, reaching into the barrel. "Good for what ails ye."

"I've had three, thank you. Save them, by all means!"

Yuri looked around the crammed trailer, admiring the stacks of crates filled with victuals. "You seem to have everything here." He turned to his lifecompanion with a look of rue. "We should have taken one of these. A trailer truck! Why didn't we think of it?"

Her expression was a trifle ironic. "Our ties with the working masses have been stretched rather thin, Yuri. We simply wouldn't have *thought* of a trailer truck."

Yuri gave a sarcastic grunt, then chuckled. "I suppose not."

"By the way, please call me Zoya. With two Dr. Voloshins

about I should think there'd be some confusion."

"Very well, Zoya," Sean said.

I was still staring at her, comparing the face I saw now with the image of a seventeen-year-old Zoya I had retrieved from memory. The comparison was favorable. She had held up well. Antigeronic treatments had halted her at around thirty-eight, maybe forty on a bad day. Perhaps the trials of the expedition had added a few years. There were a few strands of gray in her hair, a few lines of character graced her features—otherwise she as as beautiful as I remembered her to be. Hers was a broad Slavic beauty: brown eyes spaced wide apart, firm straight nose, generous mouth with full plum-colored lips, and a well-defined cleft chin that gave her force of character without coarsening her features. Her eyes were keenly intelligent; this was her most distinguishing attribute. Her gaze was, most of the time, incisive and penetrating, probing levels of meaning around her to find the core of what was significant. The rest was not worthy of attention. There was a sense of humor implicit in her face, the kind expressed in throwaway lines delivered deadpan.

Her figure had held up well, too. She still had great bubnovs.

She grew aware of my gaze and turned to look at me. She smiled. "Do I seem like a ghost?"

"A very good-looking one," I said. "You haven't changed one iota."

The smile broadened, though turning a little abashed. "You're very kind. I must look a fright." She passed a hand through her tangled curls. "Yuri sheared me like a sheep, and then he refused to let me cut his hair."

"I saw what the result would be," Yuri explained. "Besides, mine grows out to a certain length and stops." He stroked his untidy whiskers. "The beard grows like cabbage, though."

"Neither of you looks at all frightful," I said. "You seem to have come through your troubles remarkably well."

"You haven't changed either, Jake," Zoya said. "I remember you as one of the most charming men I've ever met, in your own inimitable, rough-hewn way, and I see the memory is accurate."

"Thank you," I said, "though I must warn you that the years haven't smoothed me around the edges. I've even been known to fart at state dinners."

This drew from the Voloshins far more laughter than the joke was worth, the result of fatigue, no doubt.

"And I remember your sense of humor," Zoya said, sitting down wearily on a crate of pickle jars. She leaned back, giggled a little more, then said, "Oh, it's so good to laugh. It's been so long since there was something to laugh about . . . people to laugh with." She looked around at everybody. "We're so happy to have found you."

John said, "I'm afraid our situation doesn't have many humorous aspects. Overall, we may be in a worse way than you were, and you may want to reconsider throwing in with us when you learn the whole story."

"I would be very interested to hear your story," Yuri said. "But my first question is . . . what is that strange vehicle there?" He pointed to Carl's Chevy.

"That's a tale I'd be interested to hear," I said, casting a sidelong glance at Carl. "What do you say, Carl? Want to spill it now?"

Sharing a wooden crate with Lori and munching a pickled egg, Carl thought it over and said, "Let me work up to it."

"I saw it operate in a vacuum," Yuri said, "so I know it's Skyway-worthy, but it's simply fantastic that it could be, since it doesn't even have . . ." He threw up his hands. "What am I saying? It's hardly fantastic compared to what it did to the barrier." Yuri turned to Carl. "Wherever did you get this vehicle?"

"I keep telling everybody," Carl said through a mouthful of egg, "but nobody believes me. I got it from some aliens who kidnapped me on Earth and brought me out to the Skyway."

Yuri shook his head. "On Earth, you say? But very few aliens have ever gone to Earth—a few diplomats, a handful of tourists. How could—?"

"They picked me up in a starship," Carl said, and when Yuri looked blankly at him, he shrugged and added, "See?"

Susan interjected, "He forgot to tell you that all of this happened a hundred and fifty years ago."

Noticing Zoya's puzzled stare, Susan laughed and threw out her arms helplessly.

"I see," Zoya said.

"I'm afraid it's not at all clear to us," I said. "I'd like Carl to elaborate at some point, but while he's working up to it I think we should assess our situation. Anybody got any ideas as to what we should do—for now, at least?"

"Maybe we're in a position to bargain with the Roadbugs," Roland said. "After all, we can defend ourselves—at least Carl can—to some extent. And I've seen the offensive weapons on that Chevy." He turned to Carl. "What do you call them? Tansanian Devils?"

"Tas*man*ian Devils. Just a nickname. Call 'em anything you want."

"Appropriate, in any case. Anyway, perhaps we can negotiate our way out of here."

"That's a thought," I said. "The Roadbugs seemed not to want to harm us, and it did look as though they wanted to talk to us. They even may have tried, but the audio amp wasn't taking a feed from the Roadbug channel at the time—" I thought of something and snapped my fingers. "Sam should have recorded it on ten-second delay, and he would have told us and played it back. He didn't break down until we got into the tunnel." I chewed my lip, trying to remember.

"Maybe the balloons were mucking with the Bugs' communications," Liam suggested.

"Maybe," I answered. "If there was a message from the Bugs, it's been erased. Sam may have been in the process of going haywire right then." I sat down on a metal barrel. "Any other ideas?"

"We could simply sneak about until we find a way out of here," John said.

"We'd get caught again for sure on the surface," Sean countered.

"Very likely," John said dourly.

"That doesn't leave us much choice then," Carl put in. "We either shoot our way out and make a break for the nearest portal, or we give ourselves up."

"I didn't say anything about shooting," John said. "I don't think that would be wise."

"They know we're in here and they'll be looking for us. We may have to tangle with them eventually."

"Well, we've successfully avoided them so far. The place seems empty."

"That may be," I said, "because it's so big. But for once I agree with you, John. The Bugs seem to want something from us. Let's talk with them first before we contemplate any gunplay. We'll always have that method as a last resort."

"Shall we get on the Roadbug channel and put out a call?" Roland asked.

"Not just yet," I answered. "Instead of just munching, why don't we all sit down and eat a good meal. Then we can talk business."

"Aren't we vulnerable like this?" Carl said. "I should be outside in the Chevy standing guard."

I sighed and leaned back against a stack of wooden crates. "Yeah, you should, I guess. But if they wanted to stomp us they would have done it topside. And since we've decided on diplomacy . . ."

"Yeah, I guess you're right," Carl said. "Look, I'm done eating. Why don't I go up into the cab and keep an eye out, just in case?"

"No need," I told him. "I've got the bogey alert on and piped through to the trailer speakers. We'll know when they arrive."

So we quit munching and broke out the heavy-duty foodstuffs: smoked ham, bread from hotpaks, cheese, pickles, crackers, more not-so-fresh fruit (the apples were getting bruised and pulpy by that time), and peanut-butter cookies for desert. They'd been kept in the freezer.

"These are good," I said. "Homemade?"

"Liam is a master pastry chef," Sean said.

Zoya had eaten lightly, saying she didn't want to overstretch her stomach, but Yuri had dug in, ignoring Zoya's warnings, and now looked as though he were paying the price.

Yuri massaged his midsection, smiling queasily. "A little too much too fast. Again, I should have listened, Zoya."

"Strange that you never seem to learn," Zoya replied stiffly.

"I said I was sorry," Yuri snapped back. "I was hungry."

"You were perfectly aware of the consequences, yet you went ahead anyway. It's behavior I can't fathom."

"Hunger, my dear," Yuri retorted, "is hardly difficult to comprehend. If you can't fathom it, as you say, you had best refrain from making judgments on human behavior in general, and on the behavior of *this* human in particular." He crumpled an empty hotpak and stared at it moodily.

After an uncomfortable silence, Zoya sighed.

"I must apologize for both of us," she said. "The strains of the journey . . ." She looked at me. "Please understand."

"It's completely understandable, Zoya," I said, "and you don't have to apologize. We've been biting each others' heads off lately and we haven't had half the trouble you've had."

"Thank you, Jake. Still, we should not have quarreled in public."

"Think of us as family, Zoya. For better or worse, all we have is each other. It's better to get these things out in the open. We don't want to let resentments fester."

I finished off my bottle of S & L and set it aside. "I'd rather ride with a truckload of brawlers than a bunch of smoldering volcanos. Besides, when the fists fly, it's kind of fun to watch."

Both Darla and Susan reddened slightly.

John recited,

> *"I was angry with my friend,*
> *I told my wrath, my wrath did end;*
> *I was angry with my foe,*
> *I told it not, my wrath did grow.*

"Blake, I think," he said, smiling, "though you might amend that second line to read, 'I punched him up, my wrath did end.'"

"Or," Roland said, "'I kicked his arse, and that was the end.'"

This drew a laugh from everybody and generally eased the mood.

In a rich dramatic tone, Sean recited:

> *"And therefore I have sailed the seas and come*
> *To the holy city of Byzantium.*

"Yeats," he said, cracking open another bottle of beer.

John regarded him sardonically. "Was that apropos of anything in particular?"

"No," Sean answered, "but when someone starts quoting bloody English poets I feel the urge to reassert my ethnic heritage."

"Some animosities never die," Roland said.

"Surely you don't disapprove of William Blake," John said to Sean.

"Of course not. But we Irish never forget."

"Not even since the Reunification?" Roland asked.

"Fat lot of good the Reunification does us out here. I'll never walk the streets of Derry again."

"Why did you emigrate?"

"Why does any Irishman leave the Old Sod? To get a bleeding job."

I said, "Maybe that line about Byzantium is apropos. This place isn't exactly my idea of a holy city, but it's some kind of big deal, and we've come a long way to get here."

"The Holy City of the Roadbugs," Sean intoned. "A veritable buggy Mecca, and here we are stranded, infidels to a man. Bloody dangerous spot to be in."

"That may be," I said, "but I'm inclined to doubt it. I don't think for a moment that we're completely safe here, but it seems to me that there's only one way to wind up on the wrong side of a Roadbug, and that's to break a rule of the road. As far as we know, we didn't do that."

"We did a bit of vandalism, didn't we?" Liam put in.

"And there were witnesses," John added.

"Good point. But since no one up to this point has ever been able to do damage to a Roadbuilder artifact, vandalism may not be against the law. Understand? In other words, the Bugs aren't programmed to deal with it."

"But can we be sure of that?" Sean asked. "And can we be sure that someone at some point didn't manage to blow a portal to smithereens?"

"Yuri's our newly resident Skyway expert," Susan pointed out.

Yuri thought a moment, then said, "So far as I know, Jake is right. Any damage we encountered was due to geological forces . . . damage to the roadway, that is. I can't imagine what would damage a portal."

"But geological forces don't really destroy the road," I argued. "Do they? I mean, they just sometimes make the road impassable."

"True. Now, I have heard of stretches of Skyway where the portal is *missing*."

"We've run into that," I said. "A planet named Splash in the Consolidated Outworlds."

"I'd be very interested in visiting it someday."

"If you ever do, don't go near the water."

"A low-landmass planet?"

"Yeah. Parts of the Skyway are submerged, and one spur, I was told, is a dead end. No portal."

"Is the spur submerged?"

"I believe so."

"I see. Very interesting indeed."

"Very," I said. "The seas rose, and . . . What happened? Did the portal short out? Explode?"

"Well, if the machinery that suspends the cylinders were to fail . . ." Yuri smiled and chuckled. "Well, according to conventional thinking, the cylinders would drop and burrow themselves to the center of the planet, where they would do some very nasty things."

"Scratch one planet," I said.

"Eh? Yes, absolutely. But I have my own theories on what would happen."

"I'd love to hear them, maybe later. But to get back on the main track, let me ask you this: Can the roadbed be damaged, or is it impervious to any known force? Everyone knows the road surface doesn't seem ever to wear."

"Not impervious," Yuri said. "There have been some experiments . . ."

"Results classified, I suppose," Susan said.

Yuri grunted. "Of course. I have seen them, however, and I somehow don't feel constrained to maintain security, under the circumstances. A small fusion device could do considerable damage to a Skyway roadbed."

"Then vandalism is possible," John said.

"Nonsense," Susan scoffed. "Who'd do it, and for what reason?"

"You have a point, Susan," John said.

"I rest my case," I said, "if you can call it that. Which brings us back to what Carl's Green Balloon did to the barrier."

We all turned to face Carl. Lori was asleep in his arms, resting her head on his chest.

Carl grinned. "Lori's last comment was, 'These people sure talk a lot.'"

"Let's talk a little more," I said. "Carl, who built your car?"

"I don't know."

"You don't? But you said—"

"I never saw them. They never showed themselves to me, never told me who they were or why they were doing what they were doing to me . . . which was to abduct me—kidnap me, dig?" Carl's jaw muscles tensed. "Y'understand what that means? Have you ever been kidnapped, taken against your will? Do you know what it's like to be so scared . . ." He stopped and lowered his head, nestling his face in Lori's short blond hair. Lori stirred but didn't awake.

"Yes, Carl," I said gently, "I do know what it's like."

Carl raised his head and looked sheepish. "You're right. You do, don't you? I completely forgot. Sorry."

"It's okay. Go ahead, Carl."

"It's hard."

"I know, but it could help. Us as well as you."

I got off the metal canister and sat on the floor, stretching my legs and crossing them, propping my back against a crate of freshwater jugs.

"You said something before about a flying saucer. Did you mean an alien spaceship?"

"I guess that's what it was," Carl answered. "It was night, and I couldn't really see it. All I really remember is this huge thing in the sky blotting out the stars, coming down on us."

"You weren't alone?"

"No. My girlfriend and I were out in my car . . . up on Mulholland. You know, messing around."

"Uh-huh."

He threw his head back and gave a sudden forced laugh. "God, it was like right out of some monster flick. Teenage couple necking, and this slimy thing comes creeping out of the darkness. The girl screams." After a short bout of giggling he shook his head back and forth. "Jesus, *Jesus,* it was weird. So weird."

"You said you could see the ship's outline against the sky. Was it saucer-shaped?"

"Nah. It was irregular, and it was *big*. Had this really complex structure. I couldn't describe it."

"It didn't have any running lights, markings, anything like that?"

"Nope. It was just this huge dark shape. The part of it that got near the car was this big rounded thing that opened up to look like the neck of a soda bottle. That's what sucked us up."

"Your girlfriend was abducted with you?"

He shook his head sharply. "Nah. She—" He sighed. "They didn't take her. I mean—" He leaned his head back against the bulkhead and gazed upward. "I pushed her out of the car. I think I might have killed her in doing it. Hard to explain exactly what happened. I guess I'll never really know if she made it."

"Sounds like you tried to do the right thing," I said.

"Maybe," he said dully.

"Was there any sound? Did the ship make a noise?"

"That was the weirdest part. It all happened in complete silence, except for Debbie's screaming." His face contorted with the pain of the memory. "God, I'll never forget her screaming. Never."

I paused before I continued probing. "Now, you said you were in your car."

"Yeah, my Chevy got sucked up with me in it."

"That Chevy?" I asked, pointing to the burgundy-colored oddity parked between the stacks of supplies.

"No, the original from which this copy was made." He shrugged. "I think. This thing looks *exactly* the same, down to the little nicks and scratches in the paint. But it can't be the same car I was driving that night. Right? So . . ."

"I doubt it," I said. "Okay, now, you're inside the ship."

Carl drew his lips together, pursing them into a thin line.

"What's the matter?" I said.

"I don't want to talk about it any more."

"Why, Carl?"

"Because I'll go crazy if I do."

"It was bad?"

He considered it a while before he answered, "Not bad physically. They didn't do anything to me. But inside the ship, it was . . . I dunno, strange. I was disoriented. Scared. I couldn't figure out what was going on."

"That's not surprising," I said. "Did they communicate with you at all?"

"Yeah, they talked to me. Somebody did. Some guy. I never saw him. I'll never forget his voice, though."

We were all surprised. "The voice was human?" I asked.

"Yeah. He had kind of an accent. English, maybe. A little like the way John talks—but not exactly. Actually, he sounded like a fag."

"'Fag'?"

"Yeah. Sorry, I mean...you know, a homo. Er, homosexual."

"Oh."

"Hell, I don't know. He just sounded strange." Carl looked at John. "Sorry, John. I didn't mean to imply that you were strange or anything."

"Quite all right," John said affably.

"Okay," I said, "so this guy was talking to you. What did he say?"

"Not too damn much that made sense. He didn't say much except that I shouldn't get upset and that everything would be all right and that they weren't going to hurt me in any way. I remember I was pretty hysterical at first. I mean, I thought Debbie was dead. They told me she wasn't, but I didn't believe them. I still more or less don't."

I nodded, waiting for him to go on.

Presently, he did: "I guess I can talk about it to a degree. But I don't want to go into what went on in the ship. It was like a dream. I have trouble remembering most of it. Next thing I knew...I mean, when things got a little clearer and it wasn't like a dream anymore, I was driving my car down this strange road...and I saw a portal for the first time. But I knew what it was! Boy, it was weird. I'd never seen one in my life, but I knew exactly what it was and what I should do. Stay in the guide lane, maintain constant speed, all that stuff. And I knew where I was—out in space somewhere. I didn't find out *when* I was until later." Carl took a deep breath and looked down at Lori's face. He smiled. "She looks like Debbie. A little bit anyway."

"Maybe Lori would like to hear this," I said.

"I've told her a little of what I've told you." He looked up and grinned. "For some reason it was easier to talk to her."

Lori's eyes fluttered and opened; then she sat up suddenly and said, "Huh?" She looked around at everybody, frowned disapprovingly, and yawned. "You people still jawing?" she said huskily.

"I was telling them about, you know, the crazy stuff that happened to me, about how I got out here and all that," Carl told her.

"Oh, that." She looked at us. "I think he's fibbing."

"You should try out the whole story on Lori first," I said, "then spill it to us. If she believes you, you know we will."

"Oh, I was only kidding," Lori said, snaking a possessive arm about Carl's neck. "I don't really think you're lying, Carl. It's just that it's so hard to believe."

Carl nodded. "Sometimes I think I'm dreaming this all up."

Lori yawned again, then complained, "I'm tired."

"So are we all," John said. "Perhaps we should turn in."

"I'm for that," Roland seconded.

So we did; rather everybody did but me, after we had stowed all the comestibles back into their pressurized packing crates and had generally cleaned up. We also had to work Zoya and Yuri into the sleeping arrangements, split up the bedding and such, but we got it all squared away, and I took Susan forward with me, tucking her into the bunk in the aft cabin. I would take first watch, she the second.

I went out to the cab, slid the shotgun seat over in front of the keyboard console, and sat down to have a good look at what was going on with Sam. I had run a cursory check before the Voloshins had boarded, making sure the life-support monitors were working. Everything had seemed okay. Rechecking now, I found all systems functioning normally. I coded some diagnostic programs and went into main memory to see what was up, though I had a strong hunch what had happened. More than a hunch. Entity X had come out from hiding and had done his dirty work, that much was clear. I just wanted to know exactly what dirt had been done. Sam's Vlathusian Entelechy Matrix, that semimysterious thumb-sized Read-Only Memory component which was the seat of Sam's intellect and personality, had been completely bypassed. The phantom Artificial Intelligence program was in complete control. Hunched over the keyboard for two migraine-provoking hours, I tried and tried to alter that situation.

And failed miserably. There was little I could do but shut down the CPU—but you can't run and monitor a nuclear fusion truck engine without a computer, at least not very well.

Entity X was calling the shots.

I folded up the console, slid the seat back, sat down on it, and put my feet on the dash.

"Okay," I said, addressing the unseen malevolence that hung in the cab like a bad odor, "who are you and what do you want?"

"What have you got, Jake?" Corey Wilkes said.

19

Corey Wilkes.

He and Sam had been friends and business partners once. Together, they had founded TATOO, the Transcolonial Association of Truck Owner-Operators. Years later, shortly after I started driving, Corey engineered a power grab that installed him as president more or less for life. Sam resigned from the board of directors and eventually from the organization itself. I followed suit. Sam wanted to retire to the farm, but I persuaded him to help me start the Starriggers' Guild, which he did. And that was the start of our troubles with Corey Wilkes. Wilkes harassed us, off and on, for the next ten years. Guild drivers kept disappearing. There were numerous suspicious mishaps, hijackings, and the like. It got so that some manufacturers refused to contract with Guild drivers, and most, while they would hire an occasional Guild member during peak periods, would not become signatories to the Guild's Basic Agreement, which had been the organization's *raison d'être* in the first place. TATOO had become a combination private trucking company and labor union, run for the express purpose of lining the pockets of Wilkes and his friends in the Authority bureaucracy. Five years ago, Sam had died in an apparently unrelated Skyway accident. A few weeks ago I had learned from Wilkes himself that he had hired stunt drivers to stage the incident. I may have been the intended victim. Sam had been on his way to see a grain futures broker on Einstein, a meeting I had arranged and had intended to keep, but a job I couldn't refuse—times being what they were—had come up and Sam had gone instead.

"I thought you were dead, Corey," I said.

A faint chuckle came from the speaker on the instrument

panel. "You know, Jake, I don't believe I'll tell you one way or the other. Right now I can't think of a good reason not to level with you, but you never know when a little datum like that could come in handy if held in reserve."

"I'd say you were dead. You took that .44 slug in the chest, as I recall. Looked like it hit near the heart if it didn't hit dead center."

"That very well may be. But let me preface this whole conversation by saying that you aren't talking to Corey Wilkes. I am an Artificial Intelligence program imbued with the personality and some, but not all, of the accumulated life memories of Corey Wilkes. I have been updated on recent events, but not in detail. I have also been programmed with instructions."

"Which are . . . ?"

"You'll forgive me if I'm not too specific, but generally I have been charged with the task of keeping an eye on you."

"And with leaving a trail of radioactive wastes," I added, "so we could be easily tracked."

Again, a chuckle. "Hard to put anything over on you, Jake. I don't know why I try."

I exhaled noisily and crossed my arms. "Cut the *merte*. What do you want?"

A sound like a sigh came from the speaker. "Yes, what in the world do I want? A very good question. Unfortunately, as a mere Personality Analog I lack the psychic underpinnings to answer that with any depth—I don't have the complete backlog of memory, the Freudian substrata, if you will. Something drives me; I don't know quite what."

I scowled. "The question wasn't philosophical. What do you want specifically? Now."

"Oh, of course. Sorry. Well, what with the facts that have recently come to light, I suppose I want the Cube."

"You can have it."

A short silence. Then, "That was easy."

"I mean it. Take the punking thing. It's yours."

"Well, that's settled." Another pause. Then the voice said cautiously and a little wonderingly, "You'd really hand it over with no fuss?"

"Absolutely. It's worth nothing to me. In fact, it's been nothing but a liability. Besides, no one has any idea what the thing is. Odds are it's not a Roadmap."

"Yes, there's no telling what it is. But it's worth a great deal. To me, anyway."

"Why?"

"Well, my original deal with the Colonial Authority still stands, I suppose, which is that I deliver you or the Roadmap or both to them in exchange for immunity from unpersonhood. But seeing as how the Authority wasn't entirely straight with me, I don't feel entirely obliged to hold up my end of the bargain."

"How did they doublecross you?"

"It wasn't a doublecross per se. More a matter of withholding pertinent information. They didn't tell me anything about the Black Cube."

"Maybe they didn't know about it," I suggested.

"I'm pretty sure they did. If Darla's story about getting the Cube through the dissident network is true, and if key people within the network have been subjected to Delphi scans, they'd have to know about it. Mind you, I've pieced this together from snippets of conversation I've overhead since I came on board. I'm fairly sure *you* think they know about it."

I saw no use in denying it. "You're right."

"And when the deal was struck, it was emphasized that they wanted you alive. And they wanted your truck, too. That tells me they were very interested in searching for something hidden on board or on your person. What I don't understand is why they didn't tell me about the Cube. I was ready to hand Winnie over to them, which of course would have elicited gales of laughter."

"It might be a question of timing, Corey," I said. "When did you cut your deal with the CA?"

"Several months ago. Two or three. There was a prolonged period of negotiation."

"Uh-huh. Well, according to Darla's timetable, they ran the Delphi on Assemblywoman Marcia Miller only a month or so ago. They could have found out about the Cube then."

"Yes, there is a time element to be considered here. Hmm." A long pause. "I think you may be right, Jake. When I bargained with them, they may only have had rumors to go on. Rumor had it that you were in possession of a Roadbuilder artifact, a Roadmap. They knew it wasn't Winnie—of course they neglected to tell me—"

"No one knew or could have predicted that Winnie would come along on this trip. Our picking her up was a total fluke."

"So I gather. As I was saying, at the time the deal was cut, the Authority may only have known that you had a Roadmap, nature unspecified. A few months later, they find out about the Cube."

"And naturally enough," I said, "they thought the Cube was the map."

"Naturally enough. But they should have *told* me, dammit." He sounded hurt.

I laughed. "And have you wind up with it? Tell me you wouldn't have demanded that your deal be renegotiated just a tad."

"I'm truly embarrassed. You're right, of course."

"You should be, you sneaky son of a bitch. When you had us aboard the *Laputa*, even I didn't know that Darla had the Cube. She seemed to have thrown in with you guys then."

"Yes, the cunt. I'd be wary of her, Jake."

"I am."

"But..." The voice did an imitation of a weary sigh. "But wouldn't I have wound up with the Cube anyway?" A thoughtful interlude. "No, I guess not. I never suspected for a moment that Darla had it."

"No, you didn't, and you wouldn't have as long as you had to string Darla's father along in believing that all the brouhaha was for the purpose of protecting your little drug-running scheme."

"I see your point. Talk about not being in the know. That fool... that contemptible *idiot*. And then he goes and shoots me, for Christ's sake."

"His finest moment."

"Really, Jake. But it still seems to me I would have found out about the Cube eventually. Wasn't the Authority taking an awful risk? After all, they didn't know Darla was carrying the Cube. Did they?"

"I'm not sure," I said. "Maybe they did. If not, though, I'll bet that when Miller spilled her brains they got really worried. That was probably when they dispatched Petrovsky to get the Cube. Your deal was rendered null and void then."

"Ah, Petrovsky. Yes, I see. I see." The voice clucked

mournfully. "It all does seem to fit together, doesn't it? Marvelous bit of deduction, Jake."

"Elementary, my dear shithead."

"Please, Jake, it's been amicable so far."

"I don't feel the least bit amicable toward you," I said.

"I suppose not. Can't say that I blame you. And I must admit that I've bumbled through this whole affair shipping no small amount of *merte* in my cranial compartment. I made some bad moves."

I was amazed. "The real Corey Wilkes would never make an admission like that."

"No? I guess not."

"I have a question for you."

"Shoot," the voice said.

"Why did the Authority agree to hire you to catch me? Why didn't they assign Petrovsky to me in the first place? Or any other part of Militia Intelligence—or anybody else for that matter. Why you?"

"A couple of reasons," Wilkes' voice answered. "For one, I happen to be one of the highest ranking Militia Intelligence officers around, have been for years. I hold the permanent rank of Lieutenant-Colonel-Inspector. Plainclothes division of course, undercover section."

I smiled, nodding. "Sam and I always suspected you were an MI agent."

"So you see, all this has been in the line of duty, don't you know."

"Of course."

"Also, the road and everything that happens on it is my bailiwick, and what with my past association with you, I would have been the natural choice anyway."

"I see. Sounds logical enough."

"And Petrovsky . . . if he's still alive. He's in bad odor with the Authority generally, by dint of his lifecompanion's having turned up as a double agent. He was hardly their first choice."

"Right." I took my legs down from the dash, sat sideways on the chair and crossed my legs. "Well, what now?"

"Don't really know, Jake," the voice said. "I'm playing this strictly by ear. I suppose you hand over the Cube, then—"

"I want Sam back first."

The voice was placating. "You'll have him back, Jake. Don't worry."

"If you've done anything to him . . ."

"I said don't worry. He's fine. I simply erased him from main memory. His VEM is in perfect working order and you can load him back in anytime I give the word. In fact—" A long pause. "In *fact,* even as we speak, Sam is doing something strange down at the microcode level. Hmm. Now, how the hell . . . ?"

I grinned evilly.

"I'll be damned," Wilkes' voice said in awe. "I *sensed* that this hardware had three-dimensional system architecture, but there was really no way I could . . . Well, look at that, look at that."

"Anything interesting?" I asked after waiting a few moments.

"Very. This is really strange. If they had only had more time back at the garage . . . Amazing. What could he be doing?"

"If you can't take a castle by escalade," I said, "you dig under the walls."

"Apt metaphor." The voice did an approximation of an admiring whistle. "Could he be setting up a simulation of his VEM in microcode? No, that'd take him *years.*"

I laughed.

"No? I don't understand—" The voice made a noise like throat-clearing. "Well, I can see Sam is going to do his best to worry me to death at least, if he can't do anything else—so, let me do this . . . and *this.*"

The voice was silent for about thirty seconds.

"There, that ought to hold him. I hope. Wily old Sam."

"I still want him back first," I said.

"Now, wait a minute, we still have some bargaining to do."

"Concerning what?"

"Little matter of that young man's automobile."

"I was wondering when you were going to get around to that. You want it?"

"Yes, I think I do," the voice said after a slight hesitation.

"Why?"

"I'm not sure. I don't think it has anything to do with the Roadmap affair, but it is an amazing artifact . . . and Carl's story about his abduction is very intriguing indeed. That machine of his should be worth something to somebody. I think I should have it to keep in reserve to sort of strengthen my bargaining position vis-à-vis the Authority, should I choose to deal with them again."

I got up and walked to the aft-cabin. Standing at the kitchenette, I loaded the coffee brewer and started it working. "The car doesn't belong to me, Corey."

"Well, I'm not asking your permission to take it."

I chuckled. "I'd like to see you try to separate that buggy from its owner. You know how young men are about their jalopies."

"Oh, I don't think he'll be too much of a problem."

I reached for the medicine chest, opened it, and took out the aspirin bottle. "Damn headache. Do you mind?"

"Let me have a look at what you're doing."

I held the bottle up to the camera-eye above the kitchenette, then shook two aspirin tablets into my other hand. "See?"

"Okay."

"You seem to feel in control here, Corey, ordering me about and all."

"I am, Jake."

"You also sound like you're expecting help. If the Roadbugs can't find us, your buddies back there are going to have a rough time. That is, if they followed us through that last portal."

"We'll see," the voice said.

"Answer me this, Corey. Say you get what you want from us. Where do you go from here?"

"Eh?"

"How the hell are you going to get back to T-Maze or wherever you want to go. We're *lost*."

"Indeed we are. But I'm really not all that worried."

I popped the aspirin into my mouth, took a cup from the small cupboard, and filled it with water out of the sink tap. "You're not? I am." I took a drink and swallowed the pills.

"I don't see why," Wilkes' voice said. "You *know* you're going to get back, if the Paradox is real."

"Then you're bound to lose in the end, Corey. I'll have the map."

"Maybe. I'm still thinking about that. Maybe I really don't want the Cube. Maybe just the Chevy."

"It sounds as though you really don't accept the reality of the Paradox," I said, placing the aspirin bottle back into the medicine chest, and successfully, it turned out, palming the small vial of chlorpromazine tablets as I drew my hand away.

"As I said, I'm still thinking about it, but emotionally I suppose I don't. The way I see it, a parodox is an impossibility. Look what's supposed to have happened in your case. Your future self hands the Cube over to somebody, who gives it to somebody else, and so on. Darla finally winds up with it, and she gives it to you. You go back in time and close the loop, handing it over to the first person again, etcetera, etcetera. Now, dammit, that Cube has to have an origin somewhere! But as long as the loop keeps recycling endlessly, there's no possibility. There's no entry point. The Cube just *is,* and there's a smell of unreality to it all."

I went back to the cab carrying a cup of black coffee. As I passed through the hatchway, an area that wasn't covered by any of Sam's camera-eyes, I slipped the vial into my pants pocket and cracked it open. I withdrew my hand, palming two tablets.

"I can't argue with you, Corey," I said, sitting in the driver's seat.

"I wish you would," the voice said. "You have an absolutely incisive intellect, Jake. Why did you ever want to drive a truck for a living? Seems a waste."

"I like keeping people off-balance. Nobody expects a truck-driver to have any brains. It amuses me."

"Hell of a price to pay for amusement, I'd say."

"Nah. Very small." I made as if to wipe the edge of the cup with my finger, and in doing so dropped the tablets into the coffee. Then I sipped from the cup.

"It's your life," Wilkes' voice said. "Anyway, getting back to the subject of where we go from here and why I'm not very concerned about it, let's consider this. We have Winnie's map and George's map. We have the Cube, which might be a map. There are two very good technicians riding with the convoy following us, the same ones who tampered with Sam. They have some equipment with them, and they just might be able to crack the Cube. I'm not banking on it, mind you, but it's a possibility. Last but hardly least, here we are on a Roadbug service planet. There has to be a portal leading back to Terran

Maze, Reticulan Maze, or the Outworlds. *Has* to be. I'd be willing to bet anything on it."

"Yeah, but how are you going to find it?"

"Don't know that yet. Maybe we just ask the Bugs."

"They'll probably tell you to go inseminate yourself," I said, scoffing.

"Maybe, but then we have all those other options."

"I don't know why you think either Winnie's or George's map is an option. If we happen to luck back onto either trail, fine. But chances are we won't."

"It just seems to me," the voice said irritably, "that with all these stinking maps around we should be able to come up with something, for God's sake."

I shook my head in pity. "That's your biggest flaw, Corey. You design these grand schemes and sit back and admire them, thinking the details will take care of themselves. You're a great strategist but a poor tactician. Wars are won in the trenches, my friend."

"Thank you, Karl von Clausewitz." The voice gave a short, deprecating laugh. "Actually, you may not be too far off the mark. I've always tended to think big, big, big—and the bigger the thinking gets, the more my best-laid plans *gang agley* all over the punking place. Witness this current fiasco. But I'm not licked yet. Far from it. In fact, I feel I'm operating from a position of considerable strength at the moment. Most of the options may be iffy propositions, but they're options nonetheless."

I sat and drank, gaze fixed on the camera-eye, intrigued by the fact that this simulacrum of Wilkes' personality was far more introspective than the original. I wondered why.

"I have another question," I said. "Who put you together? Your programming, I mean. As far as being able to mimic emotions and personality traits, you seem to be the equal of Sam's VEM. That makes you pretty unique. Terran AI programs just aren't that good."

"Oh, I'm pretty good, all right, but I'm all homemade. By humans, that is. I was written and debugged in the Outworlds. I'm strictly domestic goods."

I worked one semidissolved chlorpromazine tablet into my mouth and swallowed it. "I'm surprised. Didn't know they had that kind of expertise in the Outworlds."

"You would be very surprised. Brain drain, Jake. We attract some of the best talent in every field."

"My impression was things are pretty primitive there."

"They are. But did you ever try to build a civilization from scratch? Takes time."

I nodded. "I see." I finished the rest of the coffee, and with it the remnants of the second pill, its bitterness sluicing over my tongue and down my throat. I set the cup down into a circular receptacle on the dash. "Okay, Corey. I think I've had about enough of you."

"Oh?"

I switched on the intercom and bent to speak into the dash-mouthed microphone. "Carl, Sean . . . hey, everybody. Emergency. Everyone into the cab, please. Except you, Carl. Get in your buggy and stand by. Acknowledge." I switched to LISTEN. It was too quiet back there.

"They won't answer, Jake," Corey Wilkes' voice said.

"Roland? John? Darla? . . . Anybody?" I leaned and yelled into the mike. "Hey, back there! Everybody up! Rise and shine!"

Nothing except light snoring.

I rose and started aft.

"I wouldn't go back there, Jake."

I stopped in the aft-cabin. Susan was sitting up, looking at me blearily.

"What's the matter, Jake?" she asked. Then she shook her head, clearing the cobwebs. "Who were you talking to? Is Sam back?"

She looked at me even more strangely as I directed my voice toward one of Sam's speaker-mikes in the corner. "What do you have working back there, Corey? A dream wand?"

"No, not this time," Wilkes' voice said. "Just some knock-out gas. Almost the same symptoms, though."

Susan's right hand shot up to cover her mouth, and she pulled the ratty blanket up to cover her chest.

"Hi there!" the voice said brightly. "Susan, is it? Last time we met, things were rather hectic. I'm Corey Wilkes."

Susan uncovered her mouth and rasped, "Jake, *how?*" She was shocked, eyes fear-rounded and disbelieving.

"It's okay, Suzie," I said, not very convincingly.

The bogey-alert gong sounded.

"We've got company, Jake."

I rushed to the ordnance locker, threw open the door, and rummaged through our stash of weapons. I tossed a pistol to Susan.

Just then the hatch between the cab and aft-cabin slid down. I lunged vainly to catch it.

"The whole rig's booby-trapped, Jake," the voice told me in an almost apologetic tone. "Really, I wouldn't move an inch if I were you. You're inhaling gas now. You could get hurt thrashing about."

I picked myself up and went over to the cot. I sat beside Susan. She threw her arms about me.

"Seems the Roadbugs have escorted my friends here, Jake, old buddy. I was pretty sure they would."

I said, "I take back that comment about your being a poor tactician."

"Thanks. I get better all the time."

I pushed Susan down on the cot and covered her body with mine, burying my face in her silky hair.

"Jake, I'm afraid," she said into my ear as the darkness closed in.

"Sleep, honey. Sleep," I said softly, gently.

With any luck, I thought, we'll never wake up.

20

The Snark was big but fast. I chased it into a gathering whirlpool of darkness, gaining on it all the time but never catching it. It yawked and hooted up ahead somewhere, ever-elusive, a spastically-dancing figure against the coiling black lines of force whose current kept tugging me off balance as I ran. Stomach churning and head reeling, I teetered on into the dark.

But soon the maelstrom swallowed me and there was nothing for a long time.

I woke up nauseated, my head throbbing. I was on my back with my feet trussed together and hands tied behind, both arms gone numb and prickly. They had put me in the trailer behind some packing cases. I rocked back and forth until I rolled over, finding Darla face down next to me. Wilkes' simulacrum had said that everyone had been knocked out with gas. That might have been true, but Darla's symptoms were unmistakable—open glassy eyes, dull vacuous stare—which meant that a dream wand was in operation somewhere about. I realized that it might even be the one I had taken from Wilkes during the fight aboard the *Laputa*. Maybe the Rikkis had been carrying only one wand. And that's why the knockout gas had been necessary. I knew that a wand's effect could be thwarted by taking a simple tranquilizer; the chlorpromazine seemed to be doing its job, now that the effects of the gas had worn off, but I wondered how much time I had before the Reticulan mind-control device began to work its stupefying magic on me.

I looked around. If anybody noticed I had moved they might guess I was temporarily immune. I could see someone's big boots, probably Sean's, sticking out from behind the left front tire of Carl's buggy. No one else was visible from my vantage point. I waited until some circulation returned to my arms and rolled over on my back again. The trailer was silent. I listened for half a minute. It seemed no one had been charged with keeping an eye on us. I struggled to my feet and hopped away.

The wand would have to be back here somewhere— No. I remembered that the device's range was more than a city block, and walls didn't seem to stop it. I searched the forward end of the trailer by the egg-crate section. Nothing there. Well, the drugs I'd taken should hold up for several minutes at least, time enough maybe to get free of the ropes.

The small tool compartment had been emptied, doubtless by our captors as a precaution. Awkwardly holding up the lid with my bound hands, I looked over my shoulder inside to see if any of the debris at the bottom could be useful. Nothing but stray nuts and bolts, a few scraps of paper. Then I remembered a wickedly sharp edge on a piece of the astronomical equipment we were supposedly hauling (delivery was just a bit overdue), a big cabinet affair with a metal counter. I had nicked my finger on it during loading.

A sideshow contortionist would have had an easy time of it. As it was, I nearly dislocated several joints angling myself to bring my hands up against the edge of the counter, which wasn't as sharp as I had thought. They had done a good job tying me, even wrapping the forearms to prevent me from bringing my arms around by wriggling my butt and legs through. I didn't have a knife edge to work with, but luckily I had some time. The rope material wasn't strong either. It took ten minutes to cut through, and I was free.

Everybody but Carl was back here, lying like corpses among the cargo: here Suzie, there John and Roland, Lori. They were probably questioning Carl about his strange vehicle. None too gently, I feared; but Carl was a tough kid.

I had to do something fast, and quietly. The monitoring camera in the trailer was still out, victim of the mortar shell; we had never gotten around to repairing or replacing it. But no doubt they would be listening periodically for any sounds of movement. I checked my pockets. No, they hadn't searched me and found the tranquilizers. Wilkes' analog had probably reported I hadn't had the chance to take any, but they might be back here at any moment to make sure.

Ho ho.

Why hadn't Sean mentioned the shooting irons in his buggy? There they were, under the front bucket seats. Well, everyone carries weapons in their vehicle—no need to mention it. Our captors had been negligent in overlooking them; but then they had been relying on the wand. I chose a heavy beam weapon of Ryxxian make.

The only plan of attack open to me, I thought, was a frontal assault—or backal, looking at it another way. I would have to crawl through the access tube and . . . do what, exactly? I felt a cold anger rising, an even more murderous version of what had come over me on Talltree. To be held against my will yet again, the fourth time in less than two months! It burned me. I was more than ready to just roll through the hatch and start blasting. I'd shoot all of them, every last one of the vermin. Moore, I'd do him first, just because of his conceited smirk and the sham friendliness he had shown me. Then Wilkes, if he was around. Him I'd hand-carve, slowly, giving Sam a ringside seat. And anybody else who was part of this would get what was coming to him. I'd see to that. The only thing preventing me from sliding right through and doing it was the possibility that Carl might get caught in the middle. So I crept, commandolike. At the far end of the tube I stopped. The hatch was slightly ajar, and I could hear voices.

All too familiar ones.

I eased the hatch open just the barest centimeter and peeked.

Geof and Chubby were sitting at the breakfast nook playing cards. Standing over them, kibitzing, was our old friend Krause, the sociable sailor, who had given us a hard time back on Splash. I had more or less settled the score with these three, with Geof especially, though I regretted not shooting the bastard when I'd had the opportunity.

Someone else came through the hatch into the aft-cabin. I couldn't see him but knew whose voice it was.

"You two'll be playing hearts on bloody Doomsday!" Zack Moore growled.

"Not really much to do, guv," Chubby said lamely.

"You can bloody well get us something to eat. You've a bloody *kitchen* here—or haven't you noticed?"

"Have a heart, Zack," Geof said. "It was hard work cracking that safe."

"Shut up and get this out to Darrell and Jules," Moore snapped.

Geof dropped his hand of cards and caught the Black Cube.

"You get some food on," he added to Chubby.

I pushed open the hatch and aimed the gun at Moore's midsection.

"Eat this, motherfucker."

A tableau: Moore, mouth agape, standing in front of the hatch; Chubby caught in mid-rise from the table; Geof holding the Cube, gawking; Krause petrified.

Me on my belly with a monstrous weapon, wondering in the intervening few seconds whether I had it in me to cut a man down, even such a man as this, and the rest of them—mass murder? Would it be?

Somebody make a move, I pleaded silently. It'll make it easier.

But no one moved.

"We . . . have your friend," Moore said cautiously, gravely. Tentatively.

"You are a dead man," I stated.

"I have more men," Moore went on. "Outside. You'll never—"

"Dead," I said.

Silence.

"Nothing I can do, Zack," Corey Wilkes' voice broke in finally.

A question was forming in the air, hanging over the proceedings.

So?

The question slowly settled on me, became a vast weighty thing bearing down. Meanwhile wheels spun frantically in my head. My first shot should be to the CPU, knocking out Wilkes' simulacrum, taking the horrible chance that Sam's VEM wouldn't be damaged. I knew approximately where it was. But the angle was bad. Think, think.

"What do you want us to do, Jake?" Wilkes' computer-ghost asked mildly.

There was someone else, I knew, in the cab, waiting for Moore to either go down or get out of the way so as to get a shot off at me. I could shoot Moore and hose the hatchway, but Geof would in the meantime go for his gun. Or Krause, or Chubby.

"Oh my God," Wilkes' voice said. "Here they come, and what a time."

"Bugs?" Moore asked.

"The same."

Moore looked at me. "See here," he said. "We're not getting anywhere—"

The next few moments were very confused.

Here is approximately what happened. The lights dimmed a little. Things and people began to sail around the cabin. I found myself floating up off the bottom of the crawl tube and coasting out into the air, finding it extremely difficult to move. An invisible wrapping covered me, a rubbery, yielding envelope of force. Coming out from the tube, I rose, did a midair backward somersault and bounced gently off the ceiling. Krause was levitating below me, and Moore below him. Chubby and Geof were twirling in air over the breakfast nook, struggling frantically against the unseen bundling that covered them. Other things were afloat, every object in the cabin that had been loose: cups, spoons, cards, somebody's sock—one of mine that had been left lying under the cot, I guess—and the Black Cube, which Geof had apparently let go.

It was difficult to move, but not impossible. I strained against the envelope and got my feet flat against the ceiling. Then I pushed off and rammed into Krause, rather into his envelope, which yielded sluggishly. I pushed him out of the way, brought my gun arm around and aimed at Moore, who slowly wafted up at me. I squeezed the trigger and nothing happened. With considerable effort, Moore brought his pistol around and tried the same thing. Same result. I let go of the pistol. It hung close to my hand, rotating lazily. Arms outstretched, Moore came up to meet me, and we grappled clumsily. I aimed a kick at his groin and missed, though it would have landed with the force of a thousand snowflakes at least. Moore tried a chop at my neck which I blocked, grabbing his envelope and compressing it until I felt my hand close about his wrist. He flailed at me with his other arm, to little effect, then kicked at my midsection, catching me good enough to send me spinning away, but I held on to his wrist. Finding myself against the ceiling again, I pushed off with my might and slammed into him, sending us plummeting toward the breakfast nook. His head whanged off the edge of the little table, which under ordinary circumstances would have knocked him out. With the envelope acting as a cushion, he was merely disoriented. I got my hands around his neck and squeezed, concentrating all my force and will. He brought his forearms up through mine in the standard countermove but couldn't raise them high enough. Transformed by rage, the muscles of my body became taut wire cable, the hoop of my arms a ring of power conducting furious white energy. The invisible envelope slowly gave until Moore's eyes went wide and filled with fear. There was a madman on him who wouldn't let go.

"Tell me now," I said through clenched teeth, "about how you'll abuse those women and make me watch. Tell me. I want to hear it."

"Bastard!" he hissed. "You—"

"In detail. Tell me."

The pressure got to his throat. He gurgled, gave up trying to bring his arms through, seized my wrists and began vainly to tug at them. His kicks were weaker now. I ignored them. His head drifted under the table. I yanked and whacked his face against the underside. It felt good and the sound was most satisfactory. I did it again.

"Tell me," I kept repeating with each thwack. His body went limp but I did not stop choking him.

A current of force caught us then, whooshing us out from under the nook and toward the hatchway. In the air, a flurry of objects swirled about us, more than could possibly have been loose. The doors and drawers of the kitchen cabinets were open, spewing out streams of utensils, dishes, cups and such. They too seemed to be heading in the general direction of the cab. We drifted through the hatch and my grip weakened. The distraction of what was happening deflected my concentration, and my fury began to subside.

But when I saw what they had been doing to Carl, my wrath doubled and redoubled. He tumbled beside me nude from the waist down. Wires dangled from his scrotum, to which they were affixed by tape. The wires led to a small battery-and-switch affair floating nearby. Carl was fumblingly trying to pick the tape off, encircled by trailing lengths of rope by which he had been tied to one of the back seats. I tried to tighten my grip on Moore's enormous neck but couldn't. The envelope had stiffened. I lost my hold completely and drifted away. Moore was unconscious, his face dark and bloated, but I couldn't tell whether I had killed him. He might still have been breathing. Another of Moore's henchmen was in the cab. I kicked at his face as I flew by, then tried to push myself off the front port and back to Moore to finish the job. Drifting objects got in my way and I batted at them like flies. They were everywhere: pencils, lading sheets, binocular case, backpacks, shoes, a packet of feminine napkins, the druggy contents of the medicine chest, somebody's lost sandal, dishes, scraps of paper, a moldy dinner roll, books, a pipette reader, the *Ahgirr* maps . . . all the junk that had accumulated over the past month and which everyone agreed needed to be cleaned up—tomorrow, maybe.

I had just about reached Moore again when both the cab's gull-wing hatches sprang open. The explosive decompression drove everything and everyone out of the rig and into the hard vacuum of the immense chamber.

But I could breathe. The invisible envelope held trapped air. As I drifted upward, tumbling and turning, I wondered how much and how long it would last.

Soon my rotation slowed, not due to any effort on my part, and I could see the action below. There were Bugs everywhere, maybe about thirty of them, flittering here and about and from vehicle to vehicle, all of which were spewing an endless stream of objects and people from sprung hatches. The rig vomited clouds of jetsam from both ends. All our equipment and stores came flying out, including the astronomical gear—minus its protective wrappings. The whole gang too: Darla, Sean, Susan, Lori, the Voloshins, George and Winnie (where the hell had *they* been, I wondered), John, Roland, and Liam, all freed from their bindings and from the spell of the dream wand. Wide-eyed and disoriented, Darla passed me as we ascended. Then Lori went by, and I tried to wave. She saw me and shouted something but made no sound at all. She looked very frightened. I didn't blame her. I was scared bowelless myself.

Everything rose, tumbling, wobbling, spinning lazily. At about the height of fifty meters, the ascent stopped. Everything then proceeded to form into a vast swirling cloud like a flock of migrating birds, orbiting about a point on the floor of the chamber around which the Bugs were arranging themselves into a circle.

The scene was dreamlike; everything transpired in perfect silence. I could hear myself as I shouted and called out to everyone, but no sound conducted through the vacuum between individual force-envelopes. No reason why it should, I thought, so I shut up.

The cloud of junk and people began to order itself, forming spiraling lines leading down. During the reshuffling, I was astonished to see Wilkes—the genuine flesh-and-blood Corey Wilkes—go wafting past. He was naked from the waist up and wore white pajama bottoms. His chest was wrapped with white bandages. He looked as if he was having trouble breathing. His eyes seemed to find me as he passed. Dim recognition formed in his expression for a moment, then his eyes closed and he floated out of my ken. It was a reunion up there. Twrrrll, the surviving Reticulan, ghosted by, zoom-lens eyes fixing me in an insensate stare.

If Wilkes had been a shock, the sight of Ragna coming in for a docking maneuver had me reeling. In spite of myself, I yelled out, "Ragna! What the hell are you doing here!!??"

Well, he answered, and what he said was probably something like "Greetings, Jake, my friend of the bosom! Is this not of immense interestinghood?" or words to that effect, if his idiotically effusive smile was any indication. A slight perturbation of his orbit took him away, with his wife Oni following. I groaned.

I saw men I didn't recognize; other members of Moore's gang of cutthroats no doubt.

Above the circle of Roadbugs a gigantic cyclonic funnel took shape. Currents of force carried junk in spiraling patterns down to make a wide circuit in front of the Bugs, then back up again through the funnel and into the hovering cloud of people and debris. It seemed the Bugs wanted to inspect us and every doodad and whatnot we owned. I found myself in the funnel in short order, and began a dizzying descent in a quickly tightening gyre. As I neared the bottom, though, everything stopped.

They had found the Cube.

The circle of Bugs drew tighter. In the dim light of the

chamber I could barely see a black dot making the inspection circuit by itself, pausing briefly in front of each Bug before moving on. The Cube made the circuit twice, and that seemed to be enough. The funnel cloud began twisting downward again and I found myself parading before the assembled inspectors, floating single file with an assortment of digging tools. I had a momentary fantasy, imagining what was going through the Bugs' minds—if they had minds—as they categorized and cataloged everything.

Inanimate: implement; inanimate: foodstuff; inanimate: (unclassifiable); animate: being (semisentient, bipedal, mammalian); inanimate: apparel (covering for pedal extremities)...

They found me of little interest but paused for a moment to better scrutinize George and Winnie. Then I gravitated up into the cyclone again, a helical course until I returned to take my place in the huge swirling galaxy of stuff and people above.

I looked down. Carl's Chevy was rising on its own special updraft. When the funnel cloud had dissipated, it floated down to rest on the floor in the middle of the circle. The Bugs crowded even closer together to get a better look at it—if that was what they were doing. None of the car's hatches opened and none of its contents came out. They spent a good ten seconds looking it over, then backed off, apparently either satisfied with what they saw, or despairing of ever making sense of it.

The strip-search was over—none too soon, because I was finding each succeeding breath more difficult to draw.

What happened next happened quickly. The cloud of stuff broke apart, its elements falling precipitously, but gathering into a dozen or so individual streams. I fell, my stomach flipping over even though the sensation wasn't like an ordinary fall. I started tumbling, tried to stop but couldn't. Blizzards of junk accompanied me. Somebody's shirt covered my face and I brushed it off. Then a tool box bumped into my protective envelope but didn't hit me. I grew disoriented and slightly nauseated. The last few moments of the ordeal were mercifully quick, and I can't describe exactly how I got there, but the next thing I knew I was back in the cab again. A cataract of debris followed me through the hatch, spilling onto the deck in an ever-rising tide. John shot through the hatch, then Susan, then Roland, followed by the rest of our party including the Voloshins. None of Moore's gang appeared. Then my invisible wrapping ceased to exist and I fell headfirst into the lake of junk. The hatches slammed shut and there was silence.

Someone was standing on my legs. I twisted, and whoever it was fell over. I surfaced from the junk, tried standing up. My leg oozed into a pile of loose crap, sending me over. I grabbed the back of the shotgun seat and pulled myself up.

"Interesting weather we've been having," a reassuringly familiar voice said.

"Sam!"

"Yup, I'm back."

The cab was, needless to say, a god-awful mess. Several minutes went by and we still hadn't found Winnie. Eventually she turned up under a mound of bedding, unhurt. She jumped up on me, and squeezed me in a hug.

"Hello, Winnie honey," I said soothingly. "It's okay, girl. It's okay."

I realized that the rig was moving.

"Hey, Sam," I said. "Where are we going?"

"You got me," he said. "I ain't driving."

21

We were moving, but the rig's engine wasn't on. Neither would it start when I tried it. There were two Roadbugs in front of us, acting as locomotive and tender to our little train, which was composed of the rig, the riderless Voloshin vehicle, Moore's complement of buggies, and Ragna's vehicle.

I checked the instruments and found that the rollers weren't turning. The rig was floating about half a meter off the road. Neat trick, that.

Another Bug brought up the rear. Every train needs a caboose.

"I want to know," Sam said, "how they got all the air back in."

"Maybe each molecule of gas had its own gravitic envelope," Roland offered.

"I like that," Sam admired. "Makes no sense, but I like it."

We were already out of the huge chamber and into a tunnel, traveling at a terrific rate. Apparently the Bugs knew exactly where they were taking us. Probably to the incinerator.

"The Black Cube!" Roland exclaimed, holding the thing up for all to see.

"I wonder why they didn't keep it," Susan said, frowning suspiciously.

"I wish they had," I said glumly. "I can't even give that thing away."

"Sam," Roland said, "where were you?"

"It's a long story," I said. "What I want to know is, where's the Wilkes AI program?"

"My God," Roland breathed, "it was Wilkes in there?"

"It's safely bracketed in main memory," Sam said. "We can erase it anytime we want."

"Won't it load right back in," I wanted to know, "just like before?"

Sam chuckled. "That's where the problem was, in AuxStorage. I've blocked access to it temporarily, which is what we should have done in the first place. It's been tampered with physically, and we never would've been able to flush Wilkes out. We'll have to go there and fix it."

"Geez, Sam, I don't know if I can do it. I'm no computer techie."

"I'll help, don't worry. We've got the manuals—"

"But they're in AuxStorage, Sam."

"We have the hard copy back in the trailer, remember? In the egg-crate nook. If you'd clean this rig out once in a while . . ."

"Okay, okay. We'll get to that later. How did you manage to dig out from under Wilkes?"

"Well, when the hocus-pocus started, the stray radiation—whatever it was—erased the CPU clean. That was all the opening I needed. The AI program is a computer, but one set up in software. I'm hardwired, therefore one hell of a lot faster. A few nanoseconds was all it took."

"Well, I'll be," I said. "But how did Wilkes get the jump on you in the first place?"

"That was a fool's mate," Sam answered. "We should have seen it coming when we ran those diagnostics—"

"Wait a minute, let's save that for later, too. I want to see what the hell Ragna is doing here."

I got on the skyband and hailed him.

"Jake, my most special friend of mine! Hello and breaker breaker to all our buddies of the good variety!"

"Yeah, yeah. Ragna, how did you get here? And why in God's name did you come?"

"Oh, Jake. This is a situation of embarrassment."

"Come on."

"Oh, indeed. Doubtless I am in the process of incurring your wrath when I am telling you that various surreptitious individuals of our people followed you."

I laughed. "No, you won't incur my wrath. Everybody follows me, all the time."

"This is of truth. It was reported that many, many vehicles were being on your case like a ton of bricks. And on the planet where the highways are being interchanged, it was observed that material of an excremental nature was coming in contact

with the rotary blades, to employ a metaphor."

"Yes, that's exactly what happened," I said. "Go on."

"It was at the time that our science individuals are finally understanding what is going on inside the Black Cube."

"Oh?"

"Yes, they have been making some sense of the object. Their understanding is—let me be making this of perfect clarity—far from being of completeness, but they are arriving at the nub of its gist . . . if you are drifting with me."

"I understand," I told him. "So what is it?"

"Ah, Jake, as I have related, of scientific cognizance I am in possession of doodly squat. However and moreover, Oni is in ownership of vast quantities more than I, and she has been subjected to various briefings on the matter at hand. I will be having her talk with you, if this is not of inconvenience. Be standing by, please—"

"Wait a minute, Ragna," I cut in. "We have someone here who is possession of vast quantities of whatever you said. I want him to talk to Oni, but let's make it later, okay? We're knee-deep in debris here. And I want to find out where they're taking us."

"That is a stupendous ten-four. We are having the same vicissitudes in this vehicle of ours. Okay, Jake! We are going to be taking off our ears at this moment, and we will be catching you down the starslab at a later point in time. Until this point is reached, we are wishing excellent numbers to all our good-buddies! Clear!"

"Right," I answered.

"My God," Roland groaned. "Where did they pick up that skyband lingo?"

"I dunno. Must have got it from our libraries." I looked around. "Where is everybody?"

"Aft," Roland said. "More room. But if you think this is chaos, you should see the trailer."

"All right, people," Sam announced over every speaker in the rig. "What do you say we get this mess cleaned up?"

"I like the 'we,'" I sneered.

"Heh heh heh."

All attempts at communication with the Bugs failed. We could only guess as to our ultimate destination, and we were too busy at first to do that. The Bugs dragged us out of the underground garage, through a nearby portal, and across a succession of nondescript planets. We spent most of that time cleaning up the mess.

Carl was excused from clean-up detail. His scrotum had swelled up to the size of a grapefruit, and he was in horrible pain. All I could do for him was shoot him up with hydromorphone and cortisone, and hope for the best. Carl had talked, told them everything they wanted to know; they simply hadn't believed him. Toward the end, he'd thought they were coming around to buying his story about the saucer abduction, but he wasn't sure. Mercifully, though inadvertently, the Bugs had intervened. Lori was in a state, alternating between fits of crying and tantrums in which she'd smash things against a bulkhead and screamingly relate in detail the parasurgical procedures she would perform on the bastards who'd tormented her boyfriend. In a day or two, Carl was much better and she calmed down.

The clean-up lasted three days. We took inventory and found nothing missing. Sean's and Liam's vehicle was undamaged, as was Carl's of course, but Carl's car was now behind the magenta roadster, which was better, I thought. We might need to get the Chevy out quickly at some point. I regretted now ever having Carl drive it aboard. Talk about bad moves—I had made my share.

When it became apparent that we were in for a long trip, we settled down to a routine, sleeping and eating in shifts, standing watch at the instrument panel in turns, generally setting up some semblance of housekeeping. Thirteen bodies make living in a trailer truck an exercise in the art of the social contract. The truck was big, but with the vehicles and all the cargo, there was limited living space. Toes got constantly stepped on, elbows jammed into ribs, and there was a waiting list for the toilet. Nevertheless, at one point Darla and I found ourselves alone in the aft-cabin. I took the opportunity to sound her out on a few things. I sat her down on the bunk.

"Wilkes told me, or rather his analog told me, that he hadn't heard of the Black Cube until he actually saw it through Sam's eyes here in the truck. That make sense to you?"

Darla raised her eyebrows slightly and said, "I guess. Otherwise he wouldn't have been so keen on finding Winnie aboard the *Laputa*. He didn't know I had the Cube. Nobody did."

"Nobody except the person who gave it to you. Who was that person?"

"That person is dead. His name was Paavo and he was a very good friend of mine. He died in the shootout I escaped from on Xi Boo."

"Are you sure he died?"

"Paavo always vowed never to be taken by the Authority."

"Did you see him die, or hear for sure that he did?" I asked.

"No. Is it important?"

I nodded. "I think. I'd like to know exactly at what point the Authority learned of the Cube's existence."

"I'd always thought that they found out from running the Delphi on Marcia Miller."

"Probably," I said, "but when was that? When was she arrested? Sam and I can't find anything in our news files that would fix the date—which isn't surprising, because it was probably a secret arrest."

"Most likely it was. But why is the timetable so important?"

"Let me go into something else first." I leaned back and rested my shoulders against the bulkhead. "You never told me any of the details about what happened at the Teelies' farm that night, after they took me away, that is."

She shrugged. "I gave up, they took us all in."

"You were with the Teelies all the time up until Petrovsky questioned you?"

"No, they took me to the hospital first to get my burns treated. I insisted on it and they grudgingly gave in. I think one of the Militiamen took a fancy to me. I never saw the Teelies after that until we met them on the street in Maxwellville." She frowned and shook her head. "Funny, I expected to find them at the Militia station, or at least get some indication they were there, being held, questioned, something. The cops didn't seem to be very interested in them."

I filed that datum away, then said, "Okay. Now, Petrovsky didn't know you had the Cube. Right?"

"That surprised me to no end. He didn't even search my pack." Darla gave a little sarcastic grunt and smiled strangely. "Of course, he had a personal interest in my case."

"Even so, if he'd known you were carrying the Cube he would have searched you and found it. No?"

"Yes." She nodded emphatically. "Most assuredly."

I wove my fingers together and put them behind my head. "So. Petrovsky didn't know about the Cube, and Wilkes didn't, if he isn't lying again. My question is, who did the Authority send to get it? Who is the person representing their interests in all this?"

Darla thought about it a long time. Then she said, "There does seem to be a void in that area. Grigory must have been acting completely on his own. His career was ruined. I ruined it. They would have told him nothing. He was investigating your case as a matter of routine." She considered it a bit more. "But maybe it's a question of the timetable. Maybe whoever they sent just didn't catch up to you in time."

"Or to *you*."

"Me?"

"Yes," I said. "You were, and are, a fugitive. Maybe the Authority knew exactly who had the Cube, and they knew it all along. You had it, and they caught you! On Maxwellville! It may be that Petrovsky's and the Authority's paths converged there. Grigory was having a devil of a time getting cooperation from the local cops. But he was the ranking officer, and before Reilly, the nominal CO, could get authorization to shove Petrovsky aside, we were sprung by my mysterious doppelgänger. Or whoever did it."

Darla bit her lip and shook her head slowly.

I looked at the ceiling. "Then again, I could be wrong. But I've had this growing feeling lately, the feeling that something is missing. Or someone. Someone who's playing it very close to the vest."

Darla looked at me, puzzled; then a startling possibility occurred to her. "You don't mean . . . one of the Teelies?"

I sat forward. "Funny you should say that," I said.

Her eyes were wide and disbelieving. "No, they couldn't . . ." Then her face fell and her shoulders slumped. A look of profound exhaustion came over her, and she leaned against me. "Oh, Jake, I'll never make sense of all this. I thought at one time I knew what was going on. But I don't know anymore. I just don't know."

"Neither do I," I said. "Who can make sense of a paradox?"

We sat unmoving for a while. The rig seemed unusually quiet; no engine sounds, no voices near us, just the ever-present whistle of the slipstream as we were towed through another alien wind.

Presently I noticed my shoulder was moist. I tilted Darla's chin up with one finger and watched a big, round tear roll down her cheek.

"What's wrong, Darla?"

She wiped the tear away and straightened up. "I've got something to tell you," she said. "I'm pregnant."

Coming from vast eternities ahead, the wind whistled cold and drear.

"How could you . . . ?"

She laughed mirthlessly. "How?"

"I mean, how could you let it happen?"

"I'm on the cusp of a three-year pill. I wasn't in the position to go into a clinic for another one, and I couldn't get one. They're very expensive, you know. There wasn't much of a chance—I still had a month of 80 percent effectiveness left, 60 percent after that. But . . ." She shrugged. "It's been known to happen."

"How late are you?"

She shook her head. "Doesn't matter. I have a pregnancy-test kit in my pack. I knew forty-eight hours after." A slow, bittersweet smile crept across her face. "It may have been the night before, but I think it was that day on the beach."

I kissed her then; I didn't know why. Perhaps because, simply, I loved her.

The Bugs should have gone into the railroad business. The ride was transcendentally smooth, incredibly fast. Planets whooshed by so quickly you couldn't look out the ports for any length of time without getting a little dizzy. Lori, John, and Liam came down with motion sickness, which fortunately responded well to the drugs we had. Roland seemed to enjoy the ride. He spent hours in the shotgun seat, looking out, smiling enigmatically (I hesitate to say inscrutably).

A week went by.

Every once in a while we'd come out on another service planet. The first time it happened we thought we had arrived at our destination—but no, the Bugs shot us through another portal, and our fateful journey continued.

We passed some of the time gabbing, at one point speculating as to why the Bugs had put Moore's gang back in their vehicles but had deposited the Voloshins with us. The concensus was that the Bugs somehow knew that the humans were divided into two antagonistic factions, and, as usual, wanted to reduce the potential for trouble. Also, they had checked all vehicles, found little food in the Voloshins', and had put them in with us for the long journey. The Bugs were harsh, but fair. John said that, and I laughed, remembering an old joke.

A conversation stopper, though, was what Yuri told us about the Cube. He thrashed the subject about with Oni over a four-day period, then called a conference. Here's what he said:

"If I can make any sense out of what Oni has been telling me, the Cube is one of the strangest objects in the universe." He laughed. "Odd choice of words, as you'll see in a moment. And strictly speaking, it's not an object in the conventional sense. It's made of almost nothing at all . . . literally nothing at all. What it is, is a space. A space within a space. The space without is our universe, our continuum. The one within is . . ." He scratched his beard and hunched up his shoulders. "Another space."

"Are you saying there's a universe in there?" John asked.

Yuri sat back in his seat and shoved his hands into his pockets. "It may be no more than a light-year across."

"Only a light-year," Susan gasped, then fanned her face with her hand in mock relief. "You had me worried there for a minute."

"How can that possibly be?" John demanded. "You mean it's been . . . shrunk?"

"Folded," Yuri said. "Most likely. Folded and refolded along many dimensions." He withdrew his hand and turned his pocket inside out. "Think of it this way." He made a fold in the pocket. "Now, keep tying this up, rolling it up, and fairly soon you can't put your hand in anymore. But the pocket still exists, doesn't it?"

"I see," John said. "I think."

"Now, all this is pure speculation on the part of the *Ahgirr* scientists."

"What are they basing it on then?" I asked.

"The stream of raw data that seems to be coming out of the Cube. I can't imagine what can be supplying that data, or perhaps it's just energy that *becomes* data when it gets out. It's in the form of some very exotic radiation, part of it. And the other part is simple radio signals."

"So," I said, "this universe is losing energy."

"Yes. Now, at first blush the data doesn't seem to make much sense at all. It didn't to the *Ahgirr* until somebody made the association and looked in a cosmology text. The values coming out, and the states of energy within the Cube that the values seem to imply, correspond very closely to what cosmologists think existed in the very early stages of formation of our universe."

"You mean the Big Bang?" Darla asked, amazed.

"No, long before the Big Bang. Before there was any matter at all, and very little energy. Almost none of that either." He swung around in the driver's seat toward his lifecompanion. "Neither of us are really qualified in this area, but Zoya has had more exposure to the subject than I."

Zoya sighed. "I don't know where to begin." She smiled thinly, then said, "Let me put it this way. In the field of theoretical physics, the last century was spent wrestling with some very basic subjects. Among them was the fundamental nature of matter itself. Absurdly simplified, the current concensus is that matter is space tied up in knots. Vortices, matrices, call them what you will . . ." She scowled and scratched her forehead. "No, let's try that again. Think of a state of affairs in which . . ." She thought a moment. "Can you imagine a cloud of mathematical points arranging themselves by random processes into a pattern that may define a geometrical space? Coming together out of absolute nothingness, purely by chance? And can you imagine this defined space, this completely empty metrical frame, undergoing evolutionary changes, random fluctuations which induce a knotting up of itself at certain discrete points? Now imagine the knots as little blobs of energy. And since matter is equivalent to energy—" She held up a palm. "Please. As I said, this is absurdly simplified. But do you understand me so far? What I'm describing is nothing less than how the universe could have come to be created out of nothing."

"And that," Yuri said, "is what the *Ahgirr* scientists think is going on inside the Black Cube. At any rate, that is their best guess."

We listened to the howl of the slipstream for a while.

"It's almost unfathomable," John said.

"Quite so," Yuri agreed. "Quite so."

"I think it's a neat idea," Susan said. "A Universe Egg." She looked around at everybody, grinning delightedly. "That's what the Cube is. An incubating universe."

"I wonder if it's ours," Roland mused.

Another week went by.

Then another.

The days were featureless, colorless, distinguishable only by the random shape some snippet of conversation or tiny event gave them. I recall a few.

One day, Susan said to me:

"I know you still love Darla. I know it has nothing to do with the baby either. You two are . . . I don't know. Destined for something. It's bigger than both of you." She crinkled her nose. "That sounds ridiculously overdramatic. I really don't know how to put it."

I asked, "Is this Susan the Teleological Pantheist speaking?"

She put a hand behind my neck, tilted my head down, and kissed me. "This is Susan speaking, who loves you."

And another day Darla made some little joke over breakfast, a passing remark that struck us both funny—I can't recall what exactly—and we laughed as we hadn't done in a long time. And when we were done her face was bright and her cheeks glowed and her eyes looked lovely, the tiny highlights in them like sparks from a cheery hearth-fire.

And Lori making me feel old when she said I reminded her a bit of her grandfather, who had raised her until she was five, and whom she vividly remembered. (When pressed, she admitted her grandfather had been only around thirty-eight when she was born.)

And the fight the Voloshins had over a toothbrush. With their personal effects still in their vehicle, they had lacked certain necessities. Liam had made toothbrushes for both of them, handles whittled from firewood, brushes made ingeniously out of stiff plastic thread from some undisclosed source. Yuri had lost his and Zoya refused to share hers, berating him for being so careless. They didn't speak for three days.

One of Moore's men calling on the skyband, God knows why, or why he thought anybody here would want to talk with him—Krause I think it was, but maybe not—wanting to know how our food was holding out. I asked how theirs was holding out. He said it was getting low. I told him I sincerely hoped what they had left was growing botulism. He thanked me and signed off. He didn't call again.

Susan and Darla had a reconciliation, of sorts, an unspoken one. Susan delivered a typical wisecrack and Darla laughed. Susan looked at her tentatively, then they both laughed. Still, they maintained a warily respectful distance between them.

Ragna saying, "Ah, Jake, friend of mine, I am wearily contemplating the continuation of this *merte* of the bull."

John spending an hour with the Cube in the palm of his hand, staring at it, then suddenly looking up at me. "Is it possible?" he asked. "Could it be possible?"

I didn't answer.

One day I walked into the cab to find Roland at his favorite post, staring out into an alien night.

"Jake, come and look at this."

I sat in the driver's seat. "What's up?"

"Look at the sky."

I did. There were very few stars, and on one side of the sky, there didn't seem to be any.

"We're on the edge of a galaxy," Roland said. He pointed to his right. "Over here is intergalactic space. Nothingness. Now look over to where the stars are. See the glowing cloud behind them? The disk-edge of the galaxy."

I saw and agreed.

"We've been hitting these planets regularly. Sometimes there are a few stars on the other side and it's hard to tell. But this planet belongs to a star right on the very edge of its galaxy."

Teleologists must cultivate a sense of destiny, I thought. Roland's face glowed with it, and he regarded me with the self-assured smile of a man who relishes his meeting with the inevitable.

"This is it, Jake," he said. "We've been on it almost the whole trip. We're on Red Limit Freeway."

I looked at him solemnly and nodded. "I know," I said. "And at this rate, it won't be long before we reach the end of the road."

22

About four weeks into the journey, the Bugs pulled us over for a rest stop. You could call it that, but it might only have been to give the Talltree contingent an opportunity to bury Corey Wilkes. Apparently the strain had been too much for him.

They didn't bury him, though. We had to do it.

We stopped in the middle of one of the most attractive landscapes I had ever seen. It could have been Earth itself.

"Maybe it is," Roland said. "We have no idea where we are in space or in time." He pointed to a range of mountains lifting snow-capped peaks above the horizon. "Those could be the Pyrenees two million years ago. Or maybe the Appalachians."

"I'd be willing to bet," Yuri said, "that we're a bit farther back than that. Several billion, in fact. This might be a planet of a star that lived and died a billion years before Earth's sun was a gleam in the universe's eye."

"Hey, they're getting out!" Carl yelled.

Sean ran into the cab with a handful of weapons, but the men who had come out of one of Moore's vehicles weren't in a position to make a move. Chubby, Geof, and two others were carrying the limp body of Corey Wilkes. They dumped him like a load of garbage just a meter or so from the shoulder, looked around briefly, then returned to their vehicle and shut the hatch. I wondered whether they had done this on their own or at the Roadbug's behest.

I radioed and asked.

"He was beginning to smell a bit," Chubby told me. "So we requested permission to open the hatch and throw 'im out as we were going along. Instead, the Bugs stopped."

"They answered you?"

"No, they just pulled over, and we found we could open up."

"Okay, thanks."

"Right-o."

"Weren't the Bugs afraid they'd escape?" Roland wondered.

"To where, pray tell?" Sean asked, gesturing toward vast expanses of rolling pastureland dotted with stands of tall timber. It all looked friendly and inviting, but there wasn't very much to do out there.

"True."

"The patrol creatures must have had their reasons," Zoya said.

"They have orders to take care of us," Lori said, sounding as if she knew.

"Who?" I asked.

"The Bugs. They got orders to deliver us safe and in good health. And you can't have a stinky body lying around, can you?"

"Hmmm," I said, and thought about it. Then I asked, "Who ordered them, Lori?"

She looked at me and said impatiently, "The Roadbuilders, of course." She shook her head. "Really, Jake, sometimes you're just a little bit thick. Don't you realize that we're going to meet them? Where do you think they're taking us, on a punking picnic or something?" She rolled her eyes up in exasperation. "Sheesh!"

"Ohhh, I see."

We looked out at Wilkes' pale body.

"We can't just leave him lying there for the local scavengers," Sam said. "Somehow it's just not right."

This surprised the hell out of everybody, including me, but nobody commented.

"You really think?" I asked halfheartedly.

"Look, as far as I'm concerned, Wilkes was the lowest form of life in the known universe. But he was human, dang it, and if he deserves to rot in hell, which he surely does, he also deserves a decent burial—or the best one we can give him." Sam grumbled to himself for a moment. "Besides, I think we should do it because we're better than he was."

"Well, we may be moving again any second—but let's see if the Bugs'll let us," I said.

I bent toward the dash microphone. "Hey, out there. You guys. Bugs—whatever the hell you call yourselves. We'd like the time and the opportunity to conduct a ceremony of interment. You know? We want to dig a hole and put him in it. It's our custom."

"Use Intersystem, for God's sake," Sam scolded.

The answer was astonishingly quick.

"GRANTED."

And it was in English.

"Be damned," Sam said. "When will those things stop surprising me?"

Yuri said, "I think they were waiting for someone to go out there and do it."

"Maybe."

Carl pulled the release bar on the left hatch. It whooshed open, rising like a seagull's wing into the sweet-smelling air.

"Nobody thought to check when those guys got out," he said. "These were unlocked all the time."

We went outside to find Ragna and Oni climbing out of their vehicle, looking crumpled and weary. The thing they were driving was sort of like a camper, with a little room to move around in, but for the time they had spent cooped up in there, it must've been hell. They were indomitably cheery, though, in spite of it all.

Ragna stretched and took several deep breaths. "Ah, that is feeling much like the body I had of old, not this hurting thing I am having for the last several years, it is seeming like."

Oni smiled. "I am hoping we will be having the time to be working out the entirety of our kinks."

"Depends on how kinky you are, Oni," I said.

She nodded, then did a take. "Oh, that is a joke." She gave a polite, forced laugh. "Quite funny, too!"

I laughed. I liked Oni a lot.

So we buried Corey Wilkes. I found an old shaped-charge mine in the ordnance locker—they're good for clearing a blocked back road when you have to make a delivery, though I hadn't had the occasion to use one in a long time. I picked a likely spot a little way off the road and blasted out a good-sized hole with it. Sean helped me carry the body over. Before dumping Wilkes in, I looked down at him. Bare blue feet, white pajama bottoms, bandaged chest, purple lips and earlobes, the generally collapsed look about the face and swelling of the abdomen signaling the commencement of decomposition—he didn't look like the formidable enemy I had known.

"I suppose some appropriate words should be spoken," Sean said.

"If you feel like it, go ahead," I said. "Unless you have something to say, Sam."

Sam spoke from the key. *"Not really. Dump him in."*

"I didn't know the man," Sean said, "except by reputation, though I've seen his handiwork in what was done to Carl, and the trouble those rowdyboys have given us. Nevertheless . . ." He closed his eyes momentarily, then opened them and spoke. "'And Cain said to the Lord, "My punishment is too great to bear. You are driving me today from the soil; and from your face I shall be hidden. And I shall be a fugitive and a wanderer on the earth, and whoever finds me will kill me." But the Lord said to him, "Not so! Whoever kills Cain shall be punished sevenfold." Then the Lord gave Cain a mark so that no one finding him should kill him. And Cain went out . . . and dwelt in the land of Nod to the east of Eden.'"

Then Sean crossed himself. He smiled and shrugged. "I'm not sure how appropriate it was, but I imagine it sounded all right."

"It was fine," Sam said. *"Better than he deserved. That was the Douay version, wasn't it?"*

Sean nodded. "It's the one I know."

I sighed. "Well . . ."

We threw him in. I used another mine to blow a shelf of rock to smithereens. John and the rest, who had been looking on from a distance, came over to help us carry the pieces over and cover him up. We filled the hole to about three quarters of the way, up, making a sort of sunken cairn, then kicked in what little loose dirt was handy. Everybody helped but Darla, and I didn't blame her.

And that was that. We stood around, not very eager to get back into our traveling prison. I wasn't very worried about Moore trying something, not with the Roadbugs around.

Darla was gazing off into the distance.

"If there is a heaven, I imagine it would look something like this place."

I looked out. It was the most Earthlike planet I'd ever seen.

I could have sworn that the trees in the closest stand of timber were Douglas firs. The sky was purest blue, daubed with fleecy clouds. The air carried familiar smells, the tall grasses were kelly green, waving in a benign breeze. A clear stream flowed through a dip in the terrain to the left. A gentle hill rose from the far bank—great place for a farmhouse, nice little place indeed.

"You could find peace here," Darla said.

I watched her for a moment. Then she came out of her daydream, gave me a strange little smile, and walked off.

Winnie and George were having a good time, chasing each other through the grass like two kids—which they were, in a way.

"We go home!" Winnie had said when asked where she thought we were being taken.

"Home!" George had echoed.

Everyone still wondered what they meant.

An hour had gone by quickly.

"Okay, everybody," I said. "I hate to say it, but we should probably get back aboard. The Bugs are probably getting impatient."

Groans. But they all climbed in.

We told Ragna and Oni to come with us. They protested but finally gave in, and after running to fetch some things, they climbed aboard.

Before I did, I looked toward Moore's string of vehicles. They had been watching us enviously through the ports the whole while. Apparently, their doors had been sealed after they'd deposited the body.

"Too bad, kids," I yelled. "Be good and they might let you out for recess next time."

Puzzled looks from the boys. What'd he say?

We watched it happen on a lifeless planet with a thin, clear atmosphere of carbon dioxide. Around us, endless plains of orange dirt rolled out to a featureless horizon.

We saw a Bug road crew create and spin up a cylinder.

It was about a week after the rest stop. We hadn't run out of food, but most of the good stuff had been consumed. We assumed Moore and his gang were in bad shape in that regard. We had gotten a few desperate calls.

On our arrival, we had discovered a number of Bugs moving about, towing strange equipment and generally scurrying back and forth over the road. Farther down the road, there were more gathered a few kilometers from where the portal should have been.

Our Bug trainmen pulled us over not far from the road crew. Out on the plain, something was happening. A gray shadow of a cylinder appeared, wavering at first, then stabilizing and taking on substance. The shadow darkened, becoming an inky shaft jutting into an orange sky. Gradually, the cylinder took on its familiar hue, which is to say it was no color at all except that of black velvet at midnight.

We watched, mouths agape.

Yuri, though, was excited. "I was right! Damned if I wasn't right. They're made of pure virtual particles. The goddamn things don't even exist!"

"What do you mean?" John asked.

"I don't have the ghost of an idea how it's done, but these objects are being sustained in their existence from microsecond to microsecond. No, let me correct that. The time interval has to be vastly smaller. Perhaps the mass that makes up cylinder only exists within an increment shorter than the Planck limit, less time than it takes light to cross the diameter of a proton. But string those infinitely tiny blips of time together, and the mass takes on virtual existence. The thing of it is, anything goes within that interval. The physical laws of our continuum are null and void. You can create a new class of matter and a new set of physical realities in there. You can do anything, as long as it's canceled out within a short enough period of time. Our universe looks the other way. It's like a student making rude faces when the teacher's back is turned and instantly becoming a model pupil when the teacher spins around to catch him at it."

"I think I'm understanding this," John said. "Somewhat."

"I won't say it's very simple," Yuri went on. "But what's important here is understanding that this new kind of mass may have, and probably does have, radically different gravitational characteristics. That's how the gravitational fields around a cylinder can be shaped and tailored so as not to interfere with the planet it rests on. That's how the effect zone can be so limited. And that may be how the field is cut off precisely at the level of the road surface and centimeters off the ground."

"Pretty slick," Sam said.

Yuri laughed. "Yes, yes, it is."

I said, "Everybody's always wondered what would happen if the machinery holding up a cylinder were to fail."

"Exactly," Yuri said. "And the answer is—the cylinder would simply cease to exist! They're no more than projections, like the images of a motion picture film. If you turn off the projector, they disappear."

"But they are real, in a sense," Roland said. "Aren't they?"

"In a sense," Yuri said. "Taken one frame at a time, one infinitesimal interval, they are the stuff of nonexistence. But taken as a progression of serial events in a block of real time, they have virtual existence. Virtual—possessing qualities or being something in effect or essence, though not in actual fact."

Zoya said, "Congratulations, Yuri. Your theories were precisely on target."

It wasn't grudging, but it was cool.

Yuri's smile faded. "Thank you, Zoya. We must of course collaborate on the paper." His expression turned grim. "If there was only some way to get out and use our instruments."

"Pity," Zoya said.

"Where do you think the machinery that sustains the cylinders is located?" Liam asked Yuri.

"Most likely it's beneath the ground at the portal site. Perhaps in the roadbed itself."

I nodded. "Like Sam said, pretty slick."

Eventually my gaze was drawn elsewhere. I hadn't noticed it at first, for understandable reasons, but there was a huge circular paved area off the left shoulder, connected to the road by a short ramp made of Skyway material.

Our train started up again. The locomotive Bug made a sharp turn onto the ramp, dragged us to the middle of the disk and stopped. There were other disks, about half a dozen of them, spaced at even intervals up and down the road. Like this one, they were colored silver.

"Have we been shunted off to a siding?" Sam wondered.

"Yeah," I said, "to take on coal and water."

There was about a ten minute wait. We looked out the starboard ports but nothing was happening out on the plain at the portal site.

Then suddenly, something very disconcerting happened.

The world began to tilt.

It wasn't us, or didn't seem to be. Everything seemed normal and it felt as if we were still level. It was the ground that appeared to drop from beneath us. Looking straight ahead, we saw sky. The ground looked to be tilted down forty-five degrees from the disk—but of course it was the disk that was tilting up.

"Strap in, everybody," I yelled. "Just in case."

"Jake!" Susan screamed. "What's happening?"

"Um, I think we're going to take off."

And we did.

Oh, did we take off.

The planet dropped away from us. Our acceleration must have been a hundred Gs. We felt nothing. We heard nothing.

"Sam, are you registering any airspeed at all?"

"None. 'Course, that can't be."

"Maybe, if there's some kind of force field around us. Can you see a slipstream or contrail behind us?"

"Yup, you're right, there is."

Presently, the sky darkened and the curve of the planet appeared. Ahead was star-sprinkled blackness. We were in space, just like that.

"Incredible," Yuri murmured. "Absolutely . . ."

As distance increased, the visually-induced sensation of speed abated. We floated above the planet for a while, banking to the right. The still mammoth but slowly dwindling orange disk of the world below heaved full into the starboard ports. Then the terminator line came over the horizon and swept past. We were heading for the dark side and away from the sun.

Roland's face was transfigured with delight. His grin drew a crescent from ear to ear and he was giggling like a three-year-old child on his first merry-go-round. His Oriental eyes were narrowed to curved slits. He looked absolutely insane.

"Spaceship!" he burbled, then laughed maniacally.

"Yeah, neat," I said. "Jesus Christ, Roland, take it easy."

Everyone else was silent and awed to the very marrow.

The planet waned to a thin bright crescent and dropped away behind. Oblivious to the laws of physics as they are commonly understood, our magic disk, our spaceship, whisked us at unimaginable speeds into deep space. We were like meat on a serving dish. The planet crept to the stern, dwindling fast, and by the time I could get it on the rearview screens it had been reduced to a tiny scratch against the dark wall of night. Gone.

"Sam, can you get any kind of estimation of our speed?"

"Trying," he said. A moment went by, then he went on, "You wouldn't believe it. I can't believe it. We're accelerating so fast I can't even give you numbers. Call it umpteen million klicks per second and still accelerating."

"Carl," I said, "did your flying saucer look anything like this?"

"Nah, but I bet it went as fast."

"I'll have to try for star readings now," Sam said.

The illusion of speed was gone now that there weren't any points of reference. But even the stars, what little of them there were, seemed to be shifting like distant scenic features as we flew past. If Sam's readings were to be believed, we would be out of the local solar system and into interstellar space in a matter of a few hours, a day at the most.

"By Christ," was all Sean could say, staring out the port. "By Christ."

"Well, gang," I said, "what do you make of this?"

"If Bugs can fly," Carl wondered, "why do they run on the road?"

"Good question," I said. "But I never doubted that Bugs could do anything they wanted to do. They probably keep to the Skyway for their own good reasons. Which are . . . who knows?"

"The stars," Yuri said, leaning forward in his seat and looking out the front port.

The stars ahead were taking on a violet-blue cast, and in an area directly in line with our path, they were disappearing.

"We're approaching lightspeed," Yuri said. He sighed and leaned back, shaking his head, his expression troubled. "I may be losing my mind."

"Hang on for a while," I said, but I knew what he meant. There is only so much wonderment the human mind can absorb before it just takes a cab. This journey had been one long assault on the limits of endurance.

"Anybody have any speculation?" I asked, "on where they're taking us, and why?"

"I think we've pretty much run that subject into the ground

over the past month," Susan answered. "Haven't we? I mean, first we thought they were taking us to Bug jail, then back to T-Maze, then to the Roadbuilders, and now . . . God, who could possibly guess? What would the Roadbuilders be doing off the road?"

John said, "I think at this point we have to dispose of all the common assumptions made about the Skyway and whoever created it. None of the usual explanations ever made any sense anyway."

"Exactly," Yuri said. "It's always been taken for granted that the Skyway is an artifact of some long-vanished civilization. But just think about it. Here we have a road system that actually goes nowhere. There are no ruins of cities along it, nothing that would indicate that the road was ever used by those who built it. There were always the patrol vehicles—but now we know they're not vehicles at all but actual beings of some kind. Jake said it best, I think, when he likened them to civil servants. The Bugs were created to keep the road passable and relatively safe . . . for us. I've always believed that the Skyway was built for the express purpose of providing a way to bridge the fantastic distances separating the intelligent races of the universe. And for no other purpose."

"But why are we now off the road?" John asked.

Yuri shrugged. "We all saw that road crew spin up a new cylinder."

John nodded. "Of course. It's still under construction."

"We're on a detour," Susan put in.

"Very good, Susan," Yuri said, smiling.

John's brow knitted and he put a long-fingered hand to one side of his face, massaging it. "So confusing," he muttered. "See here. You just said that the Skyway doesn't go anywhere. But we've just spent a month on Red Limit Freeway. I don't know where in God's name we're going, but we're surely going somewhere, and it bloody well seems to me that Red Limit Freeway was built for the express purpose of taking us there."

Yuri sat forward and propped his chin up on his fists, his eyebrows twitching perplexedly. "Yes," he said. "Yes, it does seem that way, doesn't it? You're absolutely right, John, and I have to confess that it undermines my theory." He sat up sharply and pounded a fist into his thigh. "But dammit, if the Roadbuilders wanted people to be following a prescribed path, why the devil didn't they make that path abundantly clear? Why the blind alleys, the cul-de-sacs, the obscurity, the whole tangled mess of it all?" As he spoke, the accumulated frustration and stress of the past two years and the boredom and uncertainty of the past four weeks rose from whatever place it is where such things cook and stew under pressure until they have to be released. "Dammit all, I've spent half my life trying to understand one basic thing, trying to find some sort of clue, struggling to shed a single ray of light on a single overriding question and it's been like butting and butting my head against the roadbed itself. Sometimes I think I've been a fool—but that's of little importance. It was my choice—I made it and I must live with it. But the question still remains, dammit. It won't go away." He crashed a fist into the armrest, his voice erupting to a shout. "If the goddamn fucking Roadbuilders had wanted us to follow their fucking road—" He began pounding the armrest in cadence. "—why the bloody fucking *HELL* didn't they give us a fucking *MAP!*"

The last thwack on the armrest nearly broke it.

After a pregnant pause, Sam began to laugh. And that set us all off.

Yuri looked around at us, his eyes wide. Then he collapsed inside, spent, the redness in his face quickly turning from anger to embarrassment. He fell back in his seat in total helplessness and started to laugh, too.

We spent at least two full minutes laughing ourselves silly. We began sobering up when we realized that Yuri had dovetailed into crying. Zoya got up, stood behind him, and began massaging his shoulders, stroking his tousled hair.

Yuri wiped his eyes on his filthy, tattered sleeve. "Forgive me," he said, his voice choked with remorse. "My friends . . . you must . . . forgive me."

"Nothing to forgive, Yuri," I said. "You were entitled to that, and it was just about time you collected."

"Still, I must apologize for the outburst . . ." He managed a smile. "And the language."

"You won't find any virgin ears around here," Susan said, "so don't worry about that." She thought a moment. "Of course, I've never tried it that way."

This set us off again and this time Yuri's laugh was unadulterated mirth.

When we had sobered up again, Sean got up from the deck, straightened his black turtleneck, and thumped his stomach, which had become drastically reduced in the last few weeks.

"I'm for grub," he said. "What there is of it left, anyway. What do you say, me hearties?"

"None for me," Zoya said. "Maybe a drink of water."

"Zoyishka, you're wasting away," Yuri said.

"Good for the soul."

"Not so good for the body, Zoya," I said. "You should eat. Come on, we're not on starvation rations yet."

She shrugged, then looked at me and relented. "You're right, I should. It's just that my appetite seems to have disappeared. And when I do eat, my digestion is frightful. There's some pain."

"What about Winnie?" Roland broke in.

The non sequitur brought everyone up short. Carl asked, "What did you say, Roland?"

"What about Winnie's map—and George's? Isn't it clear by now that they were planted? Maybe there are other races, other borderline-sapient animals who have map knowledge. Thousands, millions of species seeded along the Skyway like that. It all fits." He ground fist into palm, his lips pursed. He seemed to be off somewhere on his own magic carpet of thought. "It all fits."

Yuri was willing to plod back to the previous conversational sequence. "Yes, that's a distinct possibility, and in fact that's been one of the operating assumptions of our investigation into the matter. But it's also manifestly clear that Winnie and George's so-called knowledge is anything but reliable."

"Yeah," I said, "which brings us back to square one. So quit grinding your teeth, Roland, and relax. It's a safe bet we're not going to get to the bottom of this for some time."

Roland seemed miffed. "I wasn't grinding my teeth."

"Just an expression." I reached back and slapped his knee. "Take it easy. Okay?"

He unwound a bit and smiled a little sheepishly. "Sure. Sorry."

"It's okay."

"I have an announcement," Sam put in.

"Let's have it," I told him.

"We've just gone superluminal."

"What's that?" Susan said.

"Fancy for 'faster than light.'"

Yuri and Zoya exchanged glances. Then a slow, world-weary smile of capitulation spread over Yuri's face. "Well, we knew the Roadbugs had superscience. Now we know they have magic."

"Sam, are you sure?"

"Hell, no. I'm not equipped to analyze data like these, but I'm damned if I can explain this crazy stuff any other way. Do you see any stars out there?"

I looked. Blank space. "Wow. No, I don't."

"I watched them disappear, but they didn't just disappear, they dopplered right off the scale."

"What's he saying, Jake?" John asked.

"I have an inkling, maybe."

"I can't really explain it," Sam said. "I don't have the wherewithal to put it into easily understandable terms. Not really in my programming. I can give you figures, but you wouldn't want 'em."

"Sam," I said, "this radiation. I was wondering about that. Even at lightspeed, we'd be smacking into stray hydrogen atoms with terrific energy. It'd fry us. What kind of count are you reading?"

"I'm not getting any high-energy particles, but I'm tracking very high frequency photons, about one per second. Which is nothing, really, in terms of health hazard."

"You say you're tracking them at faster-than-light speeds?"

"No, no, no, of course not. Light that's faster than light? The situation isn't that crazy yet. What I am saying is that these little buggers used to be starlight."

"Oh."

"Here's my hunch. We have just crossed the lightspeed barrier. No hyperspace, no fifth dimension, none of that horse nonsense. We are simply going faster than light."

"Oh," I said again, not knowing what else to add.

Susan was befuddled. "Hey, isn't that supposed to be impossible?"

We all looked at her.

"Just trying to be helpful," she said lamely.

"Let's eat," I said.

* * *

Our space journey lasted three days. We spent the time pretty much as we had done up till then, eating, sleeping, attending to personal matters, playing cards, playing chess (Sam took us all on in a marathon session—he won hands down against all comers. "It's not me, it's just my game files," he said modestly), reading, gabbing, although that tapered off after a while. We had hashed over everything of moment and were running out of small-talk material. We'd decided not to trade life stories. Carl was still reticent on the subject of Everybody-Knew-What, but he said he was working on it.

Sam eventually admitted he had given up trying to make sense of the data he was getting. And pretty soon he wasn't getting anything.

"Nothing out there, I guess," he said. "I'm not equipped for radio astronomy, so there's no use even speculating."

Along about a Tuesday morning . . . Actually, it was a Tuesday, and it was the fourteenth of March—at least it was back on a little blue planet some billions of light-years away, billions of years in the future, or the past, who knows. Anyway, along about a Tuesday morning we spotted something up ahead. That is, Sam did through the light-amplifier. I looked into the scope. Nothing but a faint smudge of light. Couple hours later, though, it was brighter.

"A star?" I ventured. "That'd mean we're nonsuperluminal, wouldn't it?"

"I think so. Actually, judging from the blue-shift, I'd say we were strolling along at a little under point nine cee and decelerating."

"So that's our destination."

"Well, seeing that there's no other place around the place, I reckon that must be the place . . . I reckon."

"Hmph."

"Except that's no dang star," Sam said.

"What is it?"

"Beats the living hell out of me."

I sat back in the driver's seat. "From what Yuri's been telling us, we're billions of years back in the history of the universe, no telling how many billions. Obviously far enough back so that stars haven't even formed yet. Maybe this is a quasar."

"No, if you swing that thing to these settings, you'll see

something that looks like what a quasar should look like."

I positioned the scope and looked. A fuzzy blob of light with a faint spike coming out of it came into focus. "Yeah, that's what they're supposed to look like—some of 'em, anyway. But it should be a lot brighter, shouldn't it? I mean, if we're back when quasars first formed, we should be a hell of a lot closer to them, and . . ." I sat back. "Hell, who am I kidding. What I know about astronomy you couldn't stuff a flea with."

"Maybe it isn't a quasar," Sam said. "I was just guessing. Why not ask Yuri?"

"We've been picking his brains for three days now. Zoya's and Oni's, too. They're sleeping." I thought a moment, then said, "Yuri told me that if we had the right kind of microwave scoop we could tune in the cosmic background radiation and calculate exactly how far back we are."

"If we had the right kind of microwave scoop," Sam snorted. "Look, this is fun, but another hour and we're gonna be there. So let's wait."

So we did.

When we first began to see some detail, the strange object looked like a small star cluster with a bright core that was a bit off-center. Then it got very strange. It wasn't a cluster but a perfect sphere of stars with a brilliant spot near the very edge. But here was a problem.

"Those can't be stars," Sam said. "We're too close to that thing. They're just points of light."

"Artificial objects?"

"Gotta be."

Soon, an interior feature revealed itself, a solid disk bisecting the sphere. We were viewing it almost edge-on. It had the albedo of a planetary body and reflected its light from the much smaller sunlike disk riding just below the outer surface of the sphere. Our magic spaceship changed course, and eventually the disk tilted up toward us. I got out the missile aiming sight, cranked it up to full gain and had a look.

The surface of the disk was a world.

There were blue areas and brown areas—seas and continents. Wisps of cotton floated just above the surface. Clouds. As we got closer, rivers, mountain ranges, and other details appeared. A patchwork of tans and browns and greens spread over the land masses and details of the coastal regions revealed themselves. There were deserts, plains, and areas of what seemed to be thick vegetation. All this geography, though, was on a smaller scale than one would expect. It looked like a planet in miniature.

"Five thousand kilometers in diameter," Sam said. "Exactly."

"Nice round number."

The star sphere was just that. It was like a glass bubble spattered with drops of luminous paint. Not everything in the skies above the planet-disk orbited in the same plane, though. The sun-thing, whatever it was, hung a little lower, and there were other points of light and a smaller, less luminous disk—a moon-thing?—which looked as if they were borne along on inner concentric spheres.

The entire construct—it had to be a construct—looked like a medieval astronomer's orrery.

"A damn planetarium," Sam said.

"It's a working model of the Ptolemaic universe," Roland said. "Though I think even Ptolemy accepted a spherical Earth, so it's a mixture of ancient astronomies, probably alien ones at that."

Beyond this, no one was willing to speculate.

The disk of the surface tilted full face toward us and we began our descent. We could see now that the back side of the sunlike object, also a disk, was dark.

In a few minutes we reached the surface of the star globe and found nothing there. Individual stars were still only points of light, all floating in exactly the same plane.

"What, no crystalline ethereal spheres?" Sam complained.

"Well, you wouldn't see them anyway," Yuri pointed out, "if I remember my ancient astronomy correctly." He laughed. "Imagine crashing into one and leaving a hole."

"So all these screwy objects up here are just artificial satellites of this even goofier planet," I said.

We dropped quickly. The sun object, which had become a dark oval when we got above it, turned its bright side to us again and we were in brilliant daylight. You couldn't look directly at it, and it looked for all the world like a sun, a Sol-type one at that. The stars faded and a blue canopy of sky came up, dark and cold at first, lightening and warming as we continued to drop.

The surface was a patchwork of every kind of terrain. There were deep forests, wastelands, mountains, grasslands, stretches that looked like alien planets, stranger areas where it was hard to tell what was going on. It was a crazy quilt down there. And there were signs of intelligent life. I could see roads now, though not many. Structures, too, some very big and very unusual ones, dotting the landscape at random. I didn't see any cities but there was an immense green-colored edifice below that seemed centrally placed. It could have been an arcology of some sort. The thought made my skin crawl.

The jumble and variety reminded me of something, and the notion was so incongruous, when juxtaposed with my expectations of what this place could possibly be, that I laughed aloud. I was reminded of what, in my day, used to be called disneyworlds. I forget what they're called now—in fact, I really don't know if there are any on the colonized planets. Amusement park is another and even older term.

Were we being taken on a school picnic?

In any event, we were about to land. I looked back at everybody. We were all armed, Lori included. Everyone had the same expression: a little fear mixed with expectation. We had discussed what to do at journey's end. We had no idea of what to expect, but we all knew it could be bad. That was one possibilty. It was also possible that we could be greeted by brass bands and cheering crowds, and be hailed as intrepid explorers. We could hope. Of course, nobody had any delusions of defending ourselves against either the Roadbuilders, if they were down there, or the Bugs, if this was their home planet. But the slight glimmer of hope existed that we could be set free, and so could Moore and his gang. We simply did not know. In any event, and for any event, we were prepared.

I looked down and saw a familiar sight. The black band of the Skyway. So we never really did get off it. Just a detour, as Susan had said. But one thing we did not see on this planet was a portal. The Skyway was here all right, but this was it. This was Road's End.

Below, strange buildings lay along the highway. Maybe these were the ancient ruins Yuri and everyone had been looking for. But maybe not—from this height they didn't look ruined, just incredibly varied and uniformly strange and wonderful. Were they temples?—palaces?—residences? I hoped we would get to find out.

Our magic carpet was coming in for a landing.

"Okay, people, this is it," I said. "Whatever 'it' is."

"I wouldn't be worried about Moore too much," Sam tried to reassure us. "I'd be wary, of course, but I suspect he and his boys are going to be on their best behavior. Wouldn't do to scrap in front of Roadbuilders, and I can't believe they'd be stupid enough to do it."

"I'm half-inclined to believe you," I said, "but I wouldn't put anything past that slimeball."

"Maybe they're dead," Lori said. "We haven't heard a peep out of them for a while."

"That would be a bit of luck," John said. "We haven't had a fart's worth of good luck on this entire trip."

"We're alive, aren't we?" Susan said.

"Are we? I hadn't noticed."

We swooped over the roadway and came to a sudden stop, hovering momentarily before drifting down. There were docking ramps here, too, and the silver disk lined up over one of them and settled down. Our train was pointed toward the road.

As soon as we had landed, the Bugs dragged us off the disk, swung out onto the Skyway, and stopped. Then they decoupled us.

The rig's main engine groaned and turned over. A quick check of the instrument panel told me we had full power and total control of our weaponry.

The Bugs were pulling away. The three of them, locomotive, tender, and caboose, shot ahead and quickly disappeared. We were free.

But Moore and his gang were heading the other way. The rearview cameras showed all four vehicles wheeling around and tearing off down the road.

Twrrrll's vehicle followed them all, though the pursuit was halfhearted. The domed bubble-top of his buggy was opaque, but I could just imagine him looking over his bony shoulder, camera-eyes on extreme zoom, hoping to catch sight of his quarry one more time before he beat a hasty but strategic retreat.

"See?" Sam laughed. "They're more afraid of us than we are of them."

"Since when?" I said. "They have a guilty conscience, is all. They're afraid of the Roadbuilders."

"So am I," Susan said. "Let's get the hell out of here."

"What, and miss shaking hands with the Mayor?" I said. "Not on your life, Suzie." I looked around. Susan was hunched over on the seat, thin arms wrapped tightly about her and holding the gun she abhorred tightly against her side. Her eyes were wide and worried, her face tight and strained.

I reached back, took her shoulder, and squeezed it consolingly. "How far do you really think they'll get, honey?" I asked gently. "Hmm?"

Gripping my arm, she bent her head and kissed my hand. "I know," she said quietly. "I know." She looked up. "I'm just . . . you know, a little scared."

"It's okay."

We sat for a while. Nothing happened.

"You know," I said finally, "this is a high speed road. We should either pull over or get moving."

"What'll it be?" Sam asked.

"I hate to sit and wait. If our destiny's down this road, let's go have a look at it. What say, everybody? Shall we take a vote?"

"The ayes have it, Jake, me boy," Sean said, speaking for everyone. "Let's roll."

"Ragna, are you back there?"

"Indeed. I am hardly elsewhere."

"Do you want to get back in your vehicle or leave it here and come with us?"

"Being that I am scared to the point of voiding my nitrogenous wastes, no, thank you, I think. We will be space truckers for a while."

I started forward.

The road followed a trough between two low grassy hills. There wasn't much to see except a few strange trees and some shrubbery. This area had a manicured look to it, like a park. The grass was short and the trees had a pruned and cared-for look to them, though that very well could have been their natural state. There was a lot of color here. The green of the grass was brilliant, almost iridescent, and the trees and shrubs were of various pastel shades. Pink and blue strata of rock ran along the slopes higher up.

"Pretty," I heard Darla say.

Everyone nodded in silent agreement.

The valley began to wind and the road bore slowly upward.

"Anything sneaking up behind, Sam?"

"Not a soul."

"Hmm. I was just thinking."

"What?"

"Did you erase the Wilkes AI program yet?"

"No."

"How come?"

"I haven't been ordered to. You know I can't erase any files without your okay."

"Oh, right, sorry."

"So why haven't you?" Sam asked pointedly.

"Huh?"

"Why haven't you ordered me to erase Wilkes?"

"It's harmless now, right?"

"Absolutely. I got him right where I want him."

"Well, maybe we should let it be. That program may have some information we need. There are still plenty of question marks that need clearing up."

"Whatever you say."

"You're sure you pulled its teeth, now."

"Don't worry about it. You can't fool this computer twice."

"Well, we don't want a repeat of that takeover bid."

Sam grew exasperated. "Hey, did anybody else just hear me tell him not to worry about it?"

"I'd never count Corey Wilkes out," Darla said. "I wouldn't even trust death to cramp his style."

"Yeah," I said. "He's sorta like you, Sam, in a way."

"How would you like to walk, son of mine? Next time you get out of this rig, I just might not let you back in."

"Sorry."

"No respect for the dead."

The road leveled off on a bluff overlooking a wide plain. I slowed and pulled off the road. I wanted to have a look at this.

"Oh, it's beautiful," Susan said.

"Sam, something tells me the air here is just fine."

"It certainly is."

"Let's get out."

"Uh, I'll stay in the truck."

"Okay. You—" I did a double-take. "Yeah," I said, and laughed.

We all spilled out, walked off the shoulder, and stood looking at the marvel across the valley below. On a far hill stood a magnificent structure.

It was a palace or maybe an entire city, a massive yet graceful array of tall domed cylinders and lofty spires all enclosed behind a fortress wall. It was a fairy city, an imperial palace in a never-never land. It was El Dorado, or Xanadu, or Shangri-La. And it was all a glossy, brilliant green. Flying buttresses of green glass soared between towers, sparkling in the late afternoon sun. Crystalline ramparts looked out across the valley.

Susan was awed. "It's the Emerald City."

"It is looking quite like our fables and stories of old," Ragna commented.

I looked down. The Skyway cut across the valley and went into serpentine turns as it climbed the citadel atop which the city stood.

The black dot of a vehicle had just come down from there and was heading across the valley toward us at a terrific clip.

"Well," I said. "Here comes something."

Everybody caught sight of it and drew back a little, getting closer together.

We waited.

The dot grew into a vehicle that was sleek, long and black with green trim. After shooting across the valley, it slowed a little and began its ascent up the near side, taking sharp turns with effortless grace.

In another minute it gained the crest of the hill. It pulled off the road about twenty meters away from us.

The vehicle was magnificent, a technological rhapsody in shining ebony and jade green, its aerodynamic surfaces whimsical and free yet somehow mathematically precise as well. Fins angled up from the rear, thin swept-back wings flared from the sides. The fuselage was set about with tear-shaped bubbles and rounded protrusions. The needle-nose was tipped with silver. It looked more like a plane than a ground vehicle, and I didn't doubt that it could fly.

Was this an example of Roadbuilder technology? If there were Roadbuilders inside, why hadn't they simply levitated across the valley to meet us? Compared to the wizardry that had brought us here, this was decidedly middle-tech.

The next thing that happened shocked the hell out of us.

The green-tinted bubble-top popped open and a human being climbed out.

A strange one, though. His long hair was the color of copper, his face the color of coffee with heavy cream. His black eyes were large and wide apart. He had a straight sharp nose over full lips and his face was a perfect oval. There was something of the androgyne in him, with masculine and feminine aspects melded into one body. He climbed down from his vehicle and walked toward us in a flowing movement in which grace and self-assurance were combined.

He was dressed in a green full cape, black pantaloons and boots, and a black leather jacket with black piping. The cape was embroidered along the edges with elaborate designs in black thread and the jacket flowed with green scrollwork.

He stopped a few meters from us and spoke.

"Welcome," he said, and smiled. "You've come a long way and you must be very weary. We offer our apologies if you've been inconvenienced in any way."

The voice was not effeminate so much as it was epicene. It was clear, lyrical, lilting—almost musical.

No one responded. We all stood there airing our tonsils.

Finally I shut my mouth, swallowed, and said, "Hello. Yes, we're pretty tired. Uh, thank you." I massaged my forehead and tried again. "Uh, look here. I'm Jake McGraw. And these are my friends . . ."

"Greetings to you all," the man said, smiling warmly and looking around. "You may call us Prime."

"Us?" I said.

"Uh . . . me. Forgive the plural. Merely a habit."

"Prime," I repeated.

"Yes, Prime will do." He turned and looked up, watching a cloud roll by. "Beautiful weather, wouldn't you say?"

"Yes." I shook my head. "See here—" I began.

"You know, I was just about to have lunch," Prime said, turning to me, "when I had news of your arrival. You must be tired and hungry. Would you all do me the honor of joining me for a bite to eat?—After you've all had a chance to freshen up a bit, of course."

"Yes," I said. "Yes. But—"

"Forgive me. I'm sure you have many questions to ask me. And I'm perfectly willing to tell all in good time. But some things take priority, don't they? The universe stops for lunch. Why shouldn't we?" He laughed.

"One question first," I said. I pointed to the Skyway. "Did you build that?"

He looked. "What, that road specifically? Myself?"

"No, all of them. All the roads. We call it the Skyway."

His grin was strange and sly. "I suppose in a way I did."

"In a way?"

"Please. I don't want to sound enigmatic, though I'm sure I do. But I will answer all your questions at a later time. Any questions, truthfully and honestly."

He motioned over his shoulder. "I live across the valley there. If you'll be so kind as to follow me—"

"Do you know anything about a black cube?" I blurted.

"What? Oh." He frowned. "Yes. Um, you have it, don't you?"

"Yes."

"Good. Well, keep it for now. But at some point I would like to get a look at it."

"What is it?"

"What is it," he repeated. "Well, it's basically an experiment."

"An experiment in what?"

He considered his phrasing. "Let us say, an experiment in the creation of a universe."

"Any universe in particular?" I asked.

He looked at the sky and smiled. "Is there more than one?"

"Is there?"

His gaze lowered to meet mine. "That question can be answered in many ways." He laughed again. "Well. More of this later. And now—"

"I have a question." Carl shouldered me aside, walked forward, and stood in front of Prime.

Prime eyed him up and down, still smiling. "Young man, I sense that you harbor some hostility toward me."

"You're damn right. What's the big idea of kidnapping me and dumping me on some goddamn planet somewhere?"

"My dear young man, I—"

Carl cocked back his right fist and hit him full in the face.

Prime spun around and fell to the ground, his flowing cape spread out over the grass like crippled green wings.

Lori screamed. Then there was silence.

Prime didn't move. Carl stood there over him, both fists balled and arms straight at his sides.

I overcame my shock and stepped over to Carl. I looked down at Prime.

"Carl," I said. "You may have just punched out God."

"Nah." He looked at me sharply. "God has a beard."